THE *Night* IS MINE

THE NIGHT STALKERS

M.L. BUCHMAN

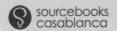
sourcebooks
casablanca

Published by Sourcebooks Casablanca, an imprint of Sourcebooks, Inc.
P.O. Box 4410, Naperville, Illinois 60567-4410
(630) 961-3900
FAX: (630) 961-2168
www.sourcebooks.com

Printed and bound in Canada
WC 10 9 8 7 6 5 4 3 2 1

DEDICATION

To my Lady, for whom all my words are written.
To my stepdaughter, for her steadfast belief.
To them both, all my heart.
To my reading group and my mentors,
I couldn't have done it without you.
To Deb and crew—what a joy!

FOR ANY INACCURACIES

My apologies.
But this being a work of fiction,
whatever I couldn't find out
I made up.

Lift *n*.
The aerodynamic force on a helicopter's rotor that provides an upward force to climb or maintain flight.

Lift *v*.
To become elevated; to soar.

Chapter 1

THE CNN FILM CREW HAD MADE IT FUN. BUT NOW...

The laptop stood balanced on a couple of empty, dull green ammo cases for the minigun. Sweaty pilots and crew stood gathered around the computer, waiting for the network to roll the clip.

Captain Emily Beale and her team rushed into the tent from the Black Hawk helicopter landing area, still in their hot, sticky flight gear, helmets clutched under their arms. Just past dawn here, late-evening news back home.

A dozen guys who hadn't been lucky enough to fly that night packed the already baking tent. They wore shorts and army green, sleeveless tees revealing a wide variety of arm tattoos. Some with girls' names, some snakes, some helicopters, all with feathered wings. The men squatted on the dirt and sand that passed for a floor, perched on benches, or stood, feet wide, with arms crossed over muscled chests.

The observation jolted Emily a moment before she shrugged it back into her mind's dustiest footlocker. Just another reminder that the entire female roster of this forward deployment included only one name—her own.

Brion Carlson came on and flashed his famous scowl, cuing his multimillion-person audience that the next clip would be fun, not war-torn hell, not drowned mother of twins, not car pileup at eleven.

Emily's free hand rested on the M9 Beretta sidearm

in her holster. Tempting. A couple of 9 mm rounds through the screen might cheer her up significantly. But then they'd all know how she felt. Be hard to laugh it off after that level of mayhem. She knew hundreds of ways to kill a person but how do you kill a newscast? Shooting a laptop didn't meet the ultimate criteria for complete suppression. She scanned the intent faces of her flightmates. Still, a bit of localized destruction held its temptations.

She'd only been in the company for two months. The first week or so, she'd been a total outsider. But as she'd proved herself on mission after mission, she'd gained acceptance, grudging at first, then not. Now, on the precarious cusp of true welcome, this.

"Hot from the fighting front, at an undisclosed location in Southwest Asia, CNN caught up with Black Hawk pilot Captain Emily Beale as she cooks up a storm for her flight crew. She's the first, and so far the only, female pilot to qualify to fly helicopters for SOAR, the elite 160th Airwing."

"Air regiment," Big John called out. Someone shushed him.

"With the Night Stalkers, as the Special Operations Aviation Regiment call themselves—"

"Damn straight," John answered and then turned to scowl at whoever had been foolish enough to try and shush him before.

"—she flies, literally, where no woman has flown before."

The clip rolled. A close-up of steak sizzling on a surface so black that it didn't reflect the scorching, midday sun. Odd place to start, but what the hell. The Black

Hawk's nose cone covering the terrain-following radar assembly really had been plenty hot to sear a steak. And the meat had tasted damn good. A humorous opening. So far she could live with this.

Then the camera pulled back.

First the nose of her chopper, which was kind of cool. Made a nice surprise for the average viewer.

Then the camera swung toward the person wielding the cooking tongs.

She groaned. Silently. But, damn! She'd given them loads of footage why she flew had answered a thousand probing questions about a woman in a man's world and this is how they started?

Ray-Bans. Blond hair running loose over her shoulders. A trick only Special Forces, SEALs, and SOAR pilots could get away with in all the U.S. military. The elite fighting teams were supposed to wear nonmilitary hair, even mustaches and beards, to blend in wherever they were inserted. SOAR pilots usually did the close-cropped military thing, but not her company. She liked the sound of that, her company. No longer the newbie on the outside looking in.

The laptop image scanned down her body as if she were a model for *Playboy* or *Hustler*. This was not what she'd signed up for. At least it would be uphill from here.

She'd made it into the Black Adders, the nastiest and toughest company that SOAR had ever fielded. They belonged to the 5th Battalion, which was the nastiest and toughest battalion, no matter what the other four claimed. That's why the 3rd Black Hawk Company of the 5th Battalion of the 160th Special Operations Aviation Regiment (Airborne) wore their hair long. It made them more like their customers, the Special Forces operations specialists they transported to and from battle. Of course, none of them minded the added bonus of being able to thumb their noses at the establishment they'd give their lives to defend.

The camera continued its slow scan down her body. Army-green tank top. Running shorts and army boots. Standard desert camp gear. She was soaked in sweat, and the clothes clung to her like Saran Wrap. A point the cameraman had made the most of, both on his pan down and back up.

But this wasn't who she was. It wasn't the point of the interview. She flew the most lethal helicopter ever devised by man, and they were turning her into a porn star. Her grip on her still-holstered M9 sidearm grew painful, but she couldn't ease off.

"Em-i-ly!" "Whoo-hoo, Captain!" "Now that's what we're talking about!" The catcalls in the tent overrode the voice-over. Attracted attention from outside the tent. More air jocks drifted in to see what was up. Is that how they thought of her every day? To react would only admit her intimidation. And that door wouldn't be opened for anybody.

She should've shot the stupid screen while she had the chance.

Even on the tiny laptop you could see good muscle definition right at her fighting weight. Not bodybuilder, though she lifted enough weights. Still, she wasn't particularly happy with how she looked. She'd never met a woman who didn't feel that way.

Did guys feel like that? This crowd seemed pretty pleased every time the camera caught one of them. A lot of macho shoulder punching, hard enough to bruise, each time one of them made national television.

The next clip showed her pulling out an emergency foil blanket, good for reflecting away the worst of the sun if you were smacked down in middle of sand dune nowhere. She'd demo-ed how to use one to hide from the sun, even digging it into the sand before disappearing beneath.

But in the next instant, she knew this broadcast didn't go there. Instead they went with her quick origami moment to create a decent solar oven from the foil. Taken her a while to figure that one out back when she flew for the 101st. They jumped to a finished loaf of sourdough bread, from some starter she'd had smuggled in. Not bad. She could live with this. Somehow.

And then the next image rolled.

Not a helicopter or flight suit in sight. How long was this stupid clip anyway? They'd dogged her heels for a full day and this was the best they could do?

Back to the solar oven. The soufflé. They wouldn't. They couldn't. They did.

A whole circle of broad-shouldered, badass flyboys standing around her with their arms crossed over bare, serious-workout chests. A solid wall of shirtless, obviously posed male flesh she'd hadn't even noticed the news crew setting up. Her tiny image on the screen lifted the chocolate soufflé from the makeshift oven. Perfect. And the desert was so frigging hot that the soufflé didn't start its inevitable collapse from cooling until after the camera moved on. The round of applause had tickled her at the time. But on the squidgy, little piece-of-crap laptop, it just made her look like a half-naked Suzy Homemaker in shades.

"Flying into battle, you know her well-fed crew will follow Captain Emily Beale anywhere because she's the hottest chef flying." In the parting shot, a helmeted pilot, visible only as a silvered visor and blue-black helmet, lifted off in a swirl of dust.

Her helmet was purple with a gold-winged flying horse on the side, and everyone in the tent knew it. It remained clamped under her arm at this moment in case they wanted to double-check. She'd had no missions the day the film crew was in camp so they'd shot that dweeb Bronson, of all useless jerks.

That couldn't be the end of the clip. But the wrap shot was perfect, the camera following Bronson high into the achingly blue sky.

All those interviews about her pride as the first woman serving in a man's world.

Not one word made it in.

Descriptions of nasty but unclassified missions that she had been authorized to discuss.

All cut.

Actually, they hadn't used a single word. She'd never spoken. Just cooked and been ogled.

And finally, to drive the hammer home, they'd used Bronson in his transport bird, not her heavy, in-your-face, DAP Hawk for the closer. When you wanted a joy ride, you called Bronson. When you wanted it done, you loaded up her MH-60L Direct Action Penetrator Black Hawk.

They had to include at least one—

"In New York's Bryant Park today…" The laughter drowned out the parade of anorexic women who probably couldn't shoot a lousy .22 without getting knocked on their narrow butts.

She pulled her pistol and let fly at the laptop. The first shot shattered the screen and flipped it off the empty ammo case. The second spun it in midair, and the third punched the computer into the sand.

A dozen guys inspected the smoldering laptop in the ear-ringing silence and then Emily's face as she reholstered the sidearm. A little more mayhem than she'd intended, but she was a pilot first, dammit.

Then, as if on cue, several of the guys fist-pumped the air simultaneously.

"Sexiest chef flying, Captain!" "They got that right!" "Whoo-hoo!"

"Well, your next thousand meals are gonna be damned MREs." She shouted to be heard over the rabble.

They hooted and applauded in reply.

"Cold egg burritos!" The very worst of the Meals Ready-to-Eat menu.

"Ooo!" "We're so scared." "Show us how to make an oven." "Sexiest chef!"

She opened her mouth to offer a few uncouth words about how much they'd enjoyed watching their own lame selves—

"'Tenshun!" The deep voice sliced through the chatter like the rear rotor of her Black Hawk through a stick of softened butter. A voice that had sent a shiver down her spine ever since she'd first heard it two months before.

They all snapped to their feet as if they'd been electrocuted. Some part of the laptop still functioned, Carlson's voice sounded into the sudden silence. "At a recent concert, the Rolling Stones—"

A booted foot smashed down and delivered the coup de grâce to the wounded machine.

Major Mark "The Viper" Henderson stood two paces inside the rolled-back flap of the tent, one foot still buried in the machine. Six feet of cliché soldier. Broad shoulders, raw muscle, and the most dangerous-looking man Emily had ever met. His straight black hair fell to his squared-off jawline. His face clean shaven, eyes hidden by mirrored Ray-Bans. Rumor had it they were implanted and the major no longer needed eyes.

After two months, she couldn't say otherwise. He always wore the shades when he wasn't wearing a helmet for a night mission.

Even the first time they'd met, as purported civilians at Washington state's Sea-Tac Airport, he had worn them. Coming out of security, newly assigned to the 5th Battalion, she'd known instantly who waited for her. She doubted another person in the crowded airport would recognize him as a soldier; they'd both been trained to blend in. But she'd recognized Major Mark Henderson as if some part of her body had known him for years.

In the tent, he swiveled his head once, the sunglasses surveying the crowd. Every man jack of them knew the major had memorized exactly who was there, what they'd said, what they were about to say—and probably knew what they'd been thinking the moment they exited their mothers' wombs. If they weren't careful, he'd start telling them what they would be thinking about during their last moment on Earth, and none of them, not even Crazy Tim, wanted to run head-on into that level of mind-blower.

"There will be no gender-based commentary in this unit. Understood?"

"Sir! Yes, Sir!" Rang out so loudly it would've hurt Emily's ears if she hadn't been shouting herself.

Chapter 2

"CAPTAIN." MAJOR HENDERSON TURNED, THE LAPTOP'S plastic shell crumbling beneath his heel with a low moan, and stepped back out of the tent into the driving sun with no sign that he would ever break a sweat.

Emily tossed her helmet to Big Bad John, her crew chief from Kentucky coal mine country. The nickname had been inevitable. Six foot four and powerfully muscled. She hustled after the major, out of the tent and across the sandy landing field.

The most common theory placed Major Henderson's mother as part snake and his father as pure viper. The very fastest, most dangerous viper, everyone added quickly. There were even debates on exactly what breed that would be.

Others claimed that he hadn't been born but rather hatched.

But she'd flown with him the first two weeks before being given her own bird, and she'd seen the two small pictures he tucked in his window every flight. Once, when he'd been out of the bird, she'd leaned in to inspect them more closely.

One a young boy wearing mirrored shades, just like his highly decorated SEAL commander father who had Mark tucked under his arm.

And the other, much more recent of Mark and his parents, all mounted on some seriously large and majestic horses, and all three wore mirrored shades. He and his father could be copies of each other, except Mark was darker, his features more sharply defined. She could see where Mark had gotten that and his straight, dark hair. His mother was a tall woman with strong Native American features and a cascade of black hair that flowed past her shoulders almost to her waist. Above them arched a carved sign that looked quite new and proclaimed: "Henderson Ranch, Highfalls, MT." They were as stunning specimens of the human race as their mounts were of the equine.

Outsiders teased their company about being the Black Adders because their company so fixated on The Viper's nickname. Henderson's pilots took it as a compliment and painted winged, striking adders on their helos, all sporting Rowan Atkinson's Mr. Bean smile. About half the winged tattoos worn by the pilots in the tent depicted striking adders, though only Crazy Tim, to no one's surprise, had placed the classic, beak-nosed Mr. Bean face permanently on his skin.

Major Henderson wasn't just the commander of the 3rd Hawk Company of the 5th Battalion SOAR. He was also the most decorated, toughest son of a bitch in the 160th Air Regiment. And, despite her first impression at the airport, he wasn't much nicer on the ground. But he had the only thing that really mattered in covert helicopter operations. He was the best.

Only the most exceptional fliers were invited to interview week at the 160th. Only the toughest survived it with a residual shred of ego intact. And of the few who made it through the pearly gates of the back lot of Fort Campbell, Kentucky, over half flunked out of the eight months of initial training. Never mind the year and a half of advanced training after you'd made the grade. Only the most terrifyingly qualified of those who survived made command.

Stories of Major Mark Henderson abounded on all sides. One told that he'd taken on a battalion of the Republican Guard during Operation Iraqi Freedom, with only his bird and his wingman's, and won.

Emily had assumed that they were just telling the newbie tall tales. But the crew stuck to the tale of two lonely choppers, totaling eight men, against five hundred troops armed with the very best the Iraqis could buy from Russia. Around Major Mark Henderson, it almost seemed possible.

Another told of the time he'd been smashed down a hundred miles behind unfriendly lines and decided to use his time awaiting rescue to blow up a few military targets. He and his three-man crew had done it running from hidey-hole to hidey-hole with a jury-rigged, four-hundred-pound, nineteen-round rocket pod torn off his chopper in the crash. His actions supposedly opened a whole section of the battlefront for easy access.

And those were before you got into the real whoppers. Tall tales edged well past surreal, one of which Emily knew from personal experience to be completely accurate. And to this day she counted herself lucky to be alive after that mission.

She caught up with Major Henderson around the midfield line. Their base camp was an old soccer stadium. Tier upon tier of concrete benches coated in flaking whitewash ringed the field. Too arid to sustain grass, the field now sprouted with a dozen-odd helicopters of varying sizes and capabilities.

Black Hawks, the hammer force, ranged down near the enemy's goal line.

A flock of Little Birds sprouted about midfield ready to deliver clusters of four Special Forces operators to almost anywhere that they were needed fast. The birds were so small that the soldiers didn't even sit in them, but rather on fold-down benches to either side. A short step to ground or a thirty-meter fast rope into a zone too hot to land.

A pair of massive, twin-rotor Chinooks, half-hidden in heat haze and thermal shimmer, lurked around the home team's goal. The playing field was owned and operated by a well-oiled, three-company mash-up of the 1st and 5th SOAR battalions.

Sentries from the 75th Rangers were perched along the topmost row of the stadium looking outward. Dust rose from every footstep and hung in the still, breathless air for hours.

She matched her stride to his. It was always nice, those quiet moments when they walked side by side. Some kind of harmony like that very first day. She'd come through the gate, bag over her shoulder, and he hadn't even nodded or smiled. Just pivoted easily on his heel and landed in perfect synch with her as they headed toward parking.

The major continued to move steadily across the dusty field toward his small command center set up by the barricaded entrance tunnel at the home team end. Why had he interfered in the tent? She could have laughed it off. Could have. Wouldn't have. Maybe the major had been right to shut down the guys' teasing, but now there'd be an even bigger wall of separation to knock down, as if being a female pilot in a combat zone wasn't three strikes already.

They reached the end of the field together, like a couple out enjoying a quiet stroll. She shook her head to shed the bizarre image. Not with her commanding officer, and certainly not with a man as nasty and dangerous as The Viper.

He stepped onto the sizzling earth of the running track that surrounded the field. They were in Chinook country now. The Black Hawks and Little Birds were but vague suggestions in the morning's heat shimmer. Down here at the command end, the pair of monstrous Chinook workhorses squatted, their twin rotors sagging like the feathers of an improbably ugly ostrich. These birds looked far too big to fly, yet they could move an entire platoon of fifty guys and their gear, or a half platoon along with their ATVs, motorcycles, and rubber boats.

"I'm sorry, sir. I know I shouldn't have discharged a firearm in camp. I'll replace the computer, but I'm a pilot and those news guys didn't…"

He stopped and turned to look at her. Not a word.

"I just…" She looked very small and insignificant in his mirrored shades. Twice.

"Captain?" His voice flat and neutral.

"I… Dammit! I'm a pilot, sir. They had no right. No bloody, blasted stupid right to do that to me. I—"

"Don't care."

Her tiny, twinned reflection dropped her jaw.

Then Major Mark Henderson did the strangest thing.

He reached up a meat cleaver-sized hand and pulled his glasses down his nose. Now she knew she was screwed. She'd never be able to joke with the guys again about the major not having eyes.

Steel gray. As hard as his body. The most dangerous-looking viper she'd ever seen.

Then he smiled. She almost fell as she dropped back a step. The smile reached his eyes and turned them the soft, inviting gray of a summer sunrise.

"Do you think I give one good goddamn about a lousy piece of hardware or about what CNN thinks? In my command, only one thing matters: are you the best flying? Period." His voice was firm, but soft and friendly. Almost teasing.

Then he shoved his glasses back in place, and the smile clicked off in the same motion. He turned back for the tent.

She tried to follow. Really she did. But two thoughts rooted her in place.

First, had The Viper really just smiled at her? Been pleasant? It would prove he was human, which didn't seem much more likely than him pulling down his sunglasses.

Second, her body felt weak and ravished by his simple gaze, though it had not raked over her like the news camera. Those gray eyes, especially when he smiled... What would she have to do to have them look at her like that again?

It still pissed her off a bit. How would he like to be called the sexiest major flying?

She got her feet moving again.

He'd probably love it—he was a guy, after all.

—~~—

By the time Emily followed him into command, Major Henderson sat at a small table spread with a large map for sector 62-15. He waved her to a stool.

Her butt hit the seat before she noticed the third man at the table.

The D-boys could do that. The ghosts of Special Forces. There were Rangers, then Green Berets and SEALs, then there was Delta Force. No one knew how many. Few of them spoke to anyone outside their own unit. She'd once heard someone call the man now seated at the table "Michael." She'd flown support for him a half-dozen times and never found out his rank or his last name. But one thing was certain: if he sat at the table, tonight's mission would not be dull.

"Operational Engagement," Henderson pointed at a narrow notch on the topographic map, "O. E. Mole." The elevation lines crowded so tightly together that the valley walls must be vertical cliffs. He spun a satellite photo in front of her. Those large hands, light and fast. She'd always been partial to big, strong hands. The way they could hold— She shook her head to clear the image and focused on the photo.

Classic Hindu Kush, the mountains of northeast Afghanistan. The desert lay below, desperately dry and hot in the wide valley. But as you climbed the cliffs, holly and cedar trees cluttered the skyline. In some places, because of the branches, flying down was almost safer than flying up, except then the enemy on the high, forested ridge could shoot down onto you.

Helicopters didn't appreciate being shot any more

than the next aircraft, but they definitely didn't appreciate being shot at from above. Most of the armor ran below and up the sides.

"Recon Team Mouse identified a cave up this notch. They have reason to believe there is intelligence inside that cave that must be recovered intact, along with several high-level unfriendlies we'd rather speak to than kill. This is tonight's target."

He pointed at Michael. "Three Little Birds will take twelve of his men to the back side of the ridge. It will take Delta a few hours to penetrate the site, so I'm having Bronson set up a FARP a dozen miles out where we can top off fuel."

Twelve Delta Force operators. If you had a crisis on your hands, you sent four of them, a disaster, six or seven. A full squadron of twelve told her exactly how important this target had been deemed by command. Bronson could handle a forward arming and refueling point, so that worked for her.

"Where am I?"

"You and I…" Both DAP Hawks. It had been weeks since a mission called for both of their heavy weapons platforms in the same place. "And Clay's pair of MH-60K transport birds. We run a noisy search-and-destroy here," Henderson put a finger on the map at the far end of the valley, "and here."

<hr/>

Mark watched her carefully as he laid out the mission, indicating key features of the terrain on the map and the tactical requirements.

Captain Emily Beale showed no surprise, no hesitation.

She captured the entire scope in a single gulp and appeared ready to go.

Michael, commander of the Delta Force group on the base, had expressed some concern about assigning Beale to a key role.

Every bit of Mark's training agreed. Except for one minor point: the way she flew. Sure, he'd heard the reports from her trainers at Fort Campbell. Even talked to her CO back in the Screaming Eagles, the 101st Airborne Assault. Hearing about the first woman who had SOAR-qualified was one thing; flying with her was quite another.

For two weeks, he'd flown her into hell as his copilot and she hadn't flinched. For the six weeks since he'd assigned her to her own bird, he'd fed her increasingly nasty missions. Her success ratio was astonishing. And when paired with Lieutenant Stevenson, who she'd insisted on having as her copilot, they were already the sharpest team he had. They'd flown together since West Point and it showed.

As far as Mark could tell, Emily and Archibald Stevenson weren't an item. That was good because of the fraternization rules in the Army Code of Conduct. There was no spark between them, just incredible flying.

The D-boy had acquiesced to Mark's judgment, but even now Mark could see him observing Beale carefully.

Mark looked at the trim blond and did his best not to think about what else he was feeling. He almost hadn't assigned her to this mission for a very different reason than the military stakes.

Mark didn't want to risk her on a dangerous mission. Could hardly stand to assign her where the personal stakes were so high.

To be fair to her, that was the factor that finally tipped the assignment in her favor rather than against. Because his mother had raised him better than that. In his command, there never had been and never would be any gender bias. He was known for that, and had probably factored into Captain Beale being assigned to his unit.

And he'd live by that, even if it would risk rather than protect Emily Beale.

Chapter 3

SIX MILES AND TWO MINUTES' FLYING TIME FROM THE D-boys' drop point, Captain Emily Beale unleashed her gunners.

"Steel!"

Big Bad John and Crazy Tim laid into the hillside with their miniguns.

The Direct Action Penetrator Black Hawk motto was, "We Deal in Steel!" No one had ever placed a chopper in the sky more lethal than SOAR's DAP Hawks.

They'd hit it lucky and spotted a couple of heat signatures walking along the ridge. No innocent shepherd would walk these hills at two in the morning. Nor start firing rifles as they broke into a run.

"Two down," Tim reported.

John chimed in. "Four ducked behind a ledge, three hundred yards at two o'clock low. Small-arms fire incoming."

She twisted the Hawk, and Archie let fly with one of their high-explosive, 2.75-inch rockets. The explosion hit the cliffside above the position. A boulder avalanche tumbled down on the bad guys and swept them away into the valley.

Big John's shouted, "Yes!" confirmed the kill. Six on the move at night would have spelled serious pain for the local 10th Mountain company in the morning. It also probably meant more were on the move.

Emily'd been keeping her eye out for the Little Birds but still barely spotted them, even with her night vision gear. Their rotor tips painting faint circles in bright green traced their static discharge on her equipment's eye. The Little Birds slithered in behind the ridge with the cave opening in it. Two D-boys per side sat on their little benches. At thirty meters up, the tiny helicopters checked their mad dash. She couldn't see them at this distance, but the D-boys would wrap one hand around the fast rope and slide down only feet apart. Five seconds to place everyone on the ground and drop the ropes. On cue, the Little Birds' two-man crews turned to run for the FARP and wait.

Once the Little Birds were gone, she and Henderson slid in perfect unison over the ridge on their side of the valley. Let the cave dwellers think the fight had moved on. Archie, her copilot, killed a couple rocks with rounds from the 30 mm cannon just to sound busy.

At two hours and twenty minutes, they ran the back side of the ridge. They took a few miscellaneous rounds shot by baddies stupid enough to underestimate a DAP Hawk. The sound of each passing bullet was instantly computer analyzed and revealed the shooter's position on the tactical displays. Big John and Tim took turns pouring a couple hundred rounds from the miniguns right back down their throats. Second volleys from the ground rarely happened.

At two hours and thirty minutes, she and Henderson roared back over the ridge with the hammer down. At 180 knots, more than 200 miles an hour, they crossed the valley in ninety seconds flat and probably weren't audible until the last fifteen. By nursing her attitude to maximize the inflow for the turbines at this altitude, she managed to arrive three full seconds ahead of Henderson. She kept her smile to herself but felt pretty damn good about that.

Emily scanned back and forth. Archie would worry about the condition of the Hawk, she kept her focus on the collection of choppers suddenly cluttering the sky.

They started taking some heavy rifle fire from down in the valley, and Henderson peeled off to deal with it. Per plan, she stayed high and back to protect Clay's birds and the three Little Birds who had returned from Bronson's refueling layover.

All went according to plan until they started loading. Twelve D-boys came out of the cave exactly on schedule, but now twenty-six people streamed from the cave mouth onto the narrow ledge that formed the only possible pickup point. Two D-boys and seven baddies, the practical limit at this altitude, piled into each of Clay's transport Hawks as they hovered a foot from the ledge. They also loaded some hefty cases and an armful of laptops.

The Little Birds dodged in and grabbed seven of the eight remaining D-boys while a cloud of fire rained down from above. Their jobs now were to be safe and far away. Two D-boys were hit but continued to return fire upward from their bench-seat perches as the Little Birds scampered along with Clay's flight.

One more Delta operator knelt in the cave mouth, busy at something. The walls were so steep that he was being shot at from almost directly above and the Hawk had no way to bring weapons to bear. She could climb up and take them head on, but there was still the one

D-boy marooned and no one left to fetch him before someone else found a good angle on him.

A loud "krump" and a massive updraft shook her bird. Henderson must have found the shooters directly below and dropped a couple Hellfire missiles in their laps to make that kind of shock wave. The gunfire from below evaporated.

She kept her eye on the D-boy as she slid forward into the narrow defile. He still knelt, safe from above just inside the mouth of the cave. The spatter of small-arms fire sounded from behind her. Her gunners had switched to their new handheld FN SCAR machine guns and were leaning out the doors to shoot upslope. Not the best, but it was all she could give them.

The rain of bullets from above meant that the D-boy would never survive a trip to the pickup ledge. Time to find another solution.

"Kick a rope."

Archie spared her a glance as Big John kicked a thirty-meter-long fast rope out the door. Anchored on a short door boom, the two-inch-thick woven rope dangled for a hundred feet below the Hawk.

Nudging the chopper forward, the sound of her rotors echoed off the walls, walls far too close on either side. The rope still hung twenty feet shy of where the D-boy crouched, now facing her from under the cave's protective overhang. Small-arms fire from above hemmed him in on three sides, the cliff wall on the fourth. In moments, someone would find the right angle and he'd be done for.

She edged in until the tips of her rotor blades couldn't be more than five feet from the cliff wall on either side, still too far.

"Spot the rear rotor for me."

Big John swore over the headset.

Emily leaned into the right foot pedal as softly as she could. The defile was too narrow for the Black Hawk to fit sideways, but she could swing the rope a little closer to the cliff wall by twisting a bit.

"Fifteen, ten, five. Damn it, Captain. Trimming trees."

For an instant she stared down through the Plexiglas window by her feet at the D-boy perched on the cliff edge ten feet from the rope and twenty feet below her. The rocks around him sparked with rifle fire from above.

It was Michael. She was close enough to recognize him with her night-vision goggles. He stared at her for a long moment before turning to finish whatever he was doing.

An RPG passed between them, somehow missing the spinning rotor blades as it passed close enough for either of them to reach out and touch. A rocket-propelled grenade would be death for all of them. It blew when it hit the slope hundreds of feet below, but she didn't flinch. Kept the rope steady ten feet off the cliff.

He finished and turned to face her. She knew he'd be assessing her as well as the tactical situation. It had been clear enough in the briefing that he didn't trust her, but she'd been assigned anyway. That meant Henderson did trust her. Well, she wouldn't let him down.

A spate of fire chased the D-boy back for a long three seconds, rattling like buckets of hail across her windshield. When it eased for a moment, he nodded his head once and leapt.

She held steady against her own downdraft swirling between the cliff walls. If he missed, he'd smack rock in three hundred feet and fall a thousand more before stopping.

"John?" Emily didn't dare break her concentration long enough to look down.

"We've got him."

She pushed her left pedal to get the tail rotor clear of the wall. Then backed up on the cyclic control and, raising the nose ever so slightly, slid backwards out of the defile. A dozen more rounds hammered against her windshield. Small arms mostly, but one big crack appeared from a heavier weapon finally brought to bear. Hopefully the Hawk's bulk shielded the D-boy, because she couldn't do anything for him dangling below her.

Then Mark Henderson roared by, almost close enough to enmesh their main rotors. He pulled his bird near vertical, giving his gunners the best line on the ridge. A stream of minigun fire burned into the baddies. In moments, the fusillade that had pounded her Hawk cut off, concentrating on the more hazardous target now close at hand. Mark gave them a quick round of rockets, and the distinct hammer of the 30 mm cannon could be heard echoing off the canyon walls.

Damn but the man was a joy to fly with. She could always count on Mark Henderson in the air. Always. And that wasn't something you could say of most men, or many at all really. Now if only he didn't insist on chapping her ass every single second they were on the ground.

She kept easing back, watching the rotors to make sure she didn't catch a tree and send them all plunging to their deaths. Once she was clear, a tongue of flame roared out of the defile right where they'd been hovering ten seconds earlier. The concussion knocked her chopper farther back.

"Damn, did we lose him?"

"Nope, he's on tight," Big John called. "Looks like he's pocketing something. Remote detonator maybe. Guessing he stayed behind to set the mines."

Dangling by one hand a thousand feet in the air, the D-boy had triggered the mines he'd left behind to destroy the cave. She leaned into the controls, backpedaling for all she was worth, the helicopter's nose pointed to the sky to give the rotors maximum rearward power. She ran the turbine engines right past redline. They roared in response as she was rammed down hard enough in her seat to hit the stops on the shock absorber.

A second blast proved her guess right: Michael's explosives triggered a massive ammo dump inside the mountain. The cliff face blew outward, spattering her bird with a pounding rattle of fist-sized rocks, and a whole section of the mountainside headed down for the valley.

They dragged the rope up with its human load and hauled ass back to base.

Chapter 4

"NICE FLIGHT, CAPTAIN."

Mark couldn't help himself. He radioed as they circled down together over the soccer stadium. He'd always been so careful not to compliment her. Keeping Emily Beale convinced she wasn't as good as he needed her to be had honed her skills even in two short months. At least that's what he hoped motivated him.

Maybe he was just being petty... But no. She'd beaten him across the valley in identical birds and still he'd complimented her. Though there wasn't enough money on Earth to make him ask her how she'd found the extra bit of speed.

"Thank you, Major."

Nice flight? He'd almost choked when she crawled into that defile under a rain of fire. One lucky shot, one moment of lost control, and she'd have eaten the cliff wall.

Any pilot good enough to make SOAR flew cool under fire. Sitting back at camp they might barf their guts out, but not in flight. And not Emily Beale. He'd never seen her with the shakes, the squeams, not even working out the kinks of a stiff neck from holding too tight.

Captain Emily Beale. Ms. Cool-as-could-be.

Would he have flown into that defile? Probably. If he'd thought of it. Would he have considered it long enough to think of it? Probably not. He'd have dismissed it out of hand as impossible. And probably left the Delta operator to pay the price for lack of any solution.

What was he supposed to do with this woman?

Even as they landed on the field, she settled her bird clean and square to the worn soccer field lines, hopped down at ease, and chatted for a minute with the D-boy she'd plucked off the cliff. He actually shook her hand and smiled before moving off toward the prisoners. More than most got from the silent ghosts of Delta Force.

A bunch of the flyboys and ground crew gathered around her. The news of the mission's success had swept through the base, and the story of the defile had already been spread by one of the Little Bird pilots. Mark could see it sweeping through the crowd.

And Beale, calm as could be, completely unaware of the men's stares, stripped her flight suit halfway down, tied the empty arms around her slim hips, and turned to inspect her bird. Peppered with hundreds of holes, one of the main rotor blades so chewed up it would need replacing, and a slow stream of black hydraulic fluid dribbled down the side of the engine housing. She climbed up with the crew chief to see where the damage originated, and thirty pairs of eyes followed her.

Hard to blame the guys. Five hundred miles from nowhere and only one woman in sight. A real stunner, too. But that wasn't the real reason they stared. She'd flown into a place no sane person would go to bring her action team out. For doing that, for protecting the team at any cost, there wasn't a man here who wouldn't throw himself in front of a bullet to save her, not even if she looked like a heifer.

Did she know that she'd mesmerized an entire base of
the toughest warriors on the planet with that single act,
never mind the dozens before it?

Did she have any idea that she'd done the same to him?

—⁓—

"What the hell is this, Captain?"

Emily rolled off her cot and hit the ground, slapping
for the gun that wasn't on her hip.

Major Mark Henderson loomed over the other side of
her cot and glared down at her.

All she wore was a braless tank tee and her underwear. But he didn't look to be in any mood to give a
damn how she was dressed or undressed.

"What the hell is what, sir?"

As she stood, he shoved out a set of orders.

> *Captain Emily Beale is hereby reassigned.*
> *Report aboard Carrier America II soonest for*
> *immediate departure.*
> *Admiral James Parker*

She read them twice more, but they made no more
sense than the first time.

"Did you put in for a transfer?" The major appeared
close to complete apoplexy. It was only the second time
she could recall seeing any emotion on his face, the first
just yesterday when he'd actually smiled at her. The jux-
taposition of the two, both directed her way, wouldn't
reconcile in her brain, making her feel as exposed as,
well, as if she was standing in front of The Viper wearing only her underwear.

"Never, sir."

"You don't know what this is about?"

"Sir, no, sir."

"Shit!" The major snatched back the sheet and glared at the order again as if there'd be any change.

"Get your damned gear together. We leave in five minutes."

As he reached the door, he hesitated but didn't look back.

"And put on some goddamn clothes."

Next time she'd sleep in bloody dress blues.

———ᨆ———

Mark shoved Beale into the copilot seat, forcing his normal copilot into the rear. In the five minutes she'd been packing and saying good-bye to her crew, he'd only grown more frustrated.

Communications had confirmed the order. The only answer he'd received from the carrier was, "All speed." There was something he couldn't ignore.

He laid down the hammer and flew in far too foul a temper to speak. Beale tried once or twice to say something, but he couldn't make himself hear the words. After an hour and a half of desert, followed by sixty miles of ocean, he scared up the carrier group.

He answered the Mini Boss in Primary Flight and swung wide to land on the aft-deck helicopter landing pad marked with a large white circle. He slammed down so hard that the shock absorbers actually bounced ten tons of helicopter back into air.

"Shit!" He cursed as they thudded back down.

"Captain Emily Beale, report to Captain Tully," came

in over Pri-Fly's air control frequency before the chopper had even settled. Whatever was going on had to be damned hot.

A crew escort in orange opened Emily's door. She was gone before Mark even had a chance to finish the shutdown.

He hadn't been able to look at her for the whole flight because every time he did, he saw the most enticing woman he'd ever met in the least amount of clothes he'd ever been fortunate enough to witness on her.

He was her commander.

He had no right to think of her that way.

Had no right to so hate the idea of losing her from his squad, from his life.

Mark punched the cockpit door window hard enough to really hurt.

Chapter 5

THE HAWK STILL ROCK 'N' ROLLED ON HER SHOCKS. Emily had never seen Major Henderson miss a landing. She'd seen him land as hard when there was reason, imminent engine failure from being shot too many times perhaps, but this one he'd just buggered. That was new. The silence on the intercom from the two crew chiefs and the copilot in the rear was deafening. Apparently they'd never seen The Viper make a flying mistake before either.

What was his problem anyway? She was the one being shipped out with no notice. Without her crew. Being sent away for who knew how long. Being away from Mark Henderson would almost be a relief.

She'd grown used to the way he was always hounding her to be better. As if she'd never measure up to a male flyer. That wasn't the problem.

The first-ever verbal compliment wasn't the problem either. He'd only ever praised her with guy-speak. Silence. Nothing to correct, so nothing to say. There was no way she'd tell him how proud that single "nice flight" made her.

The real problem was how his smile had weaseled its way into her brain, making sleep almost impossible. And when she'd finally slept, she'd dreamed of those soft, gray eyes. A little distance would be a good thing. But not reassigned.

A fully kitted swabbie appeared out of the heat haze in full, flame-retardant flight-deck suit, including helmet and orange vest, and yanked open her door.

She peeled her helmet, dumped her SARVSO survival-and-gear vest, and cracked her flight suit down the front to her gym shorts. It was even hotter on the carrier deck than inside the Hawk. Couldn't fry an egg on the deck: you'd burn it too fast. The heat pounded through her boot soles the instant they touched. She'd best get moving before the rubber melted and glued her to the spot. How could there be so much water and so much heat in the same place? The carrier and its battle group lurked a hundred miles off the coast, and the desert base was over twice that in the other direction.

The swabbie waited without even mincing from one searing foot to the other. Did the Navy give special training so he didn't just melt on the spot? Could he teach her? She was dying in shorts, T-shirt, and the wide-open flight suit.

He led her away from her helicopter across the searing deck.

During the flight, she'd tried to ask Major Henderson what was going on. She'd seen him on the radio. All he'd done was growl. Repeating that she hadn't requested any transfer or reassignment had elicited a true snarl. The trip proved tortuous, worse than trying to sneak past an antiaircraft battery, and she was glad to be out of the tiny cockpit packed solid with Henderson's anger.

Well, to hell with him. She hadn't done anything, whether or not he believed her.

As the swabbie led her up the first ladder of the

carrier's six-story command and control tower, she started thinking about what lay ahead of her rather than behind. Going to see the carrier's captain would be bad enough, but the admiral in charge of the carrier group would be right by his elbow.

Rear Admiral James Parker had shared her father's dinner table often enough that she'd have counted him a friend, if she wasn't a mere Army captain busy screwing up her career on national television. That had to be what got her sent down.

SOAR had been born in secrecy. They'd entered the public eye when they'd shown their strengths in Grenada and their weaknesses in Mogadishu. But they still tried to remain as low profile as possible. Of the eight choppers on the takedown of bin Laden, the news had only mentioned three. And not a word about SOAR. In thirty years they'd run thousands of missions that no one heard about or ever would. SOAR helicopters provided Special Forces operators with the world's best nighttime transport and protection.

The Night Stalkers shunned news as much as the Navy SEALs, and she'd hit front and center on CNN. Was that the problem? What idiot in command had even authorized the interview?

She hadn't considered that.

The moment she did, she knew the answer. Her mother would see it as a step up the social ladder. If she couldn't be in the same room as her daughter for five minutes in a row without them fighting, at least she could garner a nice social-circle boost out of Emily's unique position. And her mother had the ears of senators, newsmen, and dozens of others. A CNN piece that had nothing to do with flying or secret operations would be an easy sell for her.

"Damn!"

"Sir?"

"Nothing." She waved the swabbie on and trudged behind, the doomed woman being led to the gallows.

Her mother hadn't been trying to raise her own social status. Helen Cartwright Magnuson Beale had her sights set on a different primary mission: how to best prepare her daughter for Operation Marriage. Easy. Get her a near-enough-naked spot on CNN prime-time news. She'd probably, no, she'd certainly been in the editing room.

That's why there was nothing about flying, not one shot in her uniform or flight gear, though they'd taken enough footage of that too. That would hurt her daughter's marriage prospects.

She'd surely sold it as a "good PR piece" but, as was typical for Helen Beale, every statement had two meanings, except when it had three. Good PR for the Army and the news station, and good PR for getting her difficult daughter a husband of sufficient stature. One who would force her to stop "that foolish flying" and taking "those unnecessary risks."

The swabbie guided her toward the captain's office on the fifth floor of the carrier's tower as if Emily didn't know the way. She could trip him down a ladder or two and go hide in the bilge until the whole mess blew over. A lot of places to hide on a boat a quarter-mile long, near enough a football field wide, and a dozen decks deep.

But if she hid the rest of her life, she'd never have a chance to strangle her mother. And she'd thought that poor laptop had shown the worst of the problem.

When she'd gotten back to the tent after the meeting with Henderson and Michael, she'd found that her crew had dug a pit in the sand directly where it had landed and were waiting for her arrival to bury the machine's remains, with full honors. Most of the guys had even put on their service uniforms.

She'd cast the first handful of dirt, Big Bad John, in a big deep voice that would have sounded good on a preacher, had offered comforting words to a soldier who had served its country well but fallen while honorably performing its duty. Archie had even found a tiny American flag and presented it to her in proper triangle-folded form smaller than a silver dollar. She'd have to tell the boys they'd done good. If she saw them again.

But the problem hadn't stopped there. It had taken on a life of its own. And now she had to face the backlash.

She and the swabbie climbed the twenty-jillionth ladder-steep stair, entered a steel corridor that looked no different than the last couple dozen, and stood before a wooden door like any other except for the nameplate. "Captain." Not even "Rick Tully." Just his rank.

Getting a firm grip on her mother's throat wasn't going to happen any time soon, so she'd better shuffle the thought aside and concentrate. There was music to face right here, and she'd bet it was closer to gangster rap than string quartet.

Chapter 6

THE SWABBIE DELIVERED TWO SHARP KNOCKS ON THE captain's door, gaining Emily a call to enter. He swung open the door, dropped to a parade rest so lazy that it bordered on insolent, and shut the door behind her as soon as she'd passed in.

The air-conditioned chill of the office hammered against her sweat-soaked chest through the open flight suit. A quick glance down as she slammed to attention precisely three steps into the room revealed that, well, way too much was revealed.

Too late to do anything about it.

She snapped a salute as if she were in Class-As with a spit shine on her shoes that she could see to brush her hair in. Not scuffed boots that hadn't seen a cloth in a month, sun-faded flight suit that was once flight-crew brown but now more of a dull tan except where it sported circles of oil-stain black, and helmet hair waving and weaving down past her sweat-stained collar.

"Captain Emily Beale reporting, sir."

Captain Tully's lazy salute emphasized how disheveled she appeared, hardly worthy of a serious effort. Of course he sat comfortably in his office with its large oak desk, leather office chairs, and perfectly starched and creased khakis made so by some poor schmuck of a one-tour orderly. The place even smelled of lemon polish. Her own office measured one bucket seat wide, exactly as long as hip to pedal, and reeked of jet fuel, cordite from spent ammunition, and sweat.

"Hi, Emily."

She snapped a salute at Rear Admiral James Parker. "Hello, sir. Good to see you, sir."

He returned the salute a little less casually than the commander, but it wasn't exactly singing with respect either.

"You've certainly grown up since the last time I saw you." He had the decency not to look down her front like most guys. She'd developed two responses. If they made no comment, rare, neither did she. If they leered and went for the lame joke, she bloodied their nose but good. Usually once or twice proved sufficient to drive the message into their thick skulls.

As basic career advice, she decided not to bloody the admiral's nose even if he did start staring at her chest. For one thing, flying a helicopter would be impossible from a stockade.

"How long has it been, Captain?" The admiral's slacks and shirt were as starched and pressed as the commander's. The latter had returned his attention to his paperwork without as much as another glance in her direction.

"Four years, sir. When we were operating cleanup during that Sri Lankan mess, sir." That's when he'd personally recommended her for the Air Medal for Valor for exceptional ingenuity under pressure.

She'd been unable to fire into the rioting crowd, even when they shot at her. Against the rules to shoot up a bunch of civilians, no matter how unruly. So, she'd had her entire flight blast the crowd apart with the Hawks' downdraft. Every time the crowd tried to reassemble, she led her four Hawks to a mere dozen feet above street level, down tight between the buildings, easy prey if the crowd had a single decent shooter among them, and they'd literally blown the rioters apart with rotor wind and dust until they gave up.

"Sri Lanka. That's right. You like flying the Hawk?"

"Best bird in the sky, sir!"

"At ease, soldier."

"Thank you, sir." Was that enough permission to zip up the flight suit before the trickle of sweat between her breasts turned into an air-conditioned icicle?

Her body answered with a clear, "No," as instinct and years of training dropped her into parade rest, feet spread shoulder-wide and hands clasped behind her back, shoulders still back and chest out. The action pulled the flight suit wider open, but what was a girl to do? At least the green tee and shorts were regulation.

"You like that cooking stuff, too?"

"Always have, sir."

"I recall you were damn good at it."

"Thank you, sir." She'd cooked for him more than once at her father's house. She'd felt far more at home in the kitchen with her parents' French chef than she had in the museum-quality rooms of her mother's *Architectural Digest* house. Domicile. Work of residential art. And her mother had been much happier to have her uncomfortable daughter out from under foot and out of the public's social eye.

Emily learned to cook at Clarice's knee, French toast by the time she was five, and soloed on her first apple tart at seven. It had been a complete mess, the crust singed almost to charcoal, but she still had a Polaroid of it on

the bulletin board behind the door of her bedroom back
in D.C. She'd considered being a chef until the first time
her father took her along for a helicopter ride. One flight
and her life had been set. From that moment on, she only
cared about being best at one thing, chopper pilot.

"Richard," he turned to Captain Tully. "If you ever
have a chance to try her rack of lamb with white truffle
sauce, do. It's exquisite."

The captain merely grunted without looking up from
his paperwork.

"Nice of you to remember, sir." She filled the silence.

The admiral slid down into one of the leather armchairs. Then he waved her toward the other one.

She remained riveted to the steel plate. It was never
good when a top officer wanted a lower rank to sit in his
or her presence.

By the sheer brute strength gained from years of
hurking ten tons of armored chopper across the sky,
Emily managed to wrench herself free of parade rest and
sit in the chair. As she sat bolt upright on the edge of the
seat, the front of the flight suit billowed outward. She
grabbed at the zipper and hauled it up. So tight to her
neck that her gag reflex tried to kick in, but her hands
were already folded neatly in her lap, and she wasn't
going to do anything more to make herself look stupid.
If possible.

"I have a special assignment for you. Indefinite time
period. Completely optional, no repercussions, though I
hope that you'll consider it seriously."

Meaning she had no choice whatsoever.

Chapter 7

MARK LEFT THE EQUIPMENT CHECK TO HIS CREW. IT was a crappy call, but he was in no mood to make sure he hadn't broken a forty-million-dollar helicopter with that landing. Truth be told, the way he was acting, they'd be in no mood to let him.

As soon as he stepped on deck, he was ricocheted around by the deck crew like an old and unwanted billiard ball. The blue-jacketed chock-and-chain crew pushed him one way and pinned his bird to the deck despite the calm seas. White-vested safety guys shoved him the other and checked the chocks and looked for any fuel leaks. Two reds waited for him to move before they ran a quick inspection and dodged off to the shipboard munitions lift for resupply. The Hawk hadn't yet been restocked after last night's op at the cave.

A couple grapes, in their flame retardant suits and purple vests, waved for him to stand clear, then pulled a hose free from a handy deck hatch and started pumping JP-5 fuel to top off his tanks.

He finally found peace at the edge of the deck, just two steps from the sixty-foot drop to the Arabian Sea. Good thing the seas were calm today.

He glared up at the carrier's tower. Somewhere in there was Captain Emily Beale. If she was truly reassigned, he'd have to fill the seat on her bird. Bronson maybe. But the man was useless in combat. He'd have to reassign her bird to a carrier run until he figured out what the hell was going on.

He should be back at the base, but he couldn't let anyone else transport her. He knew it made no sense, but he didn't trust Beale to anyone else. Sure, the two of them flew side by side into life-threatening danger as often as not, but she also ranked as the most precious cargo he'd ever carried.

Knowing that the feeling made no sense made it no less true.

He turned to face the ocean, back toward Afghanistan lost over the watery horizon. Back where they'd flown together, chasing each other across the heart of the Hindu Kush, a grin of delight plastered across his face. Glad to be flying beside her even when he was losing the race.

What woman had last preoccupied his brain like Emily Beale? Okay, no one. Mary Taylor had filled his waking and sometimes his sleeping thoughts at sixteen. That she was two years older, a senior infinitely far out of his reach, hadn't stopped him. And perseverance had eventually paid off there. When he was seventeen, Laura had given him a very memorable and educational night for his Junior Prom.

Being in ROTC and a football wide receiver in college had offered him his pick of women, and he'd enjoyed every one. He'd been assigned for a couple of years to Italy, where he'd learned about the bountiful physical gifts of Italian women and their willingness to share them with a handsome American aviator. It still ranked as his first choice port-of-call for leave after his parents' ranch.

But none of them cluttered his brain like Emily Beale.

Any contentment with his lifestyle evaporated the first time he'd ever seen her. He'd come up from 5th Battalion's Fort Lewis HQ to fetch the latest newbie to graduate Fort Campbell training. Somehow a woman had made it through selection and training. The first ever, and he'd been saddled with her.

And his world had changed. Even though she'd been dressed in civvies, carrying a bright red knapsack, with her wheat-blond hair caught back in a ponytail to look like any other returning tourist, he'd known at a glance that she was the one he was there to meet.

They'd fallen into step in perfect harmony and flown that way ever since. He hadn't spoken a single word to her until they were back behind the gates of Fort Lewis because, for the first time in his life, he'd had no idea what to say to a beautiful woman.

He'd had to be careful. If he didn't want to be court-martialed and thrown out of the Army, he could never let her know how he felt. So he'd decided, as they walked side by side that first time, that in her presence he would always be pure military, pure regulation.

He wouldn't even compliment her, in case it was taken wrong. That had turned out to be a fantastic way to motivate her to excel, but it was merely a side benefit of his attempts to remain sane in her presence.

And she'd ruined him. He could work up some anger over that. Not at her, but at the circumstances that made their life. He couldn't have her. And, when he'd tried to lose himself between the generous breasts of a particularly willing Tuscan damsel on leave last month, he'd failed miserably at forgetting the slip of a blonde who could outfly every pilot in SOAR.

He stood there, in the soft breeze of the aircraft carrier's forward motion, finally admitting it.

She definitely ranked as the best pilot he'd ever flown with.

And when Captain Emily Beale flew ten tons of armored attack helicopter into battle, it was absolutely the sexiest thing he'd ever seen.

Chapter 8

"PERSONAL CHEF TO WHO?" *YOU'RE GOING MAD, EMILY.*
There's no other explanation. You aren't here sitting in a
cozy armchair in the captain's office aboard the nation's
newest aircraft carrier. You are locked in a rubber room
in a cozy white jacket with very long sleeves.

"The First Lady saw that CNN clip yesterday,"
Admiral James Parker explained. "Katherine Matthews
was quite taken with you and insists that you are the
only person she'll have."

"But I'm a combat pilot." The words choked out of
her no matter how she tried to keep her voice steady. Her
awful croak dragged the captain's attention back from
his pile of papers.

"Here now, James." Captain Tully shoved his paperwork into a folder, sealed it, and tossed it into the carved
oak outbox on his desk. "You never said anything about
taking one of Henderson's best and turning her into that,
that *woman's* nursemaid."

Listen to the captain. "One of Henderson's best."
That gave her a bit of heart. Surprised her actually, but
Emily restricted herself to a brief raising of eyebrows
before regaining control. Major Henderson specialized
in making her life a living hell. Never good enough.
In two months and over forty sorties, he'd never acknowledged a job well done but the once. He'd merely
assigned her a harder mission the next time. She'd have

to be surprised later, after she'd passed out from sitting at attention in a flight suit with a firm choke hold on her trachea.

Admiral Parker cleared his throat and didn't comment on Captain Tully's opinion of the First Lady. The military liked the President well enough; he'd done spectacularly well in cleaning up the Myanmar mess, very few troops required, no lives lost. That earned him a lot of credit with the Armed Forces. Much nicer to go home alive and in one piece; not a man or woman in the Army who wouldn't agree with that. Of course, the high mountains of Northern Afghanistan were causing him a severe headache as they had three presidents before him.

But while they might like him, they didn't much trust such a young president, and especially not his equally young and very showy wife. The latter sentiment Emily agreed with wholeheartedly, though for rather different reasons than your average soldier.

She'd never liked the First Lady, not even before they'd met.

Model at fifteen, *Vogue* cover one year later. At twenty-one, a psychology and marketing double-major at the renowned Wharton School of business in Philadelphia.

Too statuesque, too redheaded, and far too full of herself. Actually, the last point might make her a good combat pilot. She possessed the level of arrogance that only the very best air jocks cultivated. The knowledge that all of her actions were absolutely correct because they had to be, every time.

Of course, if the First Lady screwed up, there'd just be an irritated diplomat and her husband could call on the U.S. Armed Forces to clear up any little misunderstandings. If Emily messed up, people wound up very suddenly dead. Maybe she and the First Lady weren't all that different. Well, except for the statuesque and redheaded bits. Slender and blond didn't really play on the same field. Emily's height was far too emphasized by her lean physique. The First Lady was all in proper proportion and Emily didn't like her. Especially not married to the man she'd snared.

"The reason I didn't laugh off this request is very classified." The admiral dug into his pocket and pulled out a thumb drive with "Top Secret. Eyes only." emblazoned across it. As if that wasn't a walking advertisement of the worst kind saying, "Steal me."

"Captain, may I?"

It always amused her that she and Captain Tully held the same rank, but she commanded a squad of four for the Army while he commanded a ship of four thousand for the Navy. Today she wished she were a newly minted second lieutenant and none of these people had ever heard of her.

At a wave of the captain's hand, the admiral plugged the drive into the communication and conference gear that covered part of one wall and turned on the main screen.

The "Top Secret" thing was worrisome; she'd rather not see it. Her attempts to swallow nearly choked her against the too-tight zipper. She managed to ease it down a little while the two men focused on the screen, but she still couldn't breathe. She needed an oxygen bottle or perhaps a stiff drink to maintain mental operations at this altitude. Who knew that air five levels above a carrier deck had such a low oxygen content? The First Lady wanted her? To cook? It was the dumbest thing she'd ever heard in all her years of Army flying.

At the prompt, Admiral Parker typed in a ten-digit password and then, after a moment of searching, found the print authentication pad and laid his thumb on it.

Emily now knew for certain she didn't want to see whatever this was.

~~~

Emily gasped aloud as the first image after the "Classified Documents" warning flashed up on the captain's screen, then clamped her jaw shut to silence herself. Of all the faces she could possibly see, the Wicked Witch of the West Wing was the last she wanted to. Ever.

But that wasn't what had evoked her surprise.

The woman on the screen wasn't the First Lady Katherine Matthews that the world knew all too well. Cameras loved Katherine. She showed up front and center on the news so often that editorial cartoons joked about President Katherine.

But the one woman on the planet who didn't have to worry about how she looked on camera had been betrayed. The flowing red hair, intense Hollywood smile, and perfect complexion weren't in evidence at all.

The smile was missing. The glistening green eyes were closed. The red hair a snarl rather than a flounce. And the complexion was marred by a dozen bloody abrasions and cuts against a pallor gone from ivory to alabaster.

The admiral spoke, though Emily couldn't turn to look at him. It was the first time the woman had ever looked less than perfect.

"The window of the First Lady's limousine was shattered last week. We do not, I repeat, not have the attacker in custody. Apparently someone fired a spread of chipped porcelain. A shotgun blast would have done less damage, probably little more than scuff the paint job."

The next shot was a lipstick-red limousine that appeared to have the rear passenger window rolled down. The next, a close-up of the floodlit interior of the car, which glittered with a thousand glass fragments. A technician had drawn yellow arrows on the image to indicate flecks of shining white.

"High-grade porcelain, apparently from a smashed spark plug." Sure enough, the brand, model, and plant of manufacture were listed below.

"Even at a fairly low rate of impact, even the speed of a hand toss, it will cause safety glass to perform its function and fragment. Because the windows of the First Lady's personal limousine are not standard safety glass, the shattering dispersed the shards with surprising violence. The FBI theorizes that the very thing that injured the First Lady may have saved her life."

"Not making much sense with that last one, James." The captain had focused his full attention on the matter at hand.

Still inspecting the image, Emily blurted out, "The first blast created such a response…" Emily caught herself and glanced for permission to continue after she'd already begun. Not one of her safer habits.

The admiral nodded his assent.

"…that the attacker was too surprised and never fired the second shot." Emily considered the weapon itself. "Air gun probably, so it was fairly quiet. Sound and visual somehow masked so that the Secret Service couldn't locate the attacker. But an air gun with that kind of a load is only good at close range. Close enough that the explosive destruction of the window would have surprised him. Or her. The shooter stood down in the crowd, not a sniper up in a window. That takes guts or a suicidal intent."

Admiral Parker nodded for her to continue.

But she had nothing else to say. They should have caught the assailant. An air gun with porcelain shards within ten or fifteen feet of the vehicle. Enough filming crews that at least one camera should have had the right angle.

"Unless the Secret Service either knows who did it…"

"They don't. And counter-terrorism is also drawing a blank. Only the typical crazies who claim they did everything that happens called in, all missing many facts that they would have known if they'd been responsible." The admiral sounded certain. "Or…"

"Or the assailant is above suspicion. Perhaps inside the Secret Service even. Then he'd know exactly what the Service was and wasn't monitoring."

"You always were the smart one, Emily."

She clammed up. If she was so damned smart, why was she stuck on the sofa of the captain of an aircraft carrier? Smart points gathered so far this week? About minus eight.

A killer on the inside of the Secret Service? Why not just shoot the First Lady point blank? They had access. It didn't fly true.

"This was three days ago."

The next image revealed a cracked window. The one

after that, a pile of crumpled plastic next to a blooming pink rose.

"A model airplane?" The captain came out from behind his desk and moved closer to the big screen. "A MiG-21. Russian."

"From a kit company in Kentucky. This model is a fast little machine. Radio controlled. Flies at over a hundred miles an hour. Less than fifteen seconds from crossing the fence to impacting the White House."

Emily lurched to her feet as the captain stumbled forward.

"That window was the Oval Office?" The captain's voice had lowered to a deep, feral growl, belying any softness implied by his comfortable office. She must remember never to make him angry at her.

"No," Emily guessed. "The East Wing."

"Girl's on the money again. The First Lady's office, as a matter of fact. In there alone. Scared the daylights out of her. Apparently she'd glanced up at the moment it hit the window. She was frantic, screaming, and weeping when the agents broke in."

"What were they hoping to achieve with a model airplane?"

"Captain?" The admiral was looking at her. For what? How was she supposed to know?

Emily stared at the screen, and the spot between her shoulders began to itch.

"A dud." She turned to the two men. "It was a dud. Explosive charge that failed to detonate. Let me guess. M80s."

"An even dozen," he clicked to a screen showing the parts all laid out on a white cloth.

"Equivalent to nearly two sticks of dynamite bought over the counter at an untraceable illegal fireworks stand."

"Exactly. Machine-rolled like most mass-produced fireworks with no traceable fingerprints or other matter. Production lot stamped on the paper, but that tells us nothing. It was a large batch of several thousand. Enough force to blow the window and punch a fair-sized hole in the wall. The lab estimates a better than three-in-four chance of a kill if it had worked, the First Lady's desk chair is normally less than three feet from that window. The plane itself has proven untraceable, probably bought for cash at some toy store."

"Is there more?"

When the admiral shook his head, she collapsed back into her chair and the captain sat back against his desk.

"Katherine wants a bodyguard. She wants someone low profile, that's when she spotted you as a chef. That would provide you with ready access to her and the East Wing. I don't need to tell you the number of women trained in counter-terrorism who could pull this off without alerting the Secret Service."

None. No, not quite. There was one. It made sense. It made awful sense, and her head ached with every word of common sense he spoke.

She didn't like Katherine Matthews, never had. She didn't want to become a nursemaid. And most of all she didn't want to face—

"That's why they have the blasted Secret Service." Captain Tully's curse cut into the room.

"That's not what she's asking for. Because of the air-gun incident, she isn't feeling very safe in their hands. She's asking for Captain Emily Beale of the 160th Air Regiment."

"Request permission to refuse, sir?" Damn. That wasn't supposed to have turned into a question.

Rear Admiral James Parker had the decency to look uncomfortable as he reached into the inner pocket of his jacket. He handed her an envelope with her name on the front.

She didn't need to see the single sheet of paper within, or the letterhead seal it bore, to identify the author.

She'd know the handwriting anywhere.

Since before she could walk, she'd had a crush on one man, the older boy next door. How mundane was that? Her family part of the Washington power-elite inner circle, his father the Senate majority leader for fifteen years, his mother a Federal judge. She'd spent how many hours watching Mr. Junior Letterman, Mr. High School Running Back, Mr. Most Likely to Succeed?

At six, she could imitate his walk. At eight, could predict thirty seconds ahead when he'd brush his dark hair back out of his eyes, it depended less on the hair and more on how intrigued he became. By nine, she could imitate his handwriting so well that even he couldn't tell it from his own. Once for Valentine's Day she'd written love letters to thirty-two popular girls using his lumpy script, including the entire cheerleading squad. Months later he still hadn't straightened out the mess. They'd been good letters, even if she did say so herself.

But she'd been just a precocious, flat-chested twelve when he left for college and a still flat-chested sixteen when he went to Oxford for his doctorate. She hadn't graduated from flat to slender until eighteen, and he was long gone. She'd barely seen him since. Eight years younger than JFK when he took office, the youngest president in history, within five days of the youngest allowed by the Constitution. And by a landslide vote.

President Peter Matthews, her commander-in-chief, had asked her please, as a personal favor, to humor his wife's request.

She'd been right the first time, no choice at all.

Chapter 9

EMILY STEPPED BACK ONTO THE SCORCHING DECK OF the aircraft carrier but ground to a halt in the relatively safe haven against the ship's massive superstructure. Here at least there was shade, enough to mitigate the sun from devastating down to merely horrific. She eased the stranglehold of her coveralls, but it didn't helped.

Reassigned.

She'd just been reassigned to the last place on the planet she'd ever wanted to go. Sixteen hundred Pennsylvania Avenue. The White House. At the side of the First Lady, one degree of separation from the President.

Reassigned.

The word rattled around inside her like a low-energy round ricocheting inside a helicopter still hunting a target.

Reassigned. She leaned back against the wall of the superstructure before her knees gave out. And not to fly. Reassigned to goddamn cook. For the wife of President Peter Matthews, the ultimate proverbial boy next door.

She spotted Mark the moment she raised her eyes from the deck, even as an E-2 Hawkeye trapped in between them, catching the number two wire with a roar of turboprop and a wash of heat and the steamy tang of turbine exhaust.

Major Henderson glared at her from across the width of the aircraft carrier. She'd recognize him from a thousand others even at a distance through shimmering heat haze. No one walked with such power and grace, or stood with such insufferable arrogance.

Time to face The Viper. A quick calculation proved that her day had finally bottomed out. The thought offered a certain amount of freedom; she stood caught in the spin cycle, and no matter what she did, no auto-rotate maneuver would delay the imminent crash landing, so just go with the flow.

He strode to his chopper, deck crew dodging aside to let him by, snagged her duffel, and trotted across the flight line, escorted by a yellow-clad handler.

She snapped the best salute she could manage, which was pretty lame at the moment. He didn't chew her out, which was a relief, but he barely returned it which she'd had enough of already today.

But before she could bitch about it, he heaved the duffel at her. She caught it against her chest.

"What the—" Her voice disappeared beneath the roar of an F-22 Raptor going to full afterburners before the catapult fired it into the sky. She could feel her lips still moving, but even she couldn't hear what she was saying.

Only after the major grabbed her arm and dragged her back toward the closest superstructure entrance did the sounds of the deck come crashing in. She'd stepped out with no hearing protection. Had been in such shock she hadn't noticed the incessant roar as hundreds of crew manned the carrier deck during active flight operations.

He dragged her past the handlers' stations, through two sets of sound-deadening doors, and into a small rest area sporting a couple of vending machines and a handful of small tables. Echoingly vacant at the moment. He shoved her down in a chair in front of an amazing view of the

Arabian Sea and the Gulf of Oman. Vastly empty except for a couple of the inevitable support ships that danced around every carrier like a flock of seagulls with nothing better to do than bob about on the waves together.

Rather than joining her, he stood and glared at her through those mirrored shades.

Her brain wouldn't kick in. She blinked and he disappeared from in front of her. Now he'd come to gloat over her downfall. She blinked again and he was back. He thumped a soda can down on the table in front of her.

"Drink that, then tell me what the hell is going on, Captain."

She rolled the cold can across the burning heat of her forehead and cheeks. Tell him what? It was easy to remember the Top Secret banner on the video. Easy to know that this was one of those assignments that couldn't be discussed with anyone. Black Ops, and he wasn't part of the action team. Emily Beale, team of one. Totally screwed.

"Can't, sir."

"Can't or won't, Captain?"

"How do you do that?"

He narrowed his eyes at her. She could read that despite the shades.

She was tired and sick at heart enough not to care if she ticked him off.

"How do you manage to communicate your complete and utter contempt for me at the same moment you are chewing me out and threatening my rank?"

With a long sigh, he dropped into a chair opposite hers and kicked a stray into place to prop up his booted feet.

"All I know is I was rousted," he glanced down at his Kobold Phantom Tactical wristwatch, his sole ostentation other than his shades, "an hour and forty-three minutes ago. I was told to bring you and your complete kit. I'm in no mood for goddamn chatter."

"Chatter?" His word reached her brain. "Chatter! Pointless goddamn female chatter?" Emily had risen to her feet without noticing. She snagged the duffel, spinning the unopened soda into his lap with a sharp slap.

He caught it neatly and set it back on the table.

"You've never wanted me in your outfit! You'd probably rather have that idiot Bronson flying for you than me. Well, you got your wish. You've got me sent back stateside, thank you so damn much!" Actually, her mother or father had, but her chances of finding satisfaction there were so slim she might as well take it out on someone handy.

At the door, two handlers in the bright yellow vests of flight-line controllers stood frozen, blocking her exit. Before she could snarl at them, they backpedaled wide-eyed out of the room.

"No! Wait!" His feet thumped to the deck.

Henderson could go to hell. She didn't stop.

"Captain!" The major snapped out from behind her.

A decade of training jerked her to a halt. Was it possible to hate any man more?

He moved directly in front of her. Her infinitely small self glowered back at her from his mirrored shades.

"I did not assign you stateside. I never would. You're..." He stopped. If she didn't know better, she'd bet he was looking to the side as if embarrassed.

"What? I'm what? Is stateside too good for me as well? Well, here, read it for yourself."

She stopped her hand halfway to the inner right pocket of her flight suit. That was Peter's letter asking her to come to the White House as a personal favor. Both the location and the form of the request were far more information than she intended to share with Major Jerk Henderson. Let him find out from CNN like everyone else where she landed. No question remained that the painful spotlight of public attention would focus its glaring eye on the First Lady's newest toy. And that SOAR would never want her back once she'd entered the glare of that spotlight.

Emily shifted the duffel bag to her other hand and dug out the orders Admiral Parker had prepared before she'd even accepted this "voluntary" assignment.

He read the two lines aloud.

"'Captain Emily Beale, 160th Special Operations Air Regiment (Airborne), reassigned United States, detached. Board first available transport, Ramstein AFB.' Detached? What the hell does that mean?"

She snatched the orders from his hand and stepped around him. "It means I'm no longer your problem."

He moved to block her path.

She had to get away from him before she broke down. Damn him, there was no chance on Earth that he'd get to see her go all womany and weepy, and laugh about it later. "So glad to have that irritating wench out of my unit. You know she cried on me when we booted her ass."

Thumping a fist on his shoulder didn't cause his broad frame to waver in the slightest. She wanted to bury her face there and let go. All she'd ever wanted to do was fly, and they were taking that away. Surely the major would understand that. Jerk or not, he loved to fly as much as she did. It was obvious they shared that from the core of their souls.

She closed her eyes. Maybe if she counted to ten, he wouldn't be there. Yea, right. Maybe if she clicked the heels of her army boots together three times, she'd wake up in Oz and marry the Scarecrow. Maybe she'd find...

A hand cradled her face. As her father had done when she was a little girl. Without thought, just as it used to, her mind fell quiet for the first time since Henderson had flipped her out of her bunk with under two hours sleep. She turned her cheek into the comfort of the callused palm.

Lips brushed against hers. Gentle, soft, warm. The whole wretched day was slipping away. Forget the disaster that her life had become. Falling into those lips. Soft as rose petals, as intoxicating as an armful in full bloom, as strong as steel. She could—

Her eyes snapped open, and Major Mark Henderson's beautiful gray eyes were watching her from an inch away, his shades slid up into that thick dark hair she'd so often craved to toy with. His lips on hers impossibly gentle, especially because of the power of the warrior so close beneath the surface.

By reflex, before the outrageous impossibility could register, she grabbed the hand cupping her cheek. She dug her finger into the median nerve motor joint on the back of his hand, flipped it over, and lifted.

Henderson's body instinctively twisted to relieve the pain, and he crashed face-first onto one of the little tables.

Emily kept his hand twisted up behind his back,

pinning him in place. She listened to his sunglasses skit-
ter across the linoleum floor. With a small "tink," they
stopped against a chair leg. The can of soda bounced and
rolled for a moment longer before coming to a rest under
the same chair. For the space of three heartbeats, she kept
him pinned in place, ignored his muttered grunts of pain.

Was that why he'd tolerated her? Let her fly? Let her
be assigned to his unit? Because he wanted to get her in
the sack! He was so damn handsome that under normal
circumstances, she might not argue. If he hadn't been
her commanding officer. Right now, it was the eighth or
ninth thing too many this day.

She dropped his hand as if it were hotter than turbine
engine exhaust.

Before he could recover, she marched back onto
the flight deck, back where it was too loud to hear
herself think.

A yellow-clad deckhand snagged her elbow the moment she hit the flight deck and jabbed a finger toward
a jet that was number two at the catapult. Time to move.

The handler practically dragged her toward the plane
already moving into the catapult position. An F/A-18F
Super Hornet. Somebody wanted her out of the theater
of operations fast. Fine with her.

She did her best not to look back before she climbed
aboard to see if a lone helicopter pilot in a brown flight
suit and mirrored shades stood against the carrier's
superstructure. She really tried not to look.

But it didn't matter when she did, no one waited
for her.

—⁓—

Major Mark Henderson made it out the door in time to see Emily Beale slip into the Hornet. Didn't matter that the flight suit hid her shape, didn't matter that her helmeted head was already ducked out of view into the cockpit. He'd know her walk, her movements, how she entered an aircraft, how she pulled a gun, how she flew, anywhere.

One moment. One brief damned moment he'd held her. Felt her skin, even softer than he'd imagined. And her lips, someone please help him, held far more than heat, more than fire. An electric shock had stunned him down to his boots. When she'd opened those perfect blue eyes, summer-sky blue, for just that instant, he had fallen in and was gone.

Emily's Hornet, a couple hundred feet up deck, locked into the catapult. A half-dozen greenshirts scurried around the plane while the yellow-vested shooters secured the front wheel to the catapult. A white-and-black checked safety officer gave his clearance, a flurry of hand signals Mark couldn't follow traveled around the flight deck.

The plane's engine roared to life. Its dragon's maw of heat and fire diverted upward by the tilted jet-blast shield that had popped out of the deck on cue.

Suddenly, all was still and everyone danced clear.

A single shooter in yellow saluted the pilot, then lunging forward, pointed along the deck, and the controller fired the catapult. With a roar that made his body ache, she was gone. Zero to 150 in two seconds flat. Six g's. The best roller-coaster ride ever devised by man, other than a DAP Hawk helicopter in combat.

The plane pulled up its gear as it swung ten degrees to the right and climbed like only an American fighter plane could. The next one was already rolling into position as the catapult returned down the deck and the dance of color-coded deck crews started all over. When rushed, they could repeat this in under a minute all day long.

He already couldn't spot her. Gone from his life faster than could be possible. Than should be possible.

He shouldn't have done it. He was her commanding officer, for crying out loud. He'd just risked his career for that kiss. And hers, which was truly unforgivable. He hadn't even realized how badly he wanted her. Until he received the call to give her up.

And when she'd closed her eyes on so much pain, he'd given in. If he'd known how much her kiss would rock him back on his heels...

With a smile he'd do best to keep to himself, Mark Henderson decided it was worth all the risk for a kiss like that one.

He flexed his abused hand and wondered how much it was going to hurt to work the chopper's collective on the flight back. A twinge shot all the way into his shoulder where she'd torqued it around. It was going to sting like mad to fly back to base.

She really knew how to handle herself. Damn that was a turn-on. His brain tried to imagine what it would be like to tussle with a woman like that, and his body responded strongly. It made a very nice image.

He pulled the tab on the soda he'd picked up along with his sunglasses. It exploded in a cloudy spray of sugar water covering his face and chest.

Chapter 10

AT RAMSTEIN AIR BASE IN GERMANY, EMILY HAD ONE hour to sleep, shower, and change into her dress blues. The tiny government Gulfstream jet that flew her to D.C. came equipped with two pilots, a flight attendant way too good at her job to be a soldier, a very well-supplied galley, and a relentless, three-man Secret Service briefing team. And brief they did, for five hours nonstop—from "Affairs of State" the moment she sat down through "Food Security," not Food Safety, to threat-recognition protocols during the First Lady's travel, with her recent trip to Zimbabwe as an example.

"The operation manual for my Black Hawk is smaller than your briefing manuals."

The protest gained her seven seconds of blank stares from all three. Absolutely blank. The three men weren't amused, didn't care to comment, and certainly didn't care about her emotional or mental state. She'd always heard that the Secret Service required that their agents had never had or ever considered having a sense of humor. But it was incredibly daunting in real life to experience that they'd checked their laugh track at the door. Permanently.

D.C. couldn't come soon enough, until the moment the door flipped open, the stairs unfolded, and there stood Daddy on the tarmac at Andrews Air Force Base. The cold air sent a shiver up her spine. She didn't remember D.C. being this cold in midwinter, never mind the third week of September. No way this had any chance of turning out well.

Somehow it was all her dad's fault; she just didn't know how yet. She definitely didn't look forward to their fight over his part in grounding her. Maybe if she asked nicely, the three agents would take her back and brief her some more. That would certainly be less painful. But they were all bundling past her, their massive binders locked into even larger briefcases. One paused long enough to stamp her passport, but he too departed in moments.

All that remained were herself, her father, a black SUV, and the pair of agents in black who kept a twenty-four-hour eye on the Director of the FBI.

"Hi, Emily."

"Hi, Daddy." He looked good, as he always did. A little thinner, a little grayer—running the FBI could do that—but his back was straight and the daily hour at the gym still showed in how he filled out a suit jacket. The same blue eyes that stared out from her mirror every morning. She'd received her slender build and her height from her mother. From her father, the brilliant blue eyes that dragged men in and the raw determination that scared them all away.

Except Major Mark Henderson. But eight hours in transit had shed no more sense on the situation than when it had occurred. "It." Nice way to think of a kiss that had set a new standard several flight levels above any operational ceiling she'd ever imagined, never mind experienced.

The impossible gentleness from a man so strong, the

immense power she'd felt held so barely in check, had made a contrast that had set her pulse sizzling. And what she was supposed to do with that lay hidden somewhere beyond her horizon.

So, like any good pilot, she compartmentalized and shoved it aside. "Don't waste mental energy on what you can't solve, or what you were supposed to be paying attention to could jump up and kill you." So, she shoved it aside... for about the hundredth time in the last hour.

She crossed the tarmac, cool as night despite the midmorning sun. Her father's hug was as firm as it was brief.

"I'm supposed to deliver you immediately. Tried to get you a day off at home..." He shrugged, indicating that had not been a battle worth fighting.

Her father waited for her to climb into the car, and the two agents closed their doors.

Emily had hoped for an iced tea while lounging alongside the unmitigated luxury of clean water on a pool-sized scale, even if it was far too cold to swim. Not to be. She dug around in the SUV's cooler. Ice-cold bottled water. Heaven enough for her.

"I'll bet Mom will be disappointed. Who was she going to invite?"

Her father grimaced. Some lineup of overly eligible men in overly sharp business suits, no doubt.

"Well, I'm probably just going through orientation today. Tell her I'll try and be there tonight." Emily regretted it the moment she said it, but familial peace had a price you sometimes had to pay.

The SUV rolled out through the layers of security with little interference. Far too little, when compared to their hardened camp in the desert. Home soil. The U.S. didn't feel like a combat zone, despite the lessons of 9/11. The contrast creeped her out every time she took stateside leave. She knew she'd shake it off in a few days. But right now, coming from the confined world of a forward camp where you were always armed, surrounded by a "friendly" town you never entered in less than squad size, it made her twitchy. Slapping to check for her sidearm, and not finding it, didn't help. The Beretta was shoved into the top of her duffel, which an agent had dropped in the trunk.

She had to relax. Even a little would be a start.

Her father shifted in his seat to turn toward her. His secret-agent face, as she'd always teased him, abruptly, fully in place.

Or perhaps she shouldn't relax at all.

—⁓—

The FBI Director's briefing lasted barely as long as the twenty-minute ride to the White House. And it added surprisingly little to the briefing Emily had suffered through on the plane, other than the fact that her father hadn't originated the orders to get her grounded stateside. That saved them a fight and even earned him a few points. First that he hadn't and second when he adamantly insisted he'd never do such a thing. Third, that she actually believed him.

So, she'd go back to thinking he was an okay dad, in a totally committed to his work, rarely home kind of way. Though she understood that commitment now, it had been hard as a kid. It had made her rebellious, mostly against the only parent available, her mother.

How much of her flying had been her idea, and how much because her mother hated it so vocally was a question she'd stopped asking a thousand missions ago. Every protest made by Helen Cartwright Magnuson Beale had driven her daughter deeper in.

Not flying! When it had been recreational.

Not helicopters! When she'd discovered rotorcraft.

Not the military! When she'd understood they flew the very best machines.

Not West Point! When it could have been Bard or Brown or Smith.

By the time she went SOAR, her mother didn't even understand the distinctions, but it didn't matter. By then Emily's motivations had become completely her own. She loved what she did and why she did it in the present tense, even if the past tense had been a bit murkier.

For a while, this understanding, at least on Emily's part, had brought a truce into the relationship. Right until the moment her mother realized that Emily's career decision included helicopters first and men a distant second. That blew the whole mess up again. A battle, Emily knew, far from having fought its final round.

The main consideration her father mentioned that the briefing team hadn't touched on was a little freakish. Freakish even to someone inured to life on an overseas military base.

Emily was about to enter a security bubble the likes of which existed nowhere else on Earth. Inside the circle of the United States Secret Service constituted the most guarded and secure place in the world. Ironically, placing it atop the target list for every crazy on the entire planet.

Her father could shed no further light on why the
First Lady wanted a combat pilot for her chef. That
Emily would have to find out for herself.

Chapter 11

MARK HAD STARTED WITH THE CARRIER'S COMMUNICA-
tions shack. No joy. They wouldn't even let him near the
door without the day's password.

His next stop, after he'd washed off the worst of the
soda, was Pri-Fly. He managed to sweet talk his way
into the tower, since the Mini Boss on duty owed him.
Jim wore a bright blue turtleneck with "Mini Boss" in
six-inch letters across his back, and his attention was
focused on the aircraft landing over the stern.

The Air Boss, in bright yellow with his own title
stamped large, offered Mark only the briefest nod and
then turned back to watch the deck. Between them,
they juggled the flight operations from Primary Flight.
When they dropped from launching off two catapults to
one, everybody eased down and Mark judged that was
his moment.

"Hey, Jim." He'd managed to find a spot to lean not
far from the Mini Boss. "How's the wife?"

Jim glanced over and swore, but softened it with
a good smile and a punch on the arm. "What the hell
happened to you? Go swimming?" He rubbed his hand
against his pants. "Why are you sticky?"

Mark raised his mostly empty Coke can and wiggled
it. "Someone shook it."

"And you fell for it? Typical Army. You aboard tonight? Let the Navy teach you how to drink."

No alcohol aboard, but that didn't spare him the flak. "What do you need?"

"Can't I come by and ask about my cousin? Old pals, cousin-in-law, and all that?" Mark did his best to sound innocent, but could tell Jim wasn't buying in.

"Your cousin's fine. More than." He offered a wolfish grin, the kind that Christy had always elicited from men, especially her husband. "Even if you did introduce us, that's not why you're bothering me during active operations. So give. What do you need?"

Jim turned to scan the skies with his binoculars. For the moment the sky was as clear as the radar, but once a Mini Boss, always a Mini Boss.

"You shipped out one of mine about half an hour back. Can you tell me where and why?"

Jim glanced at him, then over at the Air Boss.

Commander Richards shrugged. "We should be clear for five. Be back in six."

Jim nodded toward the glass door and led them out onto vulture's row, the narrow walkway that wrapped around the tower. Mainly used for washing Pri-Fly's windows.

As soon as the door was shut, Jim turned to face him. "You don't know?"

Mark could only shake his head. He didn't like it. On a couple levels. One, that his best pilot had just been pulled and he didn't have a clue why. Two, that he cared so much about the fact that it was Emily Beale.

"Ramstein is all I know." Jim looked down as an F-18 fired off the catapult.

"Shit, Jim. I saw the orders. I already know that. What about past that point? The orders said stateside, but where?"

Jim shook his head and leaned on the steel rail facing

out toward the stern of the ship. His eyes automatically scanning the sky for incoming.

"Well, thanks for nothing, pal." Mark regretted it as soon as the words were out.

They earned him a sidelong look from Jim.

He shouldn't have even been allowed into Pri-Fly, and now he was heaping his own frustration on his friend.

Mark leaned his forearms on the rail so that they both stared aft at the glittering sea.

"Something's got you on this one."

"It's just that she's my best pilot. And I'm worried." Sounded plausible enough.

"She?" Jim shot an elbow and Mark barely blocked it.

"Eat hot lead!"

"Ooo! Touchy, touchy!" Jim started laughing, then chopped it off. "One of yours? She? Tell me you're not going there, Mark."

"I'm not going there." Only one kiss worth, and all that had earned him was a wrenched arm and a Coke shower.

"Don't go there. You know that." Jim looked around and then leaned in close. "And don't be telling me this. I can't know this. Stick around. I'll hook you up with a cute midshipman. At least she'll be in another service. Please tell me she's not part of your squad."

Mark did his best to look bland, but knew it didn't work.

Jim let out a low whistle.

"You got it bad?"

Mark shrugged.

"Aw, shit!" Jim hung his head, staring down toward the deck.

They went back to college, roommates for crying out loud. How was Mark supposed to hide anything from him?

"I got it bad the first damn time I saw her. Not that she knows that. I stayed clear." Until he'd blown it all thirty-six minutes ago.

"Shit." Jim cursed much more quietly before looking up at Mark. "Okay, here's what I know. Rear Admiral James Parker comes winging in here crack of dawn this morning. He was supposed to be rotated stateside for a couple weeks, then he's back three days later. Goes straight to the captain's office. No one's seen him since. You and your girl hit the deck about two hours later. I know where you're stationed, so the call to you had to be within five minutes of his arrival. Forty-five minutes after you smacked that puppy down," he nodded toward Mark's helicopter below, "trying to put a hole in our pretty deck, we get a call to scramble a Super Hornet two-seater for Ramstein to the head of the queue for passenger unspecified. Someone climbed aboard, I spotted a purple helmet, and we kicked them into the sky. That's it. It's all I got for you."

Mark nodded and mumbled out, "Thanks." He must really look miserable if Jim wasn't teasing him more about that landing. He'd never bounced a Black Hawk before outside of training and emergencies. Only dumb luck and the angle of arrival had kept him from bouncing them right off the side and into the ocean. He kept his attention north by west, the heading for Germany.

"Are you sure about this?" Jim broke the silence.

Mark could only shrug. Suddenly he wasn't sure about anything. Except one thing; he never should have kissed her. At least it would have remained his problem alone.

Jim stood up straight. Rather than the standard

punch, he rested his hand on Mark's shoulder for a long moment.

"Fly low, buddy mine. Way below the radar."

Jim headed back inside, but Mark stayed watching the water and the sky.

Fly low? Didn't have a lot of choice, did he? Emily Beale had just flown right off the edge of the map.

Chapter 12

THE ENTRANCE TO THE WHITE HOUSE REMINDED EMILY of her first day of basic training; thoroughly daunting. Her father had had to drop her two blocks from the security gate to save him the hassle of waiting around for her clearance. She sent the duffel back to the house with his car.

A light rain shower filled the air with sparkling light, making the September sky glitter like gold. It was the first precipitation she'd seen since rotating to Southwest Asia two months earlier, other than a couple nasty nighttime blizzards in the Hindu Kush.

The guards at the gate eyed her carefully as she kept tilting her head back to catch the shimmering raindrops on her tongue like summer snowflakes.

Let them laugh. If they'd baked their backsides in the Afghan summer... only they weren't laughing. Somewhere closer to a lethal scowl. Deadly at twenty paces. No weapons required. Suddenly she missed her flight helmet and the silvered, pull-down visor, perhaps mirrored enough to deflect their glares. Perhaps.

Of course, she'd been glared at by the best and could handle it, even if these guys had been to the same school of scowl as Major Mark Henderson. He'd graduated top of his class, no big surprise. A mental image of him giving a graduation scowl instead of a valedictory speech almost made her laugh.

One of the many Henderson legends told of a young lieutenant who'd mistakenly turned his back, thinking the major was done chewing him out. The rumor of the scowl scorch marks running up the lieutenant's backside was still passed down pilot to pilot, and it was hard not to laugh at the man, though he'd apparently been a good officer since then.

She shook her head sharply, scattering tiny raindrops in a sparkling arc from her damp hair. Why in the world was she thinking about the major? SOAR was done with her, and she'd never see the man again. Good riddance. If only that thought didn't feel like a knife to her gut. Did some part of her secretly like Major Viper Henderson? That actually did cause her to laugh aloud. Even if she didn't, clearly her hormones did.

The real White House checkpoint squatted at the end of a long, wrought-iron fence. Someone had dropped a single-wide trailer in the middle of the gate beneath a gorgeous beech tree. The trailer was unsightly on about thirty levels, right down to the off-beige color and the narrow, steel wheelchair ramps that were too steep to walk comfortably.

Four men in black suits cross-checked her ID in the computer, took a fingerprint, had her walk through a metal detector, made her check both her boot knife, not quite regulation but considered a necessity inside any zone, and the Swiss Army fold-up forgotten in her pants pocket. Felt half-naked without them. Not a good mental image in front of the burly detectives. Agents. Blacksuits. Whatever they were.

Actually, two did the work of messing with her and the paperwork. The other two stood back with a decent spread between them. All they did was watch her. Even a fast shooter would be unlikely to take down both before one could respond.

They clearly didn't know why she was really here, bodyguard in disguise. Female aviator brought in to do their job because they'd failed to protect the First Lady. She'd best keep that role to herself unless she wanted the blacksuits to really despise her. And that nickname wouldn't help either.

The briefing team had been in the dark as well. They had focused solely on her public role, a chef that the First Lady had used her influence to pull from the military because she'd been "cute" on CNN. The First Lady was notoriously whimsical, having her own lipstick-red limousine for example, and the story actually fit.

Captain Emily Beale now worked as a personal chef for the First Lady. No more, no less.

And it sucked. But, when you were all the way down, it took most of the fight out of you. Made it easy to roll with each punch to her ego.

Name. Birth date. Fingerprints. Her military ID meant nothing here.

The summer rain raised the ante to actual rainfall, beating down on the tin roof. The trailer both felt and sounded like a pressure cooker.

Last place of service. Fort Campbell, Kentucky. Let them probe all they wanted; they'd hit a dead end at a P.O. box at SOAR's main office in Michael C. Grimm Hall. SOAR never disclosed where its teams had scattered across the face of the globe. More than a few times, she'd answered a personal forwarded phone call while stationed in hell and gone, and talked as if she were looking out at the bluegrass fields. Out of habit, SOAR pilots always knew the weather and time of day at Fort Campbell for just such an occasion. As 5th battalion, she also tracked Tacoma, Washington. Easy; when in doubt, cool and raining.

The sky darkened. A real D.C.-style thunderstorm rolling through. She'd forgotten what they sounded like when they pounded in.

Current commander?

President Peter Matthews, Commander-in-Chief, U.S. Military Forces. Chew on that one, boys.

Were they pushing her just for the fun of it? She probably had higher security clearance than all four guys in the trailer. Combined. Was more trusted by her country than they were. They might guard the country's leader, she guarded the country's security and, since becoming SOAR qualified, many of her darkest secrets.

Then they tried to confiscate her chef's knives. The rolled, worn-soft leather bag was the only item she'd retained from her duffel. She'd spent most of a month's salary on this set, and she wasn't giving them over to any two-bit security guard. Okay. This was the White House. She wasn't giving them over to any four-bit security guard.

Emily bucked her way up the chain of command until she faced Agent Frank Adams, rank unknown. He didn't have the height or breadth of Major Henderson, but he had the same case of bad attitude. One that might put even the major in his place, truth be known. Though that might simply be the due to the soaking he'd received crossing over from the White House in the midst of a cloudburst.

Well, she'd learned a thing or two inside the zone herself. She planted her feet at parade rest, her dress blues perfect—well, as perfect as they ever were on her. The military really didn't know much about clothes on a female form, especially tall and thin. Her silver captain's bars polished and vertical on her collar points. Her black beret square on her head, insignia flash to the fore. Nonregulation hair bound back in a neat ponytail. The two-week-old, winged "Night Stalker" tattoo at the base of her spine well hidden, but she felt stronger for it being there beneath her hands clasped behind her back.

Mark had shown that she'd earned it, too, by how upset he'd been at losing her. Whatever snafu mangle she'd landed in, she had qualified to fly with SOAR's Black Adders and had finally belonged. However briefly. If she'd hit the pinnacle of her career at twenty-nine, then she had. But she'd always have the marker of that achievement, that strength, rooted right at the base of her spine.

"I can't cook without my knives. I'm supposed to be here to cook for the First Lady. If you must know, I'd rather be on the line with my crew, ramming my Black Hawk down some asshole terrorist's throat, but since the Commander-in-Chief chose to give that the shaft, I'm here to cook. Now, you either let me and my knives out of this nuthatch of a single-wide, or I can about-face my butt out of here and you can explain my absence to the First Lady yourself."

She bit her tongue hard. Keeping it in check had never been one of her strengths, but she'd be damned if she'd apologize. It had cost her rank more than once, which was fine by her. Too much rank, and they didn't let you fly any more.

He looked pissed. Really pissed. And this wasn't an Air-Force-base security grunt; this was the U.S. Secret Service, the baddest asses in the whole world. Even more extreme than Special Forces, some argued, because they functioned right out in the open, no cover of night, no battle gear. Even the D-boys respected them. And Delta Force operators didn't give respect to anyone who ranked less than several levels above incredibly amazing. Michael's handshake and muted "Thanks!" after she dragged him off the cliff ranked as perhaps the highest compliment of her entire career. Right up there with Henderson's, "Nice flight."

In the blacksuit world, this guy might be the toughest of them all. Mr. Agent Frank Adams, Rank Unknown, looked it, with his rough features and big hands clenching and unclenching into surprisingly massive fists.

So okay, she'd apologize a little.

"Sir."

But that was all he was going to get.

Chapter 13

First Lady Katherine Matthews's private kitchen on the third floor of the White House combined a chef's dream with a thorough undercoating of disaster. Emily couldn't stop turning around to see everything.

The decorator's motif shone in lush cherry wood and mirror-polished brass. A ring of the finest nonstick pans, cast-iron pots, and copper saucers dangled from iron hooks above a dark cherry-and-maple striped cutting block big enough to seat a party of eight comfortably. A pro-level gas range to die for, plus a griddle, an indoor grill, and a pair of wok burners. The very best kitchen machines lined a long slab of marble for baking. A windowed door led out to a sunny porch on the back side of the third floor of the residence.

Emily swung the door open, far heavier than she expected. It took a moment to figure out why. Inch-thick glass, a rude reminder that bullets, or bomb-laden model airplanes, just might come traveling this way. There was a nice place for an arrangement of herb planters. She'd get a few starts, though she had no intention of being here long enough to harvest. Better to buy plants already in full leaf.

In the cabinets, she unearthed gorgeous china in a frilly, feminine pattern of fragile delicacy, but with the bold colors suitable to a person of power. Cool and smooth to the touch, a perfect glaze over the tracery.

The pattern clearly stated part the First Lady and part President Peter Matthews. But there was no chance she'd start thinking about him.

Further exploration revealed place settings to provide quiet service for two or an unannounced crowd of two dozen. That told her one thing about her duties; be flexible, Emily. Very flexible. She froze with her hand still on the burnished-brass cabinet handle. Too flexible.

She stood in the White House.

In a kitchen.

To cook!

This world was so far from the Black Hawk cockpit she'd exited under nine hours earlier that she had to lean against the counter as a vertigo-like wave threatened to take her out at the knees.

Deep breaths. Just this morning, Mark had tossed her half-naked out of bed and dumped her in a helicopter. Dragged her to the carrier, kissed her, and not watched her go. She'd flown eight hours across nine time zones, landing in D.C. an hour earlier than she'd left the Arabian Sea. Mark had held her, kissed her nine hours ago. The change was too much. Too fast. She couldn't get her bearings. Total sleep since waking for the cave mission twenty-four hours ago; about two hours. No wonder her head was spinning. Well she'd learned how to work through far worse during the monthlong Green Platoon and the half-year Airborne training. Far worse.

Deep breaths and focus on the battle at hand. Focus on the first step. She was alive and not bleeding out. Second step. Assess. Right. Assess the kitchen. She straightened up, ignoring the spin that had felt like vertigo but she now knew to be merely lack of sleep.

Assess. Check supplies cupboard by cupboard. The stainless-steel fridge and freezer combo was huge. They were fully stocked, and not a single item of the produce looked over two days old. Five chefs could work this kitchen, if needed, but its design reflected a more intimate setting: late-night meals shared by the First Couple while perched on stools together at one end of the carrier-sized chopping-block island.

It wasn't hard to picture dashing Peter Matthews and his dynamic CoverGirl model-worthy wife sharing this kitchen wearing very little... Sooo not a good image. Peter Matthews in blue boxers made her body feel things it certainly shouldn't be feeling about her Commander-in-Chief. About her married Commander-in-Chief. Feelings she hadn't had for him since she'd graduated high school.

She'd successfully avoided him for the last nine years, since her graduation from West Point and his induction into the Senate, and yet she could remember him like it was yesterday. Tall and slender. A black mop of hair that was always slipping over his right eye. The merry twinkle in those whiskey-dark eyes. The combo had made her swoon since she'd turned six and he'd been twice her age.

For a while, she'd been able to leave him behind. That was before he became the President of the United States and her commander-in-chief. Now she couldn't turn around without finding him talking earnestly about world hunger on CNN or his photo on some commanding officer's wall.

The kitchen, Emily. The kitchen.

On the disaster side, not a single decent sauté pan.

The knives were run of the mill. The spice rack lacked any personality whatsoever. Iceberg lettuce and Big Boy tomatoes in the vegetable crisper. Not a single sauce or condiment, other than a lonely bottle of bottom-shelf ketchup and a squeeze-bottle of yellow mustard. The kitchen had all the trappings, but clearly whoever kept it stocked had never cooked in their natural-born lives.

If she was going to be marooned here, she'd be damned if she'd serve crap.

She closed her eyes for a moment and recited the Night Stalkers' motto under her breath, "NSDQ. NSDQ. Night Stalkers Don't Quit. Night Stalkers Don't Quit."

It had gotten Durant through ten days captivity in Mogadishu. Even before SOAR, it had gotten her out of the Thai jungle. It would get her through this as well. She forced her eyes open, stood at attention, and took a deep breath. With a salute directed at the earth-brown, enameled sink, for lack of a better audience, she searched out a pad and pen.

She was deep into her list of decent ingredients when one of the three doors slammed open and she leapt straight up off the bar stool. She landed in a crouched, fighting stance with her ten-inch Henckels chef's knife, the first thing to hand, cocked back and ready to throw. Her other hand part way to the boot knife she'd insisted on recovering, much to Agent Adams's displeasure.

The two agents in dark suits and narrow ties had their hands inside their jacket lapels before she froze. No question where these guys kept their weapons.

First Lady Katherine Matthews breezed into the

kitchen as if everyone sat primly together drinking tea and discussing when the Washington Redskins would finally get prettier uniforms.

Emily and the two agents relaxed in stages. The First Lady paid no attention, but neither did she reach to shake Emily's hand until the knife rested once again in the pocket of her partially unrolled leather knife case.

"I'm so glad that you decided to accept my little invitation."

The little invitation that had flipped Emily's life into inverted flight, a very unhappy place in a rotorcraft.

"I know I placed unfair pressure upon you, but having another woman by me, especially one so clearly proficient with her hands." She nodded to the agents who finally relaxed into a watchful mode closely related to parade rest, except their hands were folded in front within easy reach of their weapons. The I-look-powerful-but-relaxed stance designed to intimidate any and all who came near.

And, like Agent Adams, these were big guys. Special Forces operators and their pilots were supposed to blend in. Being five foot six might keep you out of the New York state police, but it made you a perfect fit for Spec Ops. Provided you spoke a couple languages, could run a half marathon with a full pack, and could learn explosives, medicine, or bridge building. Better yet, all three. Even Major Mark Henderson—the toughest and one of the biggest guys in the SOAR Company, other than Big John—was just six feet. She'd yet to meet a Secret Service agent under six feet.

"It gives one a feeling of safety. Thank you so much for coming."

It was hard not to feel warmed by the greeting. The First Lady, other than being even more statuesque and redheaded than Emily recalled, had a very pleasant smile. The forest-green silk blouse was open far lower than Emily would wear it, but she didn't have such a startling cleavage to show off. All the teenage wishing in the world hadn't helped on that issue.

Emily had always found Katherine to be a little creepy; too perky to be real. Or too slick to be trusted. Or… bottom line, Emily had never liked her. But how much of that was because she didn't want to like the woman married to Peter Matthews? The wife of her childhood friend deserved the benefit of the doubt. She shouldn't despise a woman she'd only met briefly at a few formal occasions. Well, not despise her too much.

"My pleasure, ma'am." Her gut instinct included a salute, but she stood in civilian country now. Besides, the First Lady still held her hand. Odd, it didn't feel awkward. In SOAR, the main contact between people other than hand-to-hand combat practice consisted of a friendly slap on the back for a job well done or someone holding the wound in your leg closed so that you didn't bleed out before landing the chopper.

"We'll have such fun together. Anything you need, anything at all, give it to Daniel." She waved a negligent flick of fingers over her shoulder without turning to look. On cue, a man about Emily's age appeared at the door.

"He's my body man," Katherine said with a throaty, flirtatious voice. "Feel free to borrow him. He can be your body man, too. I'm not possessive."

Emily gave him the once-over. And then looked

again. He was worth it. The man wasn't handsome; he
was gorgeous. Not the strength and power of Major
Henderson, but very nice to look at. A surfer-built blond.
Broad-shouldered and slim-hipped. He wore a short-
sleeved dress shirt in jewel-tone blue and a Yale tie. No
ring on his finger. Nice fingers. Slender, but not effete.
Where she'd expected lily-white office hands, he had
the muscles of someone who worked hard, or at least
worked out hard. Not Army level of course, not even in
the ballpark with Mark Henderson, but not Washington-
lawyer level either.

And for all the fitness that Daniel embodied, his
bright blue eyes showed no fool and his expression a
long-lived patience with the First Lady's introduction.
Daniel must have more than a few marbles in place to
be personal assistant to one of the most powerful women
in the world.

Emily nodded curtly to show that she'd not taken him
for granted as a blond boy toy. Hesitation as he considered, then he nodded his thanks. Guy-speak. Essential
military training. Almost never needed words once you
learned it.

Katherine clearly never had, as she was continuing to
fill the room with words. Emily figured she'd best start
paying attention.

"The President and I rarely eat together. He has such
a hectic schedule, you know. And I need someone who
can take care of my needs. They won't be burdensome.
Just myself and a few trusted advisers."

Daniel's quick roll of his eyes spoke volumes. "On
call twenty-four seven for the merest whim." He didn't
need to say it aloud.

As Katherine moved about the kitchen, it was clear she'd entered a foreign world. She pinged a manicured fingernail lightly against bright copper pans and brushed fingers across the cutting block that dominated the room. It was as if she'd never been here before.

Had never needed to make her own hot cocoa. Everything always done by magic elves about which she knew nothing and cared less. For her, an omelet and a lobster thermidor required equal amounts of effort and planning; she asked and they appeared.

"Daniel will give you warning about any major events on my schedule, though I reserve the right to call you on a moment's notice for a quick snack. Especially if I'm feeling terribly decadent." Could the woman even dish her own ice cream?

By the time Katherine was done speaking, both Secret Service agents were back at parade rest, Daniel had his tie straightened, and Emily had been graciously guided back to her bar stool. Katherine stood closer than new acquaintances would. Close as good friends might choose.

This was a skill Emily didn't have, though her mother had tried so hard to give it to her. The First Hostess made it look so easy, she must have learned it in the womb.

"And you fly too, don't you?"

"Helicopters, ma'am. Not airplanes. At least not often. I'm certified on fixed-wing F/A-18 and Harrier, transport only, but I fly helicopters." And babble like an idiot. "Black Hawks mostly. I've about a thousand hours in the Apaches and Cobras as well." Like that meant something to the First Lady.

"Isn't that marvelous?"

Yup. Didn't mean a damn thing to Mrs. Matthews. Just shoot me now.

"Well, as President Matthews and I are often traveling separately, it's such a relief that I can rely on you for both food and transportation. I feel so much better. No cooking today. Get that list you're making to Daniel as soon as possible. Tomorrow, Daniel," the First Lady addressed him for the first time, "I want her to be able to make me a shrimp quiche, egg whites only, tomato juice, and an English muffin sporting a skim of fresh blackberry jam without having to leave this room or call the main kitchen.

"You…" Katherine turned and aimed a finger at Emily suddenly enough for her to step back and sit abruptly on the stool close behind her. "Don't worry. You'll be perfect."

Before Emily could exhale, the First Lady was gone, the agents somehow a step ahead of her, whispering into their sleeve microphones, "Dragon is moving."

Dragon? No kidding.

Daniel lingered behind. "A little breathtaking?"

"She does manage to suck most of the air out of the room." Emily clamped down on her tongue, but Daniel laughed. Nice rumbly laugh.

"Not much slows her down either. Be ready for that same perfect bluster to be running as strongly at midnight as at 6:00 a.m. Which is when she expects breakfast, by the way. My office is through that door," he indicated the one the agent hadn't used, "third on the right. I'll be back in an hour for the list and to show you your apartment. You'll be on call at all times. You're one of the very few staffers with quarters in the residence. Even I don't rate that. They told you?"

She nodded, even though they hadn't. What else hadn't Agent Adams bothered to tell her? Did Adams or Daniel even know of her dual role as cook and bodyguard? No, not with an admiral personally hand-delivering the First Family's request.

She made a mental note to call Dad's driver to bring back her duffel bag.

At least Daniel didn't sound miffed about her surprise benefit. She'd assumed she'd be back in her old room at home, too often idle and easily available to her socialite, matchmaking mother. Not that her mother didn't have a fine eye for a good-looking man, but they were all far too eligible to be interested in a female helicopter pilot. And that discussion would drive her and her mother both crazy from the moment Emily walked in the door. Even tonight, she knew there'd be a couple lurking about for her first dinner home.

"On call" had defined most of her military career, so no problem there. She didn't care if the command came from the First Lady or Major Mark Henderson trying to find some new way to put her ass in a sling. He must be so glad she'd been shipped out.

Though he'd been more pissed than pleased when he read her orders. And he'd certainly fumed all the way to the carrier. Had the hard landing been on her behalf? That rated as too bizarre. She discarded the idea.

Well, she'd bet the barracks here were a step up from a mosquito-net-shrouded army cot in a sweaty desert tent that froze out around 2:00 a.m. The mosquito net wasn't for the bugs—too dry for them to survive there.

It was for the stray scorpions and snakes seeking someone warm to snuggle up with for the night. Another
reason to be glad she usually flew at night and slept
during the day.

"Is there some place I could get a few pots to start some
herbs?" She waved a hand toward the patio entrance.

"Just put it on the list." Daniel tapped the paper smartly
without having to look down and see where it was. "Man
who doesn't miss much" is what the gesture said.

Daniel started moving out the door, in motion the
moment before the First Lady's call drifted back down
the hallway.

"Then get some rest. You'll need it." He headed off.

"And watch your back." Then he was gone as
smoothly as he'd arrived.

Now what did that mean?

Chapter 14

DANIEL'S ADVICE TO REST WHILE SHE COULD CAME FAR too late. Her full shopping list had been filled in mere hours, magnificently. The best dishes always came from having the best ingredients.

After finishing the list and receiving Daniel's tour, she'd stowed her belongings in her tiny apartment. She'd slipped into her wallet the receipts for her sidearm and backup piece, being held at the gate. Then she'd hit the White House cafeteria for some lunch.

While she'd been out, a magical fairy-godmother of a buyer had transformed the all-American, iceberg-lettuce kind of kitchen into an Italian and French paradise of curly pastas and strings of garlic.

As a nice bonus, her notes to herself at the bottom of the list to buy pots and herb starts had been handled. She couldn't help sticking her nose close to the container herb garden suddenly sprouting on her patio. The tang of lemon sage, the mouthwatering sweetness of French basil, and both Turkish and Mexican oregano grew in lush abundance. A small bay tree offered fresh leaves for building a stew's heart into soul.

Somewhere around two in the afternoon, "No cooking tonight" had turned into a noisy dinner for six around the chopping block featuring antipasto, chicken flambé in brandied cherry sauce, sautéed new potatoes with garlic and fennel, and baby asparagus in truffle-infused clarified butter, with a *torta della nonna* for dessert. And all of it with a news crew jostling her elbow. Luckily for them, not the same crew who'd filmed her in Pakistan. Though they'd clearly had an agenda as they scooted most of the diners aside for one shot or posed them for another.

Just as she dropped, exhausted, onto a bar stool with her own slice of almond-crusted cheese tart, Daniel breezed in.

"Well, that was fun."

His dry tone saved her having to ask what. It had been five hours of hell for both of them. Katherine, of course, appeared fresh as a daisy and was presently having dessert and coffee on the veranda with the guests of her impromptu party.

Without asking, Daniel snagged a slice of the *torta* and dropped down across the chopping block from her. He jammed a forkful into his mouth and started to chew as he reached for the milk bottle she'd left on the table. Then he froze.

"Oh."

"What?"

"Oh." He chewed once more.

"What? Is it okay? I didn't have time to taste it." She rose to her sore feet, but he held out a hand, palm facing her, and she settled back.

He kept chewing. Then swallowed hard. He turned those pretty blue eyes on her.

"Marry me!"

"What?" Emily actually glanced over her shoulder, but they were the only ones in the kitchen.

"You must! I simply must marry the woman who

cooked this dessert." He jabbed another forkful, stuffed it in his mouth, and closed his eyes as he chewed. "I'll have to call Mother right away and tell her that I have finally met the girl of her dreams."

He opened one eye to glare at her. "You aren't married, are you?"

"No." Not that it was any of his business.

"Good." He closed his eye again and licked his lips as if some crumb might have escaped. "That's settled. April or May. Beautiful time in Tennessee. Outdoor wedding on the farm beneath the shade of the old white oak. May, I think, but early on before the heat really comes up. Rather than cake, we'll just have tier upon tier of this."

She jabbed her fork into her own dessert and tasted it. The vanilla, combined with the lightest hint of citrus from the orange zest, did make the cheese tart taste like spring.

"I've never been a woman for long engagements. And it's September now."

"Nope. Sorry. May on the farm. Calving season. New lambs. The corn just knee high. Perfect."

"Never pegged you for a farmer. Surfer boy, maybe. Bet you look damned cute in coveralls." Coveralls and nothing else.

"Farmer and Yale political science grad. I hope that doesn't destroy the wedding plans."

He took the last bite from his plate then stood while he was still chewing.

Even as he headed for the door, the First Lady's call sounded from the main room.

"What? Not even a kiss for your bride?" Emily called

after him, surprising herself. She wasn't given to flirting. Ever. It was her worst skill, but this once it came out naturally.

"Later, honey. Herself calls." And he was gone.

Handsome, charming, and funny. Certainly smart as well, have to be that and more to do his job. And she liked him, much to her surprise. A real shocker in this crazy place.

While she was wrapping the leftovers, a pair of blacksuits glided into the kitchen the way aircraft carriers glide into war zones, all fast and dangerous. Apparently they were riding much tighter herd on the First Lady than normal since the two attempts on her life. They checked the room quickly. Satisfied that no assassins lurked in the side-by-side, they blended into the background.

In moments the First Lady swept in with an air of traveling by whim rather than armed escort.

"Dear Emily. That was splendid. Mariel Anderson was really quite pushy about acquiring your dessert recipe."

"I, um, don't have one, ma'am. No easy way to carry cookbooks to the front, so I mostly make it up as I go. I could try to work it out…"

Daniel was laughing at her. Not aloud, but with his eyes all crinkled up around the edges. He'd pay for that.

"No, dear, that's perfect. I refused, saying that you were very private with your secrets, which you are. We'll have to have a girl chat one of these days. I don't think that you've put seven words together since you joined our happy little family."

A whole twelve hours earlier.

The First Lady continued rambling on as if her "girl

chat" plans were forgotten. Emily would bet her next shore leave that they weren't. A glance at Daniel, who responded with the slightest tipping of his head, confirmed it. Katherine Matthews was no one's fool, triple threat of beauty, pleasing personality, and a very sharp brain.

"That Mariel didn't give more than a few hundred thousand during the last campaign. I happen to know what her husband is worth, and I also know about her favorite congressional aide." An avaricious look crossed the First Lady's face. "But I won't bring that up for something as trivial as money."

Emily noted that the First Lady didn't say what she would trade that tidbit for. She thanked her lucky stars she wasn't part of Washington politics.

"You cooking intuitively is perfect. No evidence of little recipe cards to condemn the guilty." That dazzling smile flashed into place and Emily returned it, despite now knowing how carefully the woman controlled it. "Well done."

Emily suddenly felt ten feet tall and able to leap small buildings at the slightest provocation. She knew she was smiling foolishly, even though alarms were sounding in a dozen parts of her brain, as well as Daniel's enjoinder to "watch her back." The woman controlled what she showed to the world with impeccable care. What lay beneath didn't appear to be nearly as pretty.

"And tomorrow, I think we'll take a little journey. Do you miss flying?"

"Desperately." The word flew out of her mouth before the question fully registered. Less than, she had to think, not yet one full day since her last flight to the carrier. It felt like a year.

"Good. At seven tomorrow you're to meet with Eddie at the Marine One hangar, wherever that is. He'll check you up or out, or whatever it is they do. Once you have his stamp of approval—awkward but necessary, I apologize in advance for putting you through this, he insisted—fetch Henry and me on the South Lawn at eleven. I told Eddie not to keep you any longer than that."

She breezed out with Daniel and the blacksuits in her wake. Only two empty dessert plates remained as evidence. Emily didn't recall finishing her own. Had Daniel gotten hers when she wasn't watching?

Who was Henry? And where were they going?

She didn't care, as long as she got to fly.

She jumped up and fist-pumped the air.

It was the first good news she'd had since being dumped out of her cot by Henderson.

———— ⁓ ————

Mark knew it was stupid, even as he did it.

There'd been no mission, so he'd spent the night and the morning proving that there was little on this planet more unsuited for sleeping than an army cot when you were in a tossing and turning mood. He'd spent an hour pumping iron, taken two showers, and didn't even remember the name of either movie he'd watched.

He heard a chopper start winding up out on the field and checked his watch, 7:55 a.m. Twenty-two hours and seven minutes since he'd kissed her. He'd even spun the outer bezel of his watch so that the arrow marked the minute. How was that for sad? He almost spun it clear, but didn't.

The turbine settled into a warm-up whine. That

would be the carrier run. He jammed on his flight suit, kicked into his boots, grabbed his helmet, and arrived at the bird by 7:58. Archie Stevenson had her humming as Bronson and the two gunners secured the last of the outbound bags.

Unbelievable that they'd gotten the bird put back together so fast. Beale ran a seriously hot crew. He really should get them back on the line, and with someone other than Bronson, but today they'd served his purpose.

He tapped Bronson on the shoulder, "Take a breather. I've got this one."

Bronson tried to ask some question, but Mark just climbed into the right-side pilot seat.

First Lieutenant Archibald Stevenson III looked over at him. There was not a lot of warmth in his eyes. Mark could feel Big John and Crazy Tim glaring at his back. He wanted to protest that he hadn't been the one who'd shipped her wherever she was gone to. That he was innocent.

But he wasn't. He'd sent one of his finest crews to carrier duty after they'd done one of the bravest things he'd ever seen. And he'd kissed their captain. Good thing they didn't know that, or he might just happen to fall out of the chopper somewhere over the Arabian Sea.

"Let's just do it."

Stevenson watched him a moment longer, then jerked the bird upward hard enough to feel like a slap.

Chapter 15

TOO WOUND UP TO SLEEP, EMILY WENT FOR A WALK ON the Mall. She moseyed down to visit her old pal Honest Abe, sitting in his pillared marble cabin as he stared out over the Reflecting Pool, and glared at the Capitol where Congress had fought him almost as hard as the South. She parked her butt on Abe's front porch and watched Washington wind down for the night. A cart vendor wandered by and enticed her with three tiny scoops of truly exceptional lime gelato as the sun set. The air temperature dropped, and she soon regretted the cold gelato. It was chilly, at least to her desert-thinned blood. No one else looked dressed for the near-Arctic blast.

Tourist buses of bantering high-school kids poured through in shorts and T-shirts, harried parent chaperones dragging behind. Occasional local couples strolled through the gathering twilight. Easy to pick out the locals; they traveled in pairs, not packs.

She'd done the same herself. Come to think of it, her first kiss had been here, pressed up against the cool marble of Lincoln's seat.

Walter. Walter... Last name gone. Lawrence. Lawrence Walters. That was it. Never Larry. He'd been so emphatic about it that she'd nicknamed him "Never Larry." And it had stuck. Probably the reason Never Larry never offered a second kiss.

Given the opportunity, would Mark Henderson want

a second kiss? Would she let him if he did? Assess, that's what a pilot's good at. He was her commanding officer and never should have kissed her in the first place, they both knew it, so that could be discounted for the moment.

The kiss itself, an electric-shock kiss. She grinned back over her shoulder at Abe and gave him a private wink. That was an understatement. Her brain had switched off and her body had switched on in a single instant. Even now she couldn't say if the kiss lasted five seconds or five minutes.

No question, she'd absolutely remember if she'd ever had a kiss like that before. How could such a hard man have such a soft and gentle mouth? And that rough-palmed hand so tender and strong against her cheek.

And then she pictured the next moment. Major Mark Henderson pinned to a Formica tabletop by a hand wrenched up behind his back hard enough she knew he'd feel it for days. He'd tapped out with his free hand against the table. A training signal. Several times. Three quick taps meaning she'd gone past initial pain and into serious ouch. The last triple tap almost frantic before she let him go to collapse at her feet. Then did she check on him? No. Apologize? No. She'd stepped over him and gone.

No second kiss there, that was for sure. She considered again. But what if there were a chance?

But there wasn't. Couldn't be. And now that she identified that, she could feel all the weariness and rage of the day overwhelm her. Her commanding officer had kissed her. Taken advantage of her first moment of weakness since she'd turned twenty. The first time in nine years. She'd been weak, hurt, confused, and her commanding officer had kissed her.

It was a court-martial offense. Not that she wanted to press charges. But she couldn't go back. Not if that was all Mark Henderson thought of her, a pretty bit on the side. What next, private training missions? She'd heard that stupid offer too many times when she still flew regular Army. Groping on the flight line. Pinched—

Emily wanted to scream. It had all been so good. So happy. She'd saved Michael's life and been thanked for it. Had been told she was a good pilot by the toughest commander she'd ever been honored to fly with. A man she could truly admire and look up to, who treated her no differently than any other pilot.

And then he'd ruined it by kissing her. Well to hell with Major Henderson. When she was done with whatever nonsense her mother had landed her in, she'd put in for a transfer, for her entire crew. They'd proved themselves as the toughest team in the toughest company. Anyone would take her. And if Henderson protested, she'd threaten to go to the Military Conduct Board and then see what he said.

She'd only ever dreamed of one man's kiss. And, joke was on her, it was a man she'd never kissed. There was no question that she'd let a dozen or more relationships die before they started, all because they never measured up to that one imagined kiss. How was that for stupid? Pining after a married man who never had been and never could be hers.

She tried not to look. She tried to turn back to check on her buddy Abraham for a distraction. But she turned the wrong way and spotted the White House. She'd been pining for Peter Matthews since she was six. Twenty-three years. How was that for the definition of lost causes?

And now she worked for his wife, in the same building. The scale for masochistic had just been redefined.

But even in her daydreams, Peter's kiss had never sparked inside her. Had never ignited a flame she hadn't known lurked inside. Hadn't known a body could contain.

Where was Henderson now? Emily checked her watch. Twenty-four hours, almost to the minute, since he'd kissed her halfway around the world.

Ten a.m. there. Mark and her crew would be sleeping now. Sacked out for most of the day before rousting for dinner, flight briefing, and the night's mission. While she sat here, parked on her butt, chilling it on Abe's marbled front stoop.

Damn Henderson. She wanted his kiss; she just didn't want him. Almost as much as she didn't want to be here.

Okay, it was beyond stupid. Mark stared at a pile of breakfast he didn't want in the officers' mess aboard the carrier. Two hours from the base that reminded him constantly of her. Emily Beale had been gone a whole twenty-four hours, and Mark had already managed to estrange the best crew in the entire outfit other than his own.

Who knew what idiocy he'd think up next. Actually, he already knew what it was and couldn't believe he'd fallen so far from any hint of common sense. But knowing he was about to fall past all redemption probably wasn't going to stop him.

It was crew change for the carrier, and probably thirty guys were scattered at a dozen tables. He sat alone in the corner, staring at his tray of breakfast, contemplating his waffles and his pending stupidity.

Someone slapped him on top of the head.

He didn't bother to turn. "Hey, Jim."

The Mini Boss came around and dropped his own tray across the table from Mark.

"When did you get so dumb?"

"Born dumb."

"You got that right, bro." Jim began eating.

Mark played with his Belgian waffle, cutting it into individual squares with the side of his fork.

"You know, I had me this squirrel dog once."

"You grew up in Chicago."

"Shush! You don't mess with a good story."

Mark shrugged and began dissecting his eggs. He piled little bits of scrambled egg in each cut-off waffle square. How had she gotten so far under his skin? No one did that to him. Women were strictly catch and release. Pick 'em up, show 'em the best time he knew how so that they both enjoyed themselves, and then go their separate ways. It had always worked just fine.

What had Beale done to him? She wasn't even his type. He liked them all soft and curvy and as easy-going as a summer day. Beale was all bright and slender and edge. She never backed off. Not once in her life. Lots of edge.

"Where was I?"

"Some damn squirrel dog."

"Right. That dog couldn't track a duck to save his life. I watched a rabbit scoot between his paws once, and all he did was try to jump aside like he was scared of his own shadow. But he loved them squirrels. He'd go sniffing after them round and round a tree or a bird feeder. Any place they went, he'd try to follow. More than once I saw him staring up into the branches trying to figure out how to climb up there."

"Dumb dog. And your fake Southern accent sucks."

Jim aimed a sausage-laden fork at him, "Never said he was smart and your fake human accent sucks too, so shut up. That dog was plumb crazy about squirrels. After a time they got to know him, you see. Got used to him sniffing around because he never did anything but follow them around. So, do you know what that squirrel dog of mine did?"

"I don't care, but I'll bet you're gonna tell me."

"I'll tell you, Mark, and you will care because you are dumb like that squirrel dog. I was always the smart roommate. I got Christy, after all."

"Because I introduced you."

"But I got her."

"She's my cousin, fool. She's smart and cute and funny, but it's not like I was ever gonna get her."

"But I got her," Jim insisted once more.

Mark waved his fork in the air, "Yeah. Sure. Fine. Tell me about what the damn dog did."

"See," Jim flashed one of those grins of his that had done such a fine job of knocking Christy off her feet and into a decade of marriage and two seriously cute kids. "I told you you'd care. So, one day, I let this complete doofus of a mutt out the back door as usual. This time he walks up to one of the squirrels that's nosing around under our bird feeder and picks him up."

Mark eyed him.

"Now I'm not talking about little black squirrels. I'm talking about the big grays with the bushy tail and all." He held up his hands like a fisherman telling a dogfish story instead of a squirrel story.

"Did he kill it?"

"First he turned to look at me, so proud of himself. The big gray gone all catatonic in his mouth. Then the squirrel freaks. Starts kicking and twisting, trying to get away. I swear to you on my love of your cousin, that dog's eyes crossed as he tried to see what was going on in his own mouth. Drops the squirrel, bolts off around the house, we don't see him for hours."

Mark had to laugh. Jim always told a great story.

As his laugh eased off, Jim leaned in close, so Mark leaned in to hear.

"And the punch line? That squirrel ran about halfway back to the trees, looked around, and scooted right back to the bird feeder he'd been plundering to begin with. Damn dog never went out that door of the house again. We always had to use the front door, muddy paw prints in the hall all winter."

Mark laughed again and ate some bacon. Jim always made him feel better.

"So what's your point, buddy?"

Jim offered him another one of those beaming grins.

"The point of the story, buddy, is that Captain Rick Tully and Admiral James Parker just finished strolling through here behind your back without you ending your illustrious career by chomping down on them like a dumb squirrel dog about a classified mission involving a woman on your squad. As if they wouldn't see through that in a heartbeat."

Mark spun around, but the two men were nowhere to be seen.

He turned slowly back to contemplate his mangled breakfast. He hated to admit that Jim was right. When it came to women, he'd always been the dumb one.

Chapter 16

EMILY CHECKED THE THIRD-FLOOR KITCHEN, SHE'D left a real mess. It was past midnight and she didn't want to clean it up, but the kitchen was her domain now. Thirty-six hours straight and she was ready to crash.

She hit the lights and had to blink twice, once for the brightness and once because the room was spotless. The chopping block even looked freshly oiled. She could kiss the cleaning staff. Then she checked the fridge and noticed all the leftovers were gone as well. Ah. First Lady wouldn't want leftovers anyway. She'd have to remember to always leave the crew something extra in thanks.

She headed down the main stairs. The back stairs were well past her apartment and required doubling back half a floor. No one would be up this late at night. She took the grand staircase.

Turning the corner on the wide landing, she passed the first blacksuit before her tired brain cataloged his presence. She nearly collided with the man behind the blacksuit before someone grabbed her arm and shoved her hard up against the wide banister.

She jammed down a foot on the attacker's instep and threw an elbow hard into his sternum. He dropped to the floor with a gasp before her brain kicked in.

Two more blacksuits materialized between her and the man three stairs below. Their guns drawn. Inches from her face.

Freeze. Don't move. Stupid. Stupid. Stupid.

Which of the instructions were spoken and which her own thoughts, she didn't know, but her body got the message loud and clear. Statue. Unmoving. The black tunnel of two pistols inches from her face, as nasty a sight as she'd seen in a long while.

"Em?"

"Peter?" She only allowed her mouth to move. *Damn, not "Peter," you fool.*

"Mr. President?" She let her gaze shift for an instant off the muzzles of the .357 SIGs hovering inches from her face. It was him. More tired than he looked on television.

"Stand down, Vic."

The leading blacksuit glanced over his shoulder, back at her, then slowly returned his weapon to his holster allowing her to see clearly that the safety had been off.

They helped their downed comrade to his feet. Oh wonderful, she'd leveled Agent Frank Adams, the one who hadn't wanted to let her onto the grounds to begin with. Now she had a real chum in the service.

Then the three of them did that blur thing blacksuits did so well. One moment they were an iron shield blocking any hope of survival, and the next moment, though they were only a few feet away, she might have been alone.

Alone with…

"Hey, Em." Only Peter Matthews had ever been allowed to use that nickname. And he'd remembered it. Hopefully he didn't remember the other one. She stood a little easier as the adrenaline slid down toward a couple of shakes. Not bad this time. No one firing

RPGs at her. Hardly worth the adrenal surge and the inevitable hungover feeling.

"Good evening, Mr. President. Sorry to disturb you. I thought I was the only one up. I'll only use the back stairs from now on. I'm sorry. I just—" won't shut up. She clamped her jaw shut at his smile.

"You look good. Haven't seen you since your father's reception the night I was elected to the Senate."

Her stomach churned at the memory. Nine years ago. One of her real high moments. Twenty years old and just graduated from West Point at the top of her class. So sick at seeing him married to an overblown, high-society, Ms. Perfect wife that she'd gotten stinking drunk on champagne.

Any truly spectacular scene had been preempted when she'd passed out on her father's office couch. Where her dad and the freshman Senator had found her while seeking a place for a private word. A sodden mess in a champagne-stained dress, with puffy, red eyes. Real high times.

Her one childhood dream, the one true love of her youth, married to "that" woman. Forever after, she'd known with certainty, her marriage was to her career. Clear cut and simple. She didn't know how to be Emily Beale on the ground in an evening gown. Captain Beale, that person she understood, knew how to be. And she'd never worn an evening gown again, nor, after the next morning's spectacular hangover, touched champagne again.

"Been hiding since then." And would return to hiding at the first opportunity.

Besting one of the President's blacksuits wouldn't be

improving her relations with the Secret Service. They were already more than a little rough around the edges about having the FBI Director's daughter hovering about. The two services rarely saw eye to eye. They'd be sure she was a spy, feeding information back to her father. Nothing could be farther from the truth. Her father had taught her the keeping of secrets, not the sharing of them.

A glance showed the three were back at their posts. Here they all stood, inside the most secure building in the country, and still there was one man half a flight up, another half a flight down, and Frank Adams at the far corner of the landing, scanning the room below as if assassins lurked in every shadow. And keeping more than half an eye on her.

"Well, you certainly look good."

She knew he was just teasing. Her white pants and short-sleeved blouse looked fine under a chef's jacket, but without the jacket, left her feeling foolish here in the grandeur of the main staircase. Like a teenager who didn't know how to dress for a date. At least the hot flush that had replaced the night air's chill had cleared away all of the goose bumps.

"You look great." *Stunning conversationalist, Emily.* She'd just told the most powerful man in the world that he was hot. But damn, he was. As a teen, he'd been good-looking. Newly elected and married, Senator at twenty-six, he'd rated handsome and dashing. Now... his dark hair was tousled as if he'd just run a hand through it, covering his ears, teasing around his neck. The longest hair of any President in the past few centuries, probably since graying ponytails went out with Andrew Jackson.

Even longer than Mark's. On Peter, it looked refined; on Mark, it looked dangerous, especially with those gray eyes. Peter's eyes were dark brown. Funny, for a moment, she'd imagined his eyes were the color of Mark's. She tore her gaze away.

"It's good to see you, sir." Heat rushed to her face. She put her head down, sidestepped the President, and bolted past the blacksuits, down the stairs for safety.

When she'd regained the confines of her room, she closed the door and leaned against it. More out of breath than after a ten-kilometer run. With a pack. A full one.

Washing her face in cold water did little to relieve the heat burning her cheeks. In the mirror they looked as bright as after a day in the desert without sunscreen.

———⁓⁓⁓———

Peter watched her trot down the stairs, breezing by Vic and Frank as if they weren't there. A year in office, and he still wasn't accustomed to their constant presence. She didn't even notice. So used to high security in her chosen career that she was oblivious to something as minor as three Secret Service agents.

Emily Beale. The precocious little girl of his memory overlapped only uncomfortably with the reality of the amazing woman he'd just encountered. Her sleeveless blouse had revealed well-toned arms and shoulders, and she'd apparently stopped biting her nails. Her body definitely trim. Shapely in all the right spots. And tall. Almost eye to eye with him. She'd always been such a short little thing as a kid. When did she get so pretty and powerful?

Stunningly powerful when she'd dropped Frank,

easily twice her size, right here at his feet on the landing. That had been something to see. Funny, he hadn't noticed her until she was already planting the agent on his face, but he'd never felt fear, never felt threatened, though she looked fiercely formidable. A missile aimed and on course, to steal a metaphor from her world.

It was odd, rather sad too, that there was a side of her he didn't know. He remembered the day her parents had brought home the squalling little bundle. He'd been a part of every major event in the first dozen years of her life.

But in the last sixty seconds she'd become two different people. Did this one recall their thousand discussions as children? Or was he part of a past she'd forgotten? She'd come when he needed her, so there had to be some connection still.

He turned and continued up the Grand Staircase toward the residence with his agents in tow.

He could remember the last time he'd heard her voice. After not hearing it for nine years, he had still recognized her voice instantly. The girl grown into the woman's voice. It had happened on his third trip to the Situation Room as Commander-in-Chief, only his second week in office.

Peter turned right at the head of the Grand Staircase, careful not to look to his left as he headed for the master living room. Katherine had made it clear that the third floor and the eastern stairs were her domain. He didn't want to admit the relief when she'd declared the second floor his exclusive domain during his second day in office.

He dropped off the guys in the hall as he went into

the living room that he'd converted into his office in the residence. He hadn't bothered to mess with it, upsetting the White House decorator no end. Jim Bruckner, or his wife, had done a fine job with it during his tenure. Peter saw no reason to change the soft leather and wood decor.

He shut the door and they left him blessedly alone. He considered a beer, but they'd be waking him in four hours. He tossed his briefcase full of unread memos on the armchair and pulled an apple juice out of the fridge. He lay down on the sofa, knowing the moment he did so that he'd be spending another night sleeping there.

After kicking off his shoes, he let his mind drift back to that time he'd heard Emily's voice when he'd been expecting to hear from a combat pilot. An operation to extract a North Korean nuclear scientist had gone south. Badly. Including the backup plan. Barely seconds from losing a whole SEAL team during his third week in office, a pair of SOAR helicopters that had been training nearby swooped in out of the dark and rescued everyone under heavy gunfire. It was a pure fluke that they'd been flying in the Sea of Japan and had saved the entire operation. No injuries except one SEAL shot in the leg. The scientist and his family were safe and very useful.

Then he heard her voice on the report in. No mistaking it; he knew none better. He'd staggered from the room in shock, finding it impossible that his simplest order had sent that little girl into harm's way.

With memories of Emily Beale kicking around in his brain, he knew sleep would be elusive even at—he checked the mantel clock—1:15 in the morning. He got the best sleep aid he could find in his briefcase, a report on declining fishing off the Kamchatka Peninsula. If it didn't put him to sleep, at least it would make him stop thinking about that little girl.

That little girl who had just flattened the most senior agent of his entire guard. Hard to believe.

He'd bet Agent Frank Adams had trouble believing it as well.

Chapter 17

MARK CROSSED THE CARRIER'S FLIGHT DECK TO HER helicopter. Even here he couldn't help being reminded of Emily Beale. There sat her bird, perched ever so neatly. All fueled and armed and nowhere to go. It even had her name still stenciled beside the door. He'd told Bronson his command was only temporary so no need to put his name on her bird.

He checked his watch. Ten fifteen in the morning, just after 1:15 a.m. her time. If she was on the East Coast. Her orders had said "stateside," so that was as good a guess as any. And they'd be parked here for another hour.

He guessed that she was on a Black Ops assignment and would be back as soon as it was done. He hoped he was right. It happened, but this time felt different. He'd always been in the loop before, at least at some level.

You learned to read between the lines of your people's orders on the rare occasions when you weren't inside the loop. "Assigned to Fort Campbell, Kentucky," meant special equipment or tactical training. "Assigned to Fort Rucker, Alabama," meant extreme flight, probably with specialized night-flight training for a specific mission. "Nellis, Nevada," put you near remote and unobserved gunnery ranges for practicing high-explosives missions. The mission could then extend to anywhere in the world, but at least you knew the nature of what your people were up to.

"Reassigned stateside, detached" didn't mean squat. The unknown was killing him. If she'd crossed out of SOAR and into some other type of assignment, who knew if she'd ever make it back.

"And then you kissed her, you asshole." He whispered it to her Black Hawk. The chance of losing her into that unknown really ate at him. So what had been his totally mature response? To nearly wreck his helicopter with her aboard, then put both of their careers at risk with potential fraternization charges in exchange for seven heart-stopping seconds. Real intelligent.

Then the next thought slammed in and he was glad he wasn't standing any closer to the edge of the deck and the long fall to the ocean or he might be tempted to throw himself off.

He'd been afraid of what would happen if she didn't come back? Far more important, what would happen if she did? He'd broken a barrier of trust that he'd spent an entire career crafting, refining, and building ever higher and stronger until a TOW missile couldn't penetrate its armor.

He'd underestimated the ballistic power of a hurt woman in emotional pain. His mother's tears had always made him frantic, leaving him madly trying to fix the problem somehow, no matter how far beyond his ability. Even without tears, Emily's pain had scorched through his hard-won defenses as if they were no more than tissue paper.

"And then you kissed her, you asshole."

Would she want to come back at the end of her

assignment? Would she dare? She'd think he lurked in the shadows now, just waiting to take advantage of the only woman flying in the entire regiment. She'd ask to be reassigned elsewhere, anywhere, "except" with that sexual-harassing viper, Major Mark Henderson.

He shook his head, stopped in his tracks like a bulldog at bay. There had to be a better answer. She belonged here, 3rd Black Hawk Company, 5th Battalion, 160th SOAR. Her crew was here. Her Black Hawk.

And him.

He had to let her know it would be okay.

He couldn't call her, who knew where she'd landed. But he could write her. Email. She wouldn't get it right away, especially not if she was in the communications blackout that surrounded most Black Ops. But it would be waiting for her when she came out the other side.

He needed to borrow a computer. He turned his back on her name stenciled across the weapon of war awaiting her return and signaled a handler to get him back across the flight line.

Dear Emily, Sorry I kissed you. Your doofus commander.

Yea, that was gonna work great, especially sent from a shared military computer across a military network. Might as well publish it on a bulletin board for his court-martial hearing. Mark deleted the line and tried again.

Dear Emily Beale,

It would be easier if he felt more sorry.

Dear Captain Beale,

He regretted having done it. But he didn't regret the kiss itself. Her lips had opened to his, blooming in slow welcome. Their mouths had flowed together as if meant for each other. As if designed to be the exact and perfect fit of—

He blinked and glared at the screen.

Captain Beale,

Now what? No clue. He looked around the public comm center. In cubicled rows, sailors on break surfed the Internet, video-chatted with family, watched movies. The guy next to him was trying to get a printout of Penelope Cruz in the surf at the end of Cussler's *Sahara*.

"C'mon, Clive. Give an old boy a hand."

Not a word.

Mark stared back at the laptop sitting on the desk. It was the same model she'd shot with such awe-inspiring speed and accuracy. The woman had a grip of iron to bull's-eye the three shots one-handed and so close together. Like an Old West gunslinger. He was glad he'd glanced into the tent in time to see it.

I wish

He flexed his left hand, could still feel where she'd flipped him yesterday. Stung when he stretched for the *W* key.

> I wish to assure you that events occurring prior
> to your departure were unfortunate, strictly ac-
> cidental, and shall not be repeated.

There'd been no accident, and how unfortunate was
it to have tasted her sweet, sweet mouth? Unfortunate
in that it completely overwhelmed his senses even now.
He checked his watch. He'd been sitting here for fifteen
minutes already. He kept losing chunks of time even
imagining her.

He tried once more.

> I wish to assure you that the 3rd Company of the
> 5th Battalion of the 160th SOAR(A) will always
> honor and treat all of its members equally. I
> will uphold nonbiased treatment to the limits of
> my abilities.

Despite your testing those abilities and finding them
so lacking.

> You will be pleased to hear that the 3rd of the 5th
> stands ready to honor all men and women who
> meet the highest standards.

Even if I don't.

> I know that I speak for your crew and the entire
> 3rd Company when I say that we await your safe
> return where, as there never was before, there
> shall never again be any gender-based difference
> in treatment of the company's personnel.

He read it again. It was lame. Nothing before or again, just that one royal screwup in the middle.

> As before, I will personally ascertain that there will never be any threats to your career or position based on another's actions.

That was it. The best he could do without spelling it out for everyone to see. When she came off her current operation, when she could once again check email, she'd see his apology and should be able to read his personal promise that he'd never touch her again.

> Major Mark Henderson

He read it again. Then he spotted Big John looking for him.

He deleted the last line and replaced it.

> Mark

More personal. His personal guarantee.

It looked good. He clicked "Send" and "Okay" quickly. Only as he cleared the screen did he realize that he'd actually clicked "Delete" and "Okay" in his hurry.

Figured. He never did anything right around Emily Beale.

Even though the message was gone, he understood why he'd made the last change from his title to his name. Because he could almost hear her whispering it in his ear after they'd kissed.

Even if she hadn't.

Chapter 18

PENETRATING THE SECURITY AT ANACOSTIA NAVAL Support Facility had been a pleasure. Much quieter than Andrews, this was the home of the nation's VIP choppers. Getting in was like old home week. Emily moved slowly inward through increasing levels of security. Faster with each stage. Every layer culled away another portion of the crowds. Visitors peeled off here, then office staff, then grounds and security teams, finally only hangar-authorized personnel.

She stepped through the door and was home. The rising sun rammed into the hangar through the wide-open main doors, catching a thousand dust motes dancing over nearly two dozen choppers. A stiff breeze pushed against her as the open hangar doors funneled every bit of dew-fresh air at this small rear entrance. Along the way, the breeze picked up the smells of her life. The JP-5 kerosene, a sharp tang over the sweet slap of fresh hydraulic fluid, even the bleach of the sparkling clean concrete was an old friend.

Only standing here, in this moment, did she know what had been missing. The White House was sterile. Purged, vacuumed, polished, every night. Efficient ventilation clearing away cooking smells before they even had a chance to waft out of the kitchen.

It felt safe here, well protected. Home.

A Marine sergeant posted in the shadows just inside

the door saluted, with his other hand on his weapon. She returned the salute. Not until this moment had she understood the emptiness inside her. She'd been homesick. In two lousy days.

"I'm here for a flight check with Eddie," Emily informed him.

"Please stay here, sir." The military still hadn't adopted "Ma'am" or "Miss." He pointed at the ground.

A wide, red line boxed in the six-by-six-foot area she was allowed to occupy. She dropped her flight gear bag by her feet and settled into parade rest. Once she nodded her assent, he trotted over to a group of five men conferring over a disassembled rotor shaft. Ten feet of gleaming hardware, looked like a Cobra. Sure enough, a gutted AH-1W SuperCobra squatted against the back wall. Carts and carts of pieces all carefully racked for an overhaul inspection. She'd never flown the Super. It was the greyhound of gunships. Not well suited to covert operations, all weapon and no transport. Too inflexible a tool for SOAR, but so quick and fast that it made a welcome guest whenever the going got ugly.

The Marine snapped to attention and saluted smartly to one of them. "Air Captain Beale for a 'flight check with Eddie,' sir."

The man separated himself from the group and approached. Stiff, graying, stony faced, erect as one would expect from… his insignia came into view, from a brigadier general.

She shifted back to full attention.

"Captain!"

"General!" If a general offered snap in his or her salute, you returned snap. It felt good to be back in her dress blues. Back in a world she understood. The smell of JP-5 fuel and axle grease swirled around her in a particularly strong gust that didn't even cause the man to shift his weight. There were no overtones of cordite from spent ammo or dust from the desert, but aviation was definitely going on here. The hangar echoed from being clean and tidy. Even the grunts were in spotless coveralls. The jets, the little one that had run her across the ocean and the monster 747s and 757s used for Air Force One and Two, were over at Andrews. Only rotor-craft lived here. Gave it a nice, cozy feel.

"I'm looking for Eddie. I'm due for a flight test, sir."

"Brigadier General Edward Arnson to you, Captain." The man ground it out with a voice that could drive nails.

"Sir! Yes, Sir!" She saluted again because she didn't know what else to do. Eddie. Only the First Lady could call a Marine Corps one-star "Eddie" and get away with it. That was a hole she'd not be digging out of anytime soon. And he'd be giving the flight test? That took the wind right out of her. She'd just failed, and she hadn't even been near a helicopter yet.

"Prep the bird over there for flight."

"Sir! Yes, Sir!" Salute again. Not a glimmer of any-thing. *Move off at a fast trot. You're in it now, Beale, up to your neck.* Preflight in full service uniform. A bad morning just dying to get worse... and succeeding.

Once she looked over the three thousand kilos of flying death, Emily felt less grumpy. It was the clean-est bird she'd ever seen, parked on a concrete floor so polished she could see the Bell Huey's wavy reflection off the sealant. They didn't come out of the factory this clean, and this had to be twenty-five years old, based on its equipment.

There were patches over a couple of bullet holes. They were almost always left visible rather than being touched up. A badge of honor for the bird that had been wounded but dragged its crew to safety. That placed it as a bird that had seen action in its day. Make that over thirty-five years ago to have flown in 'Nam.

This was no carriage for the First Lady's joy ride. This was a weapon of war, one she knew better than she knew the bedroom she'd grown up in. Her first military machine, the Green Hornet. It was also a museum piece. It was perfect; it shone.

She started her circle at the pilot's door. Wheel pressure okay, no fluid seeping around the brake. The plastic tube of the fuel tester she'd taken from inside the pilot's door without even noticing rested in her hand. She poked its metal probe into the bottom of the right-hand tank. A little water always accumulated in the tanks from condensation. That could be a real problem in the sudden temperature changes from hot desert sun to the chill nights. Here in D.C., there shouldn't be enough water in this immaculate bird to even show in the tester.

Half a cup with no line of gas floating on water. Clear as could be rather than the straw color she'd expected. She sniffed it cautiously. Pure water, not even a hint of the kerosene that made up most of jet-propulsion fuel and could make your nose feel as if it had swallowed a porcupine.

She fetched a handy, fire-red safety bucket and poured her water in.

Half a gallon later, decanted a half-cup at a time, she finally struck fuel.

So, it was going to be that sort of a test. A joker had poured water into the starboard fuel tank just for her sake. Beginner stuff.

She continued her inspection as if nothing was amiss. Fourteen problems cataloged by the time she finished her preflight inspection.

"Fourteen failures, sir," she reported at the general's sudden appearance.

"You didn't use the preflight checklist." It was a bark, not a question.

"Memorized it, sir. Hazardous to show a flashlight against a white checklist during nighttime preflight inside a zone. I keep a running count of steps to make sure I don't miss anything. One hundred and thirty-two primary points of inspection." It came out all in one breath. She did her best to hide her gasp for air at the end.

He harrumphed. Not happily.

"Fourteen failures, you say? There were only twelve."

She listed them, from water in the tank to the pebble jammed in the rear rotor.

"Johnson!" He snapped out and a young airman came running.

"List those again, miss." On this side of the line she was captain, not miss, but she wasn't about to correct a general, especially not after calling him Eddie.

She repeated them in the same order she'd seen them, noting the three she hadn't fixed for lack of tools and the one she'd been too disgusted by.

"Spare ammo case for the M60 loaded backward?"

The airman stopped her halfway through. "There's only one way to load it."

She'd heard of gunners who'd died for that mistake. Whose ships had died for that mistake. She led him to the right-hand side door and climbed into the gunner's sling chair so that she sat behind the gun and looking down at the two men. She grabbed both handles of the machine gun, a necessity when the craft was tipped over sixty degrees and turning for bear. She didn't don the harness that let the gunner stay put even when going vertical; they were parked on the perfect hangar floor after all.

A slap with her right hand popped open the weapon's breech. Simultaneously, with her left foot, she kicked open the spare ammo case bolted behind the pilot's seat. Switching hands, Emily grabbed the belt of 7.62 mm cartridges and laid it across the breech. She left it dangling there. The cartridges were facing the gunner, not the outside world. The case was in its hold-down properly, but no one had checked that the ammo rested right way around in the box.

"Give it a half twist."

She saw the General flinch. Good.

"Half a twist in the belt and you increase the jam rate by a factor of ten. And a jam at the wrong moment is lethal." The tech's eyes went wide. What were they teaching these kids?

"Proceed." General Arnson was watching her carefully, with an odd look on his face. Did he not like having one of his technicians shown up? Or was he like Henderson, yet another male who thought women only had one use? Well, she faced down fiercer men on the front line.

Still sitting behind the machine gun, she continued her list—

"A nick on the main-rotor hydraulic line? Are you sure?" The airman glared at her as if she were a fool going out of her way to be insulting.

She climbed down and indicated the engine cowling she'd left folded back. It was a serious cut. Probably a tool slip rather than a bullet, considering the distance to the nearest war zone, but she'd rather not be airborne when that let loose.

"Well, I'll be dam—"

"Marine!"

"Sir!" The man saluted the General and bolted away for his tools.

The General returned his attention to study her face and Emily suddenly wished she'd used more antiperspirant this morning.

His fierce glare held for a long moment, then he nodded.

"Well done, Captain. Shall we have a flight test in a more airworthy craft?"

Chapter 19

IT WAS BEAUTIFUL. A BELL 430 VIP EXECUTIVE model. The Rolls Royce of helicopters. Not a piece of history like the Green Hornet, not heavy or dangerous like her combat Hawk, nor massive and solid like either of the Marine One aircraft, the VH-60N Black Hawk, or the VH-53 Sea Stallion monster sitting in the center of the hangar.

The Bell was a pretty craft. She wasn't painted Marine One blah, but the cheerful blue and white of the White House seal. And luxurious. Two pilot seats forward designed for comfort, not for fourteen hours behind the lines. They were more like Barcaloungers for pilots.

The cabin sported just three seats facing each other in a space that would fit eight. Between the forward pair hunkered a mini-fridge and an entertainment center. The aft seat was actually a small leather couch with two seat belts. Very cozy.

"I'm not checked out in this craft, sir." Emily eyed it carefully. Of course she could fly the pretty thing, but that wasn't the point.

"You will be today if you intend to fly with the First Lady aboard. The bird's already preflighted." He waved a hand toward the three airmen who were just finishing with her.

Now a test of her arrogance?

"I wouldn't fly a bird I hadn't checked out myself, sir. Or personally knew the crew chief."

"Good girl. Have at it."

For the next ten minutes, one of the airmen led her through the preflight checklist and the basic emergency procedures. For the forty after that, the three men led her through everything that wasn't on the list.

"Watch for airframe corrosion, especially along this joint."

"In the first two years' models you can't really see the control-cable routing bracket and you need to run your fingers along like this to check that it's tight."

"She's a light craft, a little jumpier than you'd expect when hovering in a tailwind."

When they started talking about how different engine modifications behaved over ten thousand feet altitude, the General broke them up. Too bad. Once they'd accepted her, they'd been a font of information. Manly handshakes all around replaced any wasted words. Told them she knew they were good. Their solid grips returned the compliment.

Powering up the Bell was preschool compared to her Hawk's graduate course. Everything labeled in plain English. Switches large enough to toggle with two fingers. And three switches where she was used to having thirty. Such a simple toy, but at least it was a helicopter. Each stage of the startup sequence made her smile bigger until her cheeks were positively aching.

The momentary flash of the red warning lights when she turned the key. The thing had a key just like a car. So cute. The throttle slick and smooth beneath her hand. Then the whine and thrum. Almost sexual. The high turbine whine struggling to get the rotor through its first dozen rotations. Then, the turbine overshadowed by the beat of the blades finally slicing the air, a warm buzz transmitted through her hands and the seat of her pants as the bird came to life. The hiss in the headset as she powered-on the radios, then the abrupt click to silence as the squelch circuit kicked in.

The strangest feeling was freedom of motion. No heavy, flame-retardant flight suit. No thirty-pound survival harness and flak armor. No machine gun strapped across her chest with a half dozen ammo clips in her vest's ammo rack. Flight suit and vest were still in the bag, now tucked in an actual baggage compartment. The only item she'd kept out was her helmet. Well worn from hard use sporting the sword-wielding Pegasus beneath the crescent moon. Silver on a field of sunset purple. And only two words; "Night Stalkers." It was her single proudest possession.

She'd stroked it once for luck as she did before every flight. And caught General Arnson staring at her intently. Maybe he didn't like the Night Stalkers. A lot of regular Army didn't either, she was used to it. Well, she did, and that's what mattered. Chef or bodyguard or whatever to the First Lady was not her. Night Stalker. That was her.

In moments they were off the wheels and hovering along at three feet as she slid out of the hangar. It wasn't until she was clear that she spotted the soldier just inside the doors with a small tow cart. She glanced over at the General, but he didn't make any sign that you weren't supposed to lift off inside a hangar.

No little tow carts in Forward Ops scenarios. And

you didn't taxi out even if you had wheels because you wanted to be accelerating hard when you first became visible from your hidey-hole, usually a camo net strung between trees, or aluminum poles if you were above tree line.

She kept her three-foot hover and floated across the taxiway. Settled back to the tarmac for a quick run-up and control test before she called the tower for clearance to go. When it came, they went. No radio contact needed once clearance was issued. The tower just wanted to see your tail feathers moving out of their traffic pattern. Fast.

This machine weighed barely a third of her Black Hawk armed and manned for serious havoc, light on her rotors and remarkably responsive. The foot pedal control was practically delicate, more a ballet step than the rock 'n' roll downbeat of the Huey or the badass hip-hop of the Hawk. They slid out over Chesapeake Bay and, receiving a nod from the General, Emily laid down the hammer.

She climbed, stalled, simulated turbine failures, clawed her across the sky, and even managed to coax the bird through a loop. You never got to fly a DAP Hawk for fun, whereas this machine had been made for nothing but fun.

Not offering a word, the general finally pointed her down the Chesapeake and out toward sea.

The sun glistened off the shining water as if it went on forever, not merely to the shores of Europe and Africa. If she had the fuel, she'd fly straight across and drop in on her unit. Fly some missions, if Major Jerk weren't such a prick.

First she'd kick his butt around the field for putting

her in such a damned awkward spot. Then once more for
making her feel as if she were less of a pilot. Then once
more for kissing her and screwing with her head.

"My nephew speaks well of you," General Arnson's
first comment since they'd left the hangar.

After she'd kicked his butt good… An image of Mark
Henderson lying back on the sand, looking up at her
with those soft gray eyes. Waiting for… something.
That smile pulling at the corners of his mouth. Traveling
up to his amazing eyes. Wanting… something.

"Your nephew, sir?" Emily shook her head for a moment to clear away thoughts of what her body apparently
would like to do to Mark Henderson. She definitely
didn't want to talk about that.

And it was a checkout ride after all; she needed to
control her chopper and her hormones. But how did he
keep sneaking out of her mental footlocker?

"Major Mark Henderson says you are an exceptional pilot."

The collective actually slipped from her nerveless fingers. The blade angles flattened, and the chopper plunged
a couple hundred feet before she regained control.

"Major Henderson? Your nephew?" Was this whole
disaster a setup by Henderson? No, that didn't scan.
He'd been furious about her orders.

"He said you were the first pilot, even over his
wing commander, he would choose if he had to go
in somewhere really nasty. My nephew doesn't give
compliments lightly."

She opened her mouth. And closed it again. Nothing
had come out. She wished she could restart her brain as
easily as a turbine engine.

"Major Henderson? He doesn't give compliments ever." Her spine felt positively tingly. The major thought she was good? So careful not to compliment the female to avoid showing bias. It fit. Nothing underhanded about it. Emily decided that the compliment was intentional.

"Said you had a real habit of coming back with your bird and your crew intact from really messy places," the General continued.

Most likely, that meant the kiss was equally intentional.

"I like that in a pilot."

So did she.

Chapter 20

HENRY TURNED OUT TO BE HENRY SULLIVAN, NOW seated in the back of the Bell 430, airborne and bound for New York. A mild-mannered milquetoast of a man in charge of the First Lady's image. And a very successful man he was. She'd been on the cover of *Time*, *Vogue*, and half a dozen others. Even a nearly nude one on *Vanity Fair* that had drawn almost as much other press as it had direct sales.

"More covers than the main man himself," Daniel had informed Emily in his cheerfully conspiratorial whisper before closing them inside the helicopter and trotting back to the White House.

From the White House lawn, it was exactly one hour and seven minutes until Emily landed at the Downtown Manhattan Heliport on the New York City waterfront. Exactly one hour and seven minutes of absolute privacy as Katherine and Henry conferred in the back over the roar of the rotor blades. One hour and seven minutes interrupted by only five radio contacts with air traffic control, each lasting under fifteen seconds. They'd cleared the airspace ahead of her so she had little to do but watch the autopilot.

And think.

Major Mark Henderson had inducted her exactly as she would have initiated an unknown. First as his co-pilot, then on simple missions, then a series of escalating sorties culminating in more flights to more dangerous places than any other pilot in the squad. Until that last flight, he'd simply grunted and given her the next mission. That's what made his compliment—"Nice flight, Captain"—stand out so completely.

Emily turned at Staten Island, out over the muddy swirl where the Hudson River met the dark blue of the Atlantic. Air control aimed her for Long Island before turning a dogleg toward Manhattan.

But then Major Henderson had kissed her and changed her personal kiss-rating system completely. Imagine if any of 3rd Company ever heard that Mark had the softest, gentlest, and far away the finest kiss she'd ever enjoyed. Despite the raw steel and fire that lurked so close beneath. Perhaps because of it. It would ruin his reputation. Or maybe not, they were guys after all.

She chatted briefly with Heliport control and they plopped her out at the very end of the pier. Not the greatest amount of courtesy to show the First Lady, but the extra security was fine with Emily.

Two men in black materialized from nowhere to guard the helicopter. Two more escorted Katherine and Henry to a limo. Moments later they were gone to shop in New York's finest boutiques and salons, and Emily was cooling her heels in one of the dullest air terminals on the planet.

The last thing she wanted to do was mix with a bunch of New York heli-tourists waiting for their fun, oh-isn't-this-just-so-friggin'-cute helicopter ride to the airport when they could hop on the subway for two bucks instead. And she wasn't about to mess with the pilot's lounge where bored corporate geeks with two hundred

flights to Hartford, Connecticut, and back thought they
were God's gift to the skies and women.

But there were no books or magazines in her chopper
to distract her from Mark thoughts, and it only took her
so long to memorize the emergency-procedures manual.
This bird might be sleek, but it was far simpler than an
Apache or a Black Hawk.

Worst of all, like its more aggressive siblings, the
Bell boasted no bathroom.

She'd have to brave the terminal.

Emily was washing her hands when a military
woman walked in. No mistaking the stance, despite the
pantsuit. The black pantsuit. The woman sized her up
in a moment and, after a quick squat to discover that
the two stalls were empty, came to rest beside the next
washstand over.

"Captain…" she offered after inspecting the lapel
of Emily's dress uniform, "Beale. Assigned to the First
Lady's detail."

It wasn't a question, though Emily nodded anyway.
And spotted the radio earpiece beneath the woman's hair.

"Do you have any ID?"

"The blue-and-white Bell 430 helicopter out front with
the presidential seal on its nose isn't sufficient for you?"

Not a hint of a smile. Blacksuits. Emily slipped her
White House photo ID from a breast pocket and handed
it over.

After a moment's close inspection, it was returned.
One more scan of the room, this time actually popping
the stall doors in case someone was squatting on the
toilet in her high heels totting an Uzi, and the woman
was gone with as little fanfare as she'd arrived.

Emily followed her out into the terminal's waiting room. It was too early for the First Lady to be back unless something had gone wrong.

Clusters of plastic chairs with minimal padding were bolted in neat groups of a dozen. Twice that number of blacksuits where circulating as she became aware of the noise.

Despite the double sets of doors and obvious sound insulation, nothing disguised the heavy, four-blade hammer beat of the Sikorsky Black Hawk. Moments later, through the glass doors, Emily watched the VH-60N White Hawk, painted the white and moldy-bread green of Marine One, land in the center of the pier. A half-dozen dress Marines materialized as if teleported and surrounded the aircraft. Maybe they'd sprung up directly from the tarmac where they'd been stored years before awaiting this very moment. One opened the passenger door and folded down the two stairs. President Matthews stepped onto the landing pier.

Even through the double doors he looked tall, powerful, in control. He cast a quick glance at the blue-and-white Bell copter.

His face remained unreadable through the glass doors, though he turned again to inspect the craft. Well, Emily guessed it was unreadable to anyone else, but she knew him far too well. President Peter Matthews was not happy to see his wife's transport perched on the pier overlooking the East River.

Didn't he like his wife coming to New York?

Maybe she herself was his problem. Was he unhappy about her dropping Frank Adams? Maybe he regretted asking her to come and wished her back in her far-away desert. Well, she couldn't agree more. If she was quick, she could blend back into the women's restroom with no one the wiser.

But she'd hesitated too long.

As soon as he entered the terminal, Marine One hammered back into the sky. Good pilot, she judged by the takeoff. Not SOAR, but good. Gone off to hide somewhere more secure until needed. A phalanx of blacksuits was keeping everyone back as Peter and Chief of Staff Ray Stevens moved through the center of the terminal.

"Emily?" He stopped right in front of her. His foul expression slid slowly toward a smile. A real one. So, at least she wasn't the issue. But that meant that the First Lady was. Which made no sense at all.

"What are you doing in New York?"

"I, uh..." *Breathe, Emily, just breathe.* "Flew up on the First Lady. Flew up the First Lady on..." She blew out an exasperated breath. "I know how to fly, but you knew that. Just not how to talk."

He laughed. An easy, friendly, old pal's laugh that melted her insides several stages closer to normal.

"Ray, you go on and see the guys at IndieTech. Tell them that they have until Thursday if they want to be listened to. Make sure they get that loud and clear before you leave. 12:01 a.m. on Friday and they're out and we'll broker the Internet-2 without them. I'll be at the U.N. for about three hours. If you're back in time, you can join me. Otherwise you're stuck on the commuter train."

"I'll be here." The Chief of Staff waved and moved off. Just two agents followed him. The rest remained in a loose circle and watched the tourists who gawked and snapped photos.

"If the First Lady is shopping, she'll be hours. Come with me."

"With…" But he'd already moved off. "…you?"

When he realized she wasn't with him, he turned and smiled back at her. "C'mon, Em. It'll be fun."

Last time he'd said that had been the night before he went off to Yale. And it had been. Though she doubted today's expedition would include root-beer floats for two on the Mall while sitting on the grass across from the White House. He assuredly feeling the big brother and she the twelve-year old girl with the hopeless crush.

That night Peter had talked of dreams. Dreams of serving his country. Dreams of working in the White House. Little knowing he'd sit behind the Roosevelt desk rather than stand in front of it. Or maybe he did know.

That night was the first time that she'd thought of the larger world about her. It was the night she knew her crush was never going anywhere and that she was always going to be too young to do anything about it.

The next morning he'd gone with little ceremony, leaving her to stand by the Georgetown curbside and watch him go.

Now he stood on the sunlit sidewalk outside the front door waiting for her.

She put on a fast trot to catch up with him.

Chapter 21

"YOU REALLY DO LOOK GREAT. ALL GROWN UP IN DRESS blues. Can't get over it. How did you get so beautiful?"

Emily didn't show anything externally as they exited the air terminal. She'd been trained not to. But her insides had certainly dropped its collective jaw. Beautiful? Peter thought she was beautiful? Did Mark think so as well? Either way, it made her feel all smiley inside. A totally pointless and female reaction, but it was there nonetheless. She basked in the glow of it for a good five seconds before bashing it back into the corner with all the other pointless compliments guys had ever given her.

But a little voice poked its head back around the corner: *Peter thinks I'm beautiful?*

The President's blacksuits guided them into the second of three identical black limos. The limo didn't have any give as she climbed in. A huge mass of armor now wrapped around them and a mere mortal's weight didn't shift its heavy bulk in the slightest.

Once they were locked in, the blacksuits clambered into their own hurking big SUVs. Even a Black Hawk might have trouble against these tanks. And she'd bet there was some serious firepower lurking nearby. Then she spotted a couple of armoreds up ahead. A glance back revealed a Humvee, with the .50 cal turret gun manned, along with a flock of cars for aides and cop cars.

She went to sit in the seat across from him but he patted the place beside him.

"It's much more comfortable to face forward."

"When I flew as a gunner for training, I flew backward far more than forward, well actually mostly sitting sideways but looking back." But she settled down on the sumptuous black leather.

"Always looking at where you'd been?"

"Yes, sir."

"Peter."

"Yes, sir." She'd forgotten how easy it was to talk with him, but she was riding with the Commander-in-Chief and there were some places she couldn't go, no matter how close they'd been as children. And if she didn't think of something else soon—

"Also lagging fire, a gunman on the ground is often slow in reacting to a sudden overflight of helicopters. Ground fire usually comes from four o'clock low. Easier to spot and retaliate when you're already facing it."

"I've missed you, Em."

"Me, Peter?" He'd surprised her into using his name.

"You." His smile acknowledged the minor triumph.

She could remember every conversation since her six-year-old inquiry about letters doubling when you added "ing." And why they only did it sometimes. That was the day the boy next door had decided she had a brain and might be interesting.

When had Mark decided that? Had he decided that? Or did he still just see a pretty blonde in a flight suit? She knew one thing; there was no possible chance he had felt the same visceral shock of recognition that had coursed through her body at their first meeting. She would have seen it. All she could do was shut her mouth, because who knew what idiocy would pour forth if she opened it, and hide behind her shades for the hour-long ride to the base. She wished for once she knew what he was thinking, just once.

Peter, on the other hand, she knew like a favorite book. By the time she reached twelve years old, she knew every detail of Peter's prom dates and how naive he was about his own charm and how nice he was to the girls. He'd spoiled her rotten for other men. There were three genders out in the world: women, men, and Peter.

And that too had been partly her doing. While he'd taught her why boys her age were such jerks, she'd taught him how girls really thought, airheads and nerds alike. They'd traded guy-speak and girl-speak secrets. They'd been each other's closest advisers.

He'd even held her while she moaned and griped after her first heartbreak, the boy who'd asked her to the class roller-blade party and then been a complete jerk to her in front of his friends. Odd, she couldn't remember Mr. Jerk's name, but she remembered exactly how it had felt when Peter held her while she sniffled. She'd gotten his shirt all wet and snotty, and he hadn't complained once. Definitely a low point. She could feel the heat rising to her face at the memory.

Peter Matthews had taken his empathy into corporate America. The ultimate negotiator. Bringing lots of brains and very little ego to the table. He brokered the restructuring of NASA and the U.S. aerospace industry that had salvaged both from a plunge toward bankruptcy. But he'd claimed none of the glory for himself, and hence gotten an immense amount of it. As a Senator, he'd gone on to salvage a couple hundred thousand or something jobs in the failing auto industry.

And she'd chiseled out a life among the most testosterone-laden men in existence, the fliers and ops teams of the U.S. Special Forces. And Mark Henderson was the kingpin of them all. Why had he kissed her? And why had she smashed him into a table the moment he had?

"Funny."

"What is?"

She hadn't realized she'd spoken aloud and concentrated on the configuration of the empty seats across from them.

"What's funny?"

Not Mark. What else?

"The different paths we took." She and Peter a decade ago. She and Mark two days ago.

She concentrated on the seat across from her for something to focus on. Room for three across. The two on the sides had little fold-down tables, perhaps for work desks. Sure enough, little pinpoint lights were buried in the ceiling above.

"It is funny, isn't it?"

She glanced over, but he wasn't laughing, or even smiling. She glanced back at the three empty seats. Flying forward. With only three empty seats and a dark-tinted bulletproof shield ahead. No pilot's view. No sense of direction or terrain. No night vision. Not even RNAV beacons guiding your next move ahead. Or back.

"I'd do a couple things differently, if I had the chance again." His voice was so soft that he might not have intended for her to hear.

"Sir?"

He looked at her, and for a brief instant, her closest friend from childhood sat beside her. Looking out at her from a scared place she'd only glimpsed once or twice before. He studied her face with the same intensity she brought to air combat. Complete focus and concentration. Then the searchlight switched off and he looked forward once again.

They rode in silence for a number of blocks.

"At least one thing I'd do differently." But it was President Peter Matthews talking to himself, and she didn't dare interrupt or interpret.

"It's hard to believe how young we were, isn't it, Squirt?"

It was easy to share a laugh over her nickname.

"Remember the time I dunked you in the Reflecting Pool for calling me that?"

"Remember that the park police tried to arrest you?"

"You told them I was a street urchin who'd picked your pocket and shoved you in the water to make my getaway." She smacked his arm. Then, realizing what she'd done, felt herself go bright red again.

He chuckled and continued as if he hadn't noticed anything out of place. "And I almost let them cart you off. Would've served you right. I'd had those sneakers less than a day."

"Sneaker Boy." Then her cheeks really burned. That's what she'd called him ever since that day. That was twice in two days he'd made her embarrassed enough to blush.

Nothing embarrassed her. It couldn't. Not with where she worked. If the fly boys knew you had a limit, they'd run it over a thousand times until you wanted to curl up and die. She didn't curse or swear the way some did, most did, but she also didn't flinch at even the raunchiest jokes. And they got bad.

Never show a weakness.

Ever.

But she'd just punched the President in the arm like he was an old friend. He didn't react. If he didn't, she certainly wouldn't. It was probably a court-martial offense, punching the Commander-in-Chief. But he was an old friend. And that was a very rare commodity in this day and age.

"Simmons or one of the boys will run you back. Thanks for riding along. Good to see you, Em." He really met her eyes, even better than she'd taught him so long ago.

Then he climbed out of the car and was gone. She hadn't even noticed the car had stopped until his personal squad of blacksuits whisked him away.

As she climbed from the massive hulk, an agent indicated a black Ford four-door idling at the curb. One among dozens of vehicles they'd had in tow. She'd been right about the armor. Several serious Humvees were back in the train along with, she shuddered, an ambulance. She was inside the bubble now and wanted out. She could feel the target circle between her shoulder blades.

She climbed in copilot in the Ford and without a word, was taken back the way she'd come.

Chapter 22

MAJOR MARK HENDERSON ENTERED THE MESS TENT. Tonight's flight looked to be a long one and he needed to stoke up. He hadn't slept last night and he'd already flown to the carrier and back this morning. He'd have to dig deep to stay on the ball tonight.

The chow line stood empty, but a crowd packed around one of the tables. He grabbed a glass of juice and headed over to see what was up.

"She's on!" "Shh!" "Shut up, you mutton heads!"

A bunch of the guys had a crush on Zoe Saldana, again. They'd screened *Star Trek* and *Avatar* back to back the previous week. The guys had become absolute hounds for any interview, sneak peek, or even paparazzi photo. Happened every time. Last month it had been Michelle Yeoh, and the one before that, Marilyn Monroe. He'd always been a Sophia Loren man himself, though he hadn't complained about having to watch the others for a second.

"Raise it up!" "Can't see, damn it!"

In seconds, a bench landed on the table and a laptop was perched carefully atop it.

He felt a little off balance when he noticed that the front line of guys closest to the computer were Beale's flight crew: Archie Stevenson, John Wallace, and Tim Maloney. They'd given him the full-on silent treatment both directions this morning. He started shuffling crews in his mind to figure out how to get them back on the line. Maybe put Stevenson in the right seat. He was ready despite only two months in SOAR. Would have had his own ship if he flew with anyone less skilled than Beale. But then who to drop in his left seat? Not Bronson. Maybe—

"Captain Emily Beale," Brion Carlson blared out before offering his enigmatic smile, sending Mark's stomach through an uncomfortable flip. "The flying chef of the fighting SOAR 160th Airwing—"

"Air Regiment, you ass," Big John hissed at the screen.

"—has landed on both feet. But where this stunning blonde has landed may startle you."

The shot cut away to Emily in form-fitting slacks, a tank top, and an apron. A couple of the guys made sighing noises but were shushed. A kitchen. Big stove, sparkling pots. A cooking show?

Mark could feel his jaw clenching. What idiot would take a pilot of that skill and put her on a food show?

She poured brandy into a pan. A moment later, a burst of flame roared forth. She tossed the ingredients for a few seconds and then turned to a massive cutting block. In seconds she'd made three plates of something that looked incredible. Chicken something with flames, baby asparagus, roasted new potatoes, with a drizzle of something dark in artistic swirls. Pomegranate reduction sauce, the narrator filled in. She pushed one plate toward the camera, which zoomed in for a close-up.

"Oh, man!" "Will you look at that?" "I've never seen anything like it."

Mark had, but only in the finest restaurants. He swallowed and knew it was unfair to the base's chefs, but tonight's meal was going to suck by comparison. He took a slug of juice into a mouth gone almost too dry to swallow.

The camera pulled back as Emily slipped the other two plates across the butcher block. And then lifted to show the two diners.

Mark spit his mouthful of apple juice onto the backs of the guys in front of him who didn't notice only because they were as surprised as he was.

Two of the three most recognizable faces on the planet filled the screen. Vice President Zack Thomas and First Lady Katherine Matthews. They raised large glasses of a dusky red wine toward the chef as Carlson cut back in.

"Captain Emily Beale, First Chef of the East Wing."

Mark would have to kill someone. He started a mental list. Admiral Parker might be a good place to start. Rather than pumping him for information, as he'd have done if Jim hadn't stopped him, he could offer to pump the man full of lead. The best pilot he'd ever flown with cooking for that... that woman?

Katherine Matthews had two reputations: the public one as the poster girl for every good charity the quiet rumor-mill one of a coiled snake even a Black Adder wouldn't mess with.

He'd start with Admiral Parker, raise holy hell, and if that didn't work, he'd raise unholy hell. Something wasn't right in D.C., and if he had to he'd—

Carlson continued, "And this is a chef who can fly to wherever she wants to land."

Emily in dress blues lifting off the White House lawn in a pretty little Bell 430. The First Lady waving from a rear window.

"On a recent trip to New York—"

Then, the third of the world's most recognizable faces. President Peter Matthews holding open the door of a long, black limousine. Emily Beale flashing him one of her sparkling smiles as she climbed in.

Mark didn't hear the rest of the broadcast. Couldn't face that smile. While it had never been for him, he'd seen it on rare occasion. Knew it. Only those closest to her ever received it, and Mark would bet they never forgot it. It made Jim's dazzler look like a flashlight left on the shelf for two years too long.

He left the mess tent and slammed into some crewman or other. He mumbled an apology and kept moving.

No one to complain to. Emily Beale happy at the White House. Aiming that smile at the Commander-in-Chief. He'd never have thought she'd do that. Act some part just to climb the ladder. But what ladder? She'd refused promotions, mouthed off enough to earn a couple of demotions over the years, according to her file, but he'd thought it was so she could keep flying. Bottom line, he'd never know. She was so far gone, there was no coming back.

There was an empty spot in his gut, so empty it cramped. He pulled an energy bar out of a thigh pocket. Not a chance it would get near that spot, but he could pretend.

Chapter 23

CLEARLY THE FIRST LADY LIKED HAVING HER OWN airborne chauffeur.

Barely twenty-four hours after the New York trip, Emily once again settled the Bell 430 onto the South Lawn of the White House. It was late evening, the sunset had sparkled over the western hills as she'd flown up from Anacostia. Katherine hadn't even said where they were going; she'd simply sent Emily to fetch. Like a good lapdog, not like a captain of the U.S. Army. Already any attempt to like the woman on the President's behalf was wearing thin.

The First Lady and Daniel appeared in moments, and a Marine locked them into the back.

Emily turned and looked back between the seats. "Where to, ma'am? And you'll need to buckle up." Daniel already had.

Katherine made a quick pout but reached for the seat belt. "We're going to Jenny Williams's house out on Cape Charles."

Emily knew that was to the southeast, across the Bay. A long drive, but a short flight. Traffic control could route her there, though she hated taking up air-traffic time for directions. But she also knew the First Family had their own controller on their own frequency any time they were aloft who would be glad of something useful to do.

"Okay." She spun the turbines back up, and after

checking in with the controller, she pulled up on the cyclic and got them aloft.

They hadn't cleared five hundred feet when Emily caught the sparkle of red out of the corner of her eye, off to the right and low. An instant later, even as she was wracking the Bell 430 to the east, a trail of light rocketed from the origin point of the aiming laser that had drawn her attention.

An RPG or something else nasty.

Finally the threat warning buzzed loudly.

She punched it silent. Stupid device. Too little and way too late. The chopper didn't have a tactical display to track the threat. The radar sweep was far too slow, designed for other air traffic, not missiles in transit.

With the chopper over forty-five degrees and the collective full up, they were already two hundred yards farther from the launcher than they had been when it was fired. She twisted both throttles to the stops, and the dual turbine engines gave her all they had.

She caught a glimpse of the weapon as it crossed over the brightly lit White House lawn. It continued straight at her. Not good news. She dropped the collective, rammed it down like a posthole digger, twisting the rotor blades past flat into negative lift, and the helicopter fell like a brick.

She ignored the curses and scream from the passenger cabin. Katherine and Daniel would just have to deal.

Her seat belts let her twist against the null gravity of the chopper's fall to see. The damn missile arced to follow her, its motor burning bright against the dark sky, rather than continuing on a simple trajectory path. Really bad news. Tracking warhead.

"Marine Two, Mayday! Mayday!" Not a SAM. Too slow a track. Surface-to-air missiles rarely gave you time to think. They just fried your ass. RPGs burned all their fuel in the first second or so. This one still drove ahead.

The ground was coming up fast.

She jerked the collective back up.

Climb, damn you! The Bell didn't have the raw guts of a Black Hawk, but she was also much trimmer around the waist, a third or a quarter the weight. Some bizarre part of Emily's brain puzzled over the math. Either way it roughly balanced out, though she'd bet the Hawk would have a better chance of surviving a hit. The Bell had one fifth the max takeoff weight of the Hawk, her brain finally offered up, as if she cared. Max climb rate was normally fifty-five percent of the Hawk. This souped-up bird was still thirty percent lower than the Hawk's maximum climb rate. She needed more lift. And ached for her Hawk. Might be the last emotion she felt if she didn't solve this and fast.

"Tracking RPG fired from area of F Street behind OEOB." She'd never heard of a rocket-propelled grenade with built-in tracking ability, they were already past any small-device, wire-controlled range yet the thing kept coming. She wasn't in the mood to brood over technicalities at the moment.

The turbines shrieking past the red line, she slewed back to the left until the chopper was literally flying sideways. Standard RPGs had a range of about a thousand yards. If she could just get a half mile away before it caught up with her...

"Roger. Status?"

Stupid question. Running for her life. Toward the Capitol Building and falling sideways as she went.

She glanced back at the thing's track. Still gaining.

And then it blew.

Fifty feet out. At most. Proximity fuse rather than impact trigger.

Searing white. Scorching brilliance. Her eyes hurt worse than during a runaway thermite fire in the middle of the night. And the pain kept coming, waves of it. Building layer upon layer. For a moment she might have blacked out.

The first thing she knew coming out of it was she'd been hit.

But only her eyes hurt.

She tried a breath.

Either she was numb, or she hadn't cracked any ribs. Her limbs still responded. Her hands still rested on the controls.

Her body felt normal. Except for the two pincers of fire burrowing into her brain.

And she opened her eyes. To nothing. Not even big, bright spots. She blinked again to no effect. The pain poured through her.

The turbines still roared wide open. She eased back on the throttles before something blew out.

She keyed the mic as she fought a sudden slew of the chopper. Please let the bird be intact.

"Not an RPG. Repeat, not a rocket-propelled grenade. They launched a flashbang. A big one."

The turbines were running clean. No fatal wowing sound from the rotors either. The control felt solid, no shudder or shimmy. The craft had survived even if her sight hadn't.

Even if her sight hadn't? There was no such thing as a blind pilot. A roaring filled her ears far louder than any mere helicopter turbine. If she couldn't fly, she'd—

Emily forced the thought aside. Keeping her passengers and her bird alive were the first priorities.

"Ma'am. Katherine!" she called over her shoulder.

No response. Damn, she didn't know if she was right side up or power diving toward the White House.

"Daniel!" He better be conscious; he was her only other option.

"Uh, yea? What?"

"What's my angle of attack?"

"Your what?" His voice sounded a little strangled.

"Which way is up? I can't see."

"Not the way you're going."

"Which way!"

"Left. Left is straight up." Which meant the earth was to the right and they were falling directly toward it.

She tried to yaw ninety degrees. She just didn't know this craft well enough. She could do a ninety-degree yaw in a Hawk blindfolded.

Well, that was appropriate. Blindfolded. Blind... *Don't think. Just fly.*

"I need help. I need you to talk to me constantly about where we are and how we're flying."

The radio squawked in her ear.

"What's the condition of the First Lady?"

"Unknown. She's—"

"Don't worry about her," she cut Daniel off. "If we crash, she'll be way worse off than she is."

"I see the White House," Daniel sounded dreamy, like a sleepy tourist admiring the view. "It's over to your right and pretty far down. You're tipped to the left and the nose is up."

Damn. She'd have bet she was rolling right. A lot of beginning pilots flew out of their first clouds upside down because they trusted their inner ear over their instruments. She knew better than to trust her body signals while flying, they'd always lie about angle of attack. But dammit, she couldn't see the console to trust or mistrust anything.

"Is this level?"

"A little more. Too much!" Daniel's shout made her ears hurt. "Shit! Go back! Go back!"

Little adjustments. Little adjustments. Feel the bird. Her stomach was trailing her to the right. She leaned a little on the left foot pedal and the feeling went away.

"This is flight control. Status, Marine Two?" The controller's voice strident and demanding.

"Flying blind in the vicinity of the White House. Now if you'd shut up, I'm trying to get us back there."

"That's a negative, Marine Two. White House is crashed. Full security lockdown. Any craft attempting to land will be fired upon. Proceed Anacostia Naval Support Facility. We have a team converging on the shooter. Escort is scrambled. ETA your vicinity seven minutes."

"Seven minutes from now won't matter a tinker's damn." Not the best radio protocol but she didn't give a tinker's damn at the moment.

She heard a low groan.

"Is that the First Lady?" she shouted back at Daniel.

"She's out. And bleeding. Not much. Nosebleed

maybe. Can't see. Her arm isn't right. I'm sure it's not supposed to look like that. It looks kinda like a doll that flopped down on a pile of…"

She tuned him out as he rambled away to himself.

"Flight. First Lady is unconscious and injured. Need to land and find immediate medical."

"Reroute authorized. Proceed Walter Reed Medical Center all haste."

"Damn your eyes," she regretted that as soon as she said it. "I'm blind. Literally. Not no instruments. No vision. I'm sure not going to find a hospital—I can't even find a horizon, you damned idiot!"

That gave her a moment of silence that she used to jerk her head toward the empty copilot's seat. The headset flipped off and good riddance. Flight control wasn't going to be of any use to her.

"Daniel. You still with me, buddy?"

"Parts of me. You banged us up pretty good."

"Wear your seat belt tighter next time." No time for sympathy. "Now pay attention. I need to land, and they won't let me back to the South Lawn. What can you see? Big and wide open. And how am I flying?"

"You're going in a pretty big circle to the left, and we're tilted about twenty degrees to the right. I didn't even know that was possible."

"Neither did I." She did her best to correct it.

"I'm so glad to hear that." His voice sounded sleepy.

"Daniel! Stay with me."

"Uh, right. Just really dizzy. I think you kinda concussed me with the window."

"Someplace wide and open."

"How about the Mall?"

"Any concerts or protests tonight?"

"Not that I can see. Turn right and slow down. It's off to the right about two o'clock, but I have no idea how far down."

"Can you see my console?"

"Yeah. But none of it makes any sense to me."

Did she dare let go of the cyclic and point? She'd bet they were out of trim and she'd lose what little concept she had of their orientation if she let go.

"Two big screens right in front of me. Two dials to the right. Top one. Short, fat hand."

"How many screens?" He must have hit his head hard.

Emily was never quite sure how they got down. Daniel stuck with her, and though she smacked the Bell down the last fifteen feet, the landing was better than that carrier landing Mark had hammered hard a lifetime and two days ago. No. Yesterday morning.

Well, maybe the landing wasn't so great. One of the wheels let go. She could fell the rotors hammering against something as she shut down the engines, but they didn't shatter. She was feeling pretty woozy herself as the adrenaline rush eased off. Then her face began to throb and her feet were cold.

She started reaching around for the headset. Then she heard it.

The sweet sound of sirens.

Chapter 24

"VIPER, THIS IS OVERSIGHT."

Mark wrenched the cyclic hard left, and Richardson fired three FFAR rockets as their nose crossed over the SAM missile battery. Everything going wrong. The Little Bird that had inserted the Ranger four-man squad to check out an abandoned Russian tank had been shot down. Clay was down there in his Black Hawk trying to extract the two injured pilots and recover the Rangers before they were overrun.

The 10th Mountain had promised the area was quiet and then walked into a machine-gun emplacement that tore through their first two squads.

The second rocket hit the SAM battery, which lit the sky as it blew up.

"Viper, aye." He checked the clock. The Apache Longbow backup gunships of the 101st Airborne were still three minutes away. Completely useless.

He reefed back to the right and watched as a stream of tracers sliced through the air he'd occupied less than two seconds before.

"Enough of this shit!" He stood the Black Hawk on its nose, setting the rotors to drag the Hawk straight forward. Hopefully too fast for the ground troops to compensate. "Coming up in five, four..." He saw Richardson arming everything. One the count of zero, they lit into the baddies.

Eight rocket trails streaked from the helicopter almost straight down. Mark linked the 30 mm cannon into his vision-tracking. He spotted the howitzer emplacement in the flare of the rockets piling into the trucks and buildings. Lining up the crosshairs in his heads-up display, he unleashed the 30. Ten rounds a second of ammunition, each over an inch across, ripped into men and machine. His crew chiefs pounded a couple hundred rounds each from the miniguns in the second and a half the howitzer was in range.

The capper was the Hellfire missile that Richardson dead-centered on the howitzer. In an air-shattering explosion, the whole place was gone.

"Viper, we thought you'd want to know."

"What?" The overhead AWACS battle commanders were rarely coy. Of course, the eye-in-the-sky wasn't part of his battle. As far as he knew, the closest one was working thirty miles to the east and had no idea of the mess he had on his hands.

He circled hard and spotted thirty fighters on foot cresting the ridge above the downed MH-6 and Clay's transport Hawk. And he didn't need a close look. Didn't need to see if they had IR tags sewn into their uniforms to identify them as friendlies with his NVGs. He could tell by their movements as green silhouettes across his night-vision goggles that they weren't regular Army.

"Clay, you've got under fifteen seconds to be airborne."

"Need forty-five," was all the reply he got.

"Steel, boys!" he called over the intercom. "Hard steel!" He knew there was a .50 cal machine gun he hadn't found yet, but he couldn't let the rescue site be overrun, even if that .50 could punch some nasty holes in his own bird. The crew chiefs began burping out hundred-round splashes from their miniguns at anything that moved.

"There's been an incident stateside," Oversight's dispatcher sounded calm, as if he was busy scratching himself.

Mark really didn't give a damn about stateside at this particular moment. He kept the nose aimed at the ridge above Clay's chopper and began moving sideways so that all of the Hawk's weapons had a clear sweep of the rocky ridgeline.

"We just picked it up off the news. Emily Beale's been shot down. She's alive and in the hospital, but apparently, well…"

Mark swallowed hard.

"They say she may be blind. Sorry, Mark. Thought you'd want to know."

Mark opened the 30 mm cannon against the ridgeline. He let the whole belt of ammo run through the gun at 625 rounds per minute. The feed lasted ninety full seconds, tearing up the ridgeline and anyone trying to cross, sounding like a single sustained scream inside the chopper.

When the feed ran out, his throat felt as if he'd been the one screaming.

Chapter 25

"I KNEW YOU COULD SAVE ME."

Emily struggled to collect her thoughts.

They must have pried her out of the bird. She wasn't in her seat now.

Horizontal…

A world of wonderful.

And the First Lady was saying something.

"I knew you could."

It was nice that someone knew she could do anything. She felt all wrapped in wool and unable to weave any of it into a meaningful fabric.

Moments or hours later, someone wrapped their hand around her wrist as if looking for a pulse. Pretty old-fashioned thing to do when she could hear a machine beeping lethargically away in the background. They must have drugged her on something serious to get a pulse that slow.

"If you think that lying there faking it is going to get you a medal, forget about it." The voice was the first clear thing she heard. The grip on her wrist tightened for a moment, then released.

"Already have a couple." At least that's what she'd tried to say. And it really wasn't worth the trouble of being shot or broken to get one. She tried to open her eyes, but there was padding pressing lightly on them. And total darkness. Couldn't say that surprise or fear was rocketing through her. Whatever they had pumped into her veins didn't let her think anything much at all.

And there was a thrum on the left side of her face that made her bet she'd be in real pain if they didn't have her drugged up beyond caring.

Her eyes… The thought drifted away.

"Where am I?" It didn't sound right, even to her own ears.

"Walter Reed Hospital."

A part of what she'd said must have come out clearly. Right where she'd been told to land. There was someone she wanted to tell that, but she couldn't remember who or why.

"What? How?" *Waaa. Huuuooooowwaaa?*

"The shooter evaporated. We found the launch tube sitting in the middle of the street. Not a print, mark, bit of hair. Nothing on it. No trace. The weapon itself went missing two months ago in Nevada. Specialty piece from a research test. We've been looking for it ever since."

"Hunhuoash?" Even she couldn't translate that one, but the voice continued telling her what she needed to know.

"You got the bird down, though they're taking it back out with a crane. Both you and Daniel Darlington have concussions. You knocked my wife out cold though she's hard-headed enough to be fine. You also bloodied her nose and dislocated her shoulder, but that was okay as soon as they reset it. She's up and gone back to the residence about an hour ago. You always were a hazard, Squirt."

"Reter."

"Yup." She felt the right side of the bed sag as the President sat beside her.

"My seyes." Her voice felt a little clearer.

"You weren't kidding when you said a 'flashbang.' Lit up the whole area. Inside the Oval Office it shone like a lightning strike, and you were a couple thousand feet closer. Worse than July Fourth, which can be pretty bright in this city. Based on radar and photographic reconstruction and the few comments you made on the radio, we think a proximity fuse tripped about twenty feet away from you. Based on your sunburn, you were looking at it to your left. I've seen pictures of your eyes. Now that's a shade of red I haven't seen since the last time I got plastered at Oxford. You really gotta stay out of the sun, Em."

She could hear his voice clearly now. Hear it well enough to know. To know how much it was costing him to stay light and easy. So, even if another woman did get him, they were still close. Hell, he was sitting on her bed. It was nice. And the drugs weren't letting her worry about anything as trivial as blindness or sunburned eyes.

"A rane?" Why did they need a crane to remove her helicopter? The landing hadn't been that bad. Had it? It had.

"Big crane. You landed in the Reflecting Pool. Exact same spot as you soaked my sneakers. How did you do that?"

"Did it wit' my seyes closhed."

That got a laugh. Not a good one. Kind of a choke and gasp.

"Do it allsh the time." At least that explained why her feet had been cold. They'd been in the water.

He shifted, took her hand. Not to hold, but more playing with it to see how it worked. Their old joke. She'd always said that if she was ever bored and Peter was around, she could just give him a piece of string or a sheet of paper and be entertained for hours. He wasn't hyperactive or jittery. But there was a restlessness about him that expressed itself in stacking pennies or folding and unfolding dozens of paper airplane designs across the same sheet until the paper dissolved along the folds into a dozen shreds which he'd then rearrange into different shapes. It was what he did to keep a part of his mind occupied while his thoughts worked.

"Squirt. Why do you do this? I mean how many times have you almost killed yourself since I last saw you?"

She wanted to sit up, but didn't want him to stop playing with her fingers. It felt good. Her fingers were cold, his warm.

"You saw me yesterday, in New Shork."

"Two days ago. It's morning now."

"Shorry, couldn't see the sky."

That killed the conversation. She tried again.

"I've only had one near-death experience since New Shork." Pretty droll answer for being so drugged. She'd have to pat herself on the back when he stopped fooling with her fingers.

"I mean…" He dropped her hand and the bed shifted as he moved away.

She almost reached for him. Captain Emily Beale and the President of the United States of America. The married President of the United States. They'd clearly given her good drugs for that childhood fantasy to climb even partway to the horizon. She kept her hand where it lay, soothed and warm, resting on her abdomen. She'd pat herself on the back for making it out alive some other time.

His pacing across the room and back sounded clearly. Fast. As if something were worrying him.

"I mean since I saw you at the reception."

And she thought she could kill a conversation? Twenty years old, passed out drunk on champagne in her father's office. The FBI Assistant Director at the time. She must have been a sad sight.

"You were fresh out of West Point. Highest honors and all that. I watched. I kept track. And you did it the hard way. You volunteered—Army, Airborne, Special Forces—I can't believe you actually qualified for Special Forces, then SOAR. First woman ever to make the grade. What makes you do that?"

She did sit up. Well, slouched higher on the stack of pillows. Her head only swam a little; the drugs must be clearing out of her system. She wished she could see him. Here. At her bedside. Alone. Well, except for the flock of blacksuits he must have silently in tow somewhere about the room.

"Is the Commander-in-Chief asking me? Or Sneaker Boy?" She thought she heard a muffled laugh beyond the foot of the bed. A blacksuit with a sense of humor? Adams. Had to be. She felt a little safer for having him there, even if he despised her.

The pacing stopped. Was he close or far? Was he staring out a window in contemplation or a step away studying her intently?

She reached for the bandages over her eyes but then thought better of it. There were things she didn't want to know any sooner than she had to.

"Can't I be both?" His voice barely a whisper.

He was close.

Chapter 26

"GOOD QUESTION." EMILY CONSIDERED IT AS WELL AS her muddled brain would allow. One was the best friend she'd ever had and the first man she'd ever loved, or at least suffered a multiyear crush over. The other was a man who had married Katherine Matthews, by choice. A flashy, self-aggrandizing, social success. He'd made himself the most powerful man on the planet, with the help of a hundred million or so voters. Also the man who, by orders to others, had sent her on each mission she'd flown over the past year.

The divide was too great. She'd known the first man better than anyone alive, perhaps even himself. The other one she didn't know at all. She shoved herself a little higher on the starchy hospital pillows.

"Nope. You pick your cards and you play 'em." Most of the words came out right. Her body finally found the proper rudder control and the room stopped whirling around inside her head.

"Harsh, Squirt. You were always harsh with your rules. No gray areas."

"I'm the warrior, you're the politician. I live in the black and white. I survive there. You excel in the gray areas of negotiation and compromise and trickery I could never see."

See. Oh crap, the drugs were definitely wearing off.

"I guess I could cut Sneaker Boy a little slack. Just for old times' sake." And a distraction.

"Gee, that's big of you."

"Yea, I shnow." Okay, the drugs weren't all gone. Probably just as well or she'd be screaming her head off in panic right about now. She felt the bed sag again as he settled once more, this time closer to her feet. He began playing with her toes through the thin hospital sheet.

"Why do I do what I do?" No way was her head clear enough to explain something she didn't understand. Or maybe that would help. She shoved herself the rest of the way to sitting upright. The rudder control held, no more spins.

"Right." He wiggled her toes, first in decreasing sizes, then in increasing ones. Her extremities sent no complaints.

"Okay, past history. You were gone. Off to whatever Ivy League, Mister Too-smart-for-his-own-good sort of place you went." And Mister Way-too-old-and-too-nice-to-be-hers. That's one thing she knew about herself, she wasn't nice. How else had she survived all those years of climbing through the male military structure? She'd torn into enough newbies who'd questioned her skills to know she could be a flaming, sneaky, bad-tempered bitch when cornered. She just hid it well in public.

"I'd already jumped a grade when you left. I ground through my four years and vowed I'd never waste that much time again. Did West Point in three. Fourth year was all independent study. No one in high school or at the Point had any use for an underaged, underdeveloped punk."

"That sure changed."

"What? The underaged part?" Leave it to Peter to

work in a smooth compliment like that without the usual male bravado or staring at her chest, not that there was much to stare at even now. Though maybe he was. She couldn't tell. And leave it to her drugged-out brain not to leave a decent compliment alone. Or just say, "Thanks," and move on.

"Right, you doofus. You're old."

"You're older."

"True. Back to school."

It wasn't the way the Peter she knew had ever talked about her. To her. Too little, too late.

"Being one of the few people to ever crank out the Point in three years kinda set me up for the rules. I liked the structure. I liked knowing where the game was and that I was a player in it. A good player, even. I'm proud of what I've done. I'm proud of my flying, of my fl—"

Her throat closed on her. The drugs let go of her brain all at once, and reality crash-landed front and center. The one thing she was most proud of. The one thing she did right in this world, really right. And she needed perfect vision to get there.

Peter's hand clamped around her foot, hard. Held it tight. Anchored her in time and place. It was real. The pain of his grip was real. She focused on that for all she was worth.

"The doctors said they had to wait at least twenty-four more hours." His voice changed. Now it rang with certainty. "There are enough anti-inflammatories in you to fix the worst hangover a bull elephant ever suffered from too much jungle juice the night before."

He'd become the Commander-in-Chief who was all business. This was the other Peter, the man in charge.

She might not know him, but she liked him. Someone strong enough to take care of you when all around you was darkness. Literally.

"I brought in the best radiant-light weapons team the Army has and their top medicos. Even now they're resimulating the flash based on all available data and weapon characteristics. The best eye doctor in the country and the top neurosurgeon the Mayo Clinic could offer spent an hour with you while you were out, then half a day poking through your MRIs."

He didn't ease up on her foot. It was starting to hurt, but she wasn't going to say anything that might make him let go. Or stop telling her what she most needed to hear.

"A press-corps hack was doing standard film-clip shots on the White House lawn. He bungled the by-line completely, wrong station and messed up his own name, but his cameraman shot first-class footage. Didn't miss a single second of your flight. The flight controllers I brought over from the Marine squad to inspect the footage said the flying was beyond anything they'd ever seen. Sent it down to SOAR at Fort Campbell who agreed they wouldn't want to try to repeat that particular flight."

He'd mobilized half the country on her behalf.

"The hack wanted to broadcast the film first. The guy behind the lens gave it straight to the Secret Service right there on the grounds. I have to call the station manager about not firing his butt for that. He caught the burst on film so we have a good idea of the range and energy output. For comparison, we found another Bell 430 side window from the same production week. We had it flown down from Boston. Identical piece of Plexiglas, or as near as it gets. They're firing the weapon through it in order to estimate the amount of radiant energy that reached you."

He'd mobilized the entire country on behalf of her eyes.

"They give you better than odds-on of seeing again. They give you a fair chance of no effect once the swelling goes down. Not great, but fair. I've even talked to a team of doctors working on eye transplants. Not ready for at least another decade, if ever, but I've learned that corneal transplants are common and easy. Well, easy for these guys. You wouldn't want me to try doing it. But they insist your corneas aren't scarred."

She focused on breathing. Slow, steady, deep, she told herself. Felt as if she were breathing more at rabbit speed.

"So, we leave the bandages on until tomorrow. They offered to drug you out if it was too upsetting." He eased his hold on her foot and returned to playing with her toes.

"But…" she prompted.

He kept his silence.

"Sneaker Boy, what did you say and who did you say it to?"

His fingers stopped on her toes. She could feel his grin, even through his fingertips. It must have been something wicked to see.

"I told them they had no idea who they were messing with and that if they wanted to still have fingers to practice surgery with by tomorrow morning, they had best not mention you being weak about anything. Not around you, and definitely not around me."

"And…" There was more, though she could feel the

heat rising to her face from the first part. Hopefully there were enough bandages to hide it.

"I, um, bet them a grand each that you'd be flying within the week. I didn't give them a lot of choice on the bet, either. Every now and then, there are advantages to being the leader of the most powerful fighting force on the planet."

Chapter 27

EMILY FRETTED THROUGH THE NIGHT AND THE DAY. OR the day and the night. No real difference lying on a hospital bed wearing eye bandages. The hallways had grown quiet for a long time, then louder for a brief time, but not much. Nurses and food came and went. Then the silence had clamped down. The longest night of her life stretched out forever.

Daniel had come in briefly and done his best to be funny. But it was a quieter, more somber Daniel. After a particularly long and awkward silence, he finally whispered to her; "Never knew what being close to death meant."

Emily knew. Had faced it for the first time as her pilot had bled out in her lap while they lay hidden in the godforsaken Thai jungle. She'd had to keep his mouth clamped shut against his groans of pain so he couldn't even say any last words as he died. The opium runners who'd shot them down crisscrossed less than five feet from where she'd hidden them. She'd faced death a dozen times since, and every time as horrible. This had just been a bad scrape.

They sat together in awkward silence for a few more minutes, holding hands before Daniel complained that his concussion still pounded away at him with a roaring headache. With a final squeeze of her hand, he returned to his room.

Her parents had come. Worried. Fussed. Her mother had said several completely inappropriate things about how Emily had had such pretty eyes and wouldn't it be a pity if she could never see again.

Emily felt touched that her mother was so upset that she'd forgotten her perfect manners and felt guilty but relieved when her father escorted her mother from the room. Alone again. In the silence.

At the very darkest hour of her personal night, at the moment she longed to tear and shred the bandages, at the moment she knew for a fact she'd never see nor fly again, a hand took hers. The sudden comfort was such a relief that she cried out. And then she wept for the first time in a decade, holding the hand with all her strength between both of hers.

It was a man's hand. Not Daniel's nor Peter's. Not soft.

Powerful. Protective. Well callused. She could hold a hand like that forever and know she'd be safe to the end of her days.

The hand pulled her. Pulled her until she curled in its owner's lap.

She wept against his shoulder.

She wept while the sobs wracked her body, until the only things keeping her from flying apart were the strong arms around her. Wept until she was wrung dry. Wept until the fear left her. Wept until she remembered that Night Stalkers Don't Quit.

Emily simply curled against the man who held her, her head tucked safe beneath his chin.

Then he cupped her cheek with one of those wonderful hands and held her head ever so gently against his chest.

She knew that hand. Now that she could think, she'd known it from the first instant it had taken hers.

Major Mark Henderson. She'd wept on his shoulder like a scared little girl, not a woman playing tough in a man's world. And she'd never felt so safe in her life.

Mark Henderson, the toughest commander she'd ever had in a long line of the Army's best. A man who flew like a god. A man who she could respect. He had kissed her. That had made a memory she could enjoy.

And he'd held her when she most needed it. That created a space in her heart.

She slid a hand free and, discovering his beret, tipped it from his head, releasing that soft mass of hair. She curled her fingers into it at the back of his neck. Lifting her head, she pulled his down.

He resisted. Held back, asking without words if she was sure.

She didn't think. Didn't want to think. Didn't want to analyze, understand, calculate, and estimate. She just wanted to kiss him to know if it had been real.

She pulled him down the last half inch, and his lips met hers.

There. The electric shock hadn't been her imagination. Her memory of that fleeting moment on the aircraft carrier proved trustworthy. It rang like a great bell all the way down to her toes. He tasted of woodsmoke on winter's air. Of rich, dark, sun-baked garden earth heated by the sun. He tasted most definitely of man. Man with a capital *M* and an exclamation point besides.

When he offered to retreat, she dug her fingers in harder, kept his mouth in place against hers.

With a low moan, that could have come from a wounded animal, he gave in all at once. He buried his face at her neck and held on. Held on like a man drowning.

Emily wanted to throw her head back and howl at the sky. This man, this warrior, would do anything she asked. For this moment, in this place, she controlled the beast. And as clearly as when flying, she knew exactly what she wanted.

Dress-blue service uniform, her fingers told her. The man was wearing dress blues in her hospital room. Bet he looked damn good in them, too. All formal and broad shouldered. How he looked, though, wasn't a really big motivator at this moment. She undid the three brass buttons, shoving the jacket back off his shoulders, pinning his arms. As he struggled free of that, she pulled off the tie and unbuttoned his shirt. Finally, unable to get it clear, she yanked it off over his head.

Then she wallowed against that glorious chest. Her hands flew over the landscape until she knew each curve of every well-defined muscle. Could feel the ripple of his uncertainty as she fed upon him, rubbing her cheek on his shoulder where she'd wept her heart out minutes before. His hands, he never knew what to do with his hands, appeared paralyzed on her shoulders, neither drawing her in nor pushing her away.

A nibble on his rib cage caused a sudden twitch.

She tried it again. Twitch and a squirm.

Major Mark "The Viper" Henderson was ticklish. Oh, this was too divine.

In moments they were a snarled up mess of arms and legs struggling for purchase as he strove to protect himself.

———m———

Mark swore beneath his breath.

What was it with this woman?

He trapped her hands.

Didn't she know she was injured?

With a twist, she tucked a leg up in a move so flexible it shouldn't be possible and attacked his ribs with her toes.

Didn't she know the nurse's station stood only a dozen meters down the corridor? And the night light... No, she wouldn't know about that.

He managed to fend off the leg but lost one of the hands.

Rather than going back for his ticklish spot, she slid her hand down over his pants. He'd felt guilty for being aroused when he held her while she wept. How could so much pain be trapped in so slight a body without flying apart? But holding her, he'd felt strong and, well, aroused.

And when her hand grabbed him through his pants, his arousal snapped to full attention.

No! He wasn't going to take advantage of her. Not in her current state. Through brute force, as much against his desire as against her actions, he managed to get them back to sitting upright on the hospital bed. Still in his lap, but with her legs wrapped somehow around either side of his waist. Not the strategically safe scenario he'd been aiming for.

Gently, all the wrestling violence of hand-to-hand combat gone in a moment, she reached one hand to his face. She ran gentle fingertips over his eyes as he closed them. So gentle, as if the slightest breeze had brushed over his eyelids. Then she ran a thumb over his lips and left it there. He took it lightly between his teeth, but she pulled it back until it rested on his closed lips once more. No need to tell him to be quiet. He considered looking to see if a nurse was coming, but he couldn't turn away from her.

With the grace of a butterfly taking wing, she reached back over her shoulder and pulled the tie on the hospital gown. A shrug and it slipped free to pool in their laps, dangling from the one arm that reached to his face, but hiding nothing.

Not even in his fantasies had she looked this good— and she'd looked damn incredible in his fantasies. Dressed only in dog tags, her body awash in pale gold shadows of the night light.

He wanted to tell her how magnificent she was. How much he wanted her.

Her thumb kept his lips closed but rubbed back and forth.

A smile lit her face, only then did he put together what she was doing. She was feeling his smile because she couldn't see it.

Ever so slowly, in perfect, agonizing, movie slow-motion, she lay back into shadows. Totally open to him.

He hadn't brought any protection. Would never have thought he'd need it. And he wasn't about to go ask the nurse for any. That only left a few thousand options in his imagination. So, tonight would be about those. About her. He liked that. Completely about her. He kissed her right below the dog tags between those perfect breasts.

Chapter 28

EMILY WOKE SLOWLY, LANGUIDLY, STRETCHED OUT, and clanked her hand against the bed rail of the hospital bed. A quick brush confirmed that the sheets and hospital gown once again covered her.

"How are we feeling this morning?"

Standard nurse question. One she most certainly wasn't planning to answer directly.

"Fine." *Floating.* "No more headache." *Liquid.* "I'm hungry." Smiling with every square centimeter of her body.

Her brain offered to dismiss last night as a mere dream, after all, Mark was in Southwest Asia. And they'd never said a word. Not a single word.

Yet her body insisted she'd been wide awake every single, solitary, soaring, rocketing instant of Mark's exquisite attention to her tingling flesh. He'd taken her places she didn't know you could go and still be alive afterward. Places you could only reach with someone you trusted implicitly. She wanted the nurse gone so that she could relish every moment, every instant of—

With a blast of noise and activity, several people entered the room, easily a half dozen by all the rustling.

"Hey, Squirt." That explained it.

"Hey, Sneaker Boy." Again the barely controlled laugh from an unseen person in the room. Mark? Was he still here? Or had he departed as silently as he'd made love to her. Or at least to her body. He'd given exactly what she'd needed. Though how he came to be in her hospital room rather than—

The doctors took over. Questions about pain, none. Dizziness, none. Sleep, almost none. But she wouldn't mention that. Felt too good to mention that. Chart shows you're hungry, good. How do you feel? Frustrated enough to rip your throat out if you don't do something about these damned bandages, fantastic enough to be dubbed Queen for the Day.

They finally got down to it. Someone ordered the room lights dimmed. Someone else tipped up the bed until she was mostly sitting. And, at long last, the bandages began to come off. They kept explaining what they expected to see and the worst possible scenario.

She'd had better training so she forced herself to focus on the best possible outcome. Focus on strength, and you will be strong. Focus on weakness, and you will wind up dead.

"I see light." And she did. Vague, fuzzy, but a brightness through the remaining layers of bandages.

An excited buzz filled the room that the doctor abruptly silenced.

"Even if there is nothing wrong with your eyes, they may be a little blurry at first. You haven't used them in three days. Think of it as waking up. But I don't want you to rub them."

Not until she acknowledged his instructions would he proceed.

The last few layers came free.

The images were dim, blurry.

Each time she blinked, they became clearer. But they didn't brighten.

"Why's it so dark?" She fought to keep the fear from ripping out of her gut.

"The lights are very low in the room." She'd forgotten. A deep breath. Two. Three, and she felt a little better. She glanced sideways at the rack of med equipment, and the brightness of its dials appeared normal. She turned back and blinked a few more times.

"The focus seems good." She could clearly see two doctors, a nurse, and Peter's anxious face hovering over her. More were hidden back in the shadows.

She could see. The relief welled up inside until it threatened to bury her. Then the fears rolled forward like an advancing line of tanks. She could see, but how well? In the darkened room, everything was soft-edged. And color. Any significant loss of color acuity, and she'd be relegated to flying transports the rest of her life.

"Let's run a few tests before turning up the lights."

They swung an apparatus over her face and determined in minutes that she was 20/20. Color tests revealed no failure of rods and cones. Every time someone said, "Normal," after one test or another, the relief piled up inside her. Building broader and deeper. At first she could crawl, then stand. Soon she'd run, and if they kept going, she'd fly.

A flight surgeon came to the fore and ran his tests, tests she'd had so often that it felt like coming home. And still the room lights remained low, even if the tests were often painfully bright.

They put drops in her eyes to dilate the pupils. Peter tried to tease her about something while they waited the twenty minutes for her eyes to react. She appreciated his effort, even if it fell flat, drowned in the tension in the crowded room.

Within an hour of when they'd started, they were done with all their inspections and tests. The doctors and flight surgeon moved to step out of the room. She called them back. They'd speak in front of her or not at all.

They might as well have left the room for how much of their medical terminology she actually understood.

At long last, they broke their caucus and the flight surgeon came forward.

"Captain." He saluted her formally in the dim light. "We will officially wait three more days to be certain of no relapse. But, other than that one contingency, it is my privilege to inform you that you are certified fit for flight."

She covered her mouth with both hands to stop the scream of joy that tried to burst forth. He remained at attention until she nodded for him to finish.

"No restrictions."

She didn't stop the scream this time.

As she returned his salute, a cheer broke out in the room. Doctors, nurses, a round of applause that sounded like the accolades of thousands, though it was more likely half a dozen. Someone even riffled her hair. Peter. It had to be.

She did her best to simply smile, as for a second time tears streaked her cheeks. Emily didn't wipe her face, hoping that in the dim room nobody noticed them. She'd fly again. That was all that mattered.

They gave her dark glasses to put on. "We dilated your pupils for the tests. Don't want them to hurt when

THE NIGHT IS MINE 181

we turn on the lights." She adjusted the glasses and used the motion to discreetly wipe her cheeks.

A nurse moved toward a wall switch in the now barely discernible shadows.

As she did so, a shadow of a shadow moved through the room. Coming from a distant corner of the darkened room, he moved out the door without turning to look at her. Without anyone noticing. Even the Secret Service agents didn't turn to watch him go.

Mark.

Her hands now knew the shape of that shadow, could still feel each curve against the inside of her palm. And no one else moved like that, the powerful walk of the dominant male of the species, unchallenged wherever he roamed. And, because of his Special Forces training, near invisible in a lit room.

Then the lights flashed on and Emily was forced to squeeze her eyes shut despite the dark glasses.

By the time she could blink them open, he was gone.

The doctors and Peter moved down past the foot of her bed in what looked very much like a male-bonding session. Congratulating each other on their part of her recovery. It was her body that had done the hard work.

The nurse came over to check on her, noticed Emily's attention on the door.

She looked around, a bit surprised, her eyes finally seeking an empty chair in the far corner of the room.

"Oh, your guardian angel is gone then." Her accent had the short clip of a New Englander. "Arrived yesterday afternoon shortly after the President's visit. Sat there like a stone for the last twenty-four hours. Night nurse said he never moved. Never said a word. Didn't give his name, but he must have signed in. A lot of decoration on his uniform. I can see who it was, if you'd like."

"No. That's okay. Thanks."

Emily leaned back as Peter and the doctors laughed over their mutual triumph. She closed her eyes and did her best to picture the shadow that had left her room only after she'd been declared fit to fly.

The shadow that had sat silent vigil with her for the longest night of her life and offered his hand in comfort when most needed. Far more important than what she had taken from him afterward. She'd be forever thankful for that hand and the shoulder to cry on.

Could she have found a more unlikely guardian angel than Major Mark "The Viper" Henderson? And who knew angels could make her feel so damn happy.

Chapter 29

HE SHOULD BE SHOT. MARK DIDN'T DOUBT IT FOR A single second.

The jet engines blasted away loudly enough that he could sit in undisturbed contemplation. One idiot and eighty tons of food and medical supplies in the belly of a C-5 Galaxy. Nine hours until he switched planes at Aviano Air Base in Italy. Seven more back to the carrier.

And all he could think was that someone should take a gun to his head and put Major Mark Henderson out of his misery. If he could wipe the damn smile off his own face, it might help matters a bit. His cheeks were actually hurting.

He'd taken absolute, complete, and total advantage of a distressed woman strained far past rational consideration. It had been up to him to set the boundaries, boundaries he'd promised to uphold, and he'd blown right through every one.

Finagling, hell, demanding the three-day pass the moment he'd confirmed the news report. Calling in a hundred favors to get him to D.C. in record time. Keeping his temper as he passed through the Secret Service, which had been harder than he'd imagined, despite his uncle, General Arnson, clearing the way. He hadn't expected such a barricade around the First Lady's pilot and chef; it just wasn't that important a role.

And finally to sit and watch and wait with her through

the long afternoon, evening, and night. A blond guy with a bandage on his head had held her hand briefly, though that appeared to be more for his own comfort than hers. Parents. Various doctors. Only one or two of the more observant nurses had noticed him seated back in the shadows. His dress uniform so in place at Walter Reed that he'd blended right into the background. They'd wisely let him be when visiting hours ended.

He didn't even know why he had come. The hours stretched and he had to face that he was no medic, no doctor. He wasn't even technically her commanding officer any more. All he could do was wait, and she wouldn't even know he sat there with her.

But he'd needed to be there. To sit with Emily Beale in silence, even if that was all he could offer her. The world as a place worth defending made less sense if there weren't women like Emily Beale in it. Hell, a world without this one and only Emily Beale would suck. No better word for it. For all the hours of silence, he'd come no closer to understanding his own motives. He simply needed to be there. For her. For him.

The tears. He'd never had power against a woman's tears. How many nights had he witnessed his own mother weeping? Weeping alone after providing the brave face for his dad, SEAL Commander David Henderson, as he left on no notice for yet another don't-know-if-you'll-ever-see-me-again mission. But Dad had survived. Against all odds, survived to retirement. Now the happy couple had a horse ranch in Montana where her man led mountain tours and taught wilderness survival classes and she no longer had to cry alone in the dark.

When Beale had wept, Mark had crossed to her bed

against his own will. Stood for a handful of minutes feeling twice an idiot before taking her hand.

She had swarmed into his lap and held on like no tomorrow. He had never felt so strong, so powerful as when she'd curled against his chest as her safe place to be. And he'd never been so aroused by any woman as the one in a sheer hospital gown who smelled like springtime and the ocean salt of tears. Every breath, every gasping moment building to the next shuddering sob, had run through his hands and arms, perversely making him stronger.

He rubbed his face and looked around the echoing cargo bay of the C-5. Dozens of pallets of food and dozens more of bottled water hitting Aviano before turning south, off to some African disaster.

If only he could take back what he'd done next. But even as his hand crossed over his face, he could feel his own traitorous smile.

When she had lain back in the shadows of the soft night light, her gown lying across her lap, he'd forgotten everything else. Forgotten the nurse who had watched him for almost a minute as Beale had wept in his arms before moving quietly about her appointed rounds. Forgotten that Emily Beale was blind and in a fragile state of mind. Forgotten he was a superior officer who could destroy both their careers in an instant.

All he could see was that slender waist, those perfect breasts—how in the world had he ever imagined that he'd preferred heavily endowed women?—and those strong but lean shoulders that only a soldier could truly appreciate, could truly understand the thousands of hours of back-breaking work they represented.

He fell on her. There was no other word for it. He'd taken. Ravished. Drunken deep to the point of madness. Okay, there were other words for it.

And she had responded with moans, twists, lifting herself to him in fluid arches of muscle and flesh. And he had taken. Taken all she could give. And then taken more. Whenever he feared he'd been too rough, gone too far, she'd goaded him on.

And when she exploded, each time she unraveled in a flash of energy more powerful than any rocket flare, he could only watch and wonder at what he had achieved.

At long last, she'd curled back against him. Curled in his lap and gone to sleep like a little girl with one hand tucked under her chin. And he'd run his hand up and down the smooth, naked curve of her back. Brushed her hair from across her face so it slipped behind her ear.

She'd barely murmured when he'd dressed her back in the gown and tucked her beneath the blanket to sleep with the sunrise. A kiss to her forehead and a hand brushed over her silken, sun-gold hair had elicited the softest sigh.

No question he should be shot.

She'd woken like a satisfied cat in full morning light. Yet another revelation. An unwinding, unfolding, smug motion he'd love to watch a thousand times more.

He'd wanted to greet her. Wanted to apologize for all the lines he'd crossed last night. But he'd been riveted in his seat by the languorous way she ran her hand down the body he had so enjoyed pushing past its limits.

He'd prepared again to cross to her, but the troops arrived. Nurses, doctors, and Secret Service who had acknowledged him again with the barest of nods but the intense scrutiny of military professionals assessing everyone and everything as a potential threat.

And then the President strode in, exuding confidence. That explained the hard time the Secret Service had given him about sitting in this room.

The man wasn't a trained observer; Mark would wager he was invisible to the Commander-in-Chief. He'd chosen a chair in a corner, partly masked by a plant, with the window, now bright with daylight, just to the side so that any observer's eye would be attracted there rather than to the man made invisible by his uniform, sitting still and out of the way.

The President. Coming to see the First Lady's savior. It made sense, he'd supposed. But it was more than that. He and Beale had an ease together. An ease that was hard to discount. The President teased her, had a pet nickname, played with her toes, sat on her bed, held her hand through the tests. Was she sleeping with the President of the United States? Had been for a while by the looks of it. Was that why she'd transferred to the White House?

Then what had last night meant? Mark could feel the heat of rabid jealousy rise to his face all over again as he sat on the plane over the mid-Atlantic. Then he laughed quietly, thankful the sound became lost in the jet-engine roar. She'd used him exactly as a man would, for a quick bout of sexual relief. Done. Moving on.

She'd never said a word, not his name, nothing. Not as she lifted her hips hard against his greedy mouth, not as the aftershocks shuddered the length of her body, not as she'd curled back in his lap to sleep, the fingers of one hand hooked into the waistband of his dress slacks.

Did she even know who had so ravaged her flesh? Did she care?

Mark considered that he'd been used. That he could live with. Considered that he would probably never cross her thoughts again. That was the problem.

Clearly she was in tight with the President and all safe with him behind that notorious Secret Service wall of no news in or out. Only Clinton had been so blatant about it that they couldn't protect him.

If only he could shear her away from her boyfriend. The Commander-in-Chief was a great guy and all, but he didn't deserve Beale. Okay, there were a few more problems than that. Making glorious... he shied from the word "love." Having amazing sex? Didn't begin to cover it. Glorying in each other's bodies? Well, he'd certainly gloried in hers and she clearly hadn't minded.

How they could be together? That was still a major problem, one he hadn't solved in four days of thinking of little else.

What if he tried thinking like a pilot?

He had a clear target, never clearer, but it was way behind the lines in foreign territory.

Any number of obstacles impeded his path. Her attachment to the President would blow most people out of the game before they even reached the front lines. But Mark had plenty to worry about before that.

First, Army Command Policy Regulation 600-20, especially Section 4-14, of which he'd enjoyed breaking almost every single subsection in the night.

Second, whether or not she'd want him.

And now third, the second problem was under serious jeopardy from the commander-in-chief himself.

That simply wouldn't do. It aborted any plan of attack to solve the first two problems.

He needed to come up with something Jim would really appreciate.

First, it had to be way, way, way below the radar.

Second, it was bound to be really stupid.

Chapter 30

"MY WHAT?" EMILY HELD THE KITCHEN PHONE TO her ear.

"There is a…" A pause while Agent Frank Adams cleared his throat and snarled out his contempt for whoever he was facing. "A 'Marky Herman' here claiming to be your boyfriend. He won't hand over his ID, claims he left it back at the hotel." Frank Adams was clearly pissed. "Do you want me to shoot him?"

"Hold off on that. I'll be right down." She set the pasta water to simmer and turned off the heat under the lobster puttanesca sauce. She could spare ten minutes but not fifteen, or she'd have to start the sauce over.

Boyfriend? Marky Herman? She almost head-over-heeled down the stairs when the next thought hit. Mark Henderson? If it was, should she be thrilled? She shifted up to jog as she crossed the grounds toward the northwest gate. Or should she have Adams shoot Henderson before he turned her life into even more of a nightmare? Whatever he was doing here, nothing good could come of it. That she knew for certain.

Emily strode into the trailer, short on breath, and stopped dead in her tracks. She could feel her jaw wagging and could do nothing about it.

"Hey, babe. I knew y'all lived fancy 'round hereabouts, but this place is the limit. They wouldn't even let me borrow a phone to call my best gal."

Major Mark Henderson stood across the counter from a scowling Frank Adams.

Except it wasn't him. His hair, normally loose or tucked into a black beret, now scraggled out of a sweat-stained, Grateful Dead bandanna. A two-day beard shadowed his chin. He wore a Dallas Cowboys souvenir shirt so new that it pegged him as having just attended a game. Tattered jeans and shitkicker, alligator-skin cowboy boots that she'd never seen before and looked as if he'd worn nothing else for a dozen years.

His mirrored Ray-Ban aviator sunglasses had been replaced by the angular dark glasses Keanu Reeves had worn in *The Matrix*. He looked like a pop-culture mercenary gone bad. A wealthy one, he'd kept his Kobold watch, completing the outfit. Not just a Cowboys game, probably in a box seat.

She shook her head, trying to clear the vision. She actually had to tilt her head a little to see her ramrod-straight commander in the man who slouched against one elbow on the counter.

"Good surprise? Bad surprise? At least you could give me a kiss."

Whatever he was playing at, he was doing it under-cover. No one would recognize the SOAR major who didn't know him intimately. She'd best play along until she found out what was going on. A skill they'd prac-ticed endlessly in SERE training, where the first *E* stood for evasion.

She moved to him. "Honey! Good surprise. Really good!" The kiss threatened to grow hot. She could feel his heat pouring in and igniting her own way too fast.

Before Mark could take it any further, she turned casually and ground her heel on the top of his foot.

"It's okay, Frank. I'll get him out of your hair. Thanks." She led him out of the public side of the trailer and walked back toward Pennsylvania Avenue until they were well clear of ears, though she couldn't be sure of electronic ears. So, keep it in code.

"You can't just drop in on me here, honey." She ground out the last word. "I told you that."

"I wanted to surprise you, honeybunch, but forgot my damned ID back at the hotel. So they wouldn't let me in."

Sure. His ID would say U.S. Army all over it and clearly that wasn't the role he was playing.

"Well, I'm busy. You're about to make me ruin the sauce for tonight's dinner. And you can't come inside. What were you thinking?" He held her hand. When had that happened? The warm afternoon air swirled about them and filled her brain with the rich scent of his warm skin.

"Only thinking about you, honey."

And for the first time since he'd arrived, he actually sounded sincere. She couldn't deal with this. Not now. Not until she'd had some time to think.

"Look. Uh. I'll catch up with you later. Why don't we meet at my parents, sevenish?" Had she lost her mind? The last place she wanted him, other than the White House, was with her parents. But in her father's care was the only safe place she could think of on a moment's notice. Why the hell wasn't he back in Southwest Asia like he was supposed to be? She couldn't imagine Admiral Parker assigning him to follow her.

"Seven o'clock. Perfect!" He scooped her against him, held her tight until his heart couldn't beat without her feeling it along the entire length of her body. His kiss wasn't the tender power-packed moment of the carrier or the searing heat in the hospital. It was slow, thoughtful, teasing, like a connoisseur trying to savor and memorize a new flavor. It made her groan for want of more.

Before she could snap out of it, before her brain could focus on the fact that this was her commanding officer, even in disguise, he eased back half a breath.

"Damn, Beale. Kissing you is the best thing that could happen to a man."

And he was gone.

She knew exactly how he felt.

Chapter 31

"A SUMMONS?" EMILY REFOLDED THE DAMP TOWEL she'd been using to wipe the counter. She had thirty minutes to be in front of her parents' house to cut Mark off. She should never have warned the agents guarding her father to expect him, but she didn't feel right withdrawing that invitation either. And he'd left no number for her to call him off.

"A request, ma'am. I'm to escort you to a meeting." Mr. Frank Adams, blacksuit extraordinaire, stood at parade rest just inside the swinging door leading from her kitchen to the third-floor residence dining room.

It was nice being called "ma'am." In the military, she was either "sir" or "hey, Beale!" But in the confines of her kitchen, "ma'am" sounded nice.

Emily decided to let Mr. Frank Adams wait while she hung the towel and shut down the lights. It afforded her a moment with her back to him.

Adams was scowling at her when she turned, getting tired of waiting for her answer. An invitation from a blacksuit; that gave her pause. They were always so damn polite. So damn serious. And so damn hard to read.

And Adams had to be the most inscrutable of them all. He'd barely let her in through the front gate. Now she sized him up as an opponent. A barrel of a man with rock-solid muscle. The only way she'd dropped him last week on the grand staircase had been her embodiment

of the unexpected. A mistake she'd bet a month's pay
he'd not make again. He could snap her like a twig if he
set his mind to it.

Another possibility came to mind. Was this for real,
or was Frank Adams not above a little revenge?

"No hard feelings? I'm not about to walk into a game
of pummel-the-newbie?"

"No, ma'am. No hard feelings. We've actually added
that scenario to our training. It's easy to forget that even
someone we know as well as the FBI Director's daughter
could be turned." The vitriol dripping off that title could
stain the hardwood floor. She'd wager that somewhere in
the vast depths of Adams's calm gaze lurked a desire for
serious retribution. She'd hate to be the agent playing the
role of the trusted traitor in the next round of practices.

"No hard feelings, my ass."

He actually grinned. Mr. Blacksuit Frank Adams the
Inscrutable actually grinned. A nice smile, too. Lit up
those dark eyes a little.

"Let's just say, if you ever want to train in our sparring gym, I'd pay dearly to be the first in line."

"Careful. I might take you up on that. I'm sorry, but
I don't have time tonight." She pictured her mother left
alone with a chance to sink her claws into Marky Herman.
Helen Beale would shred such an unworthy candidate.

"I've been asked to escort you to the West Wing for
a meeting."

"The West Wing?" She hadn't been there in her six
days at the White House. Actually, two days here, two
days in the hospital, and two days of home rest.

"I would not suggest trying to skip this one."

She closed her eyes for a moment and, not liking the

image, opened them again. "Marky" would just have to deal with her mother. It served him right for showing up unannounced and uninvited.

"Should I go change?" The *puttanesca* sauce had left several long, blood-red tomato spatters down the white sleeve of her men's dress shirt. The pork roast had peppered her tan slacks with several greasy bullets while searing.

"We aren't as formal under this President as, ah…"

"But go change. Got it. I'll meet you in three minutes where I dropped you like a brick." Some part of her simply couldn't resist poking the beast.

He favored her with a nearly feral smile. "You are welcome in the Secret Service gym any time you want." If smiles could kill.

They laughed together. Briefly. Tentatively. Chopped off in unison. She'd just made an enemy into a friend. A dangerous one, but a friend.

Guy-speak. She was amazed every time it worked. Maybe she should teach classes. If she ever worked with anyone other than guys.

She headed out of the kitchen at a fast clip.

The brief glance Emily spared the mirror in her room accused her of not working out often enough.

"I knew that without your help." She was as obsessed with fitness as any SOAR pilot. Not as much as the Special Forces operators, but daily ten-kilometer runs were common practice for her squad. Diagnosis? Presently grounded, eating far too well, and feeling it even in the first week.

West Wing meeting? About what?

Perhaps with the Secret Service. That made sense. They had an office in the ground floor of the West Wing. Maybe they'd finally uncovered her dual role here as chef and guardian, and wanted to do a little cooperative planning. And she had a bridge to sell real cheap.

Much more likely, a little uncooperative planning and a power-play game. Two could play that game.

She pulled on clean slacks, fine, straight-leg, white denim, and a satin blue blouse her mother had insisted she buy because it showed a little more curve. She'd bought it because it showed a little less skin. Sandals with a frustrating little ankle strap. A quick brush of her hair and she was on the landing at two minutes and fifty-three seconds.

Agent Frank made no initial remark on her arrival. He simply stood there and looked her head to toe.

"You got a problem that I'm seven seconds early?"

"No." He looked her head to toe again, not in a leering way at least. "Just never knew a woman who could look so good so fast. You clean up nice, Captain."

"Aw, shucks, Agent Adams. Y'all say the sweetest durn thangs to a gal. Y'all trying to trip me, Agent Man?"

"Only if I want my wife to bash my brains in."

No ring. But that could be an occupational hazard. Some fliers wore them; some didn't because they might snag something at the wrong moment.

"So, you're a tame one."

"Outside the sparring ring."

She laughed one short, sharp "Ha!" before she could stop it. Then she sighed. For better or worse, she'd just made an appointment.

He accepted the challenge with something between a smile and a grimace, then turned to lead the way.

Guy-speak had its drawbacks. There was no way out once a challenge had been laid down and accepted.

She'd worry about that later. For now…

———

Emily halted at the closed door.

"Go on in."

She looked at the door and back at Frank Adams.

"Nuh-uh. You said I was going to a meeting in the West Wing."

"I never said with whom." His smile now wicked.

"That's not nice."

"Sue me."

"This wall is curved." The hallway had been trucking along just as straight as could be. Where it turned a nice clean ninety to the right, the outside corner wasn't square. It wasn't the least bit cornerish. It was roundish. Curved even.

"You lying, deceitful, obnoxious…"

"Don't say it. The President isn't a big fan of the *F* word in his White House."

"He wasn't a fan of it at eighteen either, but that doesn't mean he didn't find a use for it." On the day she'd sent him swimming in the Reflecting Pool wearing brand-new sneakers, had been particularly memorable. Though not as spectacular as the night of his junior prom when he'd discovered his dress shoes filled to the brim with grape jam. Or…

"Are you going in, or are you just going to admire the damn thing?"

Even the door was curved. Bulging outward. Pushing her away.

"You're loving this, aren't you?"

"Can't say I'm being real disappointed at this moment. Now show some balls and get in there."

"Duh, Adams. I'm female. I don't have any." But she stepped forward to show that she did.

Chapter 32

"AH, THERE YOU ARE."

Emily heard the door snick shut behind her. For that alone, Frank Adams would not escape the gym unscathed.

The Oval Office spread out before her. She'd entered near the apex. A fireplace to her left sported a portrait of George Washington above the mantel. Her buddy Abe stared down on her from the right, not looking nearly as friendly as his statue. A circle of chairs and couches filled the center of the space.

Commanding the far end of the room squatted the impossible mass of the Resolute desk. It was a psychic blow declaring, "Here is power!" There were no chairs facing it or beside it. Nowhere to sit when facing the man behind the desk. Nowhere to hide. If this President wanted you to sit in his presence, he gave up the hammer-blow force of his desk and sat with you in the central area.

If there were a corner, she'd have gravitated to it. But there weren't any to hide in. The room was oval and filled with a richness that not even money could provide. A richness of history anchored the room like an aircraft carrier anchored a strike group. This room was the seat of power, and its force radiated out into the world beyond the massive, bulletproof windows. And woe be unto those who stood in its path; this room would run them right over, whether they stood beside the President or squatted in a South American jungle.

A face resolved itself before her.

"Hi, Em. Want a soda?"

The President carried an open beer, domestic, in the bottle and offered her a 7-Up still cold in the can.

"Did you shake it first?" She kept her voice low. The room's mass made more than a whisper feel sacrilegious.

"No, you're safe this time, Em." It had been his one joke, and he'd never tired of playing it on her.

Sometimes she'd let a can explode in her hand just to get him to laugh, as if she didn't know when he'd set it up. Frequently the cans positively bulged he'd shaken them so hard. She wasn't up for that at the moment.

"Don't want to stain the rug."

"What the hell am I doing here, sir?"

His smile was that of a little boy, not the President.

"What? Didn't Frank tell you to bring dessert? I miss your desserts. Next time bring a pie. No, just kidding. Let's see…"

His phone rang and he moseyed over to his desk, comfortably at home in a place she'd only seen on TV shows. No sign of anyone to act as a buffer. Not Ray Stevens nor Daniel's counterpart, Josiah Wildhawk, the silent Cherokee who served as the President's personal body man and right hand.

Emily could really use a corner right about now. She tried to look casual by strolling along the perimeter of the room. When she passed the fireplace, she popped the can there, just in case Peter had shaken it. It opened with a little pfitz sound and settled into its traditional overly perky, bubbling sounds.

In only a few steps she'd circled most of the room, nearly walking square into an enormous grandfather

clock, polished as thoroughly as the cherry wood fur-
niture and the Resolute desk, which now loomed far
too near.

The President hung up the phone.

"This room isn't as big as it looks." She'd reached
him without intending to in less than a dozen steps.

"I know. I've always liked that. You'd think a fair-
sized yacht could slip in here unnoticed when you first
come in. Yet it's only thirty-five feet from bow to stern.
Of course, having eighteen-foot ceilings makes it a little
airier than you might expect. Still, not much room for a
decent mast."

Emily dutifully looked up at the distant ceiling, the
eagle clutching olive branches and arrows carved into
the ceiling in deep relief. A monochromatic reflection of
the design stitched into the rug that dominated the room
almost as thoroughly as the desk.

He waved her to a seat. She chose an armchair that
probably went back to Abraham. This place was really
freaking her out.

He sat in the next chair over.

It felt cozy.

Just the two of them. Right where she didn't want
to be.

His home court.

Well, she'd certainly faced down worse. Combat
mode. Let it all flow through you and over you. If you
started along the path to emotion, to anger or revenge
or pride or fear, you were toast. "I am a leaf…" she recited the old *Serenity* movie line to herself, "…watch me
soar." It had become an unofficial motto of the SOAR
Black Adders. The fact that it was the last line the hero

pilot spoke before a twenty-foot spear skewered his heart was beside the point. Or perhaps was the point. He was a pilot first and foremost and last of all.

She'd let whatever was to come wash over her. A pilot first and foremost and last of all, whatever might happen.

"I'm so glad you could join me, Em."

"Sure."

"Not very respectful there, Captain Beale." His smile was back.

"Sue me, Mr. President Matthews."

She glanced at her watch. Mark Henderson was knocking on her parents' door right about now.

Chapter 33

As HIS WATCH TICKED OVER TO NINETEEN-HUNDRED hours sharp, Mark rapped smartly on the vast door of the colonnaded Georgian home of the FBI Director. The two agents who'd frisked him at the entry had barely let him through, despite Emily calling authorization ahead. That she hadn't arrived yet was unusual for a SOAR pilot. He'd expected to see her landing at the doorstep within seconds of his own arrival. D.C. ground traffic could do that to even the best flier.

The door swept open, and he was confronted by an elegant woman almost as tall as Emily. Not with Emily's amazing blue eyes, but a testament to female beauty extending into mature years.

The brown eyes that assessed him reflected a chilling assessment. Mark almost glanced down at himself to see why before he remembered. Jet-setting bum. Right. Marky. He tried to pull his other self on like a dirty cloak.

With Emily's name as a calling card, he was whisked into the parlor where her mother's other half waited. Emily's blue eyes looked at him out of a handsome male face, blond hair gone gray. Strong shoulders filling out the director's light dress shirt, a glass of scotch in his hand.

For the count of five, they all stood assessing each other while Mark let his mouth run.

"Emmy said it would be okay if I dropped in. She should be here. Have you heard from her? I can't get enough of that girl. You've raised a beautiful daughter. And White House chef? Hoo-whee! Who knew? Damn, but man is life full of cool surprises."

Mom Beale wore a cloak of ice as she sized him up.

At the end of the five count, Dad Beale nodded to himself. A half smile cracked his face for a moment as he glanced sideways at his wife, then clicked off.

He stepped forward to shake Mark's hand. "Can I offer you a whiskey? Emily said she'd be home by now. She must have been held up." The hand Mark shook wasn't the weak grip of some desk jockey. It was hard and strong. And it didn't play games. No test of strength, but the statement was there. Clearly, his disguise hadn't fooled the Director of the FBI for a moment. Not a big surprise. Father Beale might not know who Mark was, but he'd clearly connected that his daughter hadn't sent a scruffy playboy to their home unescorted for no reason.

Mark almost asked for a soda, as Major Henderson would, but changed that to a beer, Marky's drink of choice.

Now Mom Beale was looking back and forth between them. She hadn't missed her husband's shift, but clearly didn't understand it.

She fetched him a Heineken in a chilled bottle and waved him to a chair.

"So, Marky, is it? Please tell us about yourself. It is so rare that our Emily"—strong emphasis on our—"brings home a man. And she's told us so little about you."

Not a word, he'd bet. Now to see how well his act held up.

Chapter 34

"HAVE YOU BEEN AVOIDING ME, EM?"

"Wow, Peter! Nothing like cutting to the chase." Of course, Peter Matthews never followed the rules as a boy, so why should he be any different as the President?

"There's my name at last. That's a good sign."

"I haven't been avoiding you, Peter." She offered his name carefully and distinctly. She was a grown woman and could call him by his name without becoming unglued. "My current job, at your request—"

"And you're bitter about that."

Not something she intended to admit to her Commander-in-Chief so she put her mental head down and continued.

"—At your request, is to serve the First Lady. I expected to see the two of you together more often." She'd feared and hoped she'd see him more often. "But as that isn't the case, I simply haven't seen you. And, no matter how it may seem, I've actually served under forty-eight hours inside the White House. There was that little four-day gap where I just felt like lying around with bandages over half my face."

He nodded to himself for a long moment. Watched her face closely.

He striving to be polite, and she being an obtuse bitch. There was too much history between them for this. He was her closest childhood friend, no matter that she'd spent most of her adolescence swooning over him in his absence. Emily tried to relax, even a little.

"What is it you want, Em?"

"Want a list?"

"Sure."

"It's a short one."

"Fire away."

"I want to return to the front. That's where I belong. That's where my life makes sense."

He nodded again, inspecting the toe of his shoe. He'd never been one to avoid her gaze.

"Not yet, Em. There are a few things that I need. I need you here. I need…" He drifted off, fascinated by the presidential seal woven into the rug beneath his feet.

Something was eating at him. And it felt like more than his wife's safety. She couldn't put her finger on it. However, if he didn't offer, she certainly wasn't about to ask.

He jolted from his chair so abruptly that she slammed against the back of her own in surprise. He strode to the Resolute desk and, without looking in her direction, wrote two lines on a piece of paper, signed it with a flourish, and tucked it into an envelope.

Then he returned to his seat and looked her right in the face. Right in the eyes. Not the Commander, not the President, Peter looked out at her.

"I need you to stay a little longer. I have reasons. I just can't say what they are. At first I was irritated that Katherine wanted me to remove a SOAR pilot from active duty to fulfill her whim. But once I thought about it being you, I was glad for the chance."

He must have seen the look on her face.

"I know that makes no sense to you at the moment. Let me simply state that I have guesses and I don't dare bias your observations. I need you to be smart. As smart as I know you are. As smart as a woman who flies for SOAR and manages the amazing things you do. For the last year, ever since North Korea, I've received a priority report of every flight you take. And you are beyond amazing. Colonel Gibson has recommended you for a Silver Star."

"Colonel Gibson? I don't know a Colonel Gibson." A Silver Star? When had she ever done anything to deserve that? It was the third highest combat honor in the U.S. military. A Silver Star? She couldn't breathe. She tried. Her brain tried. Her body tried. But she couldn't breathe.

"Colonel Michael Gibson of Delta Force."

Michael was a colonel?

"Your commanding officer, a Major Henderson, sent one of his own for a Distinguished Flying Cross."

A Major Henderson whose ass she'd be kicking shortly, if her mother hadn't done so already.

"I can't believe you did that. Simply amazing. I shouldn't spoil the surprise, but I guess I already have. General Brett Rogers, the Chairman of the Joint Chiefs, and I debated and chose the higher award. We approved your Silver Star just a few hours ago. Simply amazing." He shook his head for a moment.

He sat again, leaning forward so that they were close.

"I know you'd rather go, but I need you to stay a while longer. Please, Em. For me." He handed her the envelope. "Here. In case you need it. I wasn't sure when you first arrived, but I am now. I need you to figure out what's going on with Katherine."

"You mean other than the attempts on her life?"

He just pointed to the envelope.

She pulled at the unsealed flap.

"No. Read it later. When you're alone."

She folded it in half and slid it into the back pocket of her jeans beside her crumpled White House ID. Crumpled already, despite the thick plastic.

There were many things the letter could be, but she was pretty sure she knew what it was.

And she hoped to God she was wrong or she was in so far over her head, who knew where she'd come ashore.

One thing was for damn sure. If she was right, she was going to need help. Fast.

Chapter 35

MARK WAS STILL STANDING BY THE TIME EMILY arrived, appearing perfectly at ease despite a full hour of her mother's interrogation. Emily tried to unravel the tableau she observed from the hall before anyone spotted her.

Her father reading through a stack of papers from his ever-handy briefcase. Comfortable as any typical evening at home.

Mark lounging back in an Edwardian wingback chair as if it were an old car seat pulled out of some wreck and propped up beside a makeshift basketball court. An empty beer bottle and another still half full stood sweating on a cherry-wood end table. No coaster beneath. And her mother hadn't killed him or even corrected the situation. That was a degree of tolerance that Emily had never been afforded, not even as a little girl.

And her mother, perched in her usual chair, a glass of barely touched white wine held easily in her hand. She wasn't on the attack, at least not obviously. Something was wrong.

"So, Marky…" Smooth and friendly, Mom in her full-on hostess mode. "Once you're done with racing, what are your plans?"

Oh, god. Her mother was trying to reshape Marky Herman into Mrs. Helen Cartwright Magnuson Beale's image of a possible mate for her daughter. Apparently, any mate was better than her daughter's twenty-nine-year-old spinsterhood in the U.S. Army. She definitely had to break this up fast.

"Hey." She strode in fast. "Sorry I'm late. Mom, thought you had a dinner meeting at eight?"

With the closest Washington D.C.'s leading hostess ever came to being discomfited, Helen kissed Emily's cheek and took Mark's hand.

"I look forward to seeing more of you."

Sure, Emily thought, and reshaping him in your image. Not gonna happen, Mom.

Her mother rushed out to her meeting just moments later, offering Emily an ugly scowl of severe disapproval. Easy to read: "You finally bring home a boy, and this is the best you can give me to work with?" Just great. Emily would have to deal with that later.

The atmosphere of the house changed the moment her mother was gone.

Her father eyed her for a moment. "Should I leave as well?"

Emily shook her head. She'd had time to think about this. She needed help—and needed it badly. She'd been at a loss for where to turn since meeting with Peter. Now, whether or not she liked it, and she didn't, an option had presented itself.

"Can we go somewhere to talk? The three of us?"

Her father raised one eyebrow inquisitively. Mark offered a disappointed look fitting his chosen character.

"For a walk, or…" Her father trailed off.

"Or," was her only response.

This time her father turned to study Mark more carefully. Mark stood more squarely and met his gaze head on, something few could do with the FBI Director.

Finally her father nodded and turned for the door to his den.

Mark glanced her way but kept his mouth shut.

Down the stairs into the basement. She stopped Mark outside the darkroom while her father went in. She knew he was keying a code into the darkroom timer that would open the other door hidden in the far wall.

"Okay," he called softly.

She tried to take Mark's elbow to guide him in. Somehow, they ended up holding hands as she led the way. First through the darkroom where she and her father had spent so many happy hours, one of their few shared hobbies, then into the unlit room beyond.

She stopped Mark clear of the unseen door and recovered her hand in the dark.

Her father closed it. And only after it snicked shut did the interior lights came up. No revealing flash of light spilled out of the darkroom to tell where they'd gone in the basement.

It was larger than she remembered, though she hadn't been in here since the one time her father had shown it to her on her twelfth birthday. The room stretched twenty feet long and fifteen wide. Indirect lighting and soft, apricot-colored walls made it easy on the eye. A couple of bunk beds and a supply of stores lined the back wall. But that wasn't the real purpose of this room.

A couple of couches and chairs and a single computer. A computer not hooked to anything. No T-1 line here. No communications panel. A Class C security site, requiring a retinal scan to even power on the machine, never mind the voice code to unlock it. Neither of which she had or wanted.

Emily turned to the bank of switches by the door and started throwing them. At first it was a game.

Turn off the outside keypad.

Switch the lights over to battery.

The feeling shifted, and she became more Captain Beale of the 160th Special Operations Aviation Regiment and less Emily Beale of the First Lady's staff. And, even less, Squirt to the most powerful man on the planet.

She turned off the last of that feeling with the ventilation system, moving over to canned air combined with a state-of-the-art air scrubber.

The second to last caused her to finally pause.

What if her mother came home? To the best of Emily's knowledge, her mother had never been in here, though she must know of the room's existence.

To cut over this switch would be to cut her mother off from them despite any emergency. To cut off any communications from the rest of the world.

She flipped it, and her mother became an outsider. A row of lights turned green one by one as inhibitors, signal jammers, and ultra- and infrasonic noise maskers fired up. No electronic signal of any kind could penetrate this bunker from any direction.

There was one switch left, but she couldn't throw it. Wasn't authorized to. Didn't want to.

Her father had stood silently through her shutdown of the room. Now he reached past her and pressed his thumb on the fingerprint scanner beside the last switch.

"No, Daddy. That's too much."

He pulled it down.

A small screen reported, "Active defenses engaged." If attackers struck the thick, steel door with more

force than a mild kick, they'd be immediately gassed.
If unexpected pressure was applied to any of the multi-
layered walls, ceiling, or floor for more than twelve
seconds, such as a shaped charge of C4 plastique being
attached, electronic jammers and other devices that functioned less kindly would attempt to destroy any timer
or trigger. And sonic weapons would engage, probably
blowing out the attackers' eardrums and rendering them
unconscious, perhaps even killing them outright. Her
mother's hand resting on the door for more than twelve
seconds would have the same effect, but hopefully she
knew better.

They were now in a secure fort programmed to automatically defend itself against all intruders short of a
bunker-busting bomb.

No half measures. Her father's attitude was clear.
He'd always believed that. He'd trained it into her as she
now enforced it from her helicopter. "If you are going
to do something, do it completely, heart and body, mind
and soul." He must have said it a hundred times to her. A
thousand. And they were more than her watchwords for
her own actions. Those words were her favorite memory
of her father.

"Nice place you have here, sir." In that moment,
the slovenly man who did nothing to stir her blood had
been replaced. Mark Henderson stood straighter, taller,
sharper. Once in the room, his T-shirt and trademark
bandanna around his neck looked foolish, but it didn't
matter. Because now the man shone through.

"First, please allow me to introduce Major Mark
Henderson, my commanding officer. Mark, this is
my dad."

They exchanged one of those manly handshakes. She could see her father leaning in a bit with twenty years of fieldcraft and a lifetime of staying fit. At the end of it, they were both smiling.

"A pleasure, sir. I can't tell you how invaluable your daughter is. She is the best pilot I've ever had the honor of flying with. You should be very proud of her."

Emily glanced at Mark. He didn't make it sound like friendly platitudes. If General Arnson's remarks hadn't forewarned her, she'd have fainted to the floor in surprise.

Her father waved them toward the chairs.

She sat. The leather squeaking loudly, almost painfully, in the anechoic silence of the space.

"So…" Both men turned from regarding each other to look at her. "Why are we here?"

Chapter 36

EMILY CLEARLY BIT BACK AN OATH. "THAT'S MY QUESTION for you. What the hell are you doing here, Major?"

He considered answering with the truth. "I'm busy proving to my best friend how stupid I can be about one particular woman." And he might have, if her father hadn't been sitting right beside her. She'd never mentioned what her parents did for a living. He could feel his palms sweating where they rested on the arms of the chair he'd chosen across from the Director of the FBI.

Clearly he'd landed solidly in the "bad surprise" category and that knowledge came with a bitter taste he didn't like at all. It meant she really was doing the impossible, sleeping with the Commander-in-Chief despite his being married.

"I thought you might need help. That attack came too close to succeeding." *And if you weren't such a perfect pilot, it would have*. He'd seen the tape on the news, and it had scared a decade off his life.

"I have a lot of untapped leave, the front is quiet at the moment, so I put in for some time." And had cashed in yet more favors to get it on such short notice. Now he actively owed people, something he never did.

She leaned forward, elbows on knees and hands clasped. As she stared down at them, her hair swung forward and hid her face.

"Okay… Okay," clearly talking to herself.

"Can I ask what you're doing here?" He had some guesses, but they didn't make sense. She was more than chef and pilot, but he couldn't figure out what. Harem girl to the President?

"Someone is trying to kill the First Lady."

"Apparently," the FBI Director told her.

"Apparently?"

Her father nodded. "It helps keep my thinking flexible."

"Apparently," she echoed. "Apparently President Matthews wants me to find out who."

She told him about her role as bodyguard. That clearly was news to her father as well. Emily was so good at secrets, Mark thought. Who could tell what she was thinking? Did she know he was the one who'd made love to her? That was the question he really wanted to ask and couldn't. During the kiss at the White House a couple of hours earlier, he'd been relieved that she had clearly known. But now that he knew the truth about her, he just wanted to be as far away as possible.

Jim would be so proud. Mark had found new levels of dumb. He'd gone and trapped himself next to the woman he wanted, and he'd probably have to help her sneak into bed with her lover. To keep himself from breaking something, he focused on the stories she was telling of limousines, model airplanes, and highly classified light weapons.

"And the First Lady doesn't trust the Secret Service?" Her father sounded incredulous. A worst-case scenario if ever there was one.

"That's black. Actually, that's black-in-black."

Mark blanched. White operations ended up in the news. Often were even fed to the news, after the fact of course. Invasion of Baghdad, both times. Capture of Saddam Hussein. Downing of bin Laden.

Black Ops were operations that were never told to anyone anywhere at any time for any reason, except for other people with similar clearance and commitment. Like that sweet bit of flying Beale had done to fetch the defecting North Korean. That one had been chatted around SOAR, but not a single member of the outfit would ever tell an outsider. It had also been a key in his requesting her and her copilot at the end of their training.

Black-in-black. Never told to anyone outside of the action team. Ever. Those operations happened once every couple years to the unfortunate, never in their life's service for the lucky. Black-in-black never went as planned. And it was always a royal, terrifying, life-threatening mess when it slid sideways, which it did every single time.

Fourteen years in the service, ten working with Special Forces, and this was only his third. Emily knew the phrase, so she'd probably been part of one while flying for the 101st Airborne.

"So, what's the play?"

"The play? You've already chosen it for us. You're playing my ex-mercenary boyfriend who knows nothing about my real past."

Playing Beale's boyfriend was a role he'd have given a year's pay to hold, if he didn't now know what lay behind it. He could dream of a bonus track or any other special features, but not with a cheating woman.

"Okay." He did his best to swallow his disappointment. "Where are we operating?"

Chapter 37

"THE WHITE HOUSE!" THE WORDS EXPLODED OUT OF both men at once.

That's where the game was, and Emily couldn't change it.

"Wait. Wait. Wait." Mark had both hands up. "You're talking about a black-in-black military operation in the most well-known building on the planet? And, in case you've forgotten, the military is not authorized on U.S. soil. That's so illegal that I don't even know where to begin."

"He's right, dear. It would require a presidential executive order, and even that might not hold up. I'm sorry, but we can't proceed with this."

She hung her head again. She didn't want to do this. She didn't want to pretend to be with Mark. It was too dangerous to both their careers, especially because she apparently had no control when he was close. Didn't want to have control.

But she also didn't have any choice in what they were doing. Her Commander-in-Chief and the best friend she'd ever had were counting on her.

"How do you do this, Daddy?"

When the silence dragged out, she looked up at him. He was studying her closely. He nodded to himself.

"You have learned the keeping of secrets. It is different training than we have as agents. Our life is sifting secrets, unraveling them to see what lies behind. The bottom line is to just say what you are thinking and then we can go over it carefully."

"But my feelings are biased." She managed not to glance at Mark. Not knowing what he was thinking hurt. And he appeared to be cutting up pretty stiff and commander-like for reasons she couldn't fathom. Hadn't his kiss buckled her knees just a few hours earlier? Well, she wasn't about to tell him any more of her past than she was going to tell her father.

"You hate Katherine Matthews."

She felt as if she'd been punched back into her chair. "But... How?"

A soft smile touched his lips, one of those rare moments when only her father was present, without any "agent man" behind the eyes.

"Trust that I know my daughter well enough to see what she was thinking even when she was twelve years old and standing on a curb."

"Was I so obvious?" This time she did glance at Mark, but clearly he was completely at sea at the moment. Please let him stay that way.

"Only to a father who loves his little girl. Now accept that I know the bias and just say it."

She huffed out another breath, managed not to check Mark, and went for it.

"I don't hate her. I don't like her, but even more, I don't trust her. I have suspicions, but I can't confirm them on my own."

"What are they?"

This time she shook her head. "They haven't jelled yet. All I can say is there's a real itch I can't scratch and I'm not seeing where it is. I'd like to find it before it kills me."

Both men sat back at that.

Mark spoke first. "Well, we still can't operate at the White House with any sort of mission. Even you shouldn't be doing what you're doing already. Do you even know what black-in-black means?"

His tone cut at her. It hurt worse than any of her gunshot wounds had. He'd been light, funny, and his kiss had promised so much. Something had changed and now his bitterness drove at her heart.

To hell with him. She'd survived seven black-in-blacks over the past four years and prayed that number eight would be luckier than those. They'd been unadulterated hell, each and every one, despite each achieving a successful conclusion. But a black-in-black never ran as planned and it never came easy.

Placing Mark Henderson in the role of her boyfriend had sounded like a huge plus when she'd first thought of it. That was before he'd made it clear that their night in the hospital had only been about the sex.

She thought hard and fast, but she had no other options. She had signed up to play what could be an incredibly dangerous game. If even a part of her guesses came true, this was going to be a tough one. Just ten minutes after adding Mark to the team, the operation was already heading down the toilet.

Time to talk his language.

She reached into her back pocket and pulled out Peter's note. She hadn't even read it yet.

"Hate to chap your ass, sweetheart."

She handed it to her father, who read it twice

before handing it to Mark. Mark read the front twice, checked the back, the inside of the envelope, and then read it again.

"Is that genuine?"

"Care to ask him yourself?"

They both shook their heads.

Mark whispered the sentence aloud.

"'Captain Emily Beale is hereby authorized to do what she deems is necessary to ensure the security and safety of the United States of America without oversight or judgment. President Peter Matthews.'" He looked at the blank back and rubbed a thumb over the raised presidential seal letterhead.

Exactly what she'd feared Peter had done.

It was the craziest of documents. It simultaneously represented the greatest level of trust between both parties and the greatest level of danger to both parties. She could theoretically nuke the Capitol Building with Congress in session, using the power granted to her by the President. It gave her the creeps to touch the letter. She folded it back into her pocket as quickly as possible, then buttoned the flap.

"That's insane."

She nodded. Empires had fallen due to abuse of such a document.

"And, Dad, the first thing I need is help smuggling my boyfriend into the White House."

Chapter 38

MARK HAD WANTED TO BRING AT LEAST ONE WEAPON, but Emily had insisted not. Now, as he lounged once more against the counter in White House security's single-wide, he was glad he'd listened. These guys had a level of inspection he'd never witnessed before. Agent-in-Charge Adams, first-name-not-supplied, made sure Mark was practically strip-searched even though "Ms. Beale" had vouched for him.

He knew by heart the background check they were set up to find. And could answer a thousand questions about it without repeating himself, which was the first sign of a fraud. He'd been up most of the night studying.

His fake profile said it all. Rich kid. Surfer, thrill seeker, college dropout with mediocre grades in psychology and a fair set of stats in college ball. No luck trying to hook up with the NFL pros. That made up the first-level cover story. The one they were meant to drill holes in. Right down into a fictitious murky past.

Paramilitary, retired. Ex-mercenary.

Even deeper in his file, there laid unconfirmed rumors that he'd knocked over a Colombian kingpin he'd been hired to protect and pocketed a huge wad of ready cash, on the scale of two suitcases full. The weakness of the first cover and the strength of the second would distract anyone from remembering the major sitting in Beale's hospital room. Now he surfed the best beaches, played in the casinos, and… right, he was supposed to be relaxed and easy, not stressed so hard that if they decided to do an anal cavity search they wouldn't be able to get a latex-gloved finger in.

"Hey, Emma, honeybunch." He did his best Texas drawl, remembering to use the nickname they'd selected. "Em" had been violently rejected. No big surprise; it was her lover Peter's name for her.

Emily smiled brightly at him on cue.

"Did I mention that I just bought that offshore Super Boat I told you about? The one that won them two little races and that one big one down Australia way. A sweet little fifty-footer with twin 1,200-horse turbines."

He made a show of glancing at his wristwatch. Five thousand dollars of the finest watch ever built by man. He could tell that the main guy recognized it. A statement of wealth and a fixation with the military. It was marketed as designed by Special Forces, and he knew a few other guys who wore it. It was also exactly what a rich, ex-paramilitary guy would wear.

"As of…" He waited for the second hand to arbitrarily reach fourteen. "Now, I own her." He dropped his arm on the counter, leaving the watch in plain view.

"I'm having her flown up for the Florida Keys race in a couple weeks. You should come down and be my throttle man. Wear that virtually nothing string-bikini I bought you." He turned to face the agents. "Damn but she looks hot in it. She flashes that around, and ain't no one else will even remember that his throttle isn't in his shorts."

Not impressed. The only agent looking the slightest bit green with envy was a young kid who probably had less than a year since agent school. Mark wasn't real happy with this tack, but he was still furious with Beale. He'd never touched another man's woman. Ever.

It didn't take a rocket scientist to notice the extra Secret Service guards watching next door to Emily's or to learn that the neighbors were the President's parents. Now Stephen Beale's comments made sense. Emily had loved the boy next door when she was twelve and was now enjoying the bonuses of being stateside and living in the White House. Maybe he could feel a little bad for Katherine Matthews getting the short end of this stick.

And that Beale would sleep with a married man just made him sick to his stomach. Well, he'd ram this role right down Emily's throat until she choked on it. He'd make himself her personal wake-up call. And the worst part was that he still wanted her so badly. She was all he thought about, and it was making him crazy.

He flashed his grin at the kid and pulled his funky shades back down over his eyes. At least he looked the part with his desert tan and sun-burnished tips of his long, black hair serving him well.

"He checks out, sir."

Agent Adams scowled at his assistant and then went to inspect the screen himself.

Mark couldn't believe that the FBI Director had done this so fast. They'd met less than ten hours ago. Fooling a third-world *garda* only required a little fake paper and a couple of discreetly folded hundred-dollar bills. Fooling the Secret Service? His palms were sweating again and he didn't dare wipe them off. These guys would notice, and then they really would strip search him.

Then, if they washed his bicep really well, they would

remove the tattoo of crossed machine guns, the headless torso, and the curlicue "Roland" to reveal the emblem of the sword-wielding winged horse. Even a Secret Service agent would know that was the SOAR emblem.

He leaned over to the newbie and offered up in a loud whisper, "Damned if I knew she was the First Lady's personal cook when I chatted her up in that bar in Monaco. Now I'm feelin' right stupid for voting for the other guy. When I first saw her, I just thought she was hot. Look at her so prim and proper." He sent a happy leer her way, which wasn't as difficult as it should be.

Emily wore high-end stone-washed jeans that had clearly been painted on in all the right places and a blue silk sleeveless top that picked up the color of her eyes.

She returned his attention with a downward glance and then a bright reddening of her cheeks. How could anyone like her look that innocent? No one was that good an actress.

He whispered loudly to the kid, "You get her alone and she's wild, boy. Wild."

The kid did his best not to go wide-eyed.

And Emily was doing an equally poor job of trying not to look pissed.

Once they were satisfied with the X-rays of his aged, shitkicker, alligator-skin cowboy boots that he'd owned for under eighteen hours, they let him through.

"I'm sorry, honey." Emily wrapped her hand over his arm.

He slid the arm free and clamped her around the waist. A quick smack on the lips. Nice, moist, unsmiling lips. No spark. No heat. From either of them, but good for show.

"No worries, babe. Better safe than sorry."

They strolled out of the back of the security trailer and up the curving path toward the White House.

"Honey." Her voice was smooth as the salty sea.

"Yes, sugar?"

"If your hand moves one inch higher, you won't be pulling back broken, mangled digits."

"No?" He hadn't even noticed how easily his finger had slid upward to trace along the bottom edge of her bra through the sheer silk.

"No. You'll be pulling back goddamn stumps."

It was good advice. After all, he'd seen the remains of the last newbie who thought he could harass the only woman in the unit. Fastest damn trip to the medico tent he'd ever seen. She didn't wait for others to defend her. Or even give them the chance.

Compared to Captain Emily Beale, they were all too damn slow.

Chapter 39

PETER COULD USUALLY MULTITASK WITHOUT A PROBLEM. His walking tours for foreign diplomats let him be visible throughout the White House. The tours also let him stretch his legs, check in with staffers at the far corners of the vast complex, and chat with said diplomats in a more casual and, therefore, less tense mode.

But whatever excuse the new Indonesian ambassador was attempting to relay about deforestation and massive clear-cut fires in Sulawesi polluting Thailand and Singapore's air, it was all lost on him. They'd been out on the South Portico admiring the cool afternoon.

Em walked into the Jacqueline Kennedy Gardens between the residence and the East Wing arm in arm with a very handsome and powerful-looking man. She leaned in cozily to whisper and they both laughed. His long hair made him look disreputable. His angular sunglasses struck Peter as a sham.

The ambassador repeated his question. A part of Peter's mind identified the tone, the tone of a man not being listened to, who knows it. But he couldn't find the words. Couldn't find his brain.

All he could find was a cold, hard, bitter knot in his belly.

Mark felt the searing acid of anger smash into his chest and lodge there.

"There's your goddamn boyfriend."

"What?"

Mark didn't realize he'd spoken aloud. He turned her to follow the next little row of boxwood in the gardens. There wasn't a leaf out of place in the frickin' Kennedy Gardens.

He cocked his head over his shoulder. "Eight o'clock."

Ever so casually, she leaned over to whisper in his ear. Her mouth moved so close, he had to close his eyes at the scent of her sweet breath. But she didn't say anything. Instead, she was pretending a flirt so that she could look behind them.

"President Matthews?" She stopped to lean down and brush those fine-fingered hands over some bush covered so heavily in purple blooms that it looked fake. Nothing could have that much color.

"The Commander-in-Chief himself." Mark kept his back toward the man standing two stories above and fifty feet behind.

She rose to her feet. She reached for his hand. Rather than taking his, she grabbed his pinkie and ring finger and bent them backwards hard enough to make him catch his breath.

"And what makes you say that, Marky?"

"Ease off, Cap—"

She wrenched them harder.

"Ease off, Beale."

She did, but not much.

"I saw you two. In the hospital. Remember? 'Em' this and 'Sneaker Boy' that. Playing with your toes, holding your hand through all your tests. He's married, for Ch—" Mark realized his voice was rising, and he chopped it off. It was wrong. There were no two ways about it. Plain and simple wrong.

She eased off on his hand. Not as if she wanted to stop hurting him, but as if she'd forgotten about them. She still held his hand as they moseyed to the next bush, something yellow this time. Once again she knelt to smell the blooms, but despite all of her elegant lines, the action looked stiff and mechanical.

"You surmised…" She stood. Then moved ahead once more.

He half suspected that if he stopped, she'd keep moving along, showing all the outer signs of enjoying herself and not even notice his absence.

"Do he and I really look as if…"

Suddenly she snapped back into her body and turned to face him, standing toe to toe. From a distance, they might look like lovers about to kiss. Being close enough to see her expression, to watch those sky-blue eyes gone suddenly cobalt, he wondered if he was about to end up in the hospital himself.

"That's why you've been treating me like shit? You thought Peter and I were lovers? You goddamn idiot!" She turned on her heel to stride away.

He grabbed her arms to keep her in place.

"Finish it."

She shook her head and hung her face down. Her hair slid around to hide her face.

Mark lifted her chin.

Emily tried to look away, but he didn't let her. Tears swam along her eyelashes and threatened imminent release. As he kept her chin steady, her eyes shifted from hot with anger to awash with pain.

He pulled her close and held her hard. There was no way he could deal with her tears. Especially not if he was the cause.

"Don't cry." He knew he was begging.

She nodded against his shoulder.

"Oh God, please don't cry."

She shook her head against his shoulder.

But he could feel where already her tears were soaking through his T-shirt.

Chapter 40

THE PLACE WAS A LABYRINTH OF HALLS AND DOORS. Mark shoved his sunglasses on Emily to prevent any questions from passersby about why her eyes were so red.

Finally, sometime after he was sure they were lost forever in the labyrinth of the White House's lower levels and would never again see the light of day, she pulled out a key and handed it to him.

They'd come to a stop in front of a door bearing a small placard with her name.

He moved her inside and sat her on the bed. He found a tiny bath, wet a washcloth, and brought it to her. By the time he returned, she'd slid down to sit on the tile floor and leaned back against the bed.

As she wiped her face, he tried to back away. Tried to find somewhere to go, but there wasn't anywhere. There was the bed, a small desk, and a dresser that also served as nightstand. A small window covered with a soft curtain, solid enough to block vision without blocking the light brightening the room. No flowers, no pictures.

She held out the washcloth. He took it the three steps back to the bathroom and hung it on the edge of the sink. Returning, he didn't know what else to do, so he sat on the floor and leaned on the bed beside her. But didn't touch her.

"Please tell me you're done crying."

"No promises." Her voice was rough. "I've cried one other time since I was twenty, two if you count a few happy tears at being able to see, and you were there for all of them."

"Well, I don't think I can go through that again." He wasn't sure, but he thought that earned a quirk of a smile.

She took a deep breath and her hunched shoulders eased slightly. "The last time I wept before that, I'd lost the one love I never had."

"Em, sorry. Emily, damn. Emma. Gotta remember that. Emma." There hadn't been enough time to practice their roles properly. "'The one love you never had.' That sure doesn't make a boatload of sense."

She laughed this time, bitterly, and shook her head.

"No. It doesn't. But it's true anyway. President Matthews isn't my boyfriend. He was the only friend I ever had before my copilot, Archie, at West Point. Peter and I grew up together. The proverbial boy next door."

Mark listened to her story of a six-year-old with a crush, a twelve-year-old in love with a college boy, of a broken-hearted girl at twenty, watching her dream boy and best friend marry someone else. And the more he listened, the stupider he felt. He'd assumed they were lovers, not friends. How damn stupid did that make him? Even Jim wouldn't laugh about this one it was so bad.

"I'm a complete wreck as a woman. There is no way you can want me, Mark. I'm going to have Peter declare me a national disaster area."

But she'd turned back into exactly the woman he'd always thought she was. Beautiful and decent and with a heart that loved so hard.

He slid a hand around her waist and pulled her across the tile until he could tuck her under his arm. Until she leaned her head on his shoulder. He leaned his cheek on the top of her head and just let her breathing ease as he rubbed his hand up and down her back.

She wasn't a wreck; she was a miracle.

And the President was an idiot for ever letting her slip through his fingers.

—⁓—

"What is it about you, Henderson?" Emily turned her face into his shoulder, her hair moving slickly across his cheek.

"Herman, you mean. Marky Herman, surfer and paramilitary extraordinaire. Henderson must be some other guy. Should I be jealous?" With his arm around her, he could feel her breathe deeply, as if she were inhaling him until he existed only inside her body. Herman—and Henderson too, for that matter—wanted to lay her on the bed and spend a day or two making love to her.

"Yes, some other guy…" Her voice a warm soft echo against his neck. "Ravished me. When I was completely helpless."

"Yes, that sounds like the cad." She had known it was him. Everything back in alignment. Well, almost. Except for Army Regulation 600-20. He tried to make light of it, but it had been so wrong. He still couldn't make sense of how something that was so wrong could feel so right.

She breathed in again, deeply, her nose against his neck so that he could feel the cool air slipping over his skin toward her inhale.

"You were angry."

When he'd made love to her? Ecstatic, perhaps thrilled. But not angry.

"When you thought I slept with you while sleeping with a married man."

"Furious!" He could still feel the grit of it making his back teeth clench. All the anger snapped back into him, even though he now knew it wasn't true.

She sat up, pulling away from him. His side where she'd been curled so warm suddenly felt chilled despite the warmth of the day.

Those eyes inspected him. Looked at him until he wanted to look away to preserve his soul. They saw through him, inside him. No secrets were safe from those eyes.

"You gave me…" She trailed off, tipped her head to one side, and then the other, inspecting his face from several angles.

The rough edge of his tongue on two continents, Asia and North America. He'd given up trying to read her and wondered what part of himself he should protect if she decided to attack. That face he thought he knew so well had run through a hundred emotions in the last hour, had shown him a dozen new sides of the woman. The most amazing woman he'd ever met.

But, he clenched his fists in resolve, she'd had a hard day, mainly due to him, there was no way on this green Earth that he'd take advantage of her emotions again.

"A gift," she whispered.

A gift? He'd never given her a single rose.

She placed her hands on his shoulders, rested them there warm and gentle for a long moment. Then pushed him away. Well, there was his answer. She wanted nothing to do with him.

He closed his eyes against the pain. He'd never have her in his arms again.

Mark half expected another blow as she pushed him back, away from the bed, pushing him prone onto the floor. Lord knew he deserved the rejection. He'd insulted her in every way possible, worst of all questioning her integrity.

But no blow landed. Moments before his back hit the floor, she slid those fine, cool hands under his T-shirt. In one clean sweep she had it clear of his torso and over his shoulders. His bare back hit the cool tile and a cold shiver shook him.

She jerked the shirt off over his head none too nicely, nearly took his ears with it.

And there she sat, like a majestic elfin queen all long and elegant in blue silk, staring at his chest. She ran her hands along his sides, up and over his ribs, those blue eyes following the hands. Right, she'd been blind last time. Now she studied him like a terrain map before an op.

She did want him. He closed his eyes. Emily Beale wanted him. Had known it was him. Hadn't thought it was just sex. The possibilities swirled in his mind, a clutter of thoughts and fantasies he couldn't process fast enough. The fantasy born the moment she'd walked off that civilian airliner two months ago.

Her hands continued their slow tracery, slid over his ticklish spot without attacking but with a small circling to acknowledge the moment. Continued until his mind quieted and all he knew in the whole world was where her palms ran over his skin.

She lifted a hand. But when he opened his eyes, she covered them with her hand. Then she folded his T-shirt and placed it over his eyes. Blinding him.

He reached for her, but she slapped his hands aside. He went to slide a hand up her leg, and his pinkie twisted painfully in her grasp. He backed off. Only had to tell him twice. He wasn't a complete idiot.

Nothing, and more nothing. The tension built. The silence. Her sweet weight rested across his hips, but she didn't move.

No sounds. Nothing except his own heartbeat, a racing patter that ebbed and flowed, unsteady. Finally, in between the sound of his own heart, he could hear Beale's breathing. Calm, steady. Always so calm and steady, except that one night.

He finally became aware of the tiny shift of her weight with each breath. He'd never been so aware of a woman, never wanted one so badly. Like his helicopter, an awareness that extended past any boundary as trivial as skin and nerves. He understood a problem with the Hawk long before any sensor could reflect it. When flying, he knew how the wind would kick before it blew. A perfect mesh of man and machine.

His connection to Beale extended past heat, past arousal. It extended into the quiet, and the dark.

A tiny shift. A moment before…

A feather couldn't be as soft as what touched his chest. It brushed over him, his skin rippling in its wake. The sensation maddening. What could it possibly…

Hair. Her hair hung loose, and she brushed it back and forth over his chest. In the dark and silence, he could see her in his mind's eye, could see her brushing her hair back and forth over his chest.

Is this what she had felt? Alone in that bed. And then a touch from the darkness. He had no fear, his sight could be returned by tossing aside a T-shirt. But he could feel the kindness behind Beale's ever-so-gentle action.

A feathered kiss on the center of his breastbone slammed into him. No one had ever done more than offer him sex. He'd never wanted more than that. Captain Emily Beale was offering him more. A vision of something. Of himself? Is this how she saw him? Kind? Everyone called him a hard ass, his commanders to his face, his crews to his back.

Beale held a different vision.

When she lay down upon his chest, he almost died. She'd shed that silk blouse and sheer cotton bra he'd glimpsed the edge of but twice. Skin to skin. Just curled there. So quiet, for so long, he wondered if she'd gone to sleep.

Safe. Quiet. Safe.

Then she shifted ever so slowly, one way and then the other. Rubbing his chest with hers, at first like a she-serpent sliding slowly over the sand. Her operational tempo increased slowly, building layer upon layer until she writhed against him like a living thing gone mad.

She ground her hips against his erection. Slid her body across his. Nuzzled his neck. Drove her fingers into his hair, scrubbing her fingernails in his scalp until even the sensation of her hips faded beneath the glorious massage.

—٭٭٭—

Mark actually whimpered as Emily unzipped his jeans. Moaned like a winter windstorm over the desert when she freed him and slid him between her breasts and nipped him with her teeth.

Emily kept him in suspense, not once or twice, but drove him to the edge a half-dozen times. When she finally drove him over, his entire body shuddered. Shuddered exactly as hers had done in that hospital bed.

She held him as he released, writhed, moaned, relaxed, sagged, and finally lay still gasping for breath.

Emily lay with her head on his stomach, her eyes closed. She had returned the gift he'd given her. Done her best to return it in kind. Sex for sex.

Now they were even.

Why did that thought make her heart want to break?

Chapter 41

"SO, HOW DO YOU WORK THIS THING?"

"This thing" was how the First Lady typically referred to the Bell 430 helicopter. Right now it was perched on the South Lawn and they were alone except for a small flock of blacksuits hovering about. Emily sat in the cockpit rechecking the preflight checklist. Trying not to fumble over the logical steps that weren't there for this bird. No terrain radar. No infrared targeting systems. No...

No further attacks had been made on the First Lady, and she was eager to fly again despite her own experiences that night. As was Emily. She hadn't heard from her "boyfriend" yet. She was making him sleep at a hotel, had sent Mark on his way when she'd headed to the kitchen to make dinner last night. They were supposed to get together later this morning, and then Katherine had called for the helicopter.

Emily looked at the First Lady standing beside her open door. A flowery top and tight designer jeans, her red hair caught in a jaunty ponytail and rippling down her back. And a close circle of blacksuits. The Secret Service had doubled the First Lady's detail until it rivaled the President's.

Shielding her eyes from the sun, Katherine stuck her head in Emily's door rather than simply climbing into the back of the helicopter.

"It works by magic." Emily's standard reply when someone asked how she pulled off a particular maneuver.

"No, I mean really."

"Oh." Not the most professional response to give your boss. "Climb on in the other side and I'll show you."

The First Lady circled the nose for the left-hand seat. Emily hopped out and slid the passenger door to the main cabin shut while Katherine climbed in and settled herself. One of the blacksuits latched the copilot's door once he saw Katherine was securely belted.

"You really want to try this?"

"You make it look so easy."

"I've been doing it since I was sixteen."

"At sixteen, what was I doing? Hmmm… That would be boys. I was also doing boys. And maybe boys."

"You make it look so easy."

The First Lady laughed aloud.

Emily bit the inside of her cheek. "That wasn't quite how I meant it."

"No, no." Katherine shook her head and patted Emily's knee. "That was perfect."

"I mean, I watch you with diplomats or staffers, the Vice President, or a new security guy. You make them, I don't know, comfortable. I was always a loner."

"Well, then, Miss Emily Beale, who was kind enough to come and be my chef and guardian and save my life last week, we'll make a trade. You teach me about this, and I'll teach you about that. Deal?"

The First Lady held out her hand. Emily took it gladly. Her grasp was warm, and while not strong, it was solid. Hard not to like a person who shook hands that way. Daniel's advice to watch her back rose up once again. And that moment of avarice in the kitchen when she'd considered blackmailing a donor's wife.

But there was no question about the First Lady having been attacked or her repeated appreciation for Emily saving her. Emily needed some quiet to think about this. But, between Mark's arrival, and scheming late into the night with her father, and, oh yeah, actually cooking at the White House, she hadn't had much thinking time.

"Is your arm okay?"

In response the First Lady waved it about.

"Now. Teach me."

"Okay. Where to start?" She tried to remember back to her first time in a helicopter. A simple machine, a radio transponder and a half-dozen gauges with a shared cyclic. That had boggled her sixteen-year-old mind. And then she'd flown and been hooked for life.

"First rule. All this stuff on the dashboard and on the console between us…" She pointed at the mass of switches running back between their seats. "Just ignore it. I'll take care of all that stuff. Today, you have only two things to worry about. The joystick between your knees—it's called a cyclic—and what's out the window.

"Don't worry. The cyclic is directly attached to mine." She wiggled hers, and the one in front of Katherine moved. "So, don't worry about crashing us. I won't let you. Just don't press any of the buttons on the top."

Radio, autopilot, and other controls peppered the wide knob on top of the joystick. On second thought, Emily slapped a half-dozen switches, turning off most of the functions. She started the turbines and they began their rotation up toward flight speed.

"Okay. Let's go." Katherine waved a hand toward the window.

Emily hadn't noticed that dozens of White House photographers were gathering to watch the show.

"Let's go soon. I get so tired of it."

"Really? But you look like you enjoy it." Katherine acted as if she lived for it. No one was that good an actress.

"Well, it has its moments." She shrugged negligently with all the confidence of one woman chatting with another where no one else can hear them.

"Then let's make this one of them," Emily offered in a bright voice and started throwing the switches to power up the electronics. While the engines wound up to speed, she helped Katherine with the headset. It cut the whine of the turbines to about theater-during-intermission levels.

"Oh, my! These are splendid. The helicopter is always so loud."

"This is a quiet one. You wouldn't enjoy riding in my Black Hawk." She resisted the hitch that tried to enter her voice. That was another thing to discuss with Mark. If she could find out who was after the First Lady and she could get Peter to release her, did she have any chance of getting back to the line? But could she serve on the line beside Mark? There wasn't anywhere else she'd rather be, but neither did she want to be court-martialed.

"A full helmet will buffer even more than these headsets, but a Hawk's rotor beat alone can make your body sore after a few hours."

"Your voice is so clear."

"Good. That will help you listen carefully. Because

I'm not going to touch the controls, and I'll make sure those cameras can see that I'm not."

Katherine turned to stare at her with her mouth open for a moment. Then she clamped it shut and grinned wickedly.

"That would be excellent."

"First trick is slow and steady. Second trick is small movements. Wiggle the joystick a little. Feel how there's a natural center?"

"Yes." She moved it without waving it all around like most beginners.

"Good. Small movements. Very good." Emily checked the fuel flow and engine temperature in the turbines.

"In a moment I'm going to add power. That will lift us up. As I do that, push the joystick straight forward the very smallest amount you can imagine. In fact, don't even try to move it, just think about pushing it forward. That will be enough."

She looked over. The First Lady's shoulders were tense, but her fingers weren't knuckle white on the controls. Good sign.

"You can rest your left hand on the control alongside your seat. They'll be able to see that through the window. Don't actually do anything, I'll take care of that with the one beside my seat, but you can let your hand ride along."

"Does it always take two hands?"

"We have an autopilot, but it's really only smart enough to help you go straight and level. For most flying you need two hands. In combat flying, you need three."

Katherine laughed. Good.

"Okay. Are you ready?"

Katherine nodded. Breathing a little too fast to speak, but not hyperventilating.

Emily made one last check of the controls.

"Okay, here we go. Don't move it until I tell you." She set the throttle and pulled up lightly on the collective, increasing the angle of the rotor blades and thereby increasing the lift they supplied. The Bell was so responsive that they were off the skids and hovering without even feeling a change.

"Now. Just think forward. Don't push, just think it."

In a single smooth motion they lifted forward and up as Emily pulled on the collective.

"Excellent. Now think right."

She saw the First Lady's head move down.

"No. Don't look at the instruments. I'm watching those. A pilot watches outside the craft far more than inside."

She let them climb in a long, lazy spiral while she chatted with Air Traffic Control. Always good to let the local ATC know where you were and what you were up to, as if they weren't following every move and the newly assigned Black Hawk tail wasn't hovering a quarter mile back.

"Now, without raising your hands—remember it takes two to fly a helicopter—look out the left window and smile."

The First Lady did and gasped. They were about a hundred feet up, and every camera of the White House Press Corps was aimed in their direction. The reporters were waving and applauding. Emily waved back with her free hand, making it clear exactly who had the controls.

"Well, you did it. You just made the hot spot on the five o'clock news on every network out there."

"That was splendid!" Her hand wobbled and she gasped when the helicopter leaned abruptly to the left.

Emily took the joystick and waggled it to the right and back to center making the helicopter rock side-to-side.

"That's how we wave back from up here."

Katherine pulled her hands into her lap, without first checking that Emily had the controls, but that was a learned skill.

"You did really great."

"You're just saying that." But Katherine was blushing deep red, almost enough to match her hair.

"Next time you're on the Internet, search on 'idiot student crashes helicopter.' Now that was truly sad flying. You did great." She really had. Was there anything Katherine Matthews wasn't a natural at? The woman could really get on her nerves.

"How is it that you don't hate me?"

The question surprised Emily enough to turn and stare. The First Lady's eyes were focused on her intently.

"Hate me for taking you away from your people and forcing you to come back stateside and cook, of all irrelevant things?"

"It turns out it was a good thing I did."

"Yes, I'm alive because of you. I know that for a fact. A debt I'll never be able to repay, except by saying thank you once again."

"That's all that needs saying and is far more than I'm used to receiving. Usually, if you're lucky, it's a hearty 'well done' from your mission commander. The really spectacular stuff is never told. If we make the news, our assignment did not go well. If we nailed it, even you would never know."

"But how…" Katherine trailed off and looked away. Down and away. Embarrassed or afraid, going by her body language, equally hard to believe.

"How do I not hate you?"

Katherine nodded without looking up.

She had come for Peter. Had there been a different President, one she hadn't known since childhood, would she come to serve his wife at her request? Maybe, maybe not. But with Peter, there was no option.

"I could answer with the truth, that I serve at the pleasure of the President. I can't even quit if I want to. I can tender my resignation, but I know a lot of Special Forces soldiers and SEALs who have waited a year, even two or three, for their papers to come through. Having invested so much in us, they are reluctant to let us go. When I am done here, I will be reassigned. Colombia, the Philippines, Africa, I don't know. Wherever my unit is called." If they let her back in. They had to. Mark had to.

She studied the woman beside her, the first woman to capture America's heart the way Jackie Kennedy had done so long ago.

"But that's not the whole truth. I came because you asked and an old family friend said you were afraid for your life. If I can be in service of that defense, I am here."

"Lucky for me. Though I knew about you as soon as I met you. I knew you could save me. And you did."

An odd way to phrase it. The same as some memory. The hospital. The voice in the hospital. So she hadn't imagined it in her drug-induced haze. "I knew you could save me."

Katherine laid her hand over Emily's on the collective and squeezed it tightly between both of hers. The earnestness in those green eyes was unmistakable. Unquestionable.

"You are a splendid pilot, and I will get you back in your sky as soon as may be. For now, I will count you as my savior and my friend. If that's okay with you."

It was Emily's turn to look away, humbled that so great a lady could care for her. She'd never been impressed much by rank, a matter her superiors never tired of pointing out. But Katherine Matthews dwelt in a different world. One of strategy and power. Of beauty and ruthless politics. And she was offering friendship.

Emily engaged the autopilot, then returned the handclasp tightly and, for perhaps only the second time in her life, felt as if she belonged exactly where she was.

Chapter 42

"MY GOD, BEALE." MARK PERCHED ON THE STOOL IN Emily's kitchen.

His attention was riveted on his slice of fresh strawberry-and-custard tart with a honey-and-currant-jelly glaze. Under the island counter lights, it glistened. The light shone off a hundred facets of glazed strawberry as if she'd sprinkled it with gold glitter rather than the lightest grace of sanding sugar.

Daniel breezed in. And slammed to a halt when he spotted Mark. It was the only time Emily had seen surprise on his face. If she read his face right, a quick shift to disappointment. He stood in her kitchen looking like a stunned puppy, his gaze swinging from her to the rather disreputable looking character sitting at the counter.

"Hey, ya." Mark offered a hand.

"Hello." Daniel shook the hand, silently gathered a slice of tart, and retreated down the corridor to his office. He hadn't even stopped for the crème fraîche she'd made to complement it.

The reaction didn't make sense.

"He's sweet on you." Mark waved a fork toward the now closed door.

"No." They'd flirted a few times, nothing more. And she didn't have that effect on men.

Daniel couldn't have gone there, could he? Sure, they'd had fun teasing each other over a few late-night desserts. He'd told her about his family's farm and that he'd come to D.C. to support some secret farming plan that he'd been egging her on to drag out of him. He'd apparently been clerking for Senator Jamison, head of oversight for the Department of Agriculture when Katherine Matthews had spotted him and scooped him into her entourage.

Mark shrugged and returned his attention to his dessert. "How did you learn to do this?"

"My dad always had a soft spot for the sweets, I liked making him smile."

It was much nicer having him here than her earlier guest.

First Sister Jessica had been a nightmare. When the First Lady had been called away after dinner, the woman had parked herself at Emily's chopping block with a half-empty bottle of champagne. While Katherine Matthews oozed tact from every pore, Jessica Cunningham swung outrageous jealousies of Katherine like a drug-crazed loon armed with a blunt ax and running around in a slasher film.

Yet Jessica's comments hadn't all fallen flat on Emily's ears. The First Lady's sister told stories of a very different "Katty." Of a girl who always got her way. A queen bee who had to take any boy that any of her circle managed to land. The girls left crumpled in Katty's wake were mere husks of their former selves.

Jessica's inability to maintain a marriage had been laid directly at her avaricious little sister's feet. Katty had needed to seduce both of Jessica's husbands and then make sure Jessica caught them, both times, in her own marriage bed. All discussed in whispered confidential tones that wandered more and more as the level lowered in the champagne bottle, "to stiffen my resolve for being here."

Emily had poured the First Sister into bed half an hour ago, mumbling how she'd rather be dead than be here but Katty had forced her to come.

Which Katherine Matthews was the real one? The charming woman the world knew and she'd flown with? Or the hellion described by an embittered and drunk sister?

Mark snapped his fingers in front of Emily's face.

"What?"

"Where did you go?"

"Just wondering if Jessica was okay."

"Happily pickled."

"She…" Emily bit her lip. She didn't feel comfortable discussing what she'd heard, not knowing when Katherine might breeze in unannounced.

Mark dolloped the crème fraîche onto his plate. "You make dessert a religious experience. I'll convert if it tastes even half as good as looks."

"It's better." She didn't like to brag, but she liked cooking. Much to her surprise, cooking for Mark was touching her even more than when she cooked for her crew.

He took a bite, chewed, and after letting out a long sigh, opened those soft gray eyes and focused on her. Really focused. No matter how she had tried to compartmentalize him, he wasn't looking at her like a sex object. She didn't know quite how to read that look.

Army guys always saw her as another challenge to beat down. Emily Beale was always blocking their way to being the best because she had already parked at a level most of them would never reach. In the military "being best" was a major motivator. It kept her flying harder and better. But it left her feeling she was only noticed for what she could do with twenty thousand pounds of steel and av gas. While that was the whole point, it left a girl feeling, well, not very feminine.

Feminine had never been one of her concerns. The pilots didn't make her feel feminine. Female perhaps, but not feminine. Right now Mark, however...

"What are you looking at?"

Moving away to the sink didn't remove the one-two punch of his wintry-eyed consideration.

"You're—Nope. Sorry." Mark stopped himself. "There must be a better way to ask a question without, you know..."

"Asking it?"

"Right. Thanks. See, you're helpful, too. But why the hell aren't you, Beale?"

"Why aren't I what? A clue would help here, Marky."

"I was about to give the stupid speech about how pretty, smart, and wonderful you are and why aren't you married?"

"Maybe the right man hasn't asked." Coy and flippant. She waited a beat for him to ask the obvious so she could reply with a "Nope, not interested," and move on as per usual SOP. A standard operating procedure that had always worked before.

"That's crap and you know it." He poked a fork at the tart but didn't eat it.

It was crap, and she did know it. And that's why it always worked. No one expected anything else back. No one until Mark.

"What is it with you?"

"Hey. My question is on the table. No shoving it off

the edge of the counter for the First Mouse to clean up. Why aren't you at least shacked up with a guy?"

"Don't believe in that."

"You're a virgin?"

"You know better." Heat rose, bringing her up on her toes.

"Almost, close enough that I'll accept that one. You don't like 'shack up' either. One man at a time. Have to really like him before she does anything. Never lived with a guy."

It wasn't a question, and it really pissed her off.

"I've lived with hundreds. Huh." That sure didn't come out right. She cooled down a little at his smile. "Okay. I know where your seedy little mind is going."

"It's not little, but I'll grant that it's very seedy. And the U.S. Armed Forces doesn't count in this conversation. I want to know about Emily Beale, not—" He glanced at the closed doors. Right, he wasn't supposed to know more about her than she was cook and helicopter pilot to the First Lady.

She could run away again, hide behind another joke, or change the topic. But there was only so long that held up as a lifestyle. Funny, she'd never run from a fight if she had a helicopter wrapped around her, so why wouldn't she defend herself when—Question for another time.

Emily could pop him one. That might cheer her up, but it wasn't the answer to every problem.

She hooked a stool and faced him across the counter. Across four feet of solid cherry-and-maple chopping block. Across the mostly untouched slice of custard tart. Across far too little distance.

"So ask."

Chapter 43

CONFIDENT A MOMENT BEFORE, MARK WENT COY. Took another bite of Emily's tart. Closed his eyes to relish it and offered up a soft, "Damn."

"You're welcome."

That snapped him back.

"So. Why not?"

"Why aren't you?"

"Nu-uh," he waved his fork at her. "No sidelining."

"Even trade then."

He considered for a moment too long. She slipped a hand toward his dessert plate. He made a stab of defense with his fork. Without thinking, she grabbed his wrist, flipped it into a twist. Mark rolled with it and came up with his fork in his other hand and pressed it against her throat.

They both froze. Then with a rough laugh, she let go and he eased back onto his stool.

"Well, at least our reflexes are still good."

Mark waved his fork around the room. "This place is enough to drive you right over the edge of insanity. How did you get so fast, anyway?"

"You should have seen my hand-to-hand combat instructor. She was lethal. Literally. Guys would see all five foot two of her and laugh, right up until the first one stepped into the dirt training circle. After that, they didn't laugh so much."

Mark nodded, "Now, answer my damned question."

She fetched a fork, made a plate for herself, and sat down across from him.

―――⁓―――

"Why aren't you?" Emily asked.

She held up a hand to stop Mark's protest.

"No. I'm serious. You know you're incredibly handsome. You're also a decent man. And don't give me the line about military-civilian marriages never work, I've heard that too many times. And I looked at the photo you always tuck in the corner of the windshield."

"Don't miss much, do you?" He speared a strawberry and studied it, clearly thinking about how much he wanted to say. He bit down, the decision made.

"Dad taught me from knee tall that the only thing more important than your family is defending it. If I can be half the man Dad is, I'll have done well." He looked sour for a long moment, inspecting her with a half glance that she couldn't figure out how to read.

"But he sure put Mom through hell every time he left on mission. It was cruel." He hated himself for saying it, but it was true. "I've never told anyone that before. I've never even thought that complete thought before."

Emily reached out to hold his hand. They sat that way for a long time before he looked back at her. When he pulled his hand back, she felt a little lost.

Mark cleared his throat and put on a brighter tone.

"My usual answer is the same as yours, that I haven't met the right woman, though your desserts may yet convince me that I'm wrong on that account." He ate another bite and sighed again as he chewed.

"Now you're trying to make me all mushy."

"Is it working?" He looked up with interest.

"Dream on." It was, but there was no way she'd tell him that. How it affected her insides each time his eyes went soft like that.

"So, neither of us believe in military-civilian marriage working."

"And neither of us has met the right opposite partner."

Mark didn't look up. He simply concentrated on eating his tart.

No. He couldn't imply that he had. She didn't like the image of Mark with another woman. Then the image shifted. He couldn't think she was the right person. Being a woman was the one true disaster area in her life. Pilot, soldier, comrade-in-arms, sure. Woman?

"Don't you want family, Beale? Husband, home, kids?"

"No." She didn't. That was her mother's dream. Not hers. She wanted to fly, not run a Georgetown household with servants and social teas.

Mark stopped eating his tart and focused those eyes on her once again. Studied her as if he no longer knew her. As if she were a stranger he didn't want to know.

Emily turned to the fridge to get away from the slap of that gaze and snagged a bottle of Katherine's favorite Chardonnay. She'd have to remember to restock it from the pantry before she went to bed.

Two glasses and a corkscrew later, they were each armed with an overly full glass of the amber wine.

"To the single life." Mark raised his glass, clearly being ironic.

She raised hers in return, clearly not being ironic.

And took a sip.

Almost took a sip. The scent was wrong. Almond. This Chardonnay wasn't supposed to have any hint of almond. Maple and oak. A little currant. Not almond. Especially not slap-you-in-the-face bitter almond.

Almond was familiar though. Familiar as—

She slapped Mark's hand hard enough to send the glass flying from his lips to smash against the floor.

"Spit! Spit, Mark! Don't swallow! Spit it out! All of it!"

He hesitated a moment and then spit it out all over the counter and dessert.

"Did you swallow any?"

He shook his head. "What the hell, Beale? Are you enjoying beating on me?" He cradled his offended wrist.

"Spit again!" She grabbed a jug of milk from the fridge. "Now. Take a mouthful and rinse your mouth, then spit it out."

Even as he did, she grabbed the phone, and punched 911. The briefing manual on the plane over the Atlantic had included, "Emergencies, medical, on premises." Inside the White House, 911 went directly to the emergency response center of the Secret Service, not a distant police dispatcher.

"Medical team to third-floor residence kitchen. Possible poisoning."

She heard the "on our way" and dropped the phone without hanging it back up.

Mark's eyes were wider now as she crunched her way over the shattered wineglass to stand in front of him.

He was again cradling his wrist.

"How do you feel? Any numbness or dizziness?"

He shook his head carefully.

"And you didn't swallow?"

Again the slow shake of his head, but his eyes were wide as the reality of the situation sank in for him.

She threw her arms around his neck and just held him until the med team arrived a few eternities later.

Chapter 44

"Nothing to report really," Emily kept wanting to duck her head. As if someone were continually firing rounds of live ammo just over her head to teach her how to crawl. The Oval Office was really creeping her out. Way too much power came from here and way too much of it radiated to out there. She stood at an uneasy parade rest before the Resolute desk.

Peter rocked back and forth in his chair and fooled with his pen, taking it apart and putting it back together again.

"If I knew why you really wanted me here, it might help, but then again maybe not. All I can report, you already know. Two apparent attacks in the past two weeks."

"Apparent?"

"Helps keep my thinking flexible." She'd almost attributed it to her father, but some hesitancy made her stop without doing so. She was running a secret operation. She had no idea what it was, but it made her want to keep each secret compartmentalized until she had a handle on it.

Peter rose to his feet and began circling the room.

"If I may ask, sir, why am I really here?"

"Ask that again using my name, and maybe I'll answer." He swung past George and headed for Abraham in a slow lap of the room.

Too many unknowns and she was getting sick of them. Washington and its goddamn games.

She stepped to block his way near the grandfather clock.

He came to a halt just a foot away.

"How about you answer the damn question or I pop you one, Sneaker Boy."

Peter laughed aloud. A good laugh. A friendly one.

"That's my Em. My, but I've missed you. C'mon." He took her hand and led her toward the couch. With a last-second maneuver she managed to land in the armchair next to the couch. They were still close enough to hold hands, if she hadn't drawn hers back.

Peter sat back, propped one ankle on the other knee, and finally looked the dignified man of the office she'd expected to meet since her arrival here. The soft light by the sofa made his face friendly and approachable. But she could see that at this moment, he wasn't Peter; he was President Matthews. Comfortable in this insane office. He'd grown to fit here. In a place she never would.

"One," he folded his hands and rested them in his lap like a man well content with life. "You are perhaps the smartest person I've ever met."

Emily squeaked. It was meant to be a squawk of protest, but it came out as a squeak.

This tickled Peter no end.

"Don't try to deny it. Valedictorian at West Point. They had to develop a whole special program for you. You used to run circles around me despite being half a dozen years younger."

She had. She'd just thought he hadn't noticed. She'd never made herself dumber around him. He wasn't like so many men who needed to be the smartest in the room.

Peter had always egged her on, though she'd thought it was her own secret that she could do both his math and his English homework as fast as he could, despite the difference in age.

"Two." He'd clearly taken her silence as having won the argument and hadn't lost the fact he was making a list. He'd always been partial to lists. For a time she'd enjoyed disrupting them, but he was no dummy either and would come back to them, often hours or days later at the exact point he'd left off.

"You are perhaps the bravest woman— Scratch that. You are the bravest person I've ever met."

She spent much of her time feeling naive and clueless, which was her true state even if he didn't know it.

"Third, let's face it," his voice softened. "I like having you here. More than I expected. I like you, Em."

Not Squirt. Not Beale. Em. It just sounded right when he said it.

And if Mark had been right about Daniel's feelings, had he also been right about Peter's?

Now that was a real problem.

Chapter 45

MARK TRIED NOT TO FEEL SO DAMN CHEERFUL. AFTER all, he'd just been sprung from a night in the hospital under observation for possible aftereffects of cyanide poisoning. Okay, that didn't add much to the cheerful side of the balance, other than not waking up dead this morning. But it really wasn't the key.

The key was, it was a beautiful September morning. The air held that first taste of fall that would wash across D.C. over the next month. And he was walking along the street holding hands with Emily Beale. If he could just remain in this space, in this moment, he'd be content, perhaps for a long time.

However, he knew it wasn't going to last but two more doors down the street, ending when they arrived at her parents' house for breakfast.

Balance. All of his thoughts today seemed to be about balance, as if he couldn't get the payload centered right for safe flight. Who'd have thought that one of his closest brushes with death, out of hundreds, would be in the third-floor kitchen of the White House Residence? He'd had no way to fight back. He'd just had to lean into Emily's shoulder and try not to shake, try not to show his fear at dying when she was so close or his raging anger that someone had nearly killed his Emily as well.

He couldn't help thinking of her that way. His Emily. Like that was going to happen. She didn't want family for one thing. It was impossible. He looked at the strength of his mom and dad's marriage and couldn't imagine wanting anything less. And Emily cared so deeply. She did her best to hide it, but he'd seen it in her concern for her crew, for the people they guarded with each flight, and for him the night before.

No wild sexual romp in a hospital bed. Instead, she'd simply arrived beside his bed as the last doctor left and the last nurse turned down the lights. Drooping, shattered with nerves and exhaustion, she collapsed into a chair as if she meant to stay.

He'd simply moved to the side of the bed away from her and raised the sheet on her side. She'd kicked off her sandals and curled up beside him on the narrow mattress. Before he could finish tucking the sheet around her, she'd been asleep against his shoulder. He rested his cheek on her hair, thinking there'd be no way to sleep while he held her.

And he'd woken to sunlight with her still curled in his arms, his cheek still against the golden wonder of her hair. She woke with that same languid, comfortable, lazy motion that she'd had while he'd watched from the far side of her hospital room. His whole body throbbed as he felt the wonder that was the woman in his arms come back to life.

Yet, as soon as she fully woke, a different Emily took her place. As if she tucked one away for storage and let another one out. She hadn't touched him again until they'd checked out, taken a car to her parents', and were walking up the block together. Holding hands for show.

Her parents. She knocked on the door and they waited

rather than just walking in. Was that what she thought family was? A sideways glance at her impassive face didn't reveal any clues. Captain Emily Beale stood solid in full control. He tried squeezing her hand as if to reassure her but received no response.

The door opened, and Helen Cartwright Magnuson Beale opened the door. Seven in the morning, and she'd clearly already spent some serious time putting herself together. And a lot of time frosting up on Mark's behalf.

Emily had survived breakfast. She didn't know how, but she had. Her mom was still on the rampage. Did Mark have a PhD or a master's? Not even a bachelor's? Did he have any special skills, something he really enjoyed? As if she were going to sponsor him to a Mercedes dealership if he'd been into cars. He liked going fast? Had he ever thought about forming a NASCAR racing team?

Emily had to give Mother points, she struggled so hard for flexibility on her daughter's behalf, though it was clearly eating her up inside to imagine this bum with her only child. And Mark scored serious points for the act; her mother's legendary tenacity never even scratched down to the secondary paramilitary profile. But that wasn't why they'd come.

Her dad had taken one look at her and known. He too had settled in for the duration, biding his time.

The breakfast ended abruptly when her mother's secretary came to remind her of a charity meeting and she rushed out. The first round had been more of a tie. This round she'd give the score to Mark for sheer survival, but Helen Beale was by no means satisfied or happy with the lack of potential in this long-haired bum her daughter had dragged through the door.

The moment her mother was safely out of the house, her dad turned for the stairs and led them back into the conference room in the cellar.

"Well, that was fun." Her father settled into his chair. "So, another apparent attempt?"

"Apparent?" Mark snapped, clearly not as casual about his near poisoning as he'd like her to believe. His raised voice rang in the small room.

"It keeps the thinking flexible," she and her father spoke in near-perfect unison.

"Screw flexibility." Mark's voice was little more than a low growl. "If Emma wasn't one of the ten percent of people who can smell potassium cyanide, she'd be dead right now."

He sounded more upset on her behalf than his own. He'd held her while she slept. And she'd felt safe there. So safe she'd never wanted to leave. After waking up, she'd had to crash down her shields. At the moment, life was far too dangerous to believe anywhere was safe, no matter how it felt. No matter how his sleep-warm and gown-clad body had molded against hers.

Her father looked over for her response.

"What? He's right. We both almost ended up dead. We were lucky."

His gaze remained on hers, finally he gave that little head shake, as if she didn't have the lesson right yet but he was going to leave it for her to puzzle out. What had always ticked her off as a girl now felt insufferable to the woman. She opened her mouth but he raised his hand to stop her.

"I have some information. I did a little digging on my own, hoping to spot a flaw." He reached over to the computer desk and picked up a slim blue folder she hadn't noticed before.

"Neither of you are authorized to read this, and yes, before you protest, I do know your clearance ratings. Better than you do and they're top rate. I'm proud of you, honey. But…" he waved the folder. "This is still above your clearance level."

He drummed his fingers on it, while studying space over her left shoulder. Clearly he wanted her to read it but didn't like to break his own rules.

"Remember President Matthews's note?"

Her father startled when she spoke.

"I forgot about that."

He studied her in silence for an interminable moment longer, then handed the file to her.

She wanted to hand it back. It was like picking up a doll in the desert. Was it a lost toy, or a land mine designed to remove a curious child's hands and create another burden on the opponent's society?

"It probably doesn't matter. It was classified by an idiot who couldn't properly code his own sneakers. This was the only inner-team member I couldn't trace back at least a half decade in his or her association with the First Family."

No name on it, just a number and a security rating that she indeed did not have. Mark moved closer to look over her shoulder. She could smell him, feel him hovering just inches away.

Reluctantly, she opened the folder and stared down at the picture.

Daniel Drake Darlington the Third.

There was a sharp headshot and a dozen other odd photos, going back to when he was maybe seven and driving a tractor from his father's lap. She'd been right. He did look good in just coveralls.

"It was a false lead. Your Daniel is what he claims, Tennessee farmer."

My Daniel. For no longer than a quick flirt or two.

"I could have told you that, Dad. I'd trust him absolutely." Emily flipped the photos aside, including the cute one of him dressed up as a Halloween pirate circa age ten and the most daunting one, damn he looked good in a tux, with a drop-dead gorgeous brunette labeled, "Senior Prom."

Mark offered a low whistle of appreciation. She considered offering a sharp elbow to his ticklish spot.

"On what do you base that, Emily?"

She thought for a moment. Be objective. Analyze.

"He was in the helicopter with me."

"Maybe he's part of a suicide attack."

"He's the only reason we made it to the ground alive. Sorry, Dad. Doesn't play out. He's clean."

Her father grunted his acquiescence.

"You're probably right. His file is just so clean it squeaks, which always makes me suspicious. He's also Yale, summa cum laude, environmental science, and Georgetown political science major. He's a very bright boy."

"Knew that. Hard to miss once you've talked to him." She turned the next sheet. Apparently a list of every girl he'd ever dated. Emily felt dirty but couldn't help scanning it. Natasha Williams for the senior prom, dated eight months, brief career as a fashion model, and now a homemaker married to an insurance salesman with four kids. Mary Harris, sophomore year at Harvard, now on her third husband, criminal defense lawyer in Austin, Texas, eleven months.

Each one traced to the present day. She knew background checks were thorough, but did they really need to know that his longest relationship was eighteen months and he'd never lived with a woman? Or that he was still friends with a woman as beautiful as Natasha?

She did her best to turn the page as if it were of no interest.

"He's also very motivated."

A list of research papers written while clerking for Senator Jamison, the head of oversight on the Department of Agriculture. Some published, a couple in *Nature*, and a number of them classified. The titles were fairly meaningless to her.

Daniel came to the First Lady's attention when she was sleeping with Senator Jamison's son. She almost turned for the next page, but Mark stopped her with a touch on the arm.

Emily doubled back and checked the date.

Two years ago.

Katherine had been married to Peter for ten years.

"Thought that might get your attention. That's why it received the high secrecy classification tag."

She read on quickly, nothing bad. Absolutely nothing. He was no more than he seemed.

The last page had a number of notes on it. Apparently he and six other farmers were starting a Slow Food Southeast Chapter, local crops served locally and all that. In two weeks, the First Lady was supposed to fly down and inaugurate the chapter. Emily thought about her flight schedule. It was there. But it was simply labeled, "visit Daniel's farm."

One of the marginal notes stated, "Reason D. Darlington in D.C." He spent three years of his life, much of that putting up with Katherine Matthews, for his farm and his friends' farms. Honorable man of the land.

She flipped back to the "Liaisons" page. Someone had probably been paid to think up that title for a scandalous sex sheet. She hoped her father had never seen hers, but she assumed she had one somewhere. You don't get to be either the FBI Director's daughter or a SOAR pilot without your life being a pretty open book. It wasn't any longer than Daniel's, but her "liaisons" were even briefer.

"Not there," Mark confirmed.

The name wasn't on the list. It wasn't all that long a list.

"You won't find her there. Katherine Matthews has apparently never slept with Daniel Darlington, at least not to the best of our knowledge."

Emily hid a smile by rubbing her hand thoughtfully across her mouth. She'd always figured that Daniel had played Katherine's sex slave at one time or another without really connecting that it would be an adulterous affair to do so. She liked him better for not having succumbed.

~~~

With no great insights, they gave up on it for now.

As they were leaving the darkroom, her father pulled Emily aside. Mark discreetly continued up the stairs.

Stephen Beale looked at her, really studied her face for a long moment. Then he laughed softly and wrapped his arms around her tightly.

She held on. He hugged her so rarely that she'd learned to cherish each time. She had to lean down for her head to rest on his shoulder. At whatever height, her father's shoulder had always ranked as the safest place in the world.

At least until she met Mark. Now there was an odd comparison.

After another squeeze, her father pushed her back until they were facing one another again. His smile was all soft and fatherly, an expression even rarer than his hugs.

"Care to let me in on the joke?" she asked.

"Nope." He shook his head. "But you'll get there, honey." He pulled her head down to kiss her on the forehead and then led her up the stairs to where Mark waited.

Chapter 46

MARK LOUNGED AGAINST THE KITCHEN COUNTER. HE hated waiting. It was the worst part of any assignment. Get into position and wait for the blockheads in the Pentagon or the White House to get off their damn butts and give a "go" clearance. Nine operations out of ten were never authorized when that last second finally reared its ugly head.

He looked over his shoulder toward the West Wing. This was where those "blockheads" lived. Never really thought about that before. Never been in the building. Only a few hundred feet and about eighteen layers of security over that way, men were planning which missions he flew and which he didn't. Were planning the fate of his squad; their missions, their lives…

And here Beale was, just tap-dancing around the kitchen working up pastrami sandwiches.

He'd die if something didn't happen soon.

And he'd die if he didn't get one of those sandwiches soon. They looked awesome.

Two days sitting around being Beale's pretty boy, and not a damn thing had happened. In or out of the bedroom. She'd made love to him. Once. There was no other word for it. Made him feel depths he didn't know he possessed. He could spend the rest of his days trying to give back even a tenth of what she'd given him, knowing he'd never succeed.

But she was having none of it. Not a grope, touch, or kiss. Not a shoulder rub. Not a hand held except in public. His barriers had come down, layer upon layer that he'd built over the years without knowing. And hers had raised. Innumerable tiers of impenetrable defense surrounded Captain Emily Beale. She'd been warmer toward him when he was just her commanding officer chewing her out for being merely incredible on some mission.

And no sign of the First Lady, his assigned target to investigate, watch, protect. The captain's—Emily's—Ms. Emma Beale's instructions had been less than clear, despite the time they'd spent hashing out the operation with her father.

Mark had thought that was a new step in their relationship. Going home to meet the parents. Of course, the whole parents thing had been a fiasco because he couldn't be himself. He had to be Marky Herman, playboy. Her dad had been a square, real stand-up guy who clearly loved his daughter immensely. At least he'd known, had seen through the disguise so fast that Mark could only marvel. Beale must have been one hell of a field agent. But Emily's mother hated his guts, and that didn't sit well at all.

Something was wrong in the East Wing but they didn't know what. Was Katherine's life in danger? Daniel's? Beale's or the President's?

Or the unvoiced suspicion? Clearly Beale had an idea, but she claimed that she didn't trust her own judgment. Her theory was too impossible. She waited for independent confirmation from him. So he watched everything twice as hard and had no idea what she was thinking.

The other problem was that he hadn't met anyone except Daniel as the guy breezed through the kitchen like a blond lightning bolt.

And now this! Whatever madman had attacked four times, apparently didn't care who got caught in the crossfire. Some schmuck had tried to shoot down his Emily, then poison her. Mark wanted to meet that man. Real soon.

The waiting was crazy-making. Watch everything. Trust nothing. And be ready to die in the middle of walking down a flight of stairs.

The only thing that made him crazier was Beale. Did she know how sexy she was, puttering around the kitchen trying to kill time? In public they held hands, kissed, sparked off each other like small-arms fire off tanks. In private, nada. Zilch. *Niente*.

She dropped a sandwich in front of him.

Okay, there were a few bonuses to being a fake lover to a beautiful woman who could cook.

Kosher dill wedge, pastrami on toasted Jewish rye, and a frosted mug of root beer. Homemade potato chips; who knew where the hell potato chips came from, and his girl could cook them from scratch. In many ways she was even more terrifying in the kitchen than on the flight line.

He snarled a thanks.

"Hey, honey. You need to get out a bit."

They both knew he couldn't leave. Had to be there whenever the moment arrived. If it ever goddamn arrived.

"You and your stupid-ass ideas. You don't even know what it means to run a black-in-bl—"

The kitchen door slammed open, the one he'd been

watching for two days. And a pair of lethal-looking Secret Service agents in perfect black suits breezed in. He slapped for a weapon but thankfully didn't find one. Before he'd even completed the gesture, they both had him in their sights. He'd seen D-boys with less speed.

"Whoa." He put his hands up in clear view and then remembered his role here. "Whoa there, pardner. Sorry for the slap." He indicated where his holster wasn't, turning his hip forward to make sure they both could see, without lowering his hands. "Old habits, you know."

They hadn't moved.

"Whew!" He shook his hands out and lowered them to his side. "Been a long time since I had to draw. Didn't know that was still hardwired inside me." They'd have definitely cracked down to his former paramilitary cover story by now so not much point in hiding it.

He wiped his brow, chastened that his hand came away damp with sweat. The boys holstered their M1911s. They packed serious stopping power.

"Sorry, honey." Emily came to his side and patted his brow with a clean kitchen cloth. "They greeted me the same way."

"Yes, except I was about to be skewered by a chef's knife," the older and tougher-looking agent remarked with a touch of chagrin in his voice. Then he looked at Mark with a "but you ain't nothing, boy" glare. Their contempt confirmed the death of his first-layer cover story. Hopefully, finding the much richer second layer would make them think they'd discovered the truth and stop them from working to go any deeper. Warriors hated paramilitary the same way cops hated vigilantes.

And freelancers like his second-tier cover story claimed him to be—guns for hire, mercenaries—were the lowest form of life on the planet in their books.

And then she breezed in.

Beale's briefing on the First Lady had been thorough. Her background. Her charm. Her innate grace and style. Her slightly domineering tendencies, which Mark translated as "screaming bitch," though Beale insisted otherwise. But there was one thing the captain never mentioned.

The First Lady was Hot.

With a capital *H*!

She packed a one-two punch of raw sexuality that maybe Beale had missed, but it hit his testosterone head on. This was a mature woman with a body built to last. Long, flowing red hair and cream skin right out of any man's fantasy. And tall. Almost as tall as Beale. With powerful curves that strained and pressed against the imagination.

"Is this him?" Katherine Matthews closed in until they were inches apart and her perfume filled his brain. Not some spicy new scent from J.Lo or the decadent luxury of Chanel. This was warm woman. One who knew exactly how good a woman and a bit of lavender soap could smell without any additions.

"You were right, Emily. He is very cute." She ran a finger over his three-day beard. "Very cute."

The caress was warm and promised more than a woman could possibly deliver. Except maybe this one.

She passed him by and parked herself on a stool at the counter.

He pulled himself together and sat back in front of

his untouched sandwich. Emily was offering him the evil eye.

Hey! He hadn't done the flirting; the First Lady had. And he could pick her out in his peripheral vision just inches to his left. Her curves registered deep in his body. And her hand, perfectly manicured, but with no finger-nail polish. He'd have expected electric, fire-engine, come-get-me red. The simplicity of those apparently naked hands was a siren call he bet few had resisted.

Emily's scowl was heating up. She either intended to play the p.o.-ed lover or she really was annoyed about it. He did his best to act the lover caught in the act of ogling another woman and took a mouth-stuffing bite of his sandwich before he could say something stupid.

"Damn!" He managed to mumble as the hot Swiss cheese threatened to sear off the roof of his mouth. "Thas sho gud!"

Emily smiled as if the morning sun had just washed over her face. And in that instant, in that simple action, she washed all of Katherine Matthews out of his brain. He knew she loved serving food, making others happy with it. But the sheer joy his gasping remark had elicited lit her up brighter than a desert sunrise. It was the most incredible thing he'd ever seen.

He kept chewing, even closing his eyes briefly to appreciate the interplay of strong, stone-ground mustard and smoked beef brisket with the perfect amount of garlicky sauerkraut. Incredible.

When he could finally think, the first words out of his mouth were, "Any man that doesn't do his damnedest to marry you is an absolute idiot."

And he meant it, which shocked him to the depths of

his bachelor soul, despite wanting family. That was for some other day. At this point in his life, he was strictly a catch-and-release guy. No one would make that mistake with Emily Beale.

"Well, lover, that's sweet." She almost purred, then leaned over to Katherine whom he'd momentarily forgotten. "See, I told you he was cute. I hit him between the ribs with my chicken piccata. Then before he could recover, I socked him with a one-two of the Duke's braised short ribs and Sophia Loren's veal parmigiana."

Right, slap him upside the head, that's what she was doing. And doing very well. His script said to get close to the First Lady, not to Emily Beale. He took a long slug from the frosted mug of root beer. An exquisite combination with pastrami. It was hard to think with that much flavor in your mouth.

He leaned over until his shoulder brushed against Katherine's and offered in a sotto voce whisper, "Then, after dinner one night, I asked about the sourdough starter for her flapjacks. Good move, huh?"

"Good move," the First Lady offered in return. Again all that silky smooth. He knew that type of voice well, as he'd gone to a lot of work to cultivate it himself. The question was, did it improve or impair the picture? On one hand it was sexy as hell, as his body and his heart rate were loudly informing him. On the other, he knew exactly—exactly!—what lay behind it. A lot of promise, a lot of delivery, and not the slightest drip of personal involvement. Sex with her would be as meaningless as it was wild. A weapon that she wielded the way Beale wielded a helicopter.

He could see Beale searching for a proper rejoinder,

but she didn't have it in her. A dozen years in this man's Army, if you included her time at the Point, and she was still at heart a sweet girl. Wouldn't have expected that of her, but there it was all over her face.

"Then I showed her my other moves," he rescued the break in the rhythm of flirting before Beale fell face-first into it. "That went well, too. As you can imagine."

The First Lady nudged his shoulder back. "Oh, indeed I can. Indeed I can."

He'd just bet.

Chapter 47

"EVERY INTUITION YOU HAD ABOUT HER IS TRUE. THAT woman is a serious piece of work. Ha! Imagine running into that in a dark bar." Mark paced back and forth across Emily's tiny White House apartment, four steps to the antique side table with its small bouquet of chrysanthemums, through the bathroom door, to the shower stall, and back.

"Keep your voice down." She stopped his excited strides with a hand on his chest. "Not here." Emily placed her palm over Mark's mouth and he kissed the center of it.

For a moment, just a moment, she let herself drift in the engulfing sensuality of Mark's lips against her palm. Of their own volition, her fingers wrapped around to cup his cheek. To have him so close, so present every day. Knowing he'd watched over her darkest hours. Knowing his body better from only two encounters than any other man she'd ever—

"No." More a caress than a refusal. "No." She dug deep and found her voice. The last three days had wound her up even more than Mark; she was simply better at hiding it. She could see him fraying at the seams, but thankfully, he didn't appear able to see her doing the same. Relief washed over her that the second phase of their plan finally had begun. The release from worry left her giddy and susceptible to suggestion.

Well, not suggestion. More to caresses or—There went her brain again.

"No!" She dragged her hand free. She stepped back and could feel the pain that caused both of them. "I'm not going there with you. You're my CO. And especially not while…" she waved a hand to indicate the building that spread about them.

"At least there's hope for me." His growl didn't sound faked. "Let's go for a walk." His high humor of a moment earlier had washed away, and now she found herself caged with an angry tiger.

Katherine was off to a dinner so they were free for the evening. Emily snagged a light jacket and held open the door before he could change his mind. In moments, they were out past the barriers and entering the warm afternoon light.

Only when they were halfway across the Mall and had passed through four very large tourist clumps did she dare speak. They were drifting along between two high school classes being herded toward the Washington Monument. A cluster of giggling teenage girls brought up the tail of the group ahead. And the cluster behind included several dozen third-graders. This was as close to her father's panic room as she'd find for making the conversation difficult to record.

She reached for his hand to pull him in close, only to realize he already held hers. Had been holding it. Ever since they'd left her room. Part of the role. Make it appear natural and cozy. But he did it so well, it had felt so natural. She hadn't even noticed the transition. That same hand that had held hers in the hospital. Now she could feel the tension in it, the instant connection to his emotions through that simple contact. For a few more moments, she let herself enjoy the sensation of walking hand in hand with her boyfriend on a quiet D.C. evening.

Nice fantasy. Forget about it, girl.

"Now, back to reality. What were you saying?"

Mark cleared his throat and almost dropped her hand as if suddenly uncomfortable, a superior officer holding hands with one of his underlings. She held on because she cared about how they looked, not how they felt. At least that's what she told herself, and she almost believed it.

"First La—"

"No names."

"She," his voice little more than a low growl. "She is one manipulative, conniving, convincing, charming, sexy-assed lady." But not all low growl.

"She impressed you?"

"Impressive lady. Haven't had my own tricks worked on me that well in a long time, probably not since Denise Hartnagel in kindergarten. Now there was a man-killer." He offered her the stupid look of a man head over heels in love for a moment before chuckling.

"We are in so much trouble on this one, gal. Do you know how deep in you are?"

Emily thought she knew but wanted his assessment.

"The wine thing?"

One case of a stuffy nose or just a little less knowledge about how that Chardonnay was supposed to smell, and she'd never have detected the potassium cyanide.

"I wouldn't be surprised if she planted it to have you killed so that it would look as if someone were attacking her."

"There's a comforting thought." She fought down

the shiver that had nothing to do with the sun setting. Though not totally successfully, as Mark answered by squeezing her clasped hand for a long moment.

Then her brain kicked in, "But—"

"Right. But! That would mean she was the one behind the plot to kill herself."

"Or apparent attempt to." Emily rolled her father's words around in her head, but the thought didn't want to settle yet. She'd had the idea that maybe Katherine had done the attacks herself but couldn't come up with why. Especially when they had so nearly succeeded. She'd decided they must, somehow, be attacks by Peter but she couldn't stand that thought. Mark was contradicting that, to her relief.

He had also just confirmed that the itch she had around Katherine Matthews might have some basis.

"If she could use a person and toss them aside so easily…" The first group of kids peeled off, headed up the monument, their pass tickets clutched desperately in sweaty hands.

She and Mark circled the monument slowly, passing between the massive stone monolith and the circle of benches holding those who had arrived before their timed ticket's mark. A group of girls lay on their backs on the stone with their feet up against the monument's base. They looked for all the world as if they were about to start walking up the vertical face. A friend snapped photos with a camera turned vertically.

Emily glanced skyward. The monument appeared to taper upward forever, its top still sunlit, sparkling far above. That would take real magic to climb. She knew the feeling.

"So, if Kath—"

Mark glared at her briefly.

"So, if She was willing to waste my li—" There had to be an easier way to do this. It was easy enough when they were flying. Go military.

"If our target of interest is willing to waste an asset such as me, such as my father's daughter, then what is her target of interest?"

"You tell me, honey. You've been doing the field-work on this one. Me? I'm just the itinerant boyfriend of some babe."

"Babe?" No one had ever called her a babe, except for a few of the newbies who'd learned better real fast.

"I'm a twenty-nine-year-old woman who is way past—"

"Being a cutie and now deep into babeland. A babe who looks even hotter in dress blues than an apron, I might add."

"You may not." For one thing it was making her blush. For another, if he kept complimenting her and teasing her like this, she might let her guard down around him. No matter what else, he was still her once—and hopefully future—commanding officer. Though the present was foggy… No. She couldn't risk going there. Not with how she already felt about this man.

"Maybe…" She searched for a return to the subject as they followed a fresh set of high-schoolers east along the mall toward the Capitol. "Maybe she's into cheap thrills."

"Murder's usually a pretty spendy thrill. Generally has a lot of hard time associated with it." Mark winked at a little blonde who had slowed down at the back of the pack, causing her to blush wildly and return to her friends. By the time she dared look back, Mark had led Emily deep into a crowd of Japanese tourists headed toward the World War II Memorial.

"It's the light weapon that makes a hole in that. That came closer to, um, bringing about the demise of herself rather than me. I can't make it scan." Emily let her eyes casually sweep the crowd, but even if any of them spoke English, none were paying them any mind.

"You're right on that." Mark harrumphed unhappily and stopped to stare up at the sky. "No airplanes."

Several of the Japanese tourists noticed him looking up and checked out the darkening October sky themselves. A couple took pictures of it. They'd get home and look at the blank blue photo and wonder, "What was I thinking when I took this?" Emily covered her mouth to keep from laughing.

"Peter's in his big white home. Twenty-five kilometers around him are no-fly. It's the clearest airspace on the East Coast, a real pleasure to fly in."

"Twenty-five klicks? About a minute and a half for a subsonic cruise missile. Twenty seconds for a Sidewinder if you could get within the fifteen-klick range to launch it."

"It's not considered polite to point out the defense-system fallacies of the house you're a guest in."

Mark nodded. "Point taken. Never thought of it that way. Seems all so safe with the men in black stalking about."

"And the bubble follows him, too. That's why the motorcades always book out of the airports so fast. As long as he's there, nothing flies."

"And you're enjoying this?"

Now there was an interesting thought. Did she enjoy being inside the "bubble" her father had warned her about the day she landed? Perhaps she did. She'd grown up as the daughter of a senior FBI agent, then assistant director, then director. She'd spent most of her life in the center of very heavily protected forward bases and training camps as secret as any terrorist training center.

"What if—?" Mark studied a massive willow tree as if it were the most fascinating thing he'd ever seen. He focused so intently on whatever he was thinking that he dropped her hand to cross his arms over his chest. She resisted the urge to move closer and slip her fingers around the crook of his elbow to stay close.

"Am I going to like this?"

Mark shrugged, "Probably not, but what do I care? You won't let me get you between the sheets, so if I offend you, it won't make a whole lot of difference in our blissful domestic arrangements."

His failure in that quest was really bothering him, which was kind of sweet. But she needed him to stay on track so she definitely wouldn't tell him that his proximity was working on her defenses far more successfully than he knew.

"Okay. What is it I'm not going to like?"

"What if she wants to look endangered? I mean, come on. Who brings a top military pilot in as their personal chef? She could have anyone."

Before Emily could even work up a halfhearted snarl in defense of her cooking, he cut her off.

"You cook almost as good as you look, which is saying one hell of a lot. But personal chef to the First— well, you know who. That's world-class credentials.

You focus on culinary arts for a couple decades, open a couple of four-star restaurants, and that may earn you a one-in-a-thousand shot at it. You study helicopter operations for those same years, and you ain't even close. If you're looking for something that doesn't scan, that's it. It's a setup, and so far she's called all the shots, some of them literal."

"You really think she's the one behind whatever is happening?"

He continued to stare at the tree, nodding slowly. "It's my current theory."

They were in sight of the Reflecting Pool. Too many memories of Sneaker Boy on the north side, so she aimed them south. A mess. She was a complete mess. Mark wanted her, perhaps Peter as well. Her career was screwed up. And her life had nearly been screwed up twice now in a very permanent fashion.

Someone had to save her from this.

Someone had to...

Mark made a noise but she raised a hand to silence him.

Someone had said to her... something. She could almost picture it. No image came clear. There was no movie of the brain to connect the line to. No visual—

"Ha! That's it!"

"What?"

"I was blind."

"And now you see. Should I break into a chorus of 'Amazing Grace' for you?"

She punched Mark's arm. Hard. With some knuckle in it on the nerve center.

He raised a fist to return the favor. She grabbed it, applied pressure behind the thumb, and twisted it sharply. He dropped to his knees before she bothered to let him go.

"I was blind, still drugged, and in the hospital."

He staggered upright, massaging his offended hand.

"But I remember Katherine saying to me, 'I knew you could save me.' She said it again on the helicopter, the next time we flew together. She knew ahead of time that we'd be attacked. That I could—"

They'd stopped when she dropped him to the ground, and a crowd of tourists now came from behind and had to swarm around them like a herd of camera-eyed ants.

"That's why I'm here." Emily half-closed her eyes, trying to see more clearly, but the thoughts came slowly, a word at a time. "That's why she wanted me."

"Why?"

"She wanted a dupe who could protect her against her own attempts on her life. Who better than me, a female SOAR pilot?"

"Well, she didn't actually do them personally."

Emily started off again.

"But what if she did?"

"How?" That finally stopped Mark from massaging his wrist.

Emily searched in her mind, trying to visualize Admiral Parker's initial briefing.

"Remember the picture I showed you of the limo?"

"Shattered glass. Little spark-plug porcelain bits on the floor. No shooter found. That's what you said."

"Picture it." She waved her hand at the golden sky as if it were a window. "You're a shooter standing outside her limousine. You point and fire. Those fragments cause an intensely reactive shattering of the glass. Where are the little fragments of porcelain going to end up?"

"Outside on the ground." Mark's voice was soft as he got the image.

"But they didn't. They ended up inside. Katherine shattered the window herself, from the inside, maybe just by throwing a handful of porcelain chips."

"And was injured by the unexpected reaction of the glass's violent shattering." Mark nodded as the piece fit. "But what about the plane?"

They paused and stared across the Tidal Basin at the Jefferson Memorial, awash in floodlights overpowering the evening.

"They never found the radio controller. They never found who launched it. Some accomplice lets it fly from well outside the fence, beyond the main cameras. Then he or she drives up to the White House gate. Perfect alibi. He's chatting with gate security as the First Lady flies the plane directly at her own window. If someone had thought to look in her desk drawer after the attack, they'd probably have found the controller. It was planned as a dud. Designed not to explode on impact with her office window."

Mark grabbed her upper arm, dragged her about, and began heading north.

"Where are we going?" She dug in her heels.

"FBI. Or Secret Service. I don't care, but we have to tell them."

"Tell them what?"

Mark stumbled to a halt.

"The highest-profile attacks in the history of the White House, actually occurring inside the grounds, and we're going to claim that they were staged by the most popular First Lady since Jackie O.? That some accomplice 'unknown,'" she made quote marks in the air with her fingers, "fired a light weapon at her helicopter, dropped it on the ground, and walked into the back door of the Executive Office Building?" She turned away and continued their progress toward the Lincoln Memorial.

"To make matters worse, only seven people in the world know why I'm here, and only two know about you."

Mark harrumphed. "Then who is the unknown? Vice President Zack Thomas? Kath—"

Emily nudged him in the ribs.

"She," Emily emphasized the word, "certainly flirts enough with him. Do we claim that they want to kill off Peter and take over the big white home? No one would believe a word."

Emily could feel the world spin. As if she were the center, standing directly on a new pole of rotation, carrying them all in a circular orbit except her. Somehow she'd stepped right into the middle of the mess.

"But I don't get why she's doing it."

"Who cares? Let's get you out while we still can."

Chivalrous of Mark, really. Mr. Alpha Male protecting the poor, helpless female.

More of the spinning pieces clicked into place. Were beginning to fit.

"Or we could just wait. She'll reveal herself eventually. Make a mistake."

Mark huffed in exasperation. "I'm not a huge fan of that option."

"Not your operation."

He sighed again. "Well, at least I'll have more time

to work my wiles on you. You have to give in at some point. I'm a pretty charming guy, you know."

"Dream on, big boy."

Even though she was there, she couldn't figure out how Mark did it.

One moment, they had wandered into the eeriest of the Washington monuments, the Korean War Memorial. Full dusk had arrived, the surrounding trees plunging them into a premature night. Only the faintest of lights broke the darkness. Life-sized bronze foot soldiers were frozen in midstride. Rifles to the ready, ponchos draped fitfully over battle gear. Eyes watchful for the enemy. And then, your eyes focused on the wall behind the soldiers. And the hundreds, perhaps thousands, of men marching forward out of the etching into the graveyard of war.

These were the men she had chosen to join. They had died in the tens of thousands, now nameless except to those who once loved them.

Would she one day be part of such a memorial? Would her name be carved on the Night Stalker memorial in front of Grimm Hall for her mother to visit and touch once a year?

The next moment, Mark had her pressed against that wall, his mouth on hers, one hand at the small of her back and the other sliding inside her jacket and over her breast. And she wasn't complaining.

She leaned her head back, exposing her throat, hoping he would ravage it. Just take her. And he did. His hands explored in ways that sent shivers of heat coursing up her spine as her pulse thundered into her brain. Rolling her head to the side, offering him more of her neck, she saw the images carved in the marble. All of those legions of soldiers.

With a sharp shove, she managed to force a breath of space despite her body's scream for anything but distance.

"Not here. Not now."

Mark growled and didn't back off. He leaned in again, but as the hunger had momentarily left his eyes. She could see them focus past her at the dead who marched from the marble.

He swore violently and strode away until he stood frozen among the bronzed figures on patrol. Lost in the shadows. Head hanging. Little more than a statue himself.

Emily took a deep breath, seeking a strength she didn't find, then rearranged her clothes and moved to his side. This time she did tuck her hand around his elbow and hold it close.

He nodded slowly, once. Twice. Then they moved off together without any further word.

Her head cleared a little as they moved back toward her old buddy Honest Abe. Cleared until Mark's kiss wasn't the only thing she could feel. Until the memory of his lust-clouded eyes wasn't the only thing she could see. She did her best to pick up the conversation where they'd left off.

"Waiting around wouldn't be my first choice either. If we're right, I'd rather avoid the risk of dying in whatever game she cooks up next. They're a little on the hazardous side for my taste."

Mark's voice sounded rough as he too fought for control. "Then let's do something simple—find out why she's doing it. If you find the reason, the motive might prove the actions."

"That's where we need to look. What is she getting out of it?"

Chapter 48

THE FIRST LADY HAD JUST WHISKED OFF TO VISIT A friend in Colorado for a weekend and taken Daniel along. Beale's father had insisted that he'd known Zack Taylor for twenty years and there was no possibility of his being involved in Katherine's plans. Once again they were stalled.

Mark found himself at loose ends and didn't like it. Beale was making him completely stir-crazy. He understood her refusals. Even inside the protective shell of the Secret Service, there wasn't the privacy, the freedom. Her kitchen far too public, her tiny apartment too claustrophobic. This crazy place was pressing in on his brain so hard that he wanted to scream.

They'd gone for a walk through the White House gardens together just to have something to do. They walked in silence, Emily so distracted by her own thoughts that she'd have walked into a tree if he'd let her.

They turned up the next path and Mark froze.

Agent Frank Adams stood not a dozen feet away scowling at him.

Emily practically jumped out of her skin.

"Didn't mean to spook you."

"Sure you did." Emily recovered her voice quickly.

His smile for her was easygoing, even friendly. "Okay, you caught me. Surprised it worked."

Mark was pretty surprised, too. Beale was normally unflappable.

"Thinking deep thoughts. Where you headed?"

"I'm just off shift, heading to the gym. Want to join in?" Agent Adams was completely ignoring Mark. So whatever this was, it wasn't about him.

"The gym?" Beale was rolling some idea around on her tongue.

Mark looked back and forth between them. There was a subtext going on here that he was missing. Clearly they weren't talking about a workout.

"Sure," Emily answered her own question. "The gym, as long as Marky can come. It'll give us a chance to find out."

"Find out? What?" Adams waved for her to lead him down the garden path toward the east entrance.

Who'd be standing afterward, of course. They were talking about a sparring match. Against this guy? She had to be kidding. Mark was pretty sure he wouldn't want to try taking on a top Secret Service agent. He needn't worry; Adams wasn't any more interested in him than a bug.

Beale didn't bat an eye as she answered the agent.

"Why, who's prettier of course."

Adams grunted. "Damn. Lost that race before we even got out the gate."

The Secret Service headquarters was a short six-block walk away. Emily did her best to keep the talk light. She and Adams were both D.C. kids in a city of transients. Discussing the changes in architecture, monuments, and most significantly, the mood of the city, was fun. The blacksuits' headquarters was an imposing, block-long megalith of brick and glass in the midst of a long row of imposing buildings of brick and glass. Even so, it stood out.

As they entered the doors, she leaned over to Mark and whispered in his ear, "Remember who you aren't."

He startled slightly and then smiled at her, "Uh, right. Sure, babe." Good thing she'd reminded him.

Adams signed them in and led them into the complex and down a broad marble-and-granite corridor tastefully lit from the recessed edges of false columns of black stone. Clearly designed to absolutely humble any guest.

"Nice," she managed, with the word completely sticking in her throat.

"Shooting range down those stairs." He indicated a double-wide staircase off to the right. Several agents moving up and down the treads.

"How long were you in SOAR?"

"I am," she hit the word hard, "in SOAR. Two years, if you include training. Seven flying for the Screaming Eagles before that. And I will be in SOAR after you've retired and they're wrapping wet nappies around your butt." Damn it! She was still a pilot. Just on some kind of screwed-up, unwanted sabbatical that now had her hunting ghosts behind every presidential portrait.

"Touchy. Touchy. So, you're saying I probably don't want to shoot against you."

She clamped down on her tongue. This was a senior blacksuit she was facing. "Um, tell you what. I'll take you on, automatic weapons .50 caliber and above. Especially weaponized vehicles."

He grunted and continued down the hall. "Okay, that wouldn't exactly be something we practice much down in the basement."

"No. But I've taken a fair number of your snipers out on the Fort Benning range. And they learned how somewhere."

Adams laughed and turned down a short hall. "It's hard to remember from minute to minute that a beautiful young woman like you is also a highly trained soldier. Today, though, we're going to see just what the Secret Service has that you helicopter jockeys don't."

"Yeah, squat. Squat and diddly."

All he did was point at a door marked for gender.

"Through there. You'll find clothes for guests over in the far-right corner. See you inside."

Chapter 49

MOST OF THE BLACK T-SHIRTS HAD A BIG "USSS" LOGO. Mark couldn't find one with no logo.

Agent Adams merely grunted when Mark pulled it on inside out so that the logo didn't show. He'd been trying to figure out how to play this for the whole walk over while Beale made nice-nice with Adams. Clearly some grudge match going on here and his role was to be invisible. He was surprised they'd let him in the building at all, even if only to the gym. It said something of how highly they thought of Beale. He could play it as jet-setting playboy-wimp, but the Secret Service had surely drilled past that facade by now. So, Mr. Paramilitary-cocky-as-can-be stud. He could get into that role.

He scared up some shorts and figured his sneakers would be good enough.

The door on the far side of the locker room led to a true wonder. SOAR did a lot of cross-country running; the worse the weather, the better the workout. A SOAR gym consisted of a set of free weights in the corner of a hangar. Volleyball and hoops were common pastimes. The three battalion headquarters had serious setups, but with the current operational tempo they were almost never parked there.

The Secret Service gym dedicated whole sections to different equipment. A banked track encircled the massive room. Eight lanes wide with a couple dozen agents spread out around the course. Rings, bars, and horses. Clearly, agility mattered. Weights, cycles, steppers, every machine imaginable.

Everything in excellent repair, all showing signs of active use. And in the center of the room a broad, clear area, heavily padded with bright blue mats. Wrestling, grappling, sparring, martial arts. Seventy people could take a class there, though right now only two couples and one threesome were using the mats.

"Cool setup." He did his best to sound casual.

Adams grunted at him again, making it absolutely clear that he didn't care in the least what Marky Herman thought.

Then Beale came out the next door over. Somewhere she'd found a T-shirt marked "Army" that clearly no one knew was there, or it would have been purged or used for target practice. It was a size or two small and made his insides quiver like Jim's stupid squirrel dog that had caught the scent. The black running shorts exposed miles of beautiful, well-toned leg. He didn't have to pretend for a second to be blown away by how good she looked.

"Let's warm up a bit first." Adams's voice sounded just a little bit rough, and Mark couldn't blame him. After a quick set of stretches on bars conveniently located nearby, they all set off at a slow jog.

Adams let Emily set the pace, and Mark dutifully followed along.

She opened up a bit after the first kilometer.

By the second kilometer she hit her stride. Mark knew it well as they often trained together. At this pace she could run with little change for two hours without

water. Six with water. Ten with water and energy bars.
It wasn't especially fast, but it was a mile-eater nonetheless. He wanted to push ahead, show Adams a thing or
two about field training, but Emily caught his gaze and
gave a short shake of her head.

Mark cursed, managing to keep it under his breath.
No matter what his instincts told him, he wasn't part of
their contest. It would be unfair of him to push ahead
and drive the challenge when he wasn't a part of it. He
heeled in alongside through four kilometers, a shade off
his normal stride, which made it pretty frustrating.

He followed them to the weight machines. Adams
chucked water bottles at each of them from a small fridge.

"You take cold water for granted. Still amazes me
every time." Beale said it a moment before he would
have. Right. His role. Florida, Australia, Italy, plenty of
cold water. His best bet, he decided, was not to speak at
all until this was completely over.

"How long were you over there? Wherever you were."

So, there were limits to how much Adams had uncovered about Beale.

"For the last couple months. Hot. Sweat-in-your-sleep
hot. And dry and dusty like you wouldn't believe. For
six months before that, hot and humid like Mississippi
never saw."

Adams dropped his empty bottle in the recycling
bin beside the mini-fridge and walked over to a weight
machine. He pulled the pin and moved it down a good
ten weights. If Beale tried to match a load like that, it
would simply lift her off the ground, but Adams starting yanking away on it with the ease a D-boy operator
would show.

Mark went to a setup and inserted a pin thirty pounds over Adams. At Beale's glare he shoved it up another twenty pounds. He'd regret that, but there was no backing off now. So she'd pegged him for the wimp role. Nope. No way. Not Mark Henderson, not even Marky Herman.

"That's warm-up weight?" Beale focused on Adams, giving the man respect and drawing his attention away from Mark. Damn her for playing fair. He wanted to wear the man down a little before Beale faced him in the ring. She went to a machine facing him and set the pin about sixty pounds lighter than Adams had.

"Gets me started." *I'm showing off a little, but not very much.*

"Don't think I'm going to try wrasslin you."

"Don't chicken on me now, Army. You're on my turf."

"You two are going to try the mats?" A guy of Adams's build, but clearly only a few years out of school, stopped spinning his cycle nearby.

"Army, meet Steve. Steve, Army."

No point in introducing Mark; he was too far beneath contempt. He did his best not to grunt as he started pressing the stack. That extra fifty pounds was going to be a mistake if they did this for long.

She nodded a greeting to Steve and her thanks to Adams.

Decent of him. Better that neither of them had a name, even inside here. What people didn't know, they couldn't tell.

"Oh, this is gonna be good." The young guy pinned his pinkies between his teeth and let out a shrill whistle.

Emily kept pulling her weights and so did Frank. Mark kept his moving in unison with Adams, not that anyone was paying him any attention. His muscles were starting to burn already. Every other agent in the room stopped and looked around. Being obviously the only two people ignoring the signal, all eyes soon locked on them. About thirty guys and maybe a dozen women. The crowd ranged from teenybopper undercovers to grizzled old warhorses.

Most went back to their workouts but kept looking around to see if Adams and Emily had moved yet.

"Warm?" Adams's grin looked dangerous.

"Getting tired?" She shot back without slowing her workout.

Steve was right: this was gonna be good. Mark would bet on Beale any day, but looking over the head White House blacksuit, maybe he'd hedge his bet.

Adams pulled five more reps then let the bar drop with a clang against the stops. A room-ringing announcement as clear as a starter's bell.

"No. You?"

She shrugged acquiescence, dropped her own weights loudly, and waved for him to lead the way.

Adams pointed at Mark, as he eased his load down against the stops. His muscles on fire.

"Steve. Keep an eye on this guy. A close one."

Steve nodded, and Mark recognized the look. He wouldn't be going anywhere Steve didn't want him to go.

Adams turned his back on them and stepped up on the near edge of the mats.

She moved so fast that no one had time to shout a warning.

Chapter 50

FRANK ADAMS HIT THE MAT FACE-FIRST WITH A LOUD smack as Emily rolled out from where she'd cut him off below the knees.

He rolled onto his back.

Catcalls followed her as she scrambled around and caught a fistful of hair and pulled down toward the mat, keeping him pinned.

Mark could see that Adams's eyes were watering and he winced in sympathy. He knew she played dirty, had a recent reminder of that when trying to protect his ticklish spot while wrestling in her hospital bed.

Adams didn't know. At least not until now.

"Doesn't hurt if you don't move," Beale told him.

He reached up a pair of meaty paws.

She pulled down on his hair.

"Impasse?" he managed to croak out.

"Depends. Broken voice box?" She waved her free hand in front of his face.

"Or not?" He lunged up against the pull on his hair and caught her thumb in his teeth.

This was going to get ugly fast if she didn't do something. Mark almost laughed when she began tickling his chin with her free fingers.

"Cootchy, cootchy, coo!"

He did join the laugh that ran around the circle of

observers. He tried exchanging a friendly look with Steve but only received Arctic chill in exchange.

She let go of Adams's hair and he released her thumb. They both rose to their feet and backed carefully apart as he rubbed his scalp and she checked the teeth marks that didn't quite break skin.

"You fight dirty, Army."

"Way I was taught, Blacksuit."

"Ha!"

So, he liked the nickname and was going to tear her apart for it. Or, he hated the nickname and was going to tear her apart for it. Fun pair of choices. Everyone in the room circled up. Sending one of the President's personal guards to the mat was about to earn her more than she'd probably bargained for.

Maybe Steve was a betting man.

They both spiraled slowly inward until, just beyond grapple range, he shifted his stance.

"Don't fool that easy." She continued her circle back around the other way.

He resumed his.

Mark was mesmerized by the moves. She had the speed and Adams the strength. Not that Adams was slow. But they both moved with nothing close to standardized martial-arts training. There was something else going on here.

Adams lunged. Nothing subtle. A lineman's flying grapple hoping for the quarterback sack, down, and yardage.

She dove over him and pushed down hard on his shoulders as she went by. He plowed into the mat, she recovered with a quick roll. As did he.

"Tag, you're it."

No subtlety. He was angry and lunged for her again. He planted his right foot hard.

She dodged left, away from his body mass.

He dug and turned and almost got her.

She danced away.

And the bastard smiled. He'd played mad to throw her off.

Good tactic. Mark had used it a time or two himself.

"Tricky, tricky, Blacksuit. But not good enough to get lucky, sailor." She offered a sassy, hip check to the air.

Beale sassy. He'd never seen that side of her before. Captain Emily Beale was always business. Even when she was cooking or shooting hoops with the guys, she never went female. She played as hard as a guy, and she played to win. What else didn't he know about her?

Adams leered appropriately, playing the game. Circling again, Mark finally recognized his stance. More than martial-arts training. More than field experience. It wasn't a stance. It was a lack of one.

"Street kid?" Emily asked.

Mark had barely spotted it, so how the hell had a girl from the D.C. elite?

Emily watched the irritation ripple across Adams's face.

His nod was tight. A past he didn't show. A past that whispered around the circle of his fellow agents. No one else had seen it.

She wouldn't have either, except for her bunkmate in

the twenty-six week Airborne course. Two women, two hundred men. Thirty-nine would graduate after a half year of testing and training, two were women.

Trisha O'Malley had grown up in Boston's Southie. Trisha had no rhythm of martial arts. No timing from carefully studied and perfected moves. She had tricks that no combat instructor had ever taught, all learned the hard way on the streets. Trisha had volunteered Army to get a new life. Emily had West Pointed in. But they'd both volunteered two more times before meeting, Airborne and Special Forces.

Emily would never have survived the course, except for the wispy little Irishwoman. If a woman with so many disadvantages could face down so many miles, so many tests of stamina, courage, and the pig-headed determination to succeed, how could Emily quit? If Trisha could run a 10k after four days of no sleep or food, so could she. If Trisha could shoot four fifties in a row at the end of a run, so could she. If Trisha was unbeatable in the sparring ring, she'd learn how.

And she had. Many, many, many bruises later. Street fighters had no sense of timing. No sense of if this, then that. They did whatever worked whenever it worked. She'd learned. And once the two of them had taken down eleven of the squad who didn't think women should be there to begin with.

The only class member Emily had never defeated was her friend.

Frank Adams moved as strangely on the sly as Trisha had. His feet never quite shifted where she expected. His weight adjustments as he circled made no match with the next motion. And she'd wager that she'd not get a moment's hesitation again. That wasn't a mistake he'd make twice.

He offered street fighter, fine. She shifted her own stance until it was Army manual, picture perfect.

Frank Adams paused. Didn't know what to make of it.

A probing swipe, which she blocked hard enough to raise a black and blue mark on his forearm within the hour.

A blinding foot sweep. She sidestepped and countered with a foot stomp that landed where he'd been, but not where he went.

He moved back a step, puzzling. Good place for him to be, but she knew she couldn't sustain it for long against a trained fighter.

She offered him a Taekwondo fighting stance, right down to the out-turned wrists.

He stopped, puzzling, and moved in. A blast of speed and power.

Pure luck. It was a variation on a trick Trisha had pounded into her brain after pounding it into her body. Emily had begged and begged until Trisha slowed it down enough for her to see it, learn it.

Adams's triple attack was a distraction. The high kick, the low sweep, and the grapple were all fakes. Any one of them would hurt like mad if they connected, but any pro could dodge them. The secret was that the dodge spoiled the balance and set up the defender for a sharp elbow-shoulder double-strike.

Rather than dodging, Emily turned to let the high kick hit her shoulder. It rocked her hard. But because she hadn't moved away, she managed to trap his foot.

He'd have rolled into a backflip, or at least a somersault, but she didn't let go.

She didn't twist the foot; no need to break the man's knee.

She didn't pull on it so that he'd hop along after her with both hands free to pummel her.

She pressed down on his knee so that he couldn't relieve the pressure when she shoved his foot away as hard as she could.

He landed backward in an uncontrolled crash with enough momentum to plow three of his fellow agents away from the mat's edge, including Steve.

Mark just stood there watching her with his arms folded over his chest and a huge smile plastered across his face.

~

This time Frank Adams returned to the mat slowly, and Mark didn't blame him. It took guts to face down Emily Beale; he wasn't sure he'd want to try it. He'd seen her prove a hundred times that she was the fastest person in the room and he'd seen her prove it against trained Army in dirt circles.

But to watch her in action as the spotlight show, against a man who was among the best trained fighters on the planet… Frankly he wouldn't want to go up against either of them.

And she was winning. That amazing, stunning, luscious slip of a woman had bested Adams two out of two so far.

This time Adams didn't squat.

He didn't circle.

No approach at all.

He moved into a reasonable, if unconventional fighting stance and raised a hand as if to dangle it out in front of her as a distraction.

She didn't ignore it, but neither did she follow it. Her eyes were unfocused, aimed around his middle.

He dropped a hand and began tapping a foot on the mat.

She didn't look down.

The next motion made no sense. A quick finger flick.

Mark wanted to shout a warning, but Steve shot an elbow hard enough to stop him. Mark blocked it easily, but it distracted him for the crucial moment.

Three agents leapt onto the mat.

She rammed an elbow straight back without even turning to see. She connected solidly with the first agent's solar plexus. The attacker from behind dropped with a grunt. Two more came from the sides. She grabbed their wrists and spun. Sent them both stumbling unexpectedly into the crowd.

She used their momentum as a launch at Adams.

But he wasn't there.

Mark spotted him standing off the edge of the mat. One step back.

She landed her dive and rolled up to crouch inches in front of him, a one-two strike on the verge of being unleashed to solar plexus and groin.

"Easy, Army. Easy." Adams held up both hands and wisely took another step back.

"What was that signal?" Her voice tight and dangerous.

He glanced around the room, then pointed at the two youngest in the group. Then he paused a moment to glare at Mark.

"You guys didn't hear this from me, and you," he aimed a finger at Mark, "didn't hear this at all. Training signal. For when someone is foolish enough to think they're ready. Also, in the field, a really loud cry for additional assistance."

"But I was ready."

"But you were. Damn, Army. Where did you learn how to do that? You ain't no street chick."

Emily straightened slowly.

Mark could see by how she moved that she'd been really edged. That's how she walked after combat, really nasty combat. He had the feeling he'd missed half of the nuances of the fight, no matter how closely he'd been watching. Like years ago, the first time he'd thought he was a hot-shit Army pilot freshly checked out in a new Apache Longbow. And then his uncle, General Edward Arnson, had taken him for a joyride in his Huey. Mark hadn't even followed half of the subtleties of what his uncle made the old bird do, though he could now.

"You've heard of Green Platoon and Airborne School?"

Adams whistled low. "Six months with the Rangers? Not many women through there. Didn't know any had been."

Mark kept his whistle to himself. It had been in her file; he'd simply forgotten about it. Too bizarre.

"Four have graduated. Ever. My trainer was in my class."

"Well," he wiped his hands on his shorts. "Whoever he was, he was damn good."

"Hey, Blacksuit?"

"Yep?"

"My trainer? She was a little bitty girl." She measured a height with her hand barely up to her own shoulder. "And she coulda whipped your ass but good."

Frank Adams grunted and didn't look real happy about it.

"If it's any consolation, she whipped mine every single time."

It took a bit, but finally he grinned at her.

"You're right. I do feel better. Come on." He nodded toward the fridge of cold beverages. "I'm buying."

Mark nodded in appreciation. Emily was so good that she'd turned a trouncing into friendship and respect.

Chapter 51

THEY SAT SIDE-BY-SIDE ON A BENCH NEAR THE FIRST turn on the running track. Emily had waved Mark off to the side, partly because she knew Adams wanted a moment alone and partly because Adams had earned it.

But also, the intensity of Mark's gaze had moved from his typical healthy, lustful leer toward ravenous. He'd applauded harder than anyone when Adams had bowed to her. He'd even slapped his painted-over Night Stalker's tattoo and shot her a thumbs-up, almost making her blush.

And she needed him at a distance because the fight had wound her up as well. With the way her body felt, if they weren't in the middle of Secret Service headquarters, she'd throw him down on the wrestling mat and taken all he could give and more. Regulations and missions be damned. She needed a cold shower, with ice in it.

But now it was she and Adams. In the quiet. No one near them. No one running at the moment. Most of the group were now out on the mat trying out the moves they'd seen her and Frank use. They looked like a bunch of flapping chickens with a rooster loose in the yard.

Over here on the bench, just Frank Adams, herself, and two half-empty bottles of orange juice.

"There are things you aren't telling me, Army."

"There's a whole lot of things."

"Don't like that much."

She took another slug of her juice and considered again. Black-in-black didn't allow for doubts. Too much at stake, her own life not least among them.

"I know." Her head ached worse than if he'd pinned her to the mat by her hair rather than the other way round. "I'm sorry," was the best answer she had.

He rolled his bottle back and forth between his palms. Back and forth. Back and forth.

"I know who you are, Army. I know who you were and how your father trained you. I know everything about you that isn't Black Ops and pieces of that, too. I've watched the President. I know that he care—that he thinks highly of you. That's the highest vote of confidence there is in my book. But there's something going on. And then there's that phony boyfriend of yours. But I can't put my finger on it. It's in my house, and I don't like this one bit."

He was begging. And for a man of his stature and training, that must have taken a lot. To say "no" would be a slap in the face. No other way to interpret it. She could show him the President's awful letter, the one that was ruining her life and almost certainly her career. And what would that achieve? More suspicion, more loss of trust. Tell him about Katherine? It was still laughable, based on not a scrap of proof other than some bits of porcelain on the wrong side of a window. She rifled Katherine's office but found no model-airplane radio controller.

Could she take Frank Adams alone into her confidence? Her father and Mark were all she could manage. Frank might feel it his duty to report what was going on.

And that would escalate to... Also, Peter had not chosen to confide in his closest protector.

Black-in-black operations didn't allow for such questions. It was either known or not. And the known side of the equation didn't allow for gray areas. Gray belonged on the outside, so she kept her peace.

The trap was closing over her head, and there was not a single thing she could do about it except wait. And hope her agility let her dodge the final blow as unbattered as she'd escaped the sparring ring.

"I don't like it either, Frank. And I'm sorry. I have no choice."

Chapter 52

MARK KNEW EMILY WAS ONLY TRYING TO DISTRACT him with the suggestion, but it was hard to complain. He hadn't flown in a week, not since the night Emily had been blinded and he'd come running to the States. He could feel his night-flying skills slipping away, losing that biting edge honed by constant practice.

A couple of judicious phone calls and a little begging on his part had convinced his uncle to lend SOAR two Black Hawks, and a pair of copilots and crew chiefs. His uncle had bought the line about Mark having some leave and being in D.C. to check on his temporarily reassigned Captain Beale. At least he hoped his uncle had. Either way, he'd released the birds.

Mark had left the Secret Service HQ as Marky Herman, Mr. Useless. Three cabs and two clothing changes later, he arrived at the Anacostia Naval Support Facility hangar as Major Mark Henderson of the 160th SOAR(A), which was doing wonders for his ego. No one trained for the night like the 160th, not even the Marines who flew for the President. The basic SOAR test loop lasted eight hours and included three landings. Each landing hundreds of miles apart, all over rough terrain. The entire flight had to be flown NOE, nap of the Earth, below two hundred feet.

Each landing had to be approached below radar, typically ten to twenty feet off the deck, and hit within thirty seconds of the plan. When you could do three different loops in three consecutive nights in the rain without climbing over two hundred feet or missing a mark by more than thirty seconds, only then were you considered fit for any real training.

He'd looked up Beale's record; the woman was inhuman. Two years in SOAR and she'd nailed it first time out. She'd missed the time mark a total of four times, the best record in the outfit other than his, and her timings were tighter. But it took a lot of continual practice to be able to do that. Even more without a SOAR-trained copilot. Tonight was going to be interesting.

They sat down to map a course, crossing deep into the Blue Ridge Mountains in West Virginia, then south. NOE over the heavily forested rolling terrain would keep them sharp.

Mark looked at the map. Too easy. He could feel it. He and Beale were the best, and that wasn't false modesty. Needed to up the stakes for it to be a real test.

As casually as he could muster, he said, "Let's keep it interesting. How about one fifty?"

"What's that?" One of the Marine copilots looked up at him. "We don't usually push the choppers that fast for a training run."

Emily looked at Mark for a long moment and just as casually offered, "Eighty," while tying one of her boots.

Now the other copilot looked up. "What the...? Is SOAR having a mosey contest or something? I thought you guys were supposed to be hot."

Mark ignored him and concentrated on Beale. The woman was completely nuts. He liked that about her.

"Eighty it is."

"Eighty what is?" The Marines asked in unison.

"I'll explain on the way. Clock starts in five minutes. We're first out. She's five minutes behind so that we don't follow each other."

Troops counted on SOAR's precision to deliver and retrieve. This loop had to be short. The birds his uncle had offered didn't have midair refueling probes or auxiliary fuel tanks. The crew chief positions each had a .50-caliber machine gun protruding from the gunner's window between the pilot and cargo doors. But they were locked down and held no ammo, so they were really light. Even traveling light, the Hawk couldn't go more than 368 miles without a refueling stop, so the limit was 340 with a ten-minute fuel safety margin.

Six hours to fly an eight-hundred mile loop from Anacostia to Anacostia. First leg: three hundred miles to Pope Field at Fort Bragg, North Carolina. Second leg: 250 to Fort Story in Virginia Beach, and then a short two hundred miles home.

He offered Beale a sassy salute, and she returned it in kind. They climbed into their birds, which the copilots already had humming.

"What's the big deal?" Jerry, his U.S. Marine copilot, buckled up. "Anyone here could hit those marks. Especially only going eighty."

Mark knew it was evil to smile at the boy's naiveté, but he'd only flown with other Marines so that could be forgiven.

"Well, two points. First…" Mark started a timer and pulled up on the collective. They lifted a dozen feet and began heading for the Potomac. "Assume that you're flying under live fire. You don't want to dawdle up to a hot LZ. You run the last dozen miles to the landing zone at redline. With your wheels less than ten feet up and hard evasive maneuvers."

"What's the second?" Terry's voice sounded from where he'd strapped into the crew chief's chair. He was little less cocky than his fellow Marine.

"Well, what's our current altitude?"

"Fifty feet."

"No, to the top of the rotor. Anything you show as visible to enemy fire must be accounted for."

"Okay, sixty-five feet then."

"Good," Mark engaged the FLIR, the forward-looking infrared radar, and flipped down his NVGs, the night vision goggles turning the night world a bright green. He tipped the Black Hawk's nose down and cranked up on the collective. In moments they were moving a hundred and fifty miles an hour.

"That's good because the operational ceiling for this entire flight is eighty feet." He heard two very satisfying yelps as he bounced ten feet up and moments later ten feet back down to clear the Hains Point golf course. Then laid into a sixty-degree turn and headed southwest.

─◆◆◆─

Mark watched the sky to the north. Jerry and Terry were sitting on the tarmac, their butts hitting the ground within three steps of exiting the craft. The ground crews at Pope Field had the Hawk already half full of fuel. It felt good to be at Joint Special Operations Command. Not as good as Fort Campbell, but familiar ground for sure. At least here they'd really top off the tanks. He'd landed on goddamn fumes because the Marines thought seventy gallons low wasn't worth topping off. His crew weren't the only ones glad to have it made it to JSOC.

He checked Beale's timer again. She'd radioed her start, five minutes after his to the second, and he'd marked it.

Still no sign of her. Nothing. Only silence. Not a peep on the radio. She'd be flying dark. Dark, but late. Oh, this was going to be so satisfying. He could lord this over her for days.

He'd hit just eleven seconds ahead of the agreed time, well within the thirty-second time slot.

The northern sky was still empty. He flipped down his NVGs so that he could spot her even without her running lights, as if she were in a combat zone. Still no sign.

The center of her mark was only forty-five seconds out. Unless she cracked the horizon in the next eleven seconds, she wouldn't be able to land within the thirty-second maximum.

He started beating a Eurythmics drum solo on the Black Hawk's dash. Thirty seconds to go. The window was open for one minute. He really laid in as the northern horizon stayed clear. He filled in a backbeat, *biddy biddy dah, biddy dah, biddy dah*.

Except he wasn't hitting the backbeat.

He spun and looked out the open cargo door. Beale was landing from the south, and she was coming in hot and low. Popping up to clear her gear over a parked Humvee, veering sharply at the fence line, slicing over to the landing.

Crew were ducking and running as her Black Hawk hammered sideways across the field within inches of sparking her rotor off the tarmac before she leveled out. She jerked it to a halt five feet up and floated ten tons of bird down like a snowflake in the exact center of the landing circle.

He punched the timer and swore.

Only six seconds after the mark.

"Hey, Mark, you out there?" Emily had flown the first leg silent, the way a Night Stalker always flew. But the temptation was too great.

"Just five minutes ahead of you, Beale. Right where I'll always be." His voice came like a whisper in her ear.

"And eleven seconds early. Just like a guy."

Her copilot had pretty well checked out, but the crew chief still had enough of a grip to snort with laughter. It turned to a shout as she cleared a line of oak trees. Power lines stretched across her path. She drove the collective down and skimmed beneath with a half dozen feet to spare, then swung right to clear a cow who thought pastures were for grazing. Four feet to the left, and they'd have both been hamburger. Not good.

"Well, at least we always make it to the finish." He had to grunt out the last word as he pulled some high-g maneuver. Maybe he'd found a cow, too. He must be in his final run, should be by the clock.

"That's just rude. Not taking your wingman all the way with you."

"Never had any complaints," he shot back.

Damn, she wished she could see him. It was so rare to see a master fly. Combat or training left little opportunity; she could feel the smile in his voice and knew he was in top form. Damn, she wished she could feel him, too. She'd bet good money he'd never had complaints.

Ten minutes to go.

"Don't let it go to your head." She cranked the throttle to just a few percent below redline and dropped her wheels down to ten feet. As she slewed right to clear a barn, she had to watch out that she didn't turn too hard and dig a blade tip into the manure spreader parked in the yard or the stinking pile beside it.

"I can fly all night, Beale. How about you?"

"I don't just fly. I soar."

That bought her some silence. Had she really flirted with a man before? A few times. With one she wanted so much? Not even close. She jerked back on the cyclic to pop over a truck parked out in the middle of nowhere. Lot of infrared heat in the cab showing up a glowing green in her night-vision gear. No question what was happening there.

"So, Mark. I was thinking—" Oh brother, was she thinking. At least her body was thinking. Very loud.

"Give me a clue."

"Can't! Guys never have one."

"But we have other nice weapons." His voice was a deep, smooth caress that raised goose bumps of anticipation.

Mark's weapons, she knew from experience, were very nice.

"Been admiring your arsenal in the mirror, have you?"

She popped up a bit at a road intersection to make sure she cleared the stop signs at the corners.

"Certainly been admiring yours. Makes me think about doin' some future Joint Special Operations."

He had less than twenty seconds to go. She lowered

her voice to make it as throaty as she could and breathed a little onto the microphone, "I love," she drawled out the word, "joint operations. Don't you, Major?"

"In the worst way." His voice sounded tight and a little desperate.

She slewed right, then pulled hard left to pass between a pair of billboards with the rotors almost vertical, not enough room to fly through on the flat. She actually smacked a wheel across one of the billboards. Probably left a skid mark across some politician's face. Close, she huffed out a held breath, but not much more than normal.

A glance at the timer showed Mark should almost be—

"Down. Three seconds from the mark."

"Early again, flyboy."

———∿∿∿———

He felt a little better after she hit Fort Story. He'd missed by three and she by six again. Now she only had a two-second advantage.

While the ground crews fueled up and the flight crews sat on the tarmac as if someone had cut them off at the knees, he and Emily agreed to start the last leg together, giving her a two-second head start. Simultaneous touchdown on the time mark at Anacostia was the goal.

Before they parted, he leaned his helmet against hers. Even if anyone saw them, they were just two pilots in full flight gear discussing the flight.

"I've got battle plans for a joint operation, Beale." A plan that was driving him insane.

"Really, Major? I can't imagine." So cool, so smooth. Just the way she flew. But he knew better. He'd seen the rocket-fire heat that could light her up until all she could do was moan and shudder.

"A plan to rip off your flight suit and every scrap under it." Oh, man, the image was killing him. Killing him slow. "I can show you all about right on time."

He heard her reply as much through the helmet as through his ears.

"Dream on, big boy." But her voice was rough and her breathing fast. "Besides, who says I'm wearing anything else?" Now he understood how his copilot felt, Mark felt a desperate need to sit down abruptly on the tarmac. She wasn't killing him slow, not Emily Beale. She was killing him fast.

Chapter 53

AT ONE POINT, EMILY ALMOST GAVE THE CONTROLS TO the copilot, but one look at his hands stopped her. They were fisted tightly in his lap as he stared rigidly ahead.

Focus, Beale. Focus.

She was, and that was the problem. She was focusing on Mark's rough voice and thinking about his gentle hands. That was a dangerous place to be while flying just twenty feet above the rolling seas. She was tipped far enough forward that her rotor tips were five feet closer to the water, and that was all she dared risk. The Chesapeake Bay could offer surprise chop that rose to twice normal height.

A quick glance at the FLIR showed Mark on the opposite side of the shipping channel, roughly dead even.

The clock was running. Once again, she tried to run the numbers in her brain; time, distance, power, fuel. At this speed, the load lightened by 2.9 gallons every second, 19.6 pounds every second. Even rounding to twenty pounds, she couldn't do the math for one minute. Sixty seconds. What could Mark make her feel in sixty seconds? Maybe that's what she'd do; give him sixty seconds and then they'd be done.

Insane. She wouldn't be satisfied in sixty hours. She wouldn't have begun to explore the possibilities. That's why this wouldn't work.

One time somewhere safe to blow off the intense

heat that fired between them wasn't going to do it. And courtesy of the Army code they'd both sworn to uphold, they couldn't risk being together more than that. That's why she wasn't even going to start.

Once more she tried to focus on the numbers—and barely managed to shear aside in time to avoid clipping the small sailboat out for a night sail.

———✺———

A tie. There was no other way to call it. Mark might have been a few seconds behind, or not. Perhaps she eased her rate of descent for the last ten feet, maybe he'd accelerated his descent. They were so in sync, cutting in from different sides of the base and arriving together, settling in perfect unison. Everything else aside, they hit tar together. Four seconds after the mark.

By twenty seconds after the mark, the copilots were gone, staggering like drunks. The crew chiefs tucked the birds in for the night and were gone inside of ten minutes. Hangar doors closed, floodlights out.

Mark stood, his clipboard with his maps and notes in hand. A work light hung over the briefing table in the corner. Emily looked down at her own clipboard and couldn't read a single word of her own handwriting. The questions, the doubts, the fears. She tried to hang on to them. To remember why she wasn't going to have sex with this man. Why she wasn't…

The clipboard slipped from her fingers and clattered to the concrete so loudly that they both jumped.

Mark stood there looking at her, his helmet at his feet. His flight suit was unzipped just enough to reveal the collar of an army-green T-shirt.

She knew only one thing.

Only one question filled her mind.

She had to clear her throat twice to give it voice.

"Your helicopter or mine?"

Neither of them jumped when his clipboard slipped free and clattered to ground.

——⁓⁓——

Mark covered the five steps between them faster than she could raise her arms to welcome him. He plowed into her and kept right on going until her back slammed against the chopper's pilot door. He'd have driven the air from her body if their mouths were not already clamped together, her arms wrapped around the back of his head.

Her chopper.

His mouth raged along her jawline, down her neck.

She shoved him away and tore at the release on his flight vest. Didn't bother to push it off his shoulders, but dragged down the tab on his flight suit. Rammed her hands down the front into the silken gym shorts he wore and wrapped her fingers around all that hard heat. He was so ready; well, so was she.

Emily reached for her own vest only to find that Mark had already removed it without her noticing.

For a moment he froze. His hands at a stop. Why weren't they on her? Ravaging her?

Mark stood there, the front tab of her flight suit still in his hands, pulled down past her waist. He wasn't looking at her face; he wasn't stripping her naked.

He was staring like a man struck dumb at the line of bare flesh that ran from her dog tags all the way down, revealed by the rolled back flaps of her flight suit.

"You weren't kidding." He turned his face up toward the heavens. "She wasn't kidding. Thank you, God."

Then he looked into her eyes, and she watched his turn suddenly black and feral. With a growl driven up from somewhere past speech, he dragged the suit off her shoulders and down to her ankles in a single pull. Almost before her next breath, she stood barefoot and buck naked on the smooth concrete.

He dug out some protection, tore the packet open with his teeth, and groaned like a man dying as she rolled it over him. He lifted her with those strong hands wrapped around her bare buttocks and drove into her, slamming her once more against the helicopter.

She wrapped her legs around him as he pinned her against the smooth curve of Plexiglas. One arm around his neck, and the other hand wrapped around the protruding muzzle of the .50 cal machine gun, their cries rose in unison to shatter against the hangar ceiling.

—⁓—

Mark lay against her. The only thing keeping them from sliding to the concrete was Beale's hand wrapped around the barrel of the .50 cal. He closed his eyes against the first wave of vertigo he'd ever felt. The relief too great, too immense. It filled him like a breath of cool air at high altitude when a hot summer day shimmered far below.

He raised his head to look at her; she kissed him, long, slow, and deep. A real tonsil-grabber of a kiss. She kissed with her eyes open. Those impossible eyes that could see straight to his soul inspected him. What did they see? He didn't even know himself.

She slid one foot down until it touched the concrete though he remained buried deep within her.

"Tonight," her voice little more than whisper. Rather than looking at her own watch, she took his wrist and turned it to look at his. "We have one night. Three hours. Mark, show me what we can do in three hours."

It ripped his soul open. He knew she was right. One night was all they'd find.

"What if…"

She stopped his mouth with her fingertips, then she replaced them with her lips.

The heat didn't build again with a roar and a slap. No rocket flare. No explosion echoing to his toes. Her lips rode over his, tasting like sunrise. Sunrise and sea salt.

He wrapped his arms around her and buried his face in her hair. He breathed her in until he'd filled his lungs with her. Until he'd never smell anything so sweet again.

She laid her head on his shoulder and they stood there. Still her back against the pilot's door. Unmoving except for a gentle rocking like the tops of trees on a windless day. Moving to some rhythm all their own. He had never held a woman who felt so right, so true.

He scooped her off her feet, carrying her the few short steps to the Black Hawk's cargo door. The engine cooling with quiet pings of a job well done.

A stack of blankets had been stowed at the rear for Search and Rescue survivors. Now he spread them upon the hard deck. Layer upon layer until they made a bed worthy of his lady.

He scooped her back into his arms as if she weighed nothing and set her upon the jury-rigged bed as if it were a mahogany four-poster.

Emily laid back and let her eyes drift shut.

"No." He leaned down to kiss her on each eye. "I need you to look at me. Look at me with those beautiful eyes of yours, Ms. Emily Beale."

She opened them, and he couldn't say what he saw, but it cast a mist over his mind, wrapping them in the safety of the night.

He studied her face with his lips, her neck with the back of his hand, her collarbone and that beautiful neckline with the tip of his nose.

She wore nothing but her dog tags, which was sexier than any cotton, silk, or lace he might have encountered. Lying partly on her and partly beside, he placed his ear upon her heart. He'd know that splendid double-skip beat from a thousand others now that he'd heard it.

He traced his fingertips over her breast, down her body, around her splendid curves, each such a perfect fit in his hand. Her long fingers slid into his hair and then held him close to her. So close, so tightly, that he could never live, never exist anywhere other than against her heart.

The fire of the hospital bed, the electric voltage of her apartment floor, the rocket flare of moments ago, all washed away behind their slow exploration.

He discovered her shivers when he ran his teeth over her insole, her quiet groans when he dug strong fingers into strong shoulders. She discovered how to kiss his one ticklish spot in a way that warmed rather than irritated. How to make him laugh when her smile bloomed mid-kiss.

When he discovered the tattoo across her lower back while massaging her shoulders, he couldn't help but take the time to trace every line with a gentle finger. Just the size of his palm, it was about the cutest thing he'd ever seen. The Night Stalker winged horse, with laser-vision eyes, but rather than being mounted by sword-wielding Death, a black serpent rode its back with eyes to match his steed. Beneath, in midnight blue, just four letters curved along the line of her hips: "N.S.D.Q." It was beautiful work.

They spent as much time holding each other as they did in any sexual act. She laid against him, on him, under him, and their bodies were in perfect harmony as long as they were wrapped tightly together.

When at long last he entered her, she cried out. Cried out and he swallowed the cry. He took her pleasure inside him and did his best to give it back. Again the tears rolled down her cheeks, and not all of them were hers.

He hadn't cried since before he could remember. He'd always been his dad's "little trooper." Now there was too much inside him. Too much pleasure, too much fire, too much heat, too much Emily Beale.

She swallowed his moans as he had her cries, and when they rose and rose like a rotor gaining speed for takeoff, when she wrapped her legs tight around him and he drove home, his breath wracked out of him in gasps. So sharp and full and complete that he half feared he'd never be able to move again.

And he half feared he would.

Chapter 54

THERE WERE NO WORDS BETWEEN THEM. NOT THAT they were awkward as they dressed, pulling on flight suits, tucking pant legs into boots, holstering weapons.

Emily thought it was just the opposite. They dressed exactly as they flew, exactly as they'd made love, in absolute and perfect harmony. Never had such peace washed over her as when Mark brushed at her hair with his fingers and as she strapped his watch about his wrist.

If she'd felt mellow after waking in the hospital, after he had taken such exquisite care of her body, she'd need a new word to define her feelings now. Languid. Sanguine. Glorious!

She started laughing. A giggle at first, but it built and built until it rolled about the hangar and pulled Mark into its arms and hers.

They began to dance. Some jaunty mash-up of waltz and two-step. They were stumbling, half falling, laughing in each other's arms when one of them kicked a clipboard. It skittered loudly across the floor and snapped them back to reality.

In minutes, they'd folded the blankets, stowed their gear in their bags, and left the base.

Emily dropped Mark at the curb of the first of his backward stops. It was a SOAR apartment that he'd signed out, where he kept his uniform and flight gear. He'd change to civilian and then head to a hotel room under the name Marky Herman, from which the uncouth high-roller would emerge.

The cab took her back toward the White House, but she had the driver stop and leave her at the Lincoln Memorial. It was still half an hour to sunrise, and she wanted to spend it with her old friend.

Other than a strolling security guard, there was just the two of them, Emily and her marble pal.

She wanted to… She didn't know what and almost laughed aloud, but in the silence of the pre-dawn light it felt presumptuous to laugh here.

Wandering over to the north wall, she read aloud the end of his second Inaugural speech. "To do all which may achieve and cherish a just and lasting peace among ourselves and with all nations."

She had always flown by this standard and the one on the south wall spoken a century and a half ago at Gettysburg: "That government of the people, by the people, for the people, shall not perish from the Earth."

She stared at the words, fighting the burning in her eyes. Fighting to keep focus on what she must do. She could never be near Mark again. Once this mission was accomplished, she'd have to be reassigned. Leave her crew? Leave her family? For the Black Adders were more than companions; they were family. She would take a round for any of them. And any of them would do the same for her. To leave that…

Reassigned or resign?

If she resigned, she and Mark could be together. It made her throat close to even think the word. If she resigned her commission to be with him, she'd never be able to forgive him, no matter how she wished to. That was not an answer either. Considering the reality proved too painful and she turned.

Turned and ran from the one place that had always given her hope.

Chapter 55

THE WAITING GAME OF CAT AND MOUSE CONTINUED. The blacksuits circled about her. FBI Director's daughter or not, friend of the sparring gym or not, if Emily was the cause of the unrest in the White House, they'd land on her hard.

Frank did his best to hold onto friendly, but inside of two days, all signs of trust had faded away, first into caution and finally distinct mistrust.

Then he began to stalk her. She'd become more rather than less dangerous in his mind. A street fighter had different ethics. The primary code was survival above all else. It had served her well in SOAR. Survival of the team, of her squad, of her cadre had been her guiding light. Right now she and her one-man cadre were the only ones on the inside of that team. Even her father had to be outside the veil now. None of it sat well with the blacksuit's team-player attitude. She considered a hop out to Anacostia, but too many memories lurked there in the sun and shadows. Mark became a caged animal. He didn't try to touch her when they were in private. Even holding hands in public was agony. Walking side by side they fell into an easy, comfortable, impossible rhythm and then stumbled out of it, almost tripping with the wrongness of it.

Two more long days passed while the First Lady luxuriated in the hot tubs of Aspen. Two days of knowing the wheels were coming off the horse and being unable to take any action. She'd botched the whole operation from top to bottom.

She hovered around the kitchen like a mad ghost, Banquo gone even madder than Lady Macbeth.

With Mark here, the kitchen felt even more compressed, ready to explode at the slightest spark. He wasn't even pretending to flirt with her anymore.

And she missed it. She couldn't stand to think about how much.

They'd had a silent lunch of the worst chicken-salad sandwiches ever made by woman. She'd cleaned the kitchen, and still no sign of Katherine who was supposed to be back already.

Emily circled out. Cleanup wasn't her job, but she headed out into the third floor of the residence. Checking gave her something to do. Some space away from Mark.

The First Lady's favorite lounge for entertaining was empty and immaculate. Not a stray plate or lipstick-fringed glass to be seen.

Her bedroom was dark and empty. Her private office was quiet, the door ajar, the afternoon sunlight streaming in.

Emily stuck her head in.

Naked.

Sprawled in the center of the large oriental.

Awash in a pool of slanting sunlight. Katherine's white skin and red hair a startling contrast to the tight green stitching of the massive rug.

First Lady Katherine Matthews arched in the throes of passion.

And beneath her, equally lost to the world, Chief

of Staff Ray Stevens. Best friend to the President. The
lightbulb in her head went off. There was the accomplice. Knowing that, the motive should become clear.

Emily backed away as quietly as she could. At the last
instant, she couldn't be sure, but she thought Katherine
turned to look at her with a gaze that was anything but
glassy eyed.

Chapter 56

EMILY DIDN'T REMEMBER RETURNING TO THE KITCHEN. Didn't remember trying to drag Mark out of the kitchen, out of the building, away from the city.

She did remember him digging in his heels before they'd gone even five feet across the parquet floor. Emily struggled. Pulled. Jerked.

Until finally he pinned her to the silvered face of the fridge with an arm across her shoulders, almost pressing against her throat.

"What's up, Emily? Spit it out."

She shook her head. Not here. Not…

She pushed at him, and he moved back a single step.

Hand signs. ASL, American Sign Language, was common among SOAR and Special Forces.

Lady, a gesture like tracing the line of a bonnet, *and Chief*… She couldn't remember how to sign "staff" and had to laboriously spell it out. Then she made the sign pretty universally recognizable, even without ASL training, for "sex." Two vees like peace signs slapping together palm to palm. Finally, for lack of any better symbol, she pointed emphatically toward the First Lady's office.

I thought you said she was hot for the Vice President?

She flirts with VP all the time. All the time! Circled the letter *t* for "time" before her open palm like a hand on a clock face, twice for emphasis.

And he flirts back?

WAY! Each letter punched into the air as a shout. She thought about it for a moment. *But feels just playful.* Was Vice President Thomas just *a cover*?

Mark paced off. Thinking.

Right, Army. In a jam, use your brain.

Mark paced back and forth on one side of the island, she on the other.

Twice he stopped, started to sign, and then lowered his hand, shaking his head.

Katherine Matthews was having an affair with the Chief of Staff. Flirting with the Vice President, though Emily had seen no signs of more.

And… Peter wasn't just too busy to have dinners with his wife. He and his wife were wholly estranged. Stupid! Stupid! Stupid! That was obvious, once she thought about it.

She tapped Mark's shoulder. Once you started signing, you sort of forgot you could talk.

P and *FL*, President and First Lady, then she shook her head emphatically.

She didn't need any sign language for Mark's mouthed, "Duh!"

Heat flooded her face. Okay, she should have picked that up sooner. A lot sooner, back to the moment she arrived barely two weeks ago.

But if that was the case, that meant that Peter was perhaps being more than just polite when he said how much he missed her. How much… *Don't go there, Army. Don't go there!*

Stay focused. Katherine, VP Thomas, and Chief of Staff Stevens.

Katherine did nothing by accident, but what was she doing?

And how did the attempts, or as her father insisted and she now believed, apparent attempts, on the First Lady's life fit into the puzzle?

Mark grabbed Emily and slammed her back against the fridge. In a second his mouth was on hers, one hand grabbing her behind, another under her shirt and clamped on her breast.

He swallowed any protest she made deep in her throat. Even to her ears, it sounded more like a moan.

It burned. It sizzled. It scorched out her brain and left a puddle of need in its place. She clamped both her hands hard into those firm buttocks of his and held on.

Blind! Deaf! Dumb! All she could do was feel as Mark overwhelmed her senses. He didn't attack her with lust; he attacked her with need. Not of man for woman, but of him for her. She'd howl like an alpha she-wolf if she wasn't so lost in her own pounding blood.

She inhaled, consumed, feasted.

And Mark matched her, taking as good as he gave. He held her so tightly she couldn't breathe, but that was okay. She didn't want to.

Then he pinched her breast hard. Hard enough for her to yelp if his mouth hadn't been clamped on hers.

That was nasty!

She prepared to retaliate when she heard it.

The kitchen door opened.

She concentrated on the kiss a moment longer. Leaned in, taking one last deep taste of her tongue against his. Her bones were wilting, but the memory of that pinch kept her from getting lost again.

She managed to open one eye and spotted Katherine at the door. She winked at Katherine. The First Lady winked back and then withdrew.

They held the clench a while longer, just in case. Then she tried to pull back.

Mark didn't appear interested in that. His fingers hooked deep in her bra, driving her crazy, making her half hope he'd just rip the barrier away and ravage her. The initial, brutal force of his kiss eased back to a tease that curled her toes. His body pressed hers against the fridge with need. Very evident need.

She managed to get her mouth free, and he moved down to nuzzle her neck. For a moment, she allowed herself to wallow in the sensation. She had no choice. The heat poured into her body like flaming jet fuel.

No one ever had made her feel this way. And his hands, those wonderful hands, shifted from grope to fondle to caress. She laid her head back against the refrigerator as he studied her collarbone with the tip of his tongue, her waist with his fingertips.

Of its own accord, one of her legs wrapped around his hip and pulled him tight against her. Their mutual moan echoed down inside her. She wanted him. Now. Against the wall, on the maple and cherry block, on the floor—

Then she pictured Katherine and Ray Stevens naked on the floor, and that was a splash of ice water.

Mark sensed the shift and had the decency to back away. At least in mood, if not in distance.

He rested his forehead against hers.

"Damn." Barely a whisper. "Goddamn."

She couldn't agree more.

A minute passed before her body recovered enough to unwrap her leg from his waist. Another as their hands both shifted from behind to each other's hips to limp at their own sides while their foreheads still rested against each other. While their noses still brushed.

With a strength she could never match, Mark stepped back until a single breath of air separated them, then another.

So close, she could be wrapped around him before her next heartbeat. Then she wouldn't stop. She knew. They both knew. Next time there would be no stopping themselves.

Now she had her duty. She had to go find Katherine.

Chapter 57

KATHERINE WOULD NEVER BE ACCUSED OF BEING COY.

"Your blouse is still awry, Emily." Katherine turned away to give her a moment as she entered the First Lady's office.

Emily checked, and she was right. She had Mark's damage fixed, at least mostly, by the time Katherine turned to her with two freshly poured glasses of wine.

"Girl-to-girl time, honey."

She followed the First Lady to a pair of floral-print armchairs snuggled together by one of the tall windows, running red with the lowering sun.

"Peter and I…" Katherine shrugged as she kicked off her sandals and settled in deeper. "We have an arrangement. I keep it private, and he pretends he doesn't know anything. Now you weren't planning on spoiling our little plan, were you?"

"Not me." Think fast, Em. "Who'd believe me?" Not good enough. This wasn't guy-speak world. This was the world of her mother. Of shade and nuance. Of multiple meanings revealed or implied but hidden. Or, when it really hit the fan, gal-speak mandated a forthrightness that a man could never achieve with all the guy-speak shorthand on the planet. And, in her professional estimation, it had just hit the fan. With a gut-wrenching splatter like the staff sergeant who'd walked through her tail rotors one day while not paying attention.

"You'd fire me, claiming theft, or reckless endangerment of the First Lady, or spying for a corrupt FBI Director." Suddenly what she'd meant as a joke felt all too possible. If she and Mark were right, and in her gut she knew they were, nothing rated too extreme for Katherine Matthews to do. Emily's stomach wrenched, and she did her best to wave it off by taking a sip of the wine.

The thought, "Poison!" ripped through her brain, but she suppressed it. She couldn't spit the wine back out now. As if guessing her thoughts, Katherine sipped from her own glass. Emily swallowed. After a heartbeat, then two with no side effects, she relaxed, at least on that one account.

"I'd be hit with a dishonorable discharge from the Army that I love, and my father would be ruined. I'm not likely to choose that." She did her best to slide a little bonelessly into the chair as if she too was sated by her man, rather than wound up like an overfired turbocharger by Mark's searing kiss and skillful manhandling. It was pure lust. That's all it was.

Not on the helicopter two nights ago. That hadn't been lust. He had made love to her. No other word for it.

"I wouldn't do that." Katherine's cool voice said that was exactly what she'd do. "Besides," she added brightly, "we're just two lusty girls together."

There was no way she'd bought into Mark's act.

"He still hasn't gotten you into bed?"

Well, they had. But they couldn't.

"Sure he has… we're just, um…"

"Having a few problems."

It wasn't a question but she didn't argue the point.

"I know. You obviously saw…"

"Yes. Looked like fun." Emily had to give a reason for why she and Mark were found in a tight clench less than ten minutes after Emily had observed Katherine in one of her own.

"You told your boyfriend. And he liked the idea." Katherine rolled it around on her tongue to check the taste of the idea. "You weren't so sure."

Emily hated being transparent about men. She could fib her way through the back hills of Argentina, despite being a tall blonde, and not speaking a word of Spanish, but she'd never been able to lie about men.

"He's, a, little wilder than I thought when we…"

"Hooked up. You're really far too sweet a girl. You know that."

Maybe she'd distracted Katherine. Changed the topic away from finding the First Lady and the Chief of Staff naked on the office rug.

"And you liked it, too."

Way too transparent!

"The way he can kiss, I wish he'd never, ever stop." The words slipped out without her meaning them to. She barely recognized them as her own.

Katherine settled back in her chair and sipped her wine in long consideration.

"That gives me such an exceptional idea."

Chapter 58

EMILY WAS LESS SURE ABOUT USING THE WORD "exceptional" as a part of this particular plan's definition.

She lifted off the South Lawn an hour before sunset with Mark and Katherine settled in the back. Her instructions? "Go up and fly around a bit. Act as if you're heading toward Camp David. We'll change our mind later because I have a date tonight."

Their late departure was to due to finagling time into the First Lady's schedule. Even as whimsical as she had built a reputation for being, Katherine couldn't brush off the wives of four very pivotal governors until after an early dinner of grilled sea bass on a bed of blackberry sauce swirled with strawberry sauce for contrast and a single, perfect basil leaf from Emily's rooftop herb garden to top off each portion. One way or another, Emily guessed this would be her last meal cooked at the White House. And she was almost sorry about that.

They cleared D.C. airspace and headed north by northwest. An Alfred Hitchcock image suddenly popped into Emily's mind of a biplane ending its life in a fiery crash into the side of a gasoline truck. This didn't bode well at all. The Secret Service flight that always dogged her tail cruised above and behind. Out of her visual, but clear as a bug on the windshield by radar.

Frank Adams must have thought her completely nuts. She'd found him while the First Lady was seeing her guests out of the building.

"I need you to trust me. I need you to be in the bird following me. I'm not sure what will happen, so I can't tell you." He'd hated it, but he'd gone when she'd played her last card. Not Army to Secret Service. Not Peter's crazy letter of authorization. But she'd asked it warrior to warrior. It was a kind of cred that made a higher calling. One time only, but if this didn't play out, she was finished anyway.

Now if only she could keep her nerves in place long enough to fly a helicopter.

"We're going to chat a bit back here." Katherine's voice was crystal clear over the headset. "You just do your flying thing. Okay, honey? Mama Katherine will make it all better."

"Thanks, uh…" Emily had never used the First Lady's first name. Time to break character for trust building. "Thanks, K-Katherine." It didn't come smoothly off her tongue. Maybe it merely sounded as if she weren't used to using Katherine's name.

"Good girl."

Emily muted her own microphone from the intercom system. And she heard the click of Katherine turning off the feed from the passenger cabin to the cockpit.

Or so she thought.

Emily had never liked that setting, being used to the wide-open intercom on a military flight. And now that feeling had changed from dislike to a long list of alarm signals. So, when she'd picked up the helicopter, she'd disabled the cabin switch.

—∿∿—

"Can she hear us now?" Katherine slipped her hand onto Mark's knee even as she asked the question.

"Honey?" Mark spoke into the mic.

Emily casually looked down to check her instruments, offering no response to his call. He knew she'd disabled the intercom cutoff and could hear them just fine.

"I'd have to say no."

"Can you be sure?" Katherine's voice had picked up a cooing tone somewhere along the way. She sounded a bit more… Southern.

"Well, can't say I know much about these here helleecopters." He let his fake Texas grew thicker in response, almost to John Wayne depth. "I have one idea. Hey, Em, baby?" he called out.

He didn't spot the flinch, but he could feel it through the airframe from her hands on the controls.

"She hates that nickname for reasons I haven't found out." He knew, and it was cruel, but he couldn't resist teasing her. He wasn't particularly excited about his role tonight.

"If she didn't react to that, she can't hear us."

No, she hadn't spoken. But she might try to castrate him later, so he'd have to be careful for a while.

Chapter 59

"So, you were in the military?" the First Lady cooed at Mark. Not subtle, rather a full-on mating call.

That the President had married such a wanton—

Mark curbed his thoughts and stuck to the script, the one he had to write as they flew along.

"We call ourselves paramilitary. I mean, called ourselves that. You'd probably call us, them, mercenaries. Guns for hire. To the highest bidder."

"And who's the highest bidder for you so far?"

"No one, pretty lady." Mark found it easy to slide into his lady-killer voice, but for the first time it didn't feel right.

"Yet," he added on a sour note. That was the problem. Emily Beale had spoiled all other women for him. He sat next to one of the most blatantly sexual women he'd ever met, and he couldn't stir the least interest.

"Ain't had a passel of luck getting any bids at all of late."

"Shucks." The South was pouring out of Katherine now, almost as thick as his Texas. "A pretty boy like you, I bet you have to brush them off like flies."

"Wa'al, up 'til I run upon this filly, I admit that trouble was pretty common. But when a high-class dame walks through your sights, sometimes you just have to take the shot on a wing and a prayer."

"And she's riding roughshod over you."

"A bit," Mark drawled. "A bit." She'd run roughshod right over his goddamn heart, something he thought no one had access to. His crew had called him heartless enough times behind his back that he'd decided it was true. And it had been.

"Perhaps…" Katherine's breath was heaved out with such a sigh that the First Lady's generous chest strained against the form-fitting black blouse she'd chosen for the warm fall evening.

"Just perhaps, if you could do me a favor, I could do you a favor."

"Depends on the favors." Mark blinked to refocus on her face; it was a magnificent chest as chests went. Didn't drag at his heart, but his eyes had other thoughts. *Remember the role.*

"I do like being paid. Er, did. Keep slipping up around you. As far as my Emma-girl knows, none of that is even in my past."

"Cross my heart." Katherine languidly crossed her hand over her deep, deep cleavage. "Your secret's safe with me. Under one condition."

"That is?" Mark was less certain.

"I thought all big boys sealed their promises…" Her voice went low and seductress. "With a kiss."

Mark hesitated. He knew it was wrong for the role he was playing, but he couldn't help himself. He didn't want to lose the taste of Emily's last kiss. Especially if it had indeed been their last kiss. Now there was a depressing thought.

But he'd signed up for the game. Hell, he'd gate-crashed the White House to play this particular game.

"Don't mind if I do."

He tipped their microphones out of the way, making sure to slide a finger along her cheek as he did so, and leaned in. If kissing Emily Beale was part blooming rose and part jet fuel, being kissed by Katherine Matthews was an Olympic sprint. She drove, attacked, laid out a battlefield, and took no prisoners.

This time Mark definitely felt the helicopter twitch.

Chapter 60

WHEN THEY FINALLY CAME UP FOR AIR, MARK OFFERED a long, low whistle. "Whoa, Nelly." The mic picked that up softly, then rattled and thunked loudly in Emily's ear as he moved the mic back to his mouth.

"If ol' Emma-girl there saw that, she'd crash us both into the ground but good."

"Oh, not her. I've got her right where I want her. And you, little boy with the tender lips, I need to get you right where I want you."

She was even more shameless than Emily had thought. And that was pretty shameless. Peter couldn't know about this and look the other way. If he did, then he wasn't the man she knew so well, the man that she knew he must be deep down. Katherine had probably lied about Peter knowing. It would fit.

She considered calling back to have Mark open the door and shove Katherine out. And then Frank Adams would shoot her and Mark out of the sky. Not exactly a happy ending for all.

"Under that seal, it must be one hell of a favor."

Good, Mark. Get her back on track. Things were making less sense the more Emily worked at them.

"First you. How badly do you want your Emily?"

You better nail this one, Marky, or she won't believe you.

"Wa'al," he drawled out. "You, lady, are a luscious

package of pure dy-no-mite. But Emily, she's got a slow burn there that I'd wager could last a man a whole lifetime just lighting the fuse and enjoying every damn second of it."

Emily could feel her cheeks burning and was glad she'd opted for her helmet and had the visor down rather than the lightweight headsets Katherine and Mark wore. She'd heard the guys talk about her in the barracks when they thought she wasn't around. A fair bit of smut, some pretty nice, and she'd shrugged both off.

This felt different. Even if the First Lady didn't buy that line, it made Emily's body turn pretty warm and gooey inside. Did Mark Henderson really want to spend his life with her, or was that just Marky Herman speaking?

She focused ahead and vectored off the Bolling and Dover TACANs to check her GPS course just to have something to do. Still on a clean course for Camp David, but at a mosey that must be frustrating the daylights out of Adams in the chase helicopter.

The silence stretched. It wasn't quite enough. C'mon, Mark, pick up the cue.

"Let me tell you a little bit about what I do… what I did. I expect your Secret Service boys picked up pieces of it. Maybe ten percent or so."

Good boy. Now make it sing.

"There were these two boys having a bit of a territory battle."

"Estanze and Peres."

"So much for my hidden ninety percent."

"I know everything about you there is to know."

At least the layer of his disguise that her father had designed to be discovered.

There was a brief silence, and Mark groaned softly at the end of it.

"We'll discuss this ten percent later."

Emily almost turned around. Had Katherine just groped Mark's pants?

"Lady," Mark gasped it out at the end of a long breath. "Now y'all just stop that. You're making my eyes cross, and it's right difficult to think in that state."

Yup. That's what Katherine had done. Emily had never been so forward in her life, not with any lover. Except with Mark. She had been that forward. In the hospital and in her apartment and... *Think about it later, Beale*.

Thankfully Mark was keeping his wits about him, or at least his Texas. She'd feel better if she knew that he'd faked the moan as well.

"Everyone thinks that I offed Peres, who'd hired me, and skipped with the loot. Didn't work that way. You pay me, I'm honor bound. But then Estanze upped my pay, by a whole lot. So, I took the new job. And my new honor included cutting down Peres. No real problem, just a damn drug war. Since I left, there've been three attempts on Estanze by Peres's relatives, but none of them amounted to much. To the highest bidder, I stay bought."

"And is your Miss Emily Beale a coin of trade?"

"None higher." Mark delivered that line with his voice low and so much sincerity that even Emily believed it. Could he really be serious? It had seemed clear in the helicopter. But now she didn't trust her memory, or that he had felt the same things she had. She and Mark were both animals of action. Warriors to the bone. That didn't bode well for any future either.

"One last question."

"Shoot."

Emily had been waiting for a moment like this. She and Mark had discussed the different ways it might come up. If this wasn't it, it wasn't going to happen. She flipped the mic switch on the radio. Encrypted emergency radio, it would feed to the Secret Service craft behind them as well as the tower that she'd told to keep a tape running for her entire flight.

She made sure that the return chatter would only be routed to her own earphones.

"When you 'offed' Mr. Peres, who did you set up to look like they did the deed? Certainly not you."

"No, ma'am. I didn't want all those guns after me. His number two, his chief of staff, if you will, didn't live out the next hour. Framed clean as could be."

Damn, Mark. Did you just set up Ray Stevens for the fall of whatever Katherine was planning? She should never have turned on the radio.

"My, my, my. Handsome and smart."

Katherine was doing just that. Setting up Ray Stevens to take the fall. Mark saw it before Emily did. But the fall for… what?

Mark picked up his line. "And which pin is supposed to be 'offed' by his own Chief of Staff?"

"Marine Two. What the hell is this transmission?" The tower sounded pissed.

"Maintain radio silence!" Frank Adams snapped out, then in a whisper over the airwaves, "Damn, Captain!"

She didn't dare respond. Her role in all this was silent partner.

"Ooo, very smart, big boy. Come to Mama, and as a bonus she will pay you with her all."

Emily didn't respond, but she did begin a long, lazy turn back toward D.C. She didn't want to land this snake out in the woods.

Peres's chief of staff had been framed for killing his boss. Katherine was trying to frame Ray Stevens for the killing of… his boss?

The helicopter jolted as she almost dropped the collective.

Katherine Matthews was planning to…

"You want me to murder the President but frame Ray Stevens?"

"Smart boy."

Get it confirmed again, Mark. C'mon. Get it on tape again.

"But Mrs. Matthews, if I kill your husband for you, you're no longer First Lady. It takes one mercenary to know another. What's the benefit to you?"

Katherine was so close that Emily could hear their microphones clicking together.

"Mr. Zachary Thomas will do anything this woman wants, an-y-thing. Including consoling the widow all the way to the Oval Office."

There it was. It all made sense.

"So," Mark's voice had lost most of its Texas but filled with wonder. "You're sleeping with Ray Stevens to get him to stage attacks against you to make you look threatened. You bring in my Emily to…"

"High-profile CNN girl to keep me alive through Ray's supposed attempts to kill both Peter and me. I have a photograph of him firing the light weapon that he doesn't know about. Yet."

"And then when I, um, do the deed for you, you

expose him. But you couldn't have counted on me showing up."

"You, cutie pie, were a bonus for which I will always thank your little Emily. I wasn't looking forward to killing Peter myself. He's such a bore, but he is my husband. So tried and true and all-American blue that he won't listen to a single idea of mine. I have the plan all worked out. And you can make it look like Ray took care of it."

"And then you marry Zack Thomas…"

"Who is total putty in my hands. The same way you are about to be."

The microphone picked up the distinct sound of a zipper being undone.

Chapter 61

"THAT WAS A NICE BROADCAST, MS. MATTHEWS." Mark's voice rang smooth and West Coast over the headset. All hint of Texas gone.

"Broadcast?" The zipper sound stopped, much to Emily's relief.

"You there, Captain?" Mark called to her over the headset.

She knew what he was doing. Maybe it had reached that point, but it could also be dangerous. What the hell? If you're going to unwrap the package, make sure it can't be wrapped back up. She keyed on her helmet mic.

"Right here, Mister Herman." She remembered his cover name at the last second. "All loud and clear. Secret Service reports a full record, and they're waiting for us to deliver you, Ms. Matthews, to the ground for plotting treason against the President of the United States. Apparently the Vice President is shocked and… hold on a moment…" She listened to the sudden stream of reports on the radio.

"The Chief of Staff actually stabbed an agent in the hand with a paring knife when they took him down. He was peeling an apple at the time. They may think it's treason, but I'd class it as premeditated attempted murder."

"Me personally," Mark added cheerfully, "I tend to think of it as an act of domestic terrorism. And I've never been a big fan of terrorism. How about you, Captain Beale?"

"Nope. Never a big fan, Mister Herman." Their role-playing had gone deep enough that even now she didn't reveal his true rank.

There was silence. Too much silence. Katherine wasn't protesting or denying or...

Mark yelped.

"Mark!"

Emily turned to look, and that was probably all that saved her life. A bullet whistled past her ear, bounced off the Plexiglas windshield, and ricocheted into her main screen. Sparks flew and breakers popped.

"Mark!" No response. She hadn't heard the shot that got him, but she needed to assume she was on her own. Strapped into a seat with her back turned to a loaded weapon.

She racked the cyclic right and stomped the pedal to the left.

Someone on the radio asked if she'd heard a gunshot.

The helicopter slewed sideways and the tail rotor spun clockwise. She was thrown forward against her restraint harness and sideways against the door with a loud whack. The blow made her head spin, and she was glad again she'd chosen to wear her helmet this time. She'd done it to keep her face hidden from those behind her; the anonymous-pilot-in-a-helmet routine had let her blend into the background. Now it had saved her from a nasty lump.

"You're not knocking me out this time, you bitch." Katherine spewed venom through the headset.

"What did you do to Mar—"

Another bullet zinged against the windshield and bounced off. This time it plowed a hole through the empty copilot's seat.

Emily tried to guess when the next shot was coming and rammed the collective downward. The helicopter fell like a stone. Emergency down. This rotor permitted a slight negative tilt. She now had twin, sixteen-hundred horsepower turbines driving them toward the earth. Terra firma was coming up awfully fast. Everything in the cabin that wasn't tied down floated.

Her water bottle floated out of the cup holder and smacked against the ceiling.

What she was hoping for also happened.

Not used to working in negative-gravity environments, Katherine had let her hand with the gun drift upward. A shot rang out. Two. Three. All upward by the impact sound. And no ricochet.

Earsplittingly painful in the small cabin, but not fatal. Not yet.

She'd once checked out Katherine's Kahr MK during a security review, which only had five shots. She should be out.

Emily yanked up on the collective and slammed down against her sprung seat so hard it rammed against the stops and jarred her spine. She'd be sore after this ride, if she was alive.

Another pair of shots rang out.

This time the impact sound came from below her right hand. The radios started sparking and more breakers popped. Adams, the tower, and all the other voices Emily hadn't realized were yelling for attention died with the radios.

So much for the five-shot theory. Katherine's weapon had to be small. A .357 would have punched through the windshield rather than bouncing back. Probably a .22 or a 9 mm.

She yanked the cyclic left and stomped on the right pedal. Only it didn't respond the way she expected. The lurch in her stomach didn't hurt; it only made her head swim.

What was going on with the chopper? It didn't feel right. Maybe this bird just responded poorly after a bit of abuse.

Then she heard it. A turbine whining, not spinning down. Spinning up, out of control. From seven lousy shots. Katherine got lucky. Or unlucky.

Emily pulled the throttle on engine number two and hit the fire suppressor.

Nothing. It kept whining upward. Runaway engine. Reaching down, she shut the fuel flow to the number two turbine. That killed it.

A small pistol flew over her left shoulder, where her head had been a moment before. Seecamp LWS .32. Little bigger than a deck of playing cards. Seven shots if you carried it with the chamber loaded. One had hit something vital, and this bird had far fewer redundant systems than her Black Hawk.

The Bell could fly on one engine, but not well. If one failed, the best practice was to find a place to land. Fast.

A blast ripped at her ears and her upper arm stung like a son-of-a-bitch. The forward windshield star-cracked, a spent bullet wedged in the center of the spidery lines. Mark's gun. The Beretta M9 they'd tucked aboard for the flight. Fifteen rounds and only one fired.

There was no way she was going to survive this unless the tables turned. And quickly.

"If you kill me, you'll die when we crash!" Emily shouted over the headset.

"I'm not going to jail, and I'm not going to be arrested." Katherine jammed the barrel of the gun against the bleeding wound on Emily's arm.

Emily managed not to scream at the scythe of pain; the wound must be deeper than she thought.

"Do you have any idea how close I was? Another day, maybe two. And it would be done."

Again the gun jammed into her arm, rocketing so much pain into her system that her vision tunneled for a moment.

"Damn you, bitch, I was so close!"

Katherine was out of her seat. Unbuckled. Probably kneeling on the front set of passenger seats to extend her gun into the cockpit area.

"Okay, Katherine. Don't kill me. Where do you want to go?"

Two Black Hawks were coming up close behind her. Nothing they could do from there but watch. Even a sniper, if they had one aboard, would be hard pressed to take out the First Lady through Plexiglas windows on the first try. And there'd be no time for a second try, at least none that Emily would survive.

"You're the one who knows everything. You figure it out."

"You've wounded the copter." Emily eyed the gauges. Turbine two had shut down. Number one was hot, taking the load staunchly, but not at all happy about it. They had about two hours of fuel, not that she'd last

another ten minutes. And the rudder was still mush.
She'd hit two vital systems. Civilian birds simply didn't
have the double and triple redundancy of systems that
kept military birds aloft after being shot up.

"Let's go to Camp David." Way out of range, but
all she could come up with quickly. "We'll get another,
long-range bird to meet us there. I can fly you to Mexico.
Midair refuel."

"I hate fucking Mexico."

The balance on the helicopter shifted as Katherine
moved across the rear cabin to the far window. Not a
big change in a bird this size, but enough to alter the
flying trim a few points. Definitely no longer in her
seat belt.

Emily went with it. She cranked the cyclic all the
way over and rolled the helicopter. Rolled it and rolled
it and rolled it.

She heard a scream. Two more rounds fired off with
massive roars. Thankfully, neither came forward into
the cockpit that she could detect.

Altitude was disappearing alarmingly. The White
House, to which they'd been returning as slowly as they
left, now filled more and more of her side window each
time she rolled over. Katherine must be thumping about
like a marble in a gerbil wheel. Hopefully separated
from her gun.

"What the hell?" Mark's voice was groggy and slow.
Then he exclaimed with a loud, "Oof!" as something
hit him.

"Beale! What the—? You can't do that."

"You're alive!"

"Bitch! Ouch! Goddamn it! She Tasered me! I think

you knocked her out. I think you just broke my fucking neck. Now stop it!"

She corrected as well as she could. The ground now alarmingly close.

The Bell had reached its limit. And then passed it.

Something gave with a low crunch.

"That didn't sound good." Mark's tone rang suddenly steady, exactly like a professional pilot. The calmest when the going got worst. If you listened to the black-box recordings of any airliner going down, the pilots sounded perfectly calm. Discussing engine-restart procedures, altimeter readings, and airframe integrity right up to the moment they augered into the ground. Except the final moment. Almost without variation, the last thing on black-box recordings was a soft, "Damn!"

She wasn't planning on adding to that legacy.

The chopper started spinning. The tail rotor was gone. That moment of imminent ground contact was going to happen much sooner than she'd anticipated.

She glanced out the window over her right shoulder, and the gunshot wound in her left arm screamed bloody murder.

No, the tail was still there, but the angle was wrong. It should be sticking out straight behind them, but she could see it out the window.

Rolling over toward the left side should decrease the strain. Help gravity counteract what the rotor wasn't doing.

The problem was, it made her crab sideways across the sky and lose altitude.

"Is she really out?" Emily shouted toward the back.

"Ouch. The intercom still works and I still have my headset on. Yes, she's out cold."

Emily thumbed the radio to call a Mayday. More sparks, more breakers popping. And the intercom went with it.

They needed to be on the ground and fast.

They were at five hundred feet and dropping rapidly.

She continued the sideways crab and surveyed the local area.

No answers. For once she had no answers. No way out or down. Mark had trusted her, as any passenger did, to get him back down to safety. And she couldn't.

Emily looked down at her hands. The hands Mark had held when she needed him most. They clutched two lousy little control sticks. Not enough to keep a dying machine alive from this high up.

She raised her head to look back for help. To look to Mark for an answer, or at least for forgiveness for killing him somewhere in the next thirty seconds. The despair spread over her like darkness.

Altitude around three hundred feet. Too low for a clean auto-rotate crash, especially with only half a tail. Chopper crashes were usually survivable below forty feet and above four hundred. The death zone lay in between, right where they hung.

If she'd reacted faster, sooner, they might have had a chance. But now—

Mark shouted. She couldn't make out the words, but she saw it.

A wash of light in the falling night.

The South Lawn.

Ahead and to the right. A quarter mile away. So

close. Even the Mall was out of reach. They were out of options.

Turbine one started a runaway whine. This bird had clearly never been designed to be shot at from the inside. Throttling back did nothing. This was it; death was upon them. And damn it, she wasn't ready. Emily eased down on the collective, hoping to bleed off her altitude without plummeting or creating a murderous spin.

The remains of the rear rotor wasn't doing much of a job to keep the helicopter in any sort of a line. More and more, she was spinning one direction as the main rotors spun the other.

Rock it sideways; let gravity help. Keep the strain low. If the tail boom went, it would fold up into the main rotor, and no one would be walking away, not from three hundred feet. Not even from the two hundred they were plummeting through.

Mark called out again, but with the intercom dead and the helmet covering her ears, she didn't get what he was saying. He'd have to deal. She was busy.

She nursed the collective up a fraction, testing the rotor's lift, and swore against the pain in her arm. Even the adrenaline couldn't knock all the pain out.

Now the helicopter crabbed sideways and backward in a sloping descending spiral. The South Lawn flashed across the windows, and a treacherous stand of trees swung into view. A moment later, the White House slewed across her view.

One fifty. Still too far to fall, but if the tail rotor held on a little longer…

One hundred.

Aim for the lawn. It flashed by, and she tried to fix it in her mind.

Another bad lurch and spin, but the lawn was... there!

The turbine screamed and started to come apart. She'd heard that noise once before. Over the opium fields of Myanmar. A small fan blade inside the engine had been fractured and then broken free, and it had begun dismantling the engine from the inside.

Below her, hurrying across the spreading field of summer-red poppy flowers, a half-dozen jeeps loaded with pissed-off drug runners had chased after her. While her turbine busily consumed itself. She retained few fond memories of that moment or the long days that followed.

And now, that same noise had once again come into her life. No one with guns after her this time, other than the First Lady. But the ground at seventy-five feet away looked no softer than it had in Southeast Asia. As a bonus, in about fifteen seconds, the entire airframe, including the passenger compartment, was going to be riddled with shards of flying engine metal.

Time to risk it.

At fifty feet, she swung the copter almost fully onto its left side and drove the right pedal into the floor.

For one long, horrid moment the Bell 430 shuddered. Shuddered and held.

She crossed the cyclic hard.

At twenty-five feet they righted and the tail boom let go with a scream of metal.

Jerking the cyclic back, Emily managed to get the nose up for the final impact.

They landed tail first, buffering the impact as the

remains of the tail boom crumpled. Then the baggage area, followed by the cabin frame in the rear hitting the ground, and finally the nose slammed forward and down onto the wheels.

The wheels all blew with sharp bangs as loud as gunfire, easily heard over the roar of the thrashing engine.

The hydraulic shocks rammed against their stops and then folded up into crumpled twists of metal.

The bird rocked to one side, and rotor blades pinged off the ground. Broken, crumpled, scattered like birdshot from a shotgun, a thousand little bits flung in a hundred different directions.

Without the resistance of the rotor, the dying turbine climbed into full runaway. Emily pulled throttles, threw breakers, but couldn't find the fuel shutoff. It wasn't where it was supposed to be.

Neither was the left front side of the helicopter.

The engine whined higher and higher. Then she smelled it. JP-5. Nothing quite like it. That tang and sting of incredibly volatile kerosene.

She scrabbled for the release on her belt. She had to get Mark and Katherine out. Had to save her crew.

As she reached for the door, Mark yanked it open from outside, grabbed her collar, and dragged her out.

They fell together and stumbled clear.

"Katherine!" She turned for the helicopter.

Mark latched an arm around her waist and continued to drag her away.

"She's done. Main tail-boom strut has passed sentence on her, right through the heart, if she had one. Damn woman Tasered me."

Emily let Mark drag her away as flames spurted out

of the exhaust ports on the screaming engine. A pool of liquid spread across the ground where one of the wheel struts had punched a fuel tank.

That was all she needed to see to get her feet moving.

They flew more than dove behind a heavy set of concrete stairs as the first tank went. Even self-sealing tanks could only take so much abuse. She landed on her shot-up arm and remembered the meaning of real pain in the moment before the world tunneled to black.

Chapter 62

"YOU ARE HANDS DOWN THE BEST GODDAMN PILOT I ever flew with."

Emily came to kneeling in the flower bed behind the curving concrete stair at the front of the White House. Mark stripped back her jacket to expose her shoulder, unheedful of her brief unconsciousness or the searing pain of her arm. He flexed her arm once or twice before grunting.

"Just a lousy meat shot. Barely bleeding anymore."

She glanced at the blood pouring from the wound and looked away.

He pulled free the bandanna he wore around his neck as part of his "Mr. Tropical Playboy" disguise. With a careless twist that made her teeth ache, he staunched the flow.

"That was amazing." He looked at neither her nor what he was doing. Instead, he watched the burning machine over the lip of the stairs. "There is no book on the planet that says we should be alive after that flight. The way you kept the tail boom hanging on by slewing us sideways. It shouldn't have worked."

Emily raised her visor and peered over the edge of the South Portico stairs. The outline of the helicopter glowed deep within the blazing fire that consumed it. She couldn't see any sign of Katherine's body in the heart of the flames. The First Lady had been granted her own personal funeral pyre.

The late-evening light shrouded everything not lit by the roaring blaze. They were crouched behind the stairs leading up to the South Portico. A range of trees to either side were beginning to burn.

Sirens were approaching. A lot of them, by the sound of it. A quick survey testified that the results to the general area were also less than subtle.

Another first for the White House. An inferno reaching at least as high as the White House's four exaggerated stories. A brilliant beacon drove out the dark of night. Most of the windows in the residence and the West Wing had been blown out. The only ones intact ringed the Oval Office. This face of the White House had some interesting scorch marks.

Mark followed the direction of her gaze, then shouted above the roar of the fire, "It will be the Black and Brown and White House for a while. Very urban. Very PC. One should always strive for political correctness. Especially here, don't you think?"

She ducked back down as a series of sharp cracks sounded from the fire. She grabbed the back of Mark's belt to haul him down. It must be his gun. Except for the round in the chamber, they'd just explode in place. But a stray round could fly, and she'd hate to be shot by their own armament.

"Damn it!" Mark glared in the general direction of the chopper on the far side of the concrete. "I liked that gun."

"Not me. The woman shot me with it." Emily raised her arm and its blood-soaked bandage as proof.

Another explosion, probably the other fuel tank, showered them with shredded bushes, chunks of sod, and a thousand bits of metal. A piece stung the back of her hand.

She and Mark both curled up with their hands under their arms and she kept her helmeted head down. Minimum target, no exposed flesh. Mark pulled his denim jacket over his head as well as he could while the metal rained down.

When the pattering ceased, they checked each other for flaming fragments. Their jackets showed several scorch marks but no fires.

The helicopter was silent now except for the crackle of flames. They stood to survey the remains of her crash.

Fire trucks zoomed up from who knew where. Over the roar of the fire, dozens of sprinklers were shushing out water at an amazing rate. The British had burned down the White House once. She'd take all the help she could get to make sure that an officer of the United States Army Special Operations Aviation Regiment didn't torch it to the ground a second time.

"Goddamn it, Beale. When you take a bird down, you really take one down."

The adrenaline surge hadn't worn off yet. She peeled off her helmet. A bullet crease scarred deeply along the side. The .32 caliber bullet itself was lodged in the helmet near the ear. She hadn't been thrown into the door; she'd been shot in the head by Katherine Matthews and only this good armor had saved her brain. She was going to figure out who'd created Kevlar and send her a really nice thank-you note. Emily tossed the helmet aside, and it rattled on the concrete walkway.

A real pity to destroy such a first-class craft as the

Bell 430. It had brought them down safely before it gave up the ghost.

Mark leaned in, "Black-in-black, indeed. I had no idea. You're bad. You goddamn did it! And we survived! The President will live to thank you for his life."

She wasn't sure Peter would be so terribly thankful to the woman who'd murdered his wife. But, it was starting to sink in that she'd walked away from another one. She cradled her arm for a moment. She'd have a scar. Another badge of survival.

She had made it.

Emily pumped a fist in the air, sending a sharp shot of pain into her shoulder, and laughed anyway. Once again she'd dodged the demon. She'd lost four choppers in a decade of flying, three while in the regular Army and now one with SOAR. And she'd managed to walk away from every one.

Mark grabbed her around the waist and swung her into his arms. He planted a kiss on her that was pure animal survivor. Wild, filled with heat and power. She wrapped her good arm around the back of his head and pulled him in so hard she knew her lips would be bruised.

They broke apart and stared back at the fire.

He slapped her butt good and hard. Ended it with a caress that backed up the kiss with the memory of much more.

She slapped his right back. It was a good, tight, hard butt. Just what you'd want in a hunky major. Or maybe a lover seeking to light a slow fuse. Maybe it wasn't such a big deal if she resigned. Maybe. It still didn't feel right. The answer was still too hard. She was sick of hard answers.

Adams jumped out of the Black Hawk almost before it landed on the South Lawn and started taking control of the situation.

People were slowly forming a wide circle around the First Lady's funeral pyre, their faces lit by the shimmering light. The biting odor of burning fuel predominated the night. Blacksuits were easy to pick out because they were looking everywhere except at the flames. At least half of them were facing outward, the others scanned the growing crowd carefully. Adams sent a group of four who formed up with her and Mark behind the South Portico stair. She took it as a good sign that their weapons remained holstered.

There were upward of fifteen hundred people working at the White House during the day. At nine o'clock on a fall evening, the number might be as low as a couple hundred. Still enough to make a solid human wall marking the boundary of curiosity, fear, and heat. A line of the gawkers and the horror-stricken. The firefighters moved in and put out the worst of the burning trees.

The adrenal slam of the last hour finally started slipping out through the soles of her boots and seeping into the ground. She sagged a little against Mark who kept his arm around her waist. Held her tight. Safe.

He too had gone quiet. They gathered strength from each other and watched the flames.

It was done.

For better or worse, Emily had uncovered the murderous plot, ruining any number of the most powerful politicians in the nation's Capitol, including the Vice President and the Chief of Staff.

Not to mention the First Lady.

Not many people would be shedding tears for her tonight. Emily knew she wouldn't. Nor Mark. Not even Daniel.

And definitely not—

Or would he?

There was a ripple over near the West Wing. She could just see it through the heat shimmer on the opposite side of the dying inferno. A phalanx of blacksuits cleared the crowd to either side and Peter Matthews stepped forward to view the fire.

He planted his feet solidly and stared toward the flames over crossed arms. His face unreadable.

But, she knew. Perhaps she alone of the whole crowd knew. He wasn't watching the fire.

He was looking past the heat shimmer, directly at her.

She'd have eased away from Mark, even tried to, but her lax muscles would not be stirred.

Today was the closest she'd ever come to really dying. She would never want to tell this story. She already knew that. She'd never lost control before. Never lost her head or her way. Letting them fall into the Death Zone before she'd recovered. The panic and terror she'd experienced aloft had blinded her more effectively that the flashbang.

Training had taught her how to deal with it, and she had, almost too late. She had let the fear ride through her but not take control, because she was too busy stretching her training to the very limits to survive. Fear was death. Fear led to inaction and mistakes, often fatal ones in her line of business. But maybe she could have gotten Katherine to the ground alive if she hadn't panicked for those long moments. She'd never know.

Now that she stood on solid ground, she could do little more than sag against a man of towering strength and return the inscrutable gaze of the man whose wife she'd just killed.

She'd just killed the First Lady of the United States. With luck, she'd only be cooling her heels for a few decades in Leavenworth. Wouldn't that be the perfect joke? After a decade of struggle to be the only woman to break into SOAR, if she'd ended up as the only woman in the maximum security prison of the U.S. Disciplinary Barracks at Fort Leavenworth.

Chapter 63

INSTEAD OF SENDING EMILY TO LEAVENWORTH, THEY sewed up her arm and then the U.S. Secret Service spent two very long days performing exceptionally cordial interrogation on her. They set Emily up in a stunningly luxurious, though very tightly locked, suite at the Hay-Adams. She could look out the window at the White House. Even watch the large crews removing the helicopter wreckage, then replacing windows.

By the end of the third day, all the landscaping was back in place, including the replacement of several trees she'd clear-cut with the rotor blades and scorched with fire. And the painters were about a third of the way down the facade.

The debriefing had been terribly polite and incredibly intense. A panel of four officers went over every action or reaction since the CNN crew had shown up in her life two weeks ago. And not a friendly face among them. Not even Frank Adams, though he'd found her after the fire and shook her hand. His comment that she was welcome in his gym any time was one of the nicest things anyone had ever said to her.

She, of course, knew how much to say, "Thanks."

And then she'd hugged him, leaving the gruff man with a very large smile.

The panel had her reconstruct every day, every detail at least half a dozen times, searching for who knew what inconsistency. The only thing she never discussed was the black-in-black team. That her belief had been vindicated, though not in the fashion she'd imagined, was beside the point. She simply told the panel there were items she was not at liberty to discuss.

They fought and pushed on this until late on the second day she clammed up and insisted that she had a letter to return to President Peter Matthews. After that, Emily sat in absolute silence ignoring their questions.

She was allowed to call "Marky Herman" that evening. Probably the most heavily monitored phone call since Nixon.

He'd suffered only one day of interrogation, somehow proving he was indeed a wealthy, drifting, ex-paramilitary playboy. Odd, he'd never struck her as having a single ounce of humor in his splendid bones, but apparently he'd decided to test the depths of the cover story on a lark. Her father's people had done their work well. Mark's story held, the black-in-black team still lay safely behind its shroud.

She hadn't dared risk saying anything else.

"Be sure you get home safe, babe," Mark had drawled in his fake Texas.

Home. With her crew. He'd know that was her home. He'd meant that and tucked it into as few words as possible. But she couldn't think about it now. Couldn't because he would be there and she wouldn't.

Out of the op and stuck in the Hay-Adams, she was at loose ends. Every time she turned on the TV, she saw yet another analysis of Katherine Matthews's evil, of the final flight, captured by the same photographer who'd filmed the flashbang, and the burning of the White

House's facade. Every newscaster trying to analyze the motivations and talents of the obscure and unavailable-for-comment pilot and chef, and getting nine-tenths of everything wrong.

"Be sure you get home safe, babe." Mark might as well have said, "Sorry I kissed you, babe. That was bad." Actually, now that Emily thought about it, she understood that he had. He'd said, "You're welcome back in the unit." It was an apology. Yes, it had been against regulation, risking both of their careers. But it had been so good. Especially now that she knew how hard he had struggled to protect her reputation since they first met. How hard he would struggle again not to put her career at risk if she returned. No other man had made such a noble offer, such an immense one. They just wanted to bed you, damn the consequences. Those consequences always turned out worse for the women, and she'd always walked away before they started.

Except from Mark, the most decent one of the lot. The chill warrior behind the mirrored shades might well reappear if she were ever allowed to return to the unit. But she'd know what was behind that shield. She'd know there was nothing cold about Mark's lovemaking. Nothing cold about the man within. And there lay the potential for immense trouble for them both. Maybe if—

A knock startled her, and she snapped off the TV she hadn't been watching anyway.

"I'd open the damn door if I could," she shouted at it.

Chapter 64

THE DOOR OPENED AND PETER WALKED THROUGH.

Emily and the President shuffled their feet against the Spanish tile in the foyer of the Hay-Adams suite while a team of three agents once again swept the rooms. Their inspection happened surprisingly fast. The only part that bothered her, other than the awkward silence, was when the agents entered the bedroom. The massive cherry-wood, four-poster bed had been slept in by no one, including herself. She hadn't been able to sleep during the past two days. Her adrenaline hadn't yet let go of its throttlehold around her heart.

When the agents were gone, she led Peter away from the Queen Anne furnishings of the elegant living room. Led him to the only room in the whole suite that had no outside windows, a lady's boudoir between the bedroom and the bath.

She shut both doors and pulled two chairs to face each other about three steps apart.

Peter's question was eloquent in what he didn't ask or gesture. She could still read his every movement as if it were her own.

"The other rooms all have glass windows. Even with the curtains shut, it would be very easy to record our conversation with a laser bounce. It's the most secure space I can make without having Mark bring along a signal jammer."

"Mark, as in your ex-paramilitary boyfriend?" Peter's face looked grim. And sad. Sadder than she'd ever seen.

"Mark as in Major Mark Henderson, commanding officer of the 3rd Black Hawk Company of the 5th Battalion of the 160th Special Operations Aviation Regiment. My CO."

That rocked him back on his heels. Literally. For a moment she thought he'd tip over backwards as his balance shifted, then his mind kicked in. His face changed, and she could almost hear the gears grinding in his head.

Commanding Officer. Part of the operation. Not at the White House by chance. But his cover had held up to intense scrutiny. Therefore, part of her secret team.

"No one can know that, by the way. I only let you know because, well, you placed the orders."

Secret beyond secret. Methods and techniques carefully protected because who knew when they'd be needed again. The Special Forces' most protected operational secret was not how they infiltrated into a site for an operation. Rather how they exfiltrated. How they escaped after a mission was complete. So protected they wouldn't even break cover when they were done. All of the "I'm retired so now I can tell stories" autobiographies still never gave away a single exfiltration technique. It just wasn't done.

Peter came out of his mental reverie much more smoothly than he'd entered it. There was one expression at the end that she hadn't been able to read. Then the President was back.

He nodded and bowed for her to take her seat before he did. He made it so natural and casual that she actually bowed back slightly before she caught herself.

"Don't try manipulating me. Your wife did more than enough of that." She planted her feet firmly.

"My late wife."

She flushed until her cheeks burned so hot she had to cover them with her hands, and she sank into the chair.

"I'm sorry, Peter. I—just—sorry."

"It's okay, Squirt."

Squirt. That's about how she felt. Small and insignificant. She'd worn her full dress uniform for the President and had collapsed into a huddled mess in front of Sneaker Boy. She unbuttoned her breast pocket and pulled out the letter that the blacksuits' ever-so-polite search had missed. It had been worn as soft as fabric, so the pocket must have felt empty.

She sat up and held it out.

Peter waited a moment before taking it.

"I'm sorry, Mr. President. I know the results were not what you'd intended. For that I am eternally sorry. I am willing to bear the full consequences of my actions." Stiff spine. Perfect posture. She was going to go down in exacting military style. Come what may.

The President unfolded the letter. Inspected the tattered creases that chopped the sheet in six pieces. He reread the two lines he himself had penned there.

Then he refolded it and slipped it into his own pocket.

"I'm the one who's sorry."

Sorry that Emily had murdered his wife.

"I'm the one who put you in this spot. Only it turned out to be much worse than I imagined."

"Huh?"

"Don't grunt, Squirt."

They both chuckled at the phrase from their past. It

was an instruction he'd oft repeated for her benefit, to no great effect on her tomboy manners. But the laugh fell hollow in the room and they both cut it off before it was complete.

"I repeat, 'Huh?' Sir."

"Well, with the 'sir' I guess it's okay." Peter leaned back and crossed his ankles. He could have been lounging in a meadow watching clouds go by instead of wearing a three-piece business suit in a Hay-Adams boudoir and about to pass judgment on her future.

"I'm sorry. Because I'm the one who manipulated you."

She shook her head. Couldn't see it.

"The first letter. The one James delivered. I knew you couldn't refuse. And I needed you here."

"Why didn't you just ask? You know I'd have come."

He nodded. "I did know that, but you're too black and white. You never could keep a secret worth a damn."

She could certainly tell him a thing or two about that. Black-in-blacks for three different administrations now.

"Hmm. By your imposing glare, I take it I am overstating or perhaps misstating my case. You can't play-act or hide your feelings well, as you are proving at this moment. Clearly you're much better at secret keeping than you were as a kid."

"It was only you." Emily swallowed hard and laid her heart on the table. "I always told you everything. No one else ever knew."

Peter nodded his thanks and his understanding. "But this time I needed to depend on your reactions being genuine."

"Genuine," she prompted. Somewhere in this conversation the ship she'd left harbor in had sunk outright.

Peter sat up, sat back, practically squirmed like the little boy she'd never known him to be. Mr. Comfortable had been an act. For her. She didn't like that. Not one little bit.

"I knew there was a threat."

"To Katherine."

"To me."

"Let me repeat my earlier statement. 'Huh? Sir.'"

It elicited a brief smile, but that was all.

"I guessed, couldn't prove, but guessed, that Katherine was gunning for me. I just didn't realize quite how literally. I figured there'd be a trumped-up scandal. I expected her to try forcing women into my bedroom, or some such. But it wasn't happening. I needed an eye on the inside of her operation. One that I knew was absolutely loyal to me."

"You could have trusted Daniel. All he wanted was governmental support for his farming program. He did everything for that. Banked his whole life on that. He has so much integrity he doesn't know how to be anything less."

Peter raised his eyebrows. "Good to know. I'll have a chat with him. But I needed you."

"You have the entire bloody flock of blacksuits at your command. You sent me in where you wouldn't send the Secret Service? What the hell, sorry, what were you thinking I was, goddamn Superwoman?"

"Yes."

Nothing else. Just a yes.

She blew out a hard breath. "Try that again, in simple words so a mere captain can understand what the Commander-in-Chief is saying."

"You are Superwoman incarnate. Come alive right out of the funny pages. You're a SOAR pilot, Em. The first woman in their three-decade, blood-stained, glorious history. And commander after commander has reported that you are the best they've ever seen. I needed the best. Desperately. And what was I supposed to do? Go to the Secret Service and whine about my wife not liking me?"

He laughed at himself. "Oh, certainly, that was going to work just great."

"So. You sent me…" She was feeling slow, like her brain might just be forcing the rotors around for that first aching rotation. "You sent me into Katherine Matthews's employ, in the hopes that I would spy for you and uncover an unknown nefarious plan. The fact that I killed her, ruined Vice President Zack Thomas's career, and put your Chief of Staff in jail were just side bonuses?"

"First, I'd argue that she is the one who actually killed herself. Second, I think Zack will make a comeback. He attempted to resign and I refused it. We're in negotiation right now, but he did nothing wrong. And third, Ray got what he bloody well deserved, stealing the light weapon, shooting it at a helicopter, launching the airplane, finding cyanide… How far he would go to continue sleeping with Katherine I don't even want to know. Thinking about how Katherine practically foisted him on me while I was still a senator and that I fell for it is a completely depressing concept."

"But he was Katherine's fall guy."

"Sorry, I still can't feel an ounce of pity for him. And she was my wife. I might not have had much joy in the connubial bed for the last decade, but she was my wife."

Her ship still wasn't returning from the depths, but neither was it resting easily in the dark, far below.

"You…" She could only piece her thoughts together one word at a time, as if climbing an infinite ladder. "Put. Me…"

It all clicked. She jerked to her feet and wavered there a moment. Then she burst clear of the cloud cover and could see the entire field of battle arrayed before her.

"You bastard. You used me. Just as Katherine tried to. Just as my mother always tried to. You knowingly used me to uncover your wife's madness without so much as a 'please.' You put my life in danger with no warning. I know a goddamn mission profile when I fly it. And you—" Her voice caught, and she didn't like that one bit either. Hated that she cared so much.

She stormed away and stormed back. The luxurious boudoir pressed too close. Too intimate.

"'Squirt' indeed. You used our past to keep me close. Your ever-so-nice story about the lowest point in your life being that day I lay drunk and drooling in my father's office. Pure crap! You probably don't even like pie! You deceitful, lying, son-of-a-bitch! You're worse than all the others put together! You goddamn politician!"

She headed for the door just below a run.

"Em!"

His call stopped her a step from escape. Stopped her cold. It was filled with pain and pleading and hope.

She didn't turn. Didn't move.

Peter came up close behind her, rested his hands on her shoulders.

"Em." Now it was a whisper. "I screwed up, Em."

She couldn't answer.

"In your father's study nine years ago, I made the biggest mistake of my life."

Her shoulders sagged as she turned to face him. He let his hands slide free.

"Why do you keep bringing that up?" Emily searched his face.

He looked worn. Exhausted.

"That was the worst night of my life. Drunk and passed out." She felt almost as sick to her stomach now as she had that night.

"Gorgeous. Like a fairy princess waiting to be awakened by a kiss from her prince. But he'd turned into a frog. He'd married the evil queen. Not a very seemly thing of him to do." Peter took her hand and led her over to a small carved Edwardian settee. They sank onto it side by side, she more tired than she'd ever been in her life.

They both hung their heads. Only slowly did she become aware of his gentle massage of her freezing cold fingers. Joint by joint. Playing with them. Wiggling them back and forth as if the muscles inside had no volition except that imparted from the outside.

This was the Peter she knew so well. Had so loved as a girl.

"The timing's lousy, Em. I know that. But I need to say something before you fly off again headed to who knows where."

He wiggled her thumb like a cyclic control. Left. Right. Forward. Back. Steering her down a path. What path? One of her choosing or his?

She waited. Waited in the silence that drew out until she looked up at his face to make sure he was still there.

His hazel eyes were watching her intently. Studying her like he'd never seen a woman before.

"Stay."

"Stay? That's it? Just stay?"

"Stay. With me."

She'd have risen if her feet worked. She'd have dropped her jaw if it wasn't numb.

"Katherine's been—"

"Dead two days. I know. But she left me years ago. I've been so alone. The minute I heard your voice on the radio as I sat in the Situation Room, I knew I couldn't live without you. And when I saw you on the stairs, it was one of the nicest surprises I've ever had. That was the real reason I agreed to let Katherine call you to the states. I missed you like a piece of my heart was gone. I need you here with me. Stay?"

Emily stood, dragging her hand from his. She paced across the carpet to a gilt-framed painting of something she couldn't focus on. The movement helped. Getting the blood back in her body. In her brain.

"As your mistress?"

"As my girlfriend, then my wife. Over a respectable period. We could work it out. If I have you with me, we can work out anything."

"Give up—" She couldn't say it. Give up flying? Give up SOAR? Give up the Black Adders? That didn't sound like any Emily Beale that she knew. She'd started flying to set her own course and fly along it. And now it was who she was. Her body wouldn't be her own if it wasn't crammed into a pilot's seat and pounded upon by the thudding rotor blades.

"I need to fly," she told the painting.

"You could fly," Peter rose; she could hear him. Feel him come close behind her. "Transfer to Anacostia. Fly Marine One or learn to fly Air Force One. Become my personal pilot and my personal wife."

"And give up…" *who I am.*

"Nothing."

"I need…" Something. The gilt-framed picture was still a meaningless blur before her tired eyes. She needed time to think. "Time."

"All you could ever want." Then he took her in his arms, there in the elegant boudoir of the Hay-Adams suite, and gave her the kiss she'd been craving with body, mind, and soul since before she could remember.

When they parted, when her heart stopped racing enough for her to breathe, she gave voice to the only thing she could think.

"Time."

He'd nodded. Nodded, but didn't release her.

He clearly had more words. More to throw at her, more ways to cajole and convince.

She pushed against his chest until they were a full step apart. Stopped his flow of words with an outfacing palm.

It was the hardest thing she'd ever done. The hardest answer she'd ever given. Why did the answers always have to be so impossibly hard? How to answer the best friend she'd ever had?

But in that instant, she knew the answer. Had Katherine not been a psycho, she'd have been perfect for Peter. Had been, despite being psycho. Perfect image. Perfect charm. Peter hadn't made a mistake when he married her. He'd never have reached so high without her.

Emily didn't need time. She knew the answer. And

as soon as she could feel it in her heart, she could see it in his eyes before he hung his head.

They were old friends who knew each other too well.

She kissed his cheek before turning without another word and leaving him to stand alone in the most luxurious suite of that luxurious prison.

Chapter 65

EMILY DIDN'T REMEMBER LEAVING THE SUITE OR passing by the blacksuits. She found a transport, a series of them, to get back to her family of crew, her home in the desert.

She slashed the poor crew of newbies and that idiot Bronson up one side and down the other about the condition of their bird during the flight from the carrier back to the base. She reamed everyone who came within hearing radius before crash-landing face down in her cot.

She remembered none of it.

Not until she woke up and Archie informed her she'd sacked out for two straight days.

Neither her copilot nor her crew said anything to her about her two weeks stateside, nor her rough reentry. After a few days, the laughter stopped dying the moment she entered a room. Though she couldn't bring herself to join in.

And she flew. Thank God, Mark let her fly. She flew the missions no one considered survivable. She reached enemy cells that no one had ever sighted before and she dropped her hammer on their heads, hard. For two full weeks now, she'd brought the hammer of the U.S. Army to the true infidels, those who used religion as an excuse to murder, rape, and pillage. The traitors to their own faiths as Katherine had been to her sworn vows. As a warrior, Emily understood better than most the meaning of true faith and swearing to uphold it, even at the cost of your life.

Now, late each afternoon, she sat here, high on the soccer-stadium bleachers. Away from Archie's worried looks, away from Big Bad John and Crazy Tim checking her sidewise, trying to gauge her madness.

Emily sat here and stared out at the distant mountains each afternoon before the night's operations kicked in. Her MRE, Meal, Ready-to-Eat chicken fettuccine, cooking on the scorching concrete, no need for the flameless heater. She pulled out the biscuit and Tabasco bottle. Tugged the small cellophane Candy II packet from its corner and clenched it in her fist.

She didn't belong in D.C. She didn't. But neither did she belong here anymore. What had Peter done to her?

Emily sat in the bleachers.

Alone except for the ring of sentries patrolling the highest level. Rangers, who claimed to fear no man, had learned quickly not to meet her eyes.

Alone.

"Hey there, Captain."

Almost alone.

"Hey yourself, Major."

Mark Henderson, hidden behind his mirrored shades, dropped down beside her. She'd seen those eyes. Knew those eyes and how they watched her. For the two weeks since her return, he'd been pure military with her. No gropes, no jokes, no hints of what they'd had. Not even any fake Texas tease, which she missed far more than she'd ever admit. Clearly he was trying to make her welcome and safe once more with the Black Adders.

"You don't want to be eating that, you know. Bad luck there." A brief hint of Texas and cozy familiarity. Did he resent not being free to use it as much as she missed hearing it?

She looked down at the Candy II packet crushed in her fist. No Special Forces grunt would dare eat the candy from an MRE before a mission. Seriously bad luck. She pried open her fist and let it flutter down to rest by her dusty boot.

The sun had set. Her MRE, forgotten too long on the scorching concrete, had fried and died, not that she cared. The knife-edge suddenness of nightfall in an arid desert was hacking its way across the sky. The temperature had already dropped twenty degrees to merely unbearable. It felt like heaven.

"You know…" He leaned back on his elbows on the bench behind, crossed his ankles on the bench below, and stared up at the darkening sky. "You are either the luckiest person alive or the unluckiest. And I'll be damned if I know which."

She knew where her vote would land so she kept her mouth shut.

"That mission you flew last night, even the D-boys were shaking when they got off your flight. I didn't know you could get that many bullet holes in a Black Hawk and still have her fly. Tough. Really tough."

"Me or the bird?"

He didn't reply. Clearly he'd meant both. She was back in the guy-speak world. Didn't know why she'd even asked.

The setting sun would soon be revealing Venus on its path to set in the west. If she looked a little north, she could pick out the planet with the more sensitive corner of her eye. Old pilot trick, center of your eye sees color, sides see no color but gather more light. There. As she did every night, she tried to track it until she was facing the planet square on. Too dim still, it faded away in the center of her vision. She turned her head slightly until it danced, enticingly elusive, in her peripheral vision. Her vision. Each night it gave her at least one thing to be thankful for. She could see.

Maghrib, the prayer at sunset, slipped through the air from the town that had once used this soccer stadium, before the jihad had murdered the star players and inducted the rest. Before the U.S. military had moved in. The sunset prayer wafted from the town. In a village too poor to have electricity, no massive speakers screeched the muezzin's chant into incomprehensibility. Instead, one man acted as town crier and the faithful echoed his call.

"How many of you share Katherine Matthews's wish? How many of you would rather see me dead than fighting your enemies? Rather see us all die, though you speak 'peace be onto us' in each round of prayer?" Emily half-whispered it into the night.

"Pretty morose there, babe." Mark slurred the last as luridly as he could, thick Texas and all.

She refused to answer his jibe. What was he playing at anyway? Why was he breaking his commitment to be her CO but no more? Couldn't he see how it tore her in two every time she saw him?

He let the silence linger until she could finally spot Venus head on.

"You're going stateside for a bit."

"No!" She jerked upright and faced him. "Don't send me down! I'm the best damn pilot you've got."

"Wrong, you're the best damn pilot I've ever seen. And I'm not sending you down. Ten days leave, all the Army can spare you. Get your head screwed back on. Even though the D-boys love where you can get them, they're afraid for you. Not 'of you,' Michael insisted. For you. They want you in fighting trim, not showing up dead one day because you pushed a line you shouldn't have crossed."

"But—"

"It's an order, Captain. I'm hereby ordering you to take a vacation. It can be on an Italian beach for all I care, but away from here."

He pulled the order from his pocket and handed it to her. The paper was slick and hard to unfold. Ten days, and no training courses allowed. Ten days completely off. What was she supposed to do with that?

"I want you alive. I wouldn't mind if it were for a long time. It was fun being your boyfriend, even if only for a little time." His voice drifted off to a bare whisper. "I wouldn't mind having you back."

For an instant she wondered if he meant as a flier or a girlfriend. Not a hard one to answer actually. Again, clearly he meant both.

His shades still covered his eyes, though true sunset had arrived. The moment, as measured by the Bedouin she'd lived among during a mission to Yemen, when a red thread and a blue one held a finger's width apart can no longer be distinguished by color.

She studied her hands. Mark had made a nice offer, even if they both knew it was impossible. Army

Regulation 600-20 was very clear on that point. He'd made it decently. A good man, he'd proven that by his actions. A thoughtful man, he'd proven that by how he offered but didn't push. A handsome man, every woman who'd ever seen him would agree. A man who knew who she was. That she didn't exist without her team, without her flight.

So why did she want to pound her fists against him? Hard.

"One other thing."

"Ah." There it was. "What's the other shoe?"

He laughed. A single, short chuckle. Not long, but complete. A compliment. That no matter how messed up her feelings were, her brain remained on the job.

"When you get back, I'm going to strip you of your bars."

"Wouldn't be the first time." Back a grade to first lieutenant. Not too bad for having killed the President's wife.

"Yeah. I've spoken with your Sneaker Boy pal. This time you're going to wear the damned oak leaf if he and I have to pin you down while I staple it to your naked breast."

"Oak leaf?" It took a moment, then she sat bolt upright as if she'd been electrocuted.

"No! Uh-uh! I don't want to be a major, Major. I fly. I don't command and sit back. I fly."

"Do you see me sitting it out? Bet your pretty ass you fly. As long as you're in my outfit, you fly."

That was something at least. Up a pay grade but still flying.

"I only command my one bird though, right?" She'd

never wanted more than her four-man team. Hated the feel of remote control on people's lives. And watching Mark juggle a dozen birds, with fifty crew and a couple hundred support personnel, just made her head pound.

"Wa'alll…"

She knew she was in trouble if the Texas accent was back.

"I think your copilot, Archie, is almost ready to become your wingman in his own bird."

She nodded. He was. Past due if they weren't such a good team together. She'd been flying with Archie since West Point days, and she'd miss sharing a cockpit with him.

"But first there's these two gal crew chiefs who've qualified as armaments and engineer, number two and three in Night Stalker history. They'll need someone to show them the ropes. They need someone who's the best."

That could be fun. Teaching a woman how to keep all these macho jocks in place. One good female copilot, and they'd be the most kick-ass crew the Night Stalkers had ever fielded.

"One of them's pretty hot, you know."

The elbow to his ribs didn't even take a thought. It shot out and caught him solidly enough to hurt.

She turned to apologize. Maybe her feelings really were messed up enough to need a break.

He smiled at her. The damn man smiled at her. As if he didn't know he'd just made her day. Her year.

"Y'all know something?"

"What?" She just knew she'd be flying. It was all she ever needed to know.

"Army Regulation 600-20, Chapter 4, Section 14, is ti-
tled: 'Relationships between officers of different ranks.'"

She blinked. Blinked hard. "But…"

"But what?"

Emily looked at him, back at Venus, down at her
folded hands, and back at Mark. Sex. They could have
sex without being thrown out of the Army for her being
his subordinate. Major and major. Same rank.

"But…"

This time he didn't respond. Mark let his silence wait
for her own thoughts to move less like a chopper with
its rear rotor just shot off.

She wanted Mark. So badly it made her head spin
worse than when the hallucinations hit during Green
Platoon training. But she didn't want sex. Well, not just
sex. She wanted to curl up with him in the same bed and
sleep with the perfect safety of his arms wrapped about
her. She wanted… "More."

He dug into his pocket and pulled out a second set
of orders. Venus now shone brilliant in the night, other
stars following close in her wake. Emily couldn't read
them even if he gave them to her.

But he held onto them. Drawing them back when she
reached out.

"Nope. Not yours, honey pie. Not yours, sweetest
lady I've ever met." His voice slipped from fake Texas
twang to the soft voice she'd only heard a few times
when they were alone together.

Mark unfolded the paper and adjusted his mirrored
shades as if that would help him read in the dark. He
turned the sheet top for bottom, then front to back, finally holding it sideways as if that made any difference.

"After the Washington shenanigans, I could only get five days off myself."

"Five days," Emily whispered out into the dark night. What could they do in five days? A lot. When they'd only had three hours, they'd done plenty. But she wanted... If only she knew. The words were there, but she couldn't find them.

"I'm a-figurin'..." He folded the order laboriously. "I'm a-figurin' that five days ain't really enough time for a purty little gal to plan a wedding and have a honeymoon, but if I gave you a five-day head start..." His shrug was eloquent even in the dark.

Wedding and a honeymoon.

He returned the order to his pocket and slid his glasses up into his hair. She could see the outline of his face in the starlight. Could feel him waiting in the dark.

Waiting in the place of greatest safety for any Night Stalker.

He was asking the same question Peter had.

They could fly together. Major and major.

Be together, husband and wife. Joint operations in the truest sense.

Mark's question sent a delightful shiver up her spine as warmth spread through her, melting a cold spot inside that the desert heat had failed to touch in the two weeks since her return. A hope of love and family she'd always imagined but never really believed in. Didn't believe in until the first time he'd kissed her aboard the carrier a lifetime ago.

Peter had proposed to her. That was the dream she'd always held, but the price had been so high. To abandon all that she'd trained to be. All she'd wanted since the first time she'd taken the controls of her first little Robinson two-seater. All she'd made herself be. Peter loved the precocious little girl. Or, more accurately, the memory of her. The warrior she'd become, though perhaps intriguing, was to be easily discarded in a way she would never survive.

And Peter's kiss had been… That was the other problem. She had to admit it. Finally.

It wasn't rough. Peter wasn't the rough sort. But the kiss she'd longed for all those years had taken itself for granted. He'd curled his hand around the back of her neck and dug his fingers into her hair to hold tight. He'd pulled her in, not roughly, but like a man who already knew the answer. No soul-filling warmth. No electrifying spark. Just possession. Taking for granted that she too would come to him as easily as all his successes.

"How's my timing, Emma?" Mark whispered her name into the night and cradled his hand against her cheek. That wonderful rough palm snuggled warm against her skin.

If her name had sounded good on his lips before, tonight it sounded perfect.

She rubbed her cheek against his palm. It took one warrior to understand another. He wanted her, the warrior and the flier. And he respected her enough to ask. Enough to stand against his desires, his needs on her behalf if that was her decision. If she said no, Mark would turn back into her commander. It might kill him inside, but he would do it.

He wanted the woman she'd made, the woman she'd become. Built layer by layer until she'd gained enough hard lift to reach the sky.

She ran her fingertips over his face, the details now hidden by the night. Brushed them across his eyelids, which fluttered shut as she felt the outline of those eyes that always saw her so clearly, despite the darkness that hid their color.

Mark would provide even more, sufficient lift to reach her dreams. They could fly to them together.

Her father had said she'd get there. Now that she had, it was easy to see despite the dark.

Mark wouldn't want her to be different than who she was, any more than he could be unkind. The perfect, clichéd warrior. Exactly as she'd thought of him every time she'd flown with him. Except not cliché at all. He still awaited her answer, assumed nothing. A hundred percent class act.

Emily turned until her lips were against the cup of his palm, and he sighed into the night as she kissed him there. A pent-up release of breath held against fear. Fear she might say no. As if she could. As if her heart would let her.

Without a single word of her own, with the perfect timing of her husband-to-be, she turned to straddle his lap and lay her head on his shoulder as he stroked her hair.

Sometimes the answer was easy. As easy as flying.

Read on for an excerpt from

I Own the Dawn

M.L. Buchman

Available August 2012

From Sourcebooks Casablanca

FALLING DOWN LIKE A HAMMER OUT OF THE CRYSTAL blue sky came her baby: a Black Hawk helicopter. And not just any Hawk. It was an MH-60L DAP. The Direct Action Penetrator was the nastiest gunship God ever put on Earth and only the best flew in her. Kee'd almost died of pleasure the first time she saw one—actually, she'd been about to die literally, too.

She'd spent five long years bucking her way up from infantry to get aboard. It had taken her three of those to get into SOAR and another two to get through SOAR training. Now she was here, forward operations. She'd done it, facing a DAP Hawk. No man had ever made her feel this good.

And this sweet bird wasn't fooling around. Two massive weapons' pylons stuck out from either side of the midsection. On one side she had a rocket pod carrying nineteen birds and a 30 mm cannon just in case they wanted to go mastodon hunting. On the other pylon, another rocket pod and a rack of Hellfire anti-tank missiles, three of which were missing.

Unfriendlies lay pretty close aboard here in the baking desert in bloody baking Pakistan, their base of operations a dusty bivouac fifty miles from Afghanistan's brutal Hindu Kush mountains. The surrounding town of five thousand people could be hiding anybody. The two Crew Chiefs still had their hands on the M134 miniguns peeking out of their shooting holes even while they were just a hundred feet up. The Hawk had the midair refueling probe which meant she went in way deep. Kee was down with that.

Only one group flew such a bird: SOAR. The Special Operations Aviation Regiment (airborne), the Army's 160th. The Night Stalkers. The baddest asses on the face of the sky. And she was here. She pinched her leg, on the side away from Major Muscle-head. It stung. This wasn't no dream. Wide awake. She'd done it.

They both turned away and covered their faces as a brown-out of dust washed across the field adding another layer to her too many hours of grime. Once the bird hunkered down and speech and vision were again possible, she faced him.

"That." She cocked a thumb over her shoulder. "Me." She thumped her chest with a fist. "Sir!" For good measure.

"Done!" Again that hidden laugh. "If you can talk your way past the pilot." He turned on his heel and disappeared into the heat shimmer.

So, all up to her, huh? Good. Didn't scare her none.

Kee yanked her duffle over her shoulder and tromped over to the DAP as her rotors wound down and the dust and sand settled.

Respect. She'd give that a shot first. Respect with a little help. Because, like a good soldier, she had more than one weapon in her arsenal. She tossed down her duffle and the rifle case at the edge of the rotor sweep and made sure her T-shirt lay smooth and tight on her skin so that every muscle and curve showed. Pack 'n' Rack. Six-pack abs and a good solid rack for a chest. On clear display. Her dusky skin, almond eyes, and single blond-streak in dark hair that had some kind of magic at knocking men dead. Wasn't why she had it, but it worked.

She didn't tease, it wasn't her mode. If she offered, she meant it and delivered. But having men's brains switch off around her had its advantages. She wasn't gonna be filing a letter of complaint with the chief people designer that wired men's brains to blow away like dust in rotor wash whenever they were around her. It just amused her that it worked every damn time.

The pilot climbed down, leaned in to trade a joke with his crew chief and then headed out from under the slowing rotors. He almost passed her by, but Kee snapped a sharp salute.

"At ease." No salute back.

Crap! Newbie mistake. She jerked her hand back to her side and couldn't help checking behind her, but Major Muscle was gone. She knew better, had been forward-deployed plenty to know better. In the field you never salute a superior officer. Sure way to tell a sniper who to target.

Kee dropped to parade rest, clenched her hands behind her back. Muscled arms and shoulders back focused men on a chest that wowed 'em all. Some civilian women thought they were hot, but there was nothing like a buffed-out soldier babe. And they knew it, too. Wasn't a single civilian chick ever gave her a smile when she entered a bar.

"Sergeant Kee Smith. Best damn gunner you ever met. I want on your ship, sir."

The pilot peeled off his helmet, revealing blue-green eyes and an unruly wave of soft brown hair that she'd bet never stayed under control, no matter how long a woman played with it. He opened the front of his flight suit to reveal a sweaty tee on a slender frame.

"First Lieutenant Archibald Jeffrey Stevenson III at your service. And it's not my ship. You'll be wanting to converse with the major." His voice so slow and smooth and refined, like a radio announcer on those classical stations.

Then he grinned at her, a saucy, funny grin. Started in his eyes and wandered down to his lips, ending up kind of lopsided. Not Handsome-Mr.-Major, but it made him look pretty damn cute. She couldn't help but notice that his long and lean had some nice muscle underneath; you'd expect no less from a SOAR.

The lieutenant, however, didn't even have the decency to rake his eyes down her body. The major hadn't been able to help studying her frame, she could tell despite the mirrored shades he wore as if they'd been welded there. But this lieutenant somehow managed. Either gay or self-control of steel-like strength. Came down to it, she'd be betting on the latter. What happened when that much self control let go? Now that could be worth the price of the ticket to find out.

He moved off to her right, passing so close they almost brushed shoulders. He leaned in and whispered, "Good luck. You are going to need it."

And even though she didn't turn to look at him, she knew they were smiling together for that moment.

Lieutenant Archibald Jeffrey Stevenson III, indeed. What was this woman's army coming to? Though she'd liked the way he said it, with a voice like silk.

She spotted the oak leaves on the collar of the other pilot and set aside thoughts of long and lean lieutenants with wavy hair. The major was still helmeted and chatting with the crew coming in to service his chopper. The Hawk'd been through some hard times. Tape patches showed more than a few hits on the fuselage, some of the panels had been replaced and a couple of those had patched holes, too. Now that they'd stopped spinning, she could see that one of the rotor blades was clearly newer than the other three, replaced after taking too much abuse. This bird had seen some heavy action. She moved in to check out the guns, worn hard but so immaculate you could eat off them. Her kind of weapon.

"Pretty, isn't she?" Some crewwoman's voice sounded close behind her. SOAR had women in the ground personnel, but Kee was only the second woman to ever make the grade for flight operations. Sweet candy for sure. A serpent of coiled gray had been painted across the dusky green of the chopper. The colors so close in tone made it hard to see in places, which made it appear all the more dangerous. It wrapped around the gunner's lookout window and writhed across the pilot's door. Etched in his scales was the name of the bird: "Vengeance." The serpent's head, striking forward along the nose of the chopper, sported mirrored shades. In the lenses, someone had even drawn a reflected explosion of an enemy going down hard.

"Better than sex." She rubbed a hand down the long

barrel of the 30 mm cannon. "I can't believe that bastard major wanted to slot me on the girlie-chopper. This is real flight."

"Don't like girlie-choppers?"

"Not one friggin' bit. I want this bad boy. I didn't come here to form no goddamn chick squad." She stepped forward to stare into the face of the rocket launcher. Seven fired. They'd been in some heat last night. She'd wager it hadn't turned out well for the bad guys. Night Stalkers ruled the dark.

Something kept dragging at her attention. She'd been trained to pay attention to the niggling feeling that something was out of place. Not right. It had saved her life more than once while pounding ground for the 10th Mountain Division.

Looking up, she spotted it.

"The rotor blades. They look different."

Kee could feel the maintenance chick, still behind her, focusing her attention upward.

"Thicker. Most can't see that. This is the first 'M'-mod in the theater. The MH-60M upgrade adds twenty-five percent larger engines, needs a heavier blade."

Kee whistled in admiration. "She must haul ass across the sky."

"She does."

Kee glanced over at her new companion. "Kee Smith."

The first thing she noticed was the shoulder-length blonde hair and the bluest eyes on the planet. Pretty, slender, perfect posture. Would fit in with Archibald Jeffrey Stevenson III just fine. Maybe they were hitched. Met in a frickin' hoity-toity fern bar somewhere on the Upper West Side. She dug a sparkler out of a pocket and slipped it on her left, though the lieutenant's hand had been clean. Still, could be.

The second thing Kee noticed was the worn flight suit, the battered helmet under one arm, the scuffed-up M9 Beretta at her hip, and the pair of major's oak leaves on the woman's lapels.

Kee's poker face clicked in a beat and a half too late. One woman had made it into SOAR before her. A friggin' legend. And not for spreading her legs to the top. A girl couldn't turn around without being compared to the one other woman flight-qualified in the whole regiment. That damn Major Muscle had tricked her. Tricked her into begging to get onto the girlie-chopper she so hadn't wanted. Who'd have guessed the girlie-bird would be a DAP Hawk?

Kee knew the woman's name even before she spoke in that refined voice of hers.

"Emily Beale."

Cover Me

by Catherine Mann

It should have been a simple mission…

Pararescueman Wade Rocha fast ropes from the back of a helicopter into a blizzard to save a climber stranded on an Aleutian Island, but Sunny Foster insists she can take care of herself just fine…

But when it comes to passion, nothing is ever simple…

With the snowstorm kicking into overdrive, Sunny and Wade hunker down in a cave and barely resist the urge to keep each other warm…until they discover the frozen remains of a horrific crime…

Unable to trust the local police force, Sunny and Wade investigate, while their irresistible passion for each other gets them more and more dangerously entangled…

Praise for Catherine Mann:

"Catherine Mann weaves deep emotion with intense suspense for an all-night read." —*#1 New York Times bestseller Sherrilyn Kenyon*

For more Catherine Mann, visit:
www.sourcebooks.com

Hot Zone

by Catherine Mann

—⁓—

He'll take any mission, the riskier the better...

The haunted eyes of pararescueman Hugh Franco should have been her first clue that deep pain roiled beneath the surface. But if Amelia couldn't see the damage, how could she be expected to know he'd break her heart?

She'll prove to be his biggest risk yet...

Amelia Bailey's not the kind of girl who usually needs rescuing...but these are anything but usual circumstances.

—⁓—

Praise for Catherine Mann:

"Nobody writes military romance like Catherine Mann!"
—*Suzanne Brockmann, New York Times bestselling author of Tall, Dark and Deadly*

"A powerful, passionate read not to be missed!"
—*Lori Foster, New York Times bestselling author of When You Dare*

For more Catherine Mann, visit:
www.sourcebooks.com

SEALed with a Ring

by Mary Margret Daughtridge

—⁓—

She's got it all... except the one thing she needs most

Smart, successful businesswoman JJ Caruthers has a year to land a husband or lose the empire she's worked so hard to build. With time running out, romance is not an option, and a military husband who is always on the road begins to look like the perfect solution...

He's a wounded hero with an agenda of his own

Even with the scars of battle, Navy SEAL medic Davy Graziano is gorgeous enough to land any woman he wants, and he's never wanted to be tied down. Now Davy has ulterior motives for accepting JJ's outrageous proposal of marriage, but he only has so long to figure out what JJ doesn't want him to know...

—⁓—

Praise for SEALed with a Ring:

"With a surprising amount of heart, Daughtridge makes a familiar story read like new as the icy JJ melts under Davy's charm during a forced marriage. The supporting cast, including one really unattractive dog, makes Daughtridge's latest one for the keeper shelves." —*RT Book Reviews*, 4 stars

For more Mary Margret Daughtridge, visit:
www.sourcebooks.com

SEALed Forever

by Mary Margret Daughtridge

He's got a living, breathing dilemma…

In the midst of running an undercover CIA mission, Navy SEAL Lt. Garth Vale finds an abandoned baby, and his superiors sure don't want to know about it. The only person who can help him is the beautiful new doctor in town, but she's got another surprise for him…

She's got a solution… at a price…

Dr. Bronwyn Whitescarver has left the frantic pace of big city ER medicine for a small town medical practice. Her bags aren't even unpacked yet when gorgeous, intense Garth Vale shows up on her doorstep in the middle of the night with a sick baby…

But his story somehow doesn't add up, and Bronwyn isn't quite sure who she's saving—the baby, or the man…

Praise for SEALed Forever:

"Take two strong characters, throw in some humor and a baby and you've got a perfect combination for a heart-warming romance. The suspense subplot is a bonus in this well-written story."—*RT Book Review*, 4.5 stars

For more Mary Margret Daughtridge, visit:
www.sourcebooks.com

About the Author

M.L. Buchman began writing novels on July 22, 1993, while on a plane from Korea to ride a bicycle across the Australian Outback. M.L. has been a substitute instructor for University of Washington's Certificate in Commercial Fiction program and has spoken at dozens of conferences including RWA national and BookExpo. Past lives include: renovating a fifty-foot sailboat, fifteen years in corporate computer-systems design, bicycling solo around the world, developing maps for a national franchise, and designing roof trusses, in roughly that order. M.L. and family live on an island in the Pacific Northwest in a solar-powered home of their own design.

"To Champion the Human Spirit, Celebrate the Power of Joy, and Revel in the Wonder of Love."

M.L. website: www.mlbuchman.com.